The Claws

Jason Ch

Copyright © Jason Charles 2017

No part of this book may be reproduced or transmitted in any form or by any means whatsoever without express written permission from the author.

First Edition. 2017.

Published by KDP Direct.

Printed 2017.

London.
UK.

www.jason-charles.co.uk

Author Bio

Jason Charles is a London-born playwright, poet, short story writer and novelist. In 2006 his play **Steam** opened at the White Bear Theatre in London, and was revived the following year at London's Barons Court Theatre. 2007 saw the production of his play **Rupture** at London's Kings Head Theatre, and in 2008 his play **Counterfeit Skin** opened at London's Courtyard Theatre. Due to its success it was revived there six months later. He had two more plays produced in 2009; **Estranged** at the Courtyard Theatre followed by **Beyond Flesh and Blood** at London's Tabard Theatre. The following year he rewrote the Hungarian musical **Better Than Sex** for the London stage, and in 2014 **Estranged** opened at the Tap Gallery Theatre in Sydney, Australia.
The Claws of Time is his first novel.

1

She felt like divine fingers had reached into her brain to fill it with light. But as she slowly opened her eyes, the rapture faded. Looking around a cold, musty, grey-bricked room that let in light through a narrow slit, she realised she had no idea where she was. The nerves in her face twitched along with the vermillion flames of an electric candelabra. That was the only other thing in the room apart from a large couple wearing white socks and red shorts who stood in the corner staring at her with open mouths. They spoke to her but she had no idea what they were saying, and when she tried to respond all she could do was make sounds like a baby. It was as if language had been ripped out of her.

Fear and vulnerability crept along her spine as she uncoiled herself from the foetal position she was in and used the dusty wall to climb up to her feet. She shakily made her way towards the open door, but her next memory was of being at the bottom of a stone spiral staircase looking up into the gawp of a hundred eyes. She later learned that a Beefeater carried her to the back of the Tower of London gift shop and laid her out on a bag of fluffy, beheaded Anne Boleyns.

An ambulance was called and paramedics presumed she was some sort of misguided tourist attraction due to the 'medieval-style' kirtle and headdress she was wearing. But Tower of London staff denied all knowledge of her, one of them telling the *Evening Standard* that peculiar people wondering around in period costumes were best left to battle re-enactment societies. She was admitted to nearby St Thomas's Hospital where doctors diagnosed her with severe amnesia as a result of the fall (even though she had no idea where or who she was before it) and police were brought in to try and ascertain her identity. Despite a public appeal, nobody came forward except for a woman from Snaresbrook who turned out to be soliciting for the white slave trade. A short stay in hospital led to a placement in a nearby assisted living centre where she was taught the basic living skills that had seemingly been wiped from her brain along with her memory. It was here that she named herself River after the brooding familiarity of the Thames.

The first time Nathan saw River and heard her strange story of appearing out of nowhere in the Tower of London was on television. She had made the mistake of accepting an invitation to talk about it on a daytime chat show called *Paranormal People*. The host was as incredulous as he was vacuous and the studio audience sniggered and shuffled as she spoke. The other guests were a clairvoyant who read toothpaste spits and a woman called Queenie who had video footage of her pet iguana spontaneously combusting. River had not finished her tale before the woman announced she had brought the lizard's charred corpse with her and asked why River was taking priority. As she unzipped her handbag, River unclipped her microphone and fled through waves of cruel laughter. By the time the closing credits sank, River was dismissed as just another fraud in search of reality TV fame. But Nathan was hooked.

Paranormal People was the first bit of television he watched since returning home from a solo two-week trip to Tuscany. He had gone there in search of a pair of arms to replace the ones that had recently dumped him with a text message that read: 'Dating an artist was an attractive novelty at first, but I think I need to find someone with their feet on the ground rather than their head in the clouds.' Within a few weeks she was engaged to an asbestos specialist, and Nathan returned home from Italy with nothing but a Prosecco stained splurge of the Basilica di Santa Maria del Fiore, which he threw into a Gatwick Airport dustbin. He fished it out again when he remembered that his live-in sister would be expecting a gift.

Nothing in Tuscany beguiled Nathan as much as River's curious mix of supernaturalism and beauty. He began to sketch her from memory the moment she left his television screen, and the more he drew, the more she materialized inside his head the way she had materialized inside the Tower that day. Eventually he gained the courage to telephone the television production company to see if they could put him in touch with her. They took his details, and to his shock she rang him the following morning. She told him she hoped he was someone who could help her discover her true identity. After getting over this initial disappointment, she agreed to meet him for a drink.

2

River took out the A4 journal she bought from Plaistow Poundland that afternoon and put a cross through the year on the cover 2012. If only it were that easy to erase this mess she was in. To the first page she Pritt Sticked a newspaper cutting that was now nine years old.

The Metropolitan Police are appealing to the public for help in identifying a woman who appears to have severe amnesia. The woman, who was admitted to St Thomas's Hospital yesterday morning, was discovered by tourists in the Tower of London. They reported that she was acting very strangely before falling down a stone stairwell. Hospital staff, who have named the woman 'Scarlet' after the colour of the medieval-style dress she was found wearing, say she is suffering from a rare condition where the patient loses their entire memory, including forgetting how to read and write, but they are still unsure of the cause.

She looked at the attached photograph of herself in a light blue hospital gown, her eyes resembling those of a trapped and frightened wild animal. It would have made more sense to photograph her in the medieval kirtle and wimple she was found in. Perhaps the fifteenth century undergarment and headdress had already been stolen by then, by somebody in the hospital who could see they were authentic and worth a lot of money. She wondered if the wild boar badge that she recently remembered Richard giving her just before he became king was attached to her dress. That would surely be priceless now. Re-reading the caption below her photograph, 'No information about the woman, who appears to be in her early twenties, is known,' she reminded herself of the purpose of buying this book. It was not to chronicle her complaints about how badly the twenty first century was treating her, but to record from her flashbacks the life she led in the fifteenth century, and the relationships she had with royalty.

I think the biggest difference between the 15th century and today is smell. Back then everybody stunk. Mostly of old sweat. We did not bathe much, not because we did not have baths, but because we thought God liked it when we suffered. Richard only bathed once a month, but he mostly smelled of the herbs and spices that he had me rub into his back. Whereas now we have soaps and deodorants and toothpastes and mouthwashes, in the later end of the 1400s we relied on things like dried lavender to mask our stench. On top of this, the smell of human waste hovered over every street and river. Disease was never far away. In fact my grandparents died of the plague. I knew very few people who lived beyond the age of forty, and if they did, it was because they lived somewhere isolated from regular flesh to flesh contact. Richard's mother, Proud Cis as she was known, lived to the almost unheard of age of eighty and that was because she locked herself away in Berkhamsted Castle. She isolated herself there after certain people spread rumours about her and a six foot four French archer. Slapping Richard's face on a balcony in front of hundreds of highly amused Londoners was the last contact she had with her son. She refused to even attend his coronation. But if the rumours were not true, why was her oldest son so much taller than her husband and her other sons?

River scratched her inner ear with the end of the red biro and read over her words. The confused ramblings of a crazy woman, that is what Nathan or anyone else would think if they ever got hold of this. She ripped out the page, forced breath into her lungs, and started again.

My real name is Dimiza and I was born in the small Scottish town of Inverness. Well, it was small when I was born there. From my calculations I place the year of my birth at 1461. Or 1462. I was the youngest sister of four brothers and I had to share a bed with two of them. We had a pet falcon called Grizella. Or it may have been a hawk.

She bit the pen in frustration. Why did she think this would be easy? She could already hear the laugher, the same laughter she heard in that television studio last year.

She was a joke, a freak, and may as well embrace her vocation of being a daytime TV lunatic.

Her bird gingerly climbed onto her lap, perhaps sensing her turmoil. Roger was a broken-beaked raven that decided to cling to her the day the council moved her into this flat. Both ex prisoners of the Tower of London, they were united by their miraculous gift of flight. Roger escaped those tall grey walls by secretly growing back his clipped wings, while River apparently escaped them by slipping hundreds of years through time.

Rain dribbled down her windows like slow dirty tears. She held the jet black bird as close to her chest as she could without hurting him, needing right now his warmth and affection. Time obstinately staggered on, dragging her and her pet and everything else along with it, but over her shoulder she could feel her past clawing its way up her spine. The light faded, the air cooled, and her eyes slowly rolled back for another fifteenth century flashback.

3

Time had a habit of picking Petra Sherry up by the neck and dropping her back into the nest she once shared with him. Him. That man with his cold body and stagnant heart. All she could do was stand motionless on the spot where it had caught her, close her eyes, and hope for the ghost to pass as quickly as possible. Certain smells conjured him up - acrylic paint, alcohol that slept the night, malt vinegar. She was a dead woman on the very rare occasions that somebody walked past her in the street wearing his aftershave.

Alone on her dirty bedroom carpet in a grimy pocket of south London, big red fender in hand, she begun to strum the riff of the opening track of her album. She stopped before the lyrics kicked in, because they were about him.

Dear Petra
I think you know that our relationship was never destined to work. Please don't try
to find me. Trust me, this is for the best.

Stephen

Trust. It's funny how when you repeat a word over and over again in your head it starts to mean absolutely nothing at all.

When Stephen Jude Tyburn first arrived in her seaside town of Budleigh Salterton, Petra was swimming through the emotional sanguinary of her mid twenties, and her song writing was shaping into something dark and tangled. Her lyrics choked with desperation for love, and her guitar playing became frenzied. So when her eyes swum over the thick brown hair, pale skin and Celtic irises plucked from a clover green that had moved into the rundown chalet park, this need suddenly had an obsession to feed on. While she rarely ventured beyond Exeter, from whose university she graduated with a music degree, this slightly older, handsome man had spent the past five years travelling from one coastal town to the next, painting everything he saw. Oily surrealist blurs of cliff tops, lighthouses, and coastal terrains he sold for his supper and accommodation, waiting for the day that some elusive gallery would give him that equally elusive thing called 'recognition.' For months they did not speak, but Petra would often go and watch how he interpreted the shoreline she had known since birth. His latest patron was the owner of *Salterton and Vinegar*, the town's fish and chip shop, who not only bought his canvasses but also his chip frying skills by the hour. Sometimes Petra would find a vantage-point across the street, between the telephone box and the bus stop, to watch him at work through the steamy shop window. The thrill of seeing fingers that were so delicate and easel-intricate during the day, tossing, vinegaring, salting, wrapping, and fishcake-tonguing by night.

One evening she mustered up the courage to shakily slip a CD of her songs between the jars of pickled onions and gherkins. With it she attached a letter, a few lines that, just like her lyrics, she took a long time to get right.

In her best handwriting she requested his company at Shingles, the cliff-side cafe, at four-o clock the following day. She knew this was an hour before he started his shift as she had access *to Salterton and Vinegar*'s rota through her closest friend Etta, the Norwegian drummer in her band who also worked there. The next day, after changing her outfit to match her personality and then her personality to match her outfit, she arrived early for their tet-a-tea. A tet-a-tea that never happened. His snub confirmed her worst fears about herself, that she was not attractive or interesting enough for someone like him. Through the glaze of rejection, self-loathing, anger and obsession, she continued to watch him paint from cliff tops and wrap haddock from bus stops, and now all of her songs were about him. But she never stepped foot in that shop again. Sometimes he noticed her and frowned, but she no longer cared, there was no longer anything to lose because he was never going to be hers.

That was until a newly formed London record company took an interest in her work.

Petra had sent them a demo disk of her band performing after seeing an advert in a music weekly, and its manager summoned them to an unsigned talent night they were holding in Plymouth. The gig went well and the following week *Petra Sherry and The Eleventh Hour* were the first act to sign to Stanway Records. They were keen to cash in on the 'tortured female singer songwriter' craze that Petra's songs personified.

Word of the band's signing quickly permeated Budleigh Salterton, and their local gigs were suddenly attended by more than just one man, his Doberman, and holiday makers desperate to escape DJ Dwayne's eighties cacophony at the chalet park. It was a shock to see Stephen's hazel gaze through the crowd, and not just his usual perturbed glare either. This was something entirely different, and accompanied with an invitation to meet him for a drink in *The Three Swans*.

Drawing any passion or conversation out of this laid-back beatnik was a tricky affair. As a lover he was even more distant. But unsurprisingly for a woman who turned self loathing into an art form, this only made her want him more. She was happy to just tighten his arm around her while he tried to watch television, or have her leg curled around his as he sketched a lemming from memory. She was sure that he would reciprocate in time, and even if he did not, well, he was hers now and that was all that mattered. After only a few months of being together, her skin pricked at the sight of him moving his stuff out of his chalet and into her small flat. Once he was in there with all his clothes, boots, books and paintings, she wanted to nail down the doors and windows and never disentangle her limbs from his again, but her burgeoning musical career beckoned.

Stanway were keen for their new signing to begin recording and touring as quickly as possible, and Petra had to remind herself that this was what she had always wanted.

The company hired a studio in Torbay for three weeks for them to record their debut album, which she named '*I Am Alive Save Me*'. The lyrical inspiration for the album lay on her sofa sketching lighthouses and remained there while the band set out on a national tour to promote it. The tour opened in a room above a pub in North London to a small crowd who were mostly sat on the floor, and went on to entertain audiences in dark sticky venues across Britain, before finishing with a homecoming gig at Exeter's Cavern Club. To elicit media interest and oil the tour bus wheels, Stanway released a single, the electric guitar heavy *Dead Stolen Flowers*, and although it did not trouble the charts, the song received Devonshire radio play and garnered reviews that compared Petra's stark lyrics and erratic strumming to bands like Throwing Muses and the Pixies.

Spending over a month apart did not seem to trouble Stephen, but Petra spent much of the tour feeling like a pearl crow-barred out of an oyster. Despite the appealing odour of affirmation, the singer could not wait for Exeter, where she would finally be able to wash away that agitating grain of sand. Her mother said she would be there, despite preferring *Waitrose* and *The Telegraph to* amplifiers and beer, but it was of course Stephen Jude Tyburn that she longed to see and sing to.

When that fateful night finally arrived, Petra refused to go on stage until she could see him in the audience. His attendance would be a sign of the thing she prayed flowed beneath his stoical surface - commitment. She also could not wait to sing her lyrics into the eyes of the man who wrote them beneath her skin. But, with curtain gripped and frantic eyes scouring, one hundred people amounted to nothing more than an empty room.

She wanted to cancel the show seconds before they were due on stage, but she knew that was out of the question since they had all paid to see South Devon's flavour of the month. They even sold her album in the local Tourist Information Centre, between the postcards and the seashell seabeds. Stepping out into the spotlight, she sheltered her eyes from it to try and spot him one last time, and felt her heart jaundice with every face that was not his.

Managing a small "hello" before Etta began the drum intro to *Dead Stolen Flowers*, she felt herself suffocating in the greasepaint elixir mist. She did her best under the circumstances, but without him everything was meaningless. Even by the encore she could not shake the quicksand from her feet, and as she muttered an apologetic goodnight she realised she had just given the worst performance of the tour. Backstage, Len Stanway sported a beaming smile. She wondered if he too had missed the gig as he proffered a glass of Taittinger in her direction.

"The album's gone to number 68!"

"Do you know what happened to Stephen? He was supposed to be here."

"Stephen who?"

She shook her head, bile scratching at her vocal chords.

"You must know by now that the tour sold much better that we imagine, thanks to my PR contacts."

She heard his words and saw his gold canine wink, but she wanted to flee from the venue as quickly as possible. In her head she was still searching.

"…some very generous album reviews, and a nice bit of radio play. Anyhow, I have been doing some schmoozing and I have managed to get Q Magazine interested in doing a half page article. The Exmouth Journal is here tonight, you probably already know that, and NME were at the opening night, although their review seems to have fallen by the wayside. There's a possibility Radio One might invite you into their basement for a live session, and wait for this… I am in the throes of getting you a midday slot at Glastonbury this summer."

She sipped her cheap champagne, knowing that she should be feeling something other than despair. The bassist in her band, Stuart, perked up when he heard the word 'Glastonbury', but claimed he was once in a band that performed there post-sunset, although Len argued that people had fewer expectations back then, in reference to Stuart being a lot older than the rest of them. Etta killed the buzz by announcing she was going back to her native Norway for a while as her beloved uncle had suddenly fallen ill. Len was furious, thinking of how the sudden loss of the drummer would affect his plans, not to mention a booking the following week at the *Camden Underworld*. Etta slipped out of the dressing room before he could say "one month's notice required" again, and Petra soon followed, getting a lift back to Budleigh with her mother.

Her brain's grey clouds gathered as they approached the dark windows of her flat. Mustering a thank you to the woman who was unable to muster words like, "I'm proud of you," or even, "well done," she found her door key in the bottom of the crocodile skin handbag that she bought in London's Shepherd's Bush market during the tour. Inside the cold darkness she knew it was over when she spotted the letter folded on the draining board. With her champagne stomach turning sour, she read the three lines that consigned their relationship to the cesspit she had spent her life trying to claw out of.

That night drew itself out with Sovereign cigarettes and Beefeater gin. Sleep-starvation sawed her limbs away, but she did not want the realisation that waking would bring. Although consciousness was equally unbearable.

Petra received the obligatory sympathy from her band mates but felt they did not like him anyway. And then Etta left for Norway when she needed her the most. She needed shoulders, she needed comfort, but all she was left with was a record company piling on the pressure for more songs and more shows. But without her monolithic, monosyllabic muse, all she wanted to do was lie on her sofa in the space he left behind. While she immersed herself in daytime TV harridan makeovers, Stanway tried to keep her career alive by releasing a second single from the album. But with very little radio play and Petra refusing to promote it, it sank without trace.

Leaving the flat as little as possible, she wore her abandonment like an anchor, until her mother insisted she see their local doctor. Pills were prescribed to try and replace life's meaning, and the platitude, "don't worry, you will be back to your old self in no time," infected her ears. It was not the old self she wanted, but that extremely fleeting new one, so fleeting she begun to wonder if Stephen Jude Tyburn had just been a mirage. Or a conman.

Eventually Len Stanway gave her an ultimatum - either she moved with her band to London to start work on a new album or he would have no choice but to release them from the contract. Petra was angered by the blackmail, but she realised that sliding off Devon's emotional millstone would be for the best. With nothing in her possession but a smashed up life and a cupboard full of meals that only needed hot water and a stir, she knew it was only her career that could save her now. The rest of the band were keen, especially Etta who had just returned from her uncle's Fjord-side bedside.

Days before she was due to depart, her mother bought her a farewell Bloody Mary in *The Three Swans*. Across the room, drinking a milk stout with an antique squeezebox on her lap, was a woman with false eye-lashed eyes fixed on her. Despite her grey bob, she was clearly in her twenties like Petra. Her mother grimaced at the scarlet satin gown peeled over rack-stretched limbs and black stockinged legs in black bovver boots. "Must be from the chalet park," she muttered into her Shiraz. She kissed her daughter's vodka-flushed cheek goodbye and managed a good luck, desperate to leave before the pub's live music began. Petra was surreptitiously pleased to see the back of her.

The strange squeezebox woman was the first to perform that night, and her mournful, elongated playing elicited in Petra's mind a melancholic drunk sailor sheltering under a seaside bandstand. Entranced, she disappeared with the musician into haunted places. The spell continued after the playing stopped, and by the end of the night, Smokey agreed to play on Petra's as yet unwritten second album.

After a short band rehearsal with their new member, and an even shorter farewell gig at *The Three Swans*, the band left Budleigh Salterton for a rundown Victorian terrace house in Camberwell, South London, rented for them by the record company. All further promotion of *I Am Alive Save Me* was shelved, with Petra given time to write and record 'the difficult second album.'

Sitting on her dirty Camberwell bedroom carpet, big red Fender in hand, Petra felt a glimmer of contentment seep back into rage. Rage at the record company who clearly just saw her as a mad cash cow, turning her pain into profits, but most of all at herself for still having no idea how to rip that man out of her chest.

4

River looked up at the excitable raven flying above her bed and smiled. She remembered the first time he flew in through her window, the day she moved into this block of flats. He had looked straight into her eyes as if to say "please don't send me back to the Tower." That ancient building was eerily close by and River knew from experience just how terrifying it could be, so she made him some toast and he has become a semi permanent fixture on her curtain rail ever since.

She put last night's scrambled scribbles under her pillow and climbed out from beneath her Tom and Jerry duvet. It was exactly one year to the day that she met Nathan, and he insisted on them celebrating. She could not think of anything worse. Immersed in memories and flashbacks of her fifteenth century relationships, she was finding it increasingly difficult to equate that life with this one.

Shivering in her badly insulted bedroom, she watched herself dress in the mirror. She planned to wear the dungarees, sandals and stripy top ensemble that she wore when he first saw her on *Paranormal People,* but she did not want to be that lost and fumbling woman anymore. Instead, she picked out the pure white dress that had grabbed her attention through a Brick Lane charity shop window. Eerily, her first thought on seeing it was that it was the perfect outfit to climb the executioner's scaffold in. Once again she thought about her "lost" medieval kirtle and wimple, wondering how much the hospital thief probably sold them for on EBay. The strange commoditization of time and history; medieval rat droppings were probably of interest to some modern day collectors.

With a bowl of *Coco Pops* inside her, she kissed goodbye to Roger and made her way over to Nathan's apartment on the other side of the Thames. It was a psychologically treacherous trip that she made at least twice a week.

Walking through the squirrel-littered Trinity Square Gardens, she soon fell upon the cold stare of the grey Towers of London, as familiar to her as a creepy uncle. If it were not for the unidentified paranormal protector that saved her from 1483, she was positive she would have lost her life in one of them, or on the scaffold on Tower Hill. She cursed Tower Hamlets Council for housing her so close to the place of her metaphysical transition, they should have just let her stay in that assisted living centre for the rest of her life, instead of tipping her out into this giant city with nothing but a monthly appointment with an Occupational Therapist ("Magdalena but just call me Mags") to grip onto. Speeding up her pace, she reached the Thames and looked into its green ripples. She saw a face staring back up at her and her body froze. Swirling amongst the crisp packets and debris she saw fishermen on a bridge, the turrets of a castle upon a hill, the spires of churches, and heard the cacophony of screaming seagulls and cawing gannets. *How the arms of a hunter, a man trained for battle, hold me in that icy river that flows inches from our wooden home. He is my father and it is hours before his body was ripped to pieces by what must have been a wolf.*

Through a giddy blur, she stumbled along the path to the stone steps that lead up to Tower Bridge, and the snap of passing traffic slammed her back into the urban anxiety of today.

After crossing the Thames, she passed the patch of green known as Potter's Field where the magician David Blaine had himself suspended in the air in a glass box for forty four days. It was almost nine years ago now, just after her time-transition, and she used to stand and stare at him for hours at a time, relating completely to how he must have been feeling in there. An exhibited alien. Taxidermied alive. But while she was a freak show by no choice of her own, she could not understand why somebody would want to inflict that kind of madness upon themselves.

The Thames path eventually brought her to Borough High Street, and she welcomed its security blanket of pubs, shops, banks, restaurants and internet cafes. But it was not long before the middle ages slapped her around the face again, this time with Southwark Cathedral. The building had not changed much since the fifteenth century when she would have known it as St Mary Ovarie. Out of some strange self-annihilating curiosity she cast her eyes up its great clock tower and was immediately attacked by the smell of rotten air and the sound of horse hooves. She shuddered, not from this medieval miasma, but with the knowledge that just around the corner stood another time-slider, the ruins of Winchester Palace. After watching ant-like tourists crawl over the Golden Hinde, which was a reconstruction of a ship built one hundred years after her birth and therefore of no immediate psychological threat, she turned into Clink Street and was hit by the ruins of Winchester Palace's stone window frames. Her eyes filled them with the beautiful stained glass she once admired.

As often she did, she slipped into the little newsagent across the road for some sugar comfort. While purchasing a bag of sugary strawberry cobras, she accidentally dropped a coin onto a magazine cover circling the cellulite on fifteenth century blonde celebrity queen, Elizabeth Woodville. On blinking she saw that it was actually Madonna.

Stepping back out onto Clink Street, she nodded at her old friend, the skeleton that hung in a gibbet outside the Clink Prison museum. As the prison was functional in the fifteenth century she may well have known the flesh that once coated it. Today only the haunted basement of the original prison building remained intact. Next door were the buzzers to a collection of converted Victorian warehouse apartments, her boyfriend's being one of them.

"Is that you, kitten?" purred a softly spoken voice on the intercom.

She cringed when she knew she should be set alight. "Yes. Hello."

The door buzzed and she pushed it open.

On climbing the metal steps to the third floor, she was greeted by the fiery mane of Tiana, Nathan's sister, whom he shared the apartment with.

"Excited?"

"About what?"

"Your anniversary of course."

"Oh. Yes."

There was something clown-like about her pink rouged face, bright red hair, and glace cherry lips.

"He's inside getting ready. I'm just on my way out to make my millions."

River guessed from the mammoth cello case that she was going busking.

River liked their sophisticated arty pad, bought for them on the sale of their dead grandmother's historic Berkhamsted house. She knew she could never create the same atmosphere in her own poky dwelling.

Stepping out from the abstractly adorned canvases, rustic furnishings, phallic sculptures and tawdry religious imagery, was her boyfriend. Before reaching her he studied her as if for a still life. "I just want to paint you. Is that weird?"

"How old do you think I look?"

His face visibly changed gear. "Erm. Well, we talked about this before and agreed that you're probably in your late twenties like me."

"But can you try to be more specific?"

"Twenty seven. Twenty eight. Shame you're not a tree."

"Why, so you can cut off my head and count the rings? Why does every man I get close to want to behead me?"

"Who else has wanted to behead you?"

"Richard the third, of course. I am pretty sure that's why he imprisoned me in the Tower."

Although his girlfriend's time travel claims were part of the eccentric charm that first attracted him to her, the novelty wore off when he seriously began to fear for her psychological state. He thought it best to change the subject. "How do you feel about a wander down Borough Market? We could get some fresh coffees and organic pastries and eat them by the Thames. Sound nice?"

It annoyed River when he spoke to her like a child, but bearing in mind she was reborn nine years ago, it could be argued that mentally she was.

Leaving his dark, paint peeling building for the bustling stalls radiating crepes, croissants, and ostrich burgers round the corner, Nathan grew concerned about River's silence. She would usually comment on the surroundings, enquire about his latest artwork, ask why we have thunderstorms – anything. Though on this special day River was different, diffident. "Something wrong, mon poussin?"

River turned to face him. "Can we sit down?"

"Are you tired?"

They walked to the benches below Southwark Cathedral's vast tower. "I've not been sleeping," she said as they sat down amongst the history-envious Americans and bored European students. "I've been having new flashbacks, so much more vivid than the ones I had before."

"They're just bad dreams."

"They are not bad dreams. I have them during the day."

"And what is it you are seeing now?"

"Everything I went through in the fifteenth century."

"It's just your mind playing tricks on you. We will get your real memory back for you, I promise."

"This is my real memory."

"Your real memory is not the fifteenth century."

"Of course it is. Just because it is beyond your realm of understanding, it doesn't mean it isn't true."

She wanted to ask him how an artist could be so cynical, but the medieval brickwork of the cathedral hooked her brain again and *Richard is bringing a crucifix up to his thin determined lips. He kisses the tortured Christ. Words in Latin. He kisses him again. Latin again, hushed and beseeching. He raises his deep set eyes to me, and I look away feeling as if I am intruding on the bond between God and the man I love. He says: "I would not have needed to do any of this if my brother had just looked after his health, instead of squandering it with whores and drink. His greed has created a disaster. I was happy with my life up in the north with my family and my people. I was respected and heavily rewarded. It was a good life. I did not want any of this. I never once considered taking the throne for myself, because I was content being the dutiful and loyal brother to the man it rightfully belonged to. But now, if I don't take it I risk losing everything that I have ever lived for. Taking the crown is now my only way of being safe."*

"River? … River, where have you gone?"

A black cat skulked over to them and began brushing its head against River's ankle, waking her from the trance. "I used to look at this cathedral from my prison cell window in the Tower," she said as her eyes refocused.

Nathan was about to speak, but held his tongue and put his hand on her thigh instead, feeling the thin, white cotton of her dress. River reached down to stroke the cat's head, and as she did so it took the hem of her dress into its mouth.

"Bentley," wailed an approaching young, floppy haired man who appeared to be wearing pyjamas. "I'm so sorry. She has a problem with doing this. Come on, Bentley."

Nathan tried to prize the material out of the cat's jaws, but it just made her grip tighter, looking up at River with a devil in her eyes.

"I'm so sorry," repeated the mortified man, gently tugging at the feline by the scruff of her neck. "Don't worry, she won't hurt you. She just has this funny thing with trying to possess things."

River stroked her furry belly, causing her to bare a canine. "She doesn't look very friendly."

"She's actually really lovely. I took her to an animal specialist who said I should get rid of her because she does this sort of thing all the time, but I think it's just her way of showing love."

"Is there no way of calling her off?" asked Nathan, growing impatient at his pet-owning ineptitude.

"Nathan, don't be rude. I really don't mind."

"The only way she'll let go is if we all look away and pretend we're not interested in what she's doing."

Nathan looked up at the cathedral clock tower while River took out one of her strawberry snakes. Bentley jumped onto her lap and shoved her nose into the glistening sugar.

"Oh, thank God," said the face-flushed man. "How's your dress? Not ripped I hope? Actually, don't look at it, if she thinks you care she'll latch on again."

River broke a bit of snake off for her which she snatched before leaping back to the ground. Nathan leant down to tickle her under the chin and she responded by rolling onto her back in a quarter moon shape, the snake's red tail sticking out of her mouth.

"Bentley is a strange name for a lady cat," said River.

"We named her after the Spurs player, David Bentley. My mum and I were big fans."

"There were quite a few Tottenham Hotspur fans where I grew up," said Nathan.

"Are you from north London then?"

"No. Berkhamsted."

"Richard's mother lived there," said River to no one in particular. "In the castle."

"Richard who?" Nathan asked, suspiciously.

"Richard the third. How many times do I have to tell you?"

5

Smoking her way through a packet of Sovereigns, Petra Sherry sat in the centre of the yellowing sitting room with her band disseminated around her. She looked up from the cigarette burnt carpet to meet their eyes. In Etta's she saw the same sympathy she expressed ever since the day Stephen left her; *The Day of the Black Storm*, as Petra called it on the only song she has so far written for the new album. Smokey looked anxious, while Stuart conveyed his usual impatience. "Made a start on the new songs yet?" he eventually asked, as often he did.

She ground her cigarette into the choking ashtray. "Why? Didn't you like the last ones?"

"I don't think the record company will like the colour you're turning this wallpaper," he treacherously continued.

The strained, stained room was accustomed to Petra's silent rage, but today she decided to surprise them. "Actually, I've written most of the album already. I could do with some new musicians to tell you the truth. And maybe replace some of the old ones" she added for Stuart's benefit.

There was shock all round. This divine utterance might be enough to get them off the dole, or it might even be the first in a line of utterances that marked the resurgence of their long-thwarted musical ambitions. The band's greedy eyes continued to consume their matriarch as she lit up another cigarette. And then something even more shocking occurred - Smokey, a woman so quiet the rest of the band nicknamed her 'Mousey,' began talking.

"Petra, I have heard this red haired woman play the cello at Elephant and Castle station and I have a strange feeling that she is just what you are looking for."

"I appreciate the thought," Petra replied to her Thames-green gaze. The unwaveringness of it compelled her to continue. "I suppose it won't hurt to hear her."

"You won't be disappointed."

"And nor will she, a busker invited to join a band signed to a top independent record label," said Petra.

"Yes, but for how much longer?" Stuart murmured into his chipped mug. "This tea's gone cold."

Etta walked over to the singer's threadbare armchair and embraced her. "Well done, I'm so proud of you."

"I haven't done anything yet. Mind my cigarette."

"I thought something was off, this *NME* smells of cat piss," moaned Stuart.

"It's not what it used to be," conceded Etta.

"That's what you getting for picking things up off the street," offered Smokey.

"I wouldn't have to pick *NME*s up from the street if Camberwell had a newsagent which actually sold them," said Stuart. "Couldn't they have put us in a better part of London?"

"Maybe the Dorchester was full up," Smokey threw back over her shoulder as she strode out of the room like a bloodthirsty stray on the trail of a dormouse.

"Just when you think the cat's got her tongue, you get all that," said Petra, pondering the space she left behind on the sponge-ejaculating sofa.

6

For Tiana, validation was a cascading coin and the possibility of her music having an effect on the rest of a person's day. Although, to her knowledge, her music had never had an effect on anyone's day, not even her brother's. He was so miserable these days, although he hid it every time his girlfriend came round. She resented how his despondency could only be lifted by a crumb thrown by that perpetually irritating, preternatural woman.

The most frustrating thing, Tiana thought as clip-clopping heals clip-clopped past her coveted spot at the bottom of the escalator at Elephant and Castle tube, was that she knew she could play well. She knew that she if she were given the chance, the right audience, the right venue, they would be downloading her compositions onto their portable devices in the masses. Instead of using their portable devices to block her out. But the prattling devil in her ear told her she was destined for obscurity, and when that voice spoke all she could see were the dark creatures that lived in the underworld beneath the Underground.

Something floated into her cello case. A five pound note. A five pound note! That never happened. Shocked, she stopped her string stroking to look up at her new patron: a young woman who must have been almost six feet tall sporting a slim fitting scarlet dress under a tailored black suit jacket.

"Thank you very much."

"I've heard you before," descended a castrato-edged West Country accent. "I love the cello."

"It's a beautiful instrument, isn't it?"

The statuesque woman delved into a red salmon purse and took out a card. "Your future is going to change. I am sure you have heard of Petra Sherry?"

"Is she a clairvoyant?"

"No she is not a clairvoyant. Are you not up to date with music?"

"Only classical."

She raised an eyebrow. "Well anyway, she's auditioning new musicians for her band and would like to hear you. You live locally to here."

Tiana heard no inflection to signify a question, but nodded anyway. "Yes, near London Bridge."

"She will come over tomorrow afternoon." She handed her another card and a fancy fountain pen. "Write down your address."

Tiana wrote her address down in red ink for the woman who was clearly not accustomed to pleasantries, and arranged a time for Petra Sherry to come and hear her play. As she disappeared into the sea of suits, a cold sensation remained, leaving Tiana more baffled than excited. But she was aware that this audition could well be a crucial spin of Lady Fortune's inscrutable wheel.

"Do you know any David Essex?" asked a passing briefcase.

7

"Stop fussing, Ti, everything looks fine," Nathan groaned irritably at the nervous wreck. "She is coming to hear you play, not inspect the flat."

"Everything has to look perfect," she said, emphasising her words with a slam of a blue and gold cushion. "This is an opportunity I cannot throw away."

"In that case you should be getting more practice in."

"I've been practising all afternoon."

The caustic drone of the buzzer caused Tiana to let out a cry and slip into the bathroom.

"I'll get that then shall I?"

"Bonjour," he dispassionately said into the telephone receiver.

"We are looking for somebody called Tiana Pentelow."

"Top floor, push the door," he replied before replacing it. "Let's take a look at this famous singer that no one has ever heard of then. Tiana, where are you?"

The approaching sound of high heels trotting up metal stairs reminded him of sheep climbing over cattle grids. On opening the door, Nathan was bemused by how the two women, both slender limbed and dressed head to toe in black, just glared without speaking. One of their gazes was accompanied by a slightly open mouth emitting a fog of smoke, while the other stared like a pet gecko waiting to be fed.

"Erm, hello, you must be ….Come in … My sister won't be a second."

"Smokey is my name," said a young, pallid face beneath a stark bob of grey hair. He reached out to take her scarlet-ringed hand. "And *this* is Petra Sherry."

"You're the one my sister is so nervous about meeting."

He reached his hand out to the woman, viscerally recoiling at vintage viscose fur. Instead of taking his hand, she awkwardly stepped forward to kiss him on the cheek. Unprepared for this, nor keen on physical contact with strangers, he tried to avoid as much of her mouth as possible, and ended up with it on his ear.

"I love your apartment," Petra said, knocking her cigarette out on its silver packet.

"Thank you, I designed it myself. Let me know if you want to purchase any of my paintings. They're unpriced but I am open to all three figure and four figure offers. I'm actually just off to meet my girlfriend."

"*Girlfriend*!" the word simultaneously spun out of the musicians' mouths like a magician's dagger.

Unsure of how to persevere with this odd interaction, or even how to end it, Nathan brushed past them and closed the door on their black-lined gazes. Smokey walked straight over to a shelf and grabbed hold of a photograph of River. "This will be her."

"Who? Tiana?"

"No, the girlfriend."

Before Petra could take a look, a red fountain of hair flowed from the bathroom. "I'm so sorry to keep you waiting. Where's my brother?"

"He's gone," said Petra sounding almost bereft.

"You must be Petra Sherry?"

"Unfortunately."

"Thank you so much for coming."

The woman Tiana met at the tube station did not unpeel her eyes from the picture in her hand. "Is this her? Is this his girlfriend?"

"Smokey, you're being rude."

"Yes, that's River. There are photographs and portraits of her all over the flat. My brother's an artist, you see."

"Aren't we all?" sighed Petra.

"I've made some tea if you like that sort of thing?"

Once she plucked them out of River and moistened them with Lady Grey, Tiana began bowing the composition she had chosen for the occasion. She utilised her instrument's ability to sound both sinister and soothing, warm and majestic, but every sophisticated key change, every effort to show her originality were lost on these women whose eyes were on everything but her.

Petra pointed at something in the corner of the room once she finally put down her bow. "Did he paint that too?"

"He did," Tiana replied, too deflated to actually look.

Petra went to take a closer look.

"Did you like my playing?"

"Yes," replied the Devonshire singer to a psychedelic pastel of the Thames at night. "Welcome to *The Eleventh Hour*."

8

Sitting on her kitchen floor surrounded by history books and print outs from the library computers, River gently rested her head on the black-feathered bird beside her. She craved affection and Roger was the only one in this time zone she wanted it from. Nathan refused to believe and understand that nine years ago the seven hundred year old Cradle Tower was her maternity ward, Beefeaters were her midwives, and what she actually needed from him was nurturing.

She wasn't really in the mood for it but she could feel it coming - another moving fifteenth century jigsaw piece. Her roots, her blood, instead of this ridiculously overcrowded city where only the Thames and the odd surviving medieval building feel real. A farce in which her boyfriend looks to her as his whole life when she is still grappling in the dark for her own. Pinning the limping raven to her bosom, River searched for a pen in case she needed to write notes once the flashback had spat her out.

Awaiting the pungent sensations of her medieval life, she went into the kitchen in search of something to settle her stomach. Opening the fridge and taking out the milk prompted Roger to start chirping loudly.

"Oh, Roger, I haven't fed..."... *My heart and hatred cannot be contained in this tiny cell. When I close my eyes, blood drips onto my dirty hands through the cracks in the ceiling. Measuring the length of my neck with my cold hand, I cannot see how an axe, however sharp, will remove my head in one fell swoop. At what point exactly will I die? Out of this thin arrow slit I scream at the cathedral across the Thames. My throat is sore from its pleas. What will I be like when they lead me out there? I want to be calm as I confess my sins to the priest and beg Jesus to accept my soul. Is it too late for mercy? My eyes fall onto the boats floating obliviously along the Thames. The evening is growing thicker and colder. I blacken at the endless silence, but what is worse is what I can hear right now. The sound of the guard's footsteps climbing the stone steps to my cell. My organs freeze. I curl up and close my eyes. A white light. My skin is being touched. Fear drains from my veins and love encompasses me like I have never known before.*

The intangible woman was sat motionless on the floor as if the cold from the fridge had frozen her. The bird she loved more than anything feasted happily away on bacon, cream and cottage cheese, until Nathan stood over them adorned in a tangerine jumper and holding the spare key. Stepping over a discarded tub of humus and a dirty teddy bear, he was immediately struck by two saucer sized eyes, mesmerised, apparently, by him. "River, can you hear me?" He began shaking her, scaring Roger into the open icebox.

The taxi driver took some persuading and fibbing to let her into his cab ("She's not drunk, she is just having a bad reaction to some medication") and she appeared even more zombified once they arrived at St Thomas's Hospital. He perched her on one of the neon blue chairs before going up to the counter.

"Name there, please," said the handsome Rasta receptionist before Nathan could say anything.

"It's my girlfriend, she's come over all funny. She used to be a patient at this hospital."

"She'll still have to wait along with everyone else I'm afraid."

"Do you know for how long?"

"Up to four hours."

"Four hours! But she's barely conscious. I had to get her here in a taxi."

"Did she fall?"

"No, she's … she's in some sort of trance."

He peered at her over his computer screen. "Has she taken anything?"

"Not to my knowledge."

"Ok, let me know if her condition changes. Write her name there and take a seat."

Sitting beside his girlfriend, he looked around at all the other patients. An elderly woman across the room whose arm was in a homemade silk scarf sling was watching him. She did not look away or smile when he clocked her. Beneath his anxiety lay a glimmer of hope that the doctor would finally be able to diagnose her condition and administer the correct treatment. For all his love for her, he knew she was mentally ill and getting worse, and his own internet research into her delusions and hallucinations suggested a scary array of psychoses. Fear shot through his body and he shuffled closer to her. "River, you are going to be okay." He looked up to see that other peoples' eyes were glued to a small television attached to the ceiling. He squinted at a topless, tanned, toned man opening a mosquito door and smiling at who he found behind it. Ramsay Street's bright utopia mocking London's dark, locked door spirit.

Despite growing up just thirty miles outside of London, he had always felt like a stranger in this labyrinthine city. His eyes were closed to the bitter capitalist pill that he would have to swallow if he did not sell more paintings. And River clearly did not live in 'the real world' either which, of course, is what first attracted him to her. But she was slowly becoming as cold to him as London itself. Holding her now in this comatose state was the closest they had been for weeks.

The closing theme tune of *Neighbours* chirped like a jester at a wake and after three minutes of capitalist aspiration that Nathan was too despondent to look away from it was replaced by the grey constipation of *Coronation Street*. The sling-armed woman's eyes zapped to the screen like a lizard's tongue on a fly.

"That on in the afternoon now?" asked a porter, stopping to look at the screen. "That wig really is shocking."

Nathan smirked and River muttered something to herself.

"River? Are you awake?"

She looked at him like a baby sparrow that had just fallen out of a tree. "Where am I?"

"A and E."

Her face morphed between confusion, realisation and disbelief. "Why am I here?"

"Because you were out of it and needed help."

She stood up and loomed over him. "Of all the people I thought I could trust."

"River..."

"How could you do this to me?"

"What did you want me to do, just leave you unconscious on your kitchen floor?"

"Yes, thank you. I was fine there."

"Listen to me, you *need* to see a doctor. I just want you to hear what he has to say."

"I don't need a doctor, I just need to be left alone."

"I don't even know who you are anymore." The words seemed to fall out of his mouth before he even thought them.

"What did you just say?"

Before he could respond, she turned around and departed the purple plastic Hades. He wanted to go after her, but the look she left him with was like Greta Garbo on acid.

"Split personality is it?" Nathan turned to see that the question emanated from the old woman with the homemade sling. "I have it too, sweetheart. That's why I'm here. The person I was last night went out and hurt me. I don't know exactly how I ended up with all these people inside my head and I probably never will, but according to Doctor Chop it is the biggest growing mental complaint in the city."

9

At midnight, the newly employed cellist finally arrived home after celebrating her inauguration into the *Eleventh Hour*. The band took a night bus back to Camberwell, except for their singer-songwriter who insisted on escorting Tiana back to her Clink Street apartment.

"That was sweet of you, Petra. Will you come up for a night-cap?"

"A quick one maybe."

Petra followed Tiana up the metal staircase. On opening the front door and turning on the light they were met by the silhouette of Nathan sat on the carpet cradling a bottle of Cognac. Despite the fact he had consumed more alcohol than them, he did not look a fraction as cheerful.

"Turn off the light," he growled.

"But we've got a guest, Nathan. You've met Petra Sherry."

"Oh, just Petra, please. Hello again, Nathan."

"I said turn it off."

Tiana felt she had no choice but to obey, delivering her brother back to the darkness. "Sorry, Petra, this is awkward."

"Not at all." Petra treaded softly over to the night's casualty and crouched down beside him. "Brandy is it? We drink a lot of that where I'm from."

Tiana hated seeing him like this; it reminded her of what he was like just before he met River, the days when his endless searching for love left him hopeless. She resented River for being yet another false hope.

"Where did you go?" he asked his sister over Petra's too close, ashtray hair.

"I've been out celebrating with my new band, remember?"

"Oh yes. Happy days."

"I love your paintings, Nathan," Petra persevered.

"Do you?"

"They're really impressive."

Nathan swigged again from the bottle and climbed to his feet. "I'm so glad you think so."

"Nathan, you're being rude," said his mortified sister.

"No, no, he's fine."

"As a matter of fact, that's what I'm going to do right now. Paint."

"You can't paint in this state." His sister followed him to his bedroom where he picked up his painting paraphernalia, and then brushed past her towards the front door, grabbing his brown sheepskin jacket from where he threw it.

"Nathan, where are you going, it's gone midnight!?"

He closed the door on the two musicians and clambered down the staircase into the dark and dusky streets of Southwark.

"I'm so sorry about him, Petra."

"Don't be silly. Look, Tiana, it's getting late, I might go and catch a cab."

"Oh. What about your drink? ... Let me call you a taxi at least."

"No, I'll pick up one on Borough High Street. It won't be difficult."

"Please don't go just yet. I want to show you something."

"What is it?" The impatience in her voice was suddenly palpable.

"Please sit down."

"Tiana..."

"Please. It won't take a second."

Petra quickly obeyed as if hoping to get this over with as quickly as possible.

Tiana sped off into her bedroom before returning with a CD. "Look," she said, sitting a little too close to her. "It's your album, *'I Am Alive Save Me.'* I went up to the second hand music shops on Berwick Street to find it."

Petra took the CD. There she was on the cover, lying in the Devonshire sea like a pound shop Lady of Shalott. Long black hair floating on the ripples like long strands of seaweed. On her face was a small, self-satisfied smirk, encapsulating the album's hollow concept of redemptive love.

"Why are you showing me this?"

"I've listened to all of it and I just love it. I love your voice, I love your words, I love all the arrangements. Petra, you don't know how proud I am to join your band and be a part of the follow up."

"Those songs mean nothing to me now. When I hear them now I just hear a stupid, naïve, brainless cow who knew nothing about the world. A woman singing about love just before it tore her apart. It's a joke. A sick joke."

Petra pressed her nails into her palm, and on her wrist Tiana saw scars. She gently took hold of Petra's hand, caressing her cicatrices with her thumb, before bringing her fingers up to her mouth where she delicately kissed them.

"What are you doing?"

"How did you get all these scars?"

"Why does it matter?" Her impatience was turning into anger and she disentangled herself from the unwanted human ivy.

"When was the last time you listened to your own…?"

Petra snatched the album off her and threw it on the floor. "I don't care about that record and I don't want to see it or hear it for the rest of my life. Now, if you'll excuse me." Petra's gaunt frame swung towards the front door. "I really have to go."

"But…," Tiana began, her arms reaching out like a lonesome sycamore. As Petra's heels xylophoned the stairwell, Tiana breathed in the troubadour's smoke and red wine wake.

*

Releasing his darkening spirit into the half-lit Victorian serial killer haunt of Clink Street, paints in pockets and canvass under arm, Nathan decided to reattempt St Paul's Cathedral. As he paced precariously towards Cardinal Cap Alley, which faced the cathedral across the Thames, he recalled his girlfriend's outburst. Her words cut his brain like a scalpel. However uncharacteristic her reaction was, in the clarity of twilight he could fully understand it. He had betrayed her trust.

Staring up at the tall, moonlight-glazed Georgian house where Christopher Wren was said to have lived while he designed and built the cathedral, Nathan felt simultaneously in awe and inadequate. Under a streetlight he read the plaque besides the front door: "Here lived Sir Christopher Wren during the building of St Paul's Cathedral. Here also, in 1502, Catherine Infanta of Castile and Aragon, afterwards first queen of Henry VIII, took shelter on her first landing in London." Nineteen years after his girlfriend claims to have travelled time, he thought, pressing his palm against the building, hoping to absorb some of Wren's dynamism. The front door opened and an unimpressed, grey bearded man stepped out. "Can I help you?"

"Sorry, I was just ... sorry...."

"This is a private house."

"I know. I'm not a tourist, I only live around the corner."

The man tutted and closed his door. Nathan turned to look at Wren's majestic masterpiece across the water; the huge, illuminated, architectural jewel reflected in the ripples of the Thames. But thinking about River and how she may never forgive him sent his eyes to the dark world beneath the currents.

*

Prowling, creeping and padding, Petra watched him from a close distance, carrying her heels so as not to make a sound. Damp stockinged feet on a moonlit Thames path, she knew she had not changed at all from the days she stalked Stephen on cliff edges. Nicotine-stained fingers splayed into the charged air, and she felt herself become possessed by that same hunger and ache. That helpless feeling of being controlled by the one thing she was unable to give to herself.

10

River threw the history book at the wall and collapsed onto her bedroom floor. Yet another one she could not find any trace of herself in. The events and people from her flashbacks were historically accounted for, but never her. Why does history always forget the mistresses? Fuelled with righteous anger, she opened her drawer and took out her memoir. If historians were resolute to ignore her she would have to imprint the story of Dimiza into history herself. Glaring at her face in that press cutting, all wild eyed confusion and open backed hospital gown, she drew a line through the words she had already written. Time to start again, clearly, confidently and accurately.

I grew up in the small timbre framed house in Inverness that I shared it with my three older brothers and a buzzard named Grizella. We spent most of our lives without our mother around as she worked as a seamstress and spinner in the castle that loomed over us from the top of the hill. One day a harlot who often treated my father's stag hunting wounds knocked on our door to say that he had gone missing. My brothers went out in search for him. They came home that evening and told me that a wild animal had ripped him to pieces and they found parts of his body in the mountains that overlooked Loch Ness. I could not sleep that night, but I could not cry either. The next morning I woke to discover a wolf's head on a wooden plaque hanging up in the kitchen. Blood was on its fangs and I wondered if it was my father's.

River put the end of her biro into her mouth and read it back. Fighting the self-doubt she straightened her back and continued.

All of my life I had wanted to work at that castle with my mother. I used to wave up at the arrow slits imagining that she could see me from behind them, or better still, that the duke who lived there could. He was the younger brother of the King of Scotland and to be in such close proximity to royalty prickled at my skin. My mother promised me that when I was sixteen she would get me a job there. And she did. In approximately 1477, not long after my sixteenth birthday, which we celebrated with a bowl of dried dates and a cask of ale, she led me over that drawbridge for the first time. The closer to the giant gatehouse we got, the more formidable it all became. I made sure not to display any fear to my mother because I didn't want her to change her mind. I had been waiting for this moment all my life.

Once we got to the portcullis she handed me over to a guard she knew, kissed me on the cheek and told me that she would come to visit me in my lodgings that night. I detected a glimmer of trepidation in her eyes and her attempts to blink it away.

"This way," the guard told me, walking off towards the castle's towering keep.

"Is that where the Duke of Albany lives?"

He looked down at me like he was surprised I had the gumption to speak. "This is where he has his chambers, yes. But you will never see them and you will never see him."

Instead of walking up to the lofty main entrance, we took the steps down to a basement door. Expecting to be greeted by tapestries and goblets of gold, my senses were immediately attacked by the smell of meat cooking, the sight of enormous beheaded carcasses hanging from the ceiling, and the intense heat from the gigantic black cauldrons that I thought only witches owned. A large sweaty woman pushed her big round red face into mine: "Morag's girl are you?" I nodded and she took me by the arm.

Kneading dough, chopping up stags and boar, plucking heron and beheading storks – being one of the castle kitchen's several scullions was hard work but I never complained. There was no other place in Inverness that I wanted to be, and to my silent delight, after working there for a year it was decided that I should become one of the duke and duchess's serving staff.

Overwhelmed with being in such close proximity to the man I had spent my childhood daydreaming about, I initially returned to being the timid little girl who was first led over the drawbridge. But that soon faded, and within a few days I started doing something I was instructed by the duke's chief attendant never to do – I started looking into the duke's eyes as I served him. Curiosity propelled me, plus I was desperate for him to know who I was. Ladling pigeon stew into his jewel encrusted bowl, I returned his gaze and I smiled, absorbing as much of him as possible before my transgression was noticed by another servant, or worse, his fat wife who sat beside him at the centre of the long table. I was surprised at how young he was, certainly no older than thirty. Immaculately dressed in fur and velvet, beard neat and symmetrical, nose long and thin, eyes big, grey and glimmering. I never once saw him talk to or even look at his silk seam stretching duchess.

A chicken beheader with a predilection for gossip told me that the duke was an adulterer who slept with a different mistress every night. Female staff would either fear or long for one of his henchmen to enter their bedchambers as they were sleeping, summoning them to spend the rest of the night with him. Some ladies tried their best to position themselves within his view during the day, thinking that his loving could release them from the relentless grind of castle work. As soon as I heard this I did the same.

As a child I learnt that the King of England had fallen in love with a beautiful commoner called Elizabeth Woodville after she jumped out at him from behind a tree as he rode through a forest. And now she was his queen. It was like a true life fairy tale, the fairy tale that I had always wanted for myself.

After serving the duke's table for about a month, I finally felt the coarse hands of a henchman shake me awake. Despite wanting this, I could not remember being more scared as I was led up the dark, narrow stone staircase to his bedchamber. Beyond the luscious wall tapestries and behind the long velvet canopies of his four poster bed, the duke lay naked illuminated by a half lit, half smouldering fire. Out of duty to my ambitious heart I removed my kirtle, and spent the night engulfed in hirsute aristocratic flesh.

I was sent for the following night too. And the next. He told me he loved my passion and spark, although I had no idea I possessed such qualities. Soon I was his favourite mistress and his fat, jealous wife had to make do with the cleft of downy duck feather pillows. He told me she had tried to get me thrown out of the castle but he intervened. She started locking herself in her bedchamber, crying through the door that she wanted their marriage dissolved. Alexander did not care though, and I was secretly thrilled that I was having such a dramatic effect on the royal household.

Gossip about my royal favour scuttled along the castle walls like rats. Duchess Katherine's chief lady in waiting, Gormla, similarly red faced and obese, became a tyrant towards me, no doubt with repressed jealousy. Ex mistresses who were no longer summoned bubbled over with either scorn or gratitude. I lived in daily fear of being poisoned. My mother was worried for my safety, but ultimately blamed herself for bringing me here in the first place.

One night, the duke twitched with anxiety and hardly allowed me to touch him. I begged him to tell me what was wrong and eventually he told me that he had warning from a courtier at Edinburgh Castle that his brother, the King of Scotland, thought he was plotting against him.

"Why would he think such a thing?"

"Because it's true," he replied. "Dimiza, my brother is just a wimpy old heather doll who is much more interested in fancy young tailors and handsome shoemakers than going out hunting and jostling like a real king should. I have been planning a way to get him off that throne for some time now and I've been corresponding with our youngest brother, John, and some other nobles who feel the same way."

"Are you saying you want to replace him with yourself?" I excitedly asked him, the image of myself at the Queen of Scotland jumping before my eyes.

"Perhaps."

I could see our thrones side by side in Edinburgh Castle.

"But some paranormal old hag and her pet cat seem to have put him in touch with someone who intercepted my letters. He has managed to extract a confession out of the Earl of Lennox because he could not handle a little bit of torture. John has already been arrested and I have been told his soldiers will soon be on their way for me too. I can either flee Scotland or ride to Edinburgh Castle and beg for forgiveness."

"What are you going to do?"

"I have stationed an archer at every window and I am going to leave for Paris tomorrow."

"Paris?"

"I am on good terms with the King of France, and am sure he will give me shelter. At daybreak I am riding to my castle at Dunbar and from there I will take a boat to Calais."

"What will I do when you go?"

"You are coming with me."

On hearing this, my head burned with the thrill of leaving behind those cold grey walls for a land unknown.

Looking up from her scrawl, something hooked her eye. Through her window she saw a tall woman wearing a long scarlet dress and black hood standing on the pavement across the street. She was staring straight up at her. Her skin froze and she looked away feeling both exposed and threatened. Allowing herself another glance, she saw that the woman had gone. Slowly, she got up from her chair and edged over towards the window. The emptiness of the street made her wonder if she was ever there at all.

11

If only I could touch him, Petra thought, pulling her windswept hair back from her pallid face. Wrapping her coat tight around her, she dragged on her thirteenth king size *Sovereign* of the day. If only she could hold him and whisper into his ear that somebody out there cares, cares enough not to dislodge her eyes from his troubled face for the past hour.

Every so often she photographs his delicate profile; the slightly turned up Grecian nose, the thick dark sideburns, lips pursed in concentration. God resided in the single strand of straight brown hair that crossed his jaw line. The transparent tension that lay beneath his skin, he could almost be Stephen Jude. No, he is Stephen Jude, returning to lick the injuries he inflicted on her. Something supernatural had obviously looked down on her pain and decided that it needed a salve. A salve and a saviour.

*

"Why can't I just be appreciated?" Nathan asked himself as he mixed greys with blues. Not just as an artist but as a human being. A dark, volatile, greedy, green river was engulfing the cathedral and everything else in its wake. He didn't know whether to just throw the canvass in the bin and try and get some sleep. The cold air was doing nothing to cool his thoughts. She did not care about him or his art; just her stupid, psychotic fantasies, a squashed-beak raven and a collection of antique teddy bears. So why did he still love her?

Love is a masochist.

She never even asked him to paint her.

What a narcissist.

12

River opened her memoir, picked up her red fluffy pen, and let her eyes wander out the window. Streetlights and moonlight slithered through the trees that lined the street. She could taste the fear in her breath, both at the thought of seeing that strange, scarlet dressed woman again, and at the empty page waiting to be filled. Startled, she felt something kiss her bare ankle. Looking down she saw a black feather at her heal. She slipped it in her hair and carried on with her blood red saga.

My lover, Alexander Stewart the Duke of Albany, sent his messenger off to France to inform King Louis XI that he was on his way. Not even his fat duchess knew of our departure. As I climbed aboard the narrow carvel bobbing on the tide, I thought about the family that I was leaving behind, and the possibility of Inverness Castle being captured by the king. My mother would lose her livelihood. But there was nothing I could do about that now and if I were to go back the king would probably want me dead too.

In the salty air I could smell the impending storm. While our captain was trying to control the steer, Alexander shivered and pressed his cold face against my warm breasts.

The white sails lashed noisily overhead but I was not scared. I felt sick but I was not scared.

She checked her phone just as it vibrated with a message, the sensation of technology on her fingertips very much of this century. 'River, I don't know what to say to make things better. Tell me what you want me to say.' *Nathan, what would be the point of you saying something that I have told you to say?* she thought, but did not text. Instead, she continued with her scribbles, wishing she could crawl into the pages of that life, instead of trying to make sense of two of them.

A moth eaten felt hat, a humungous hooked nose, a fish-like mouth that never smiled, and a stomach even more bloated than that of my lover's sad old wife; the King of France looked nothing like I had imagined. He was known as the Universal Spider as he had his fingers in the political pies of every country in Europe. Despite being obsessed with what people thought of him, he was a man-hater who preferred the company of his spaniels.

On arriving at his grand apartments at the Chateau du Louvre he silently lifted his fat, gold ringed fingers for Alexander to kiss. He did so and then introduced his weather-beaten crew who all bowed. Finally, I was presented as his "herbalist" (that's a new one, I thought) and I bent my knees. I avoided eye contact as that was one bed I never wanted to be summoned to.

More scheming than welcoming, within days of us arriving, King Louis insisted that Alexander marry one of his relatives, a woman named Anne De La Tour, in order to solidify the ancient alliance between Scotland and France against England. Little did he know that Alexander was now an outlaw of Scotland and already married, but agreed to his terms to guarantee his support and the lavish chateau he had housed us in. They married the following week, but fortunately never shared a bed, so I was able to remain the key female influence in his life. However, it soon became clear to Alexander that masquerading as the King of Scotland's bosom brother was never going to get him his castle back. The King of France would never assist him against his brother, so we had to find a king who would.

Alexander already had a close friend and ally in England, the Earl of Douglas, whom his paranoid brother forced out of Scotland many years previous. When Alexander wrote to him to tell him he was bent on war against his brother and needed an English base, the fervour in his reply was palpable. We departed from the chateau in the dead of the night and made our way to Calais. By the time our carvel approached the English port of Southampton, Alexander already had a meeting arranged with the King of England.

King Edward IV of England was always up for an invasion of Scotland. Their regular raids and skirmishes on English border towns made them a constant thistle in his side. An alliance with King James's rebellious brother would be highly advantageous to him if he could put him on the Scottish throne instead - under terms that suited England rather than Scotland of course. The English king had a treaty that he wanted to present to him and requested that Alexander meet him and his younger brother, Richard Duke of Gloucester, at Fotheringhay Castle near the town of Peterborough on the 12th July 1482.

River looked up at the Day-Glo colours of *Home and Away* on mute, impressed with how vividly she was able to recall and compile her medieval escapades. Or had she just absorbed too many history books? She refused to allow the question to throw her and continued.

Alexander knew this was the best chance he'd ever get of deposing his brother. He even began styling himself "King Alexander IV of Scotland." If he got rid of those bigamous marriages, was there a chance of me becoming Queen Dimiza? I dared not ask this question, but I was delighted when he told me he wanted me to attend him when he met the King of England at Fotheringhay Castle.

Alexander presented me to the King of England as his "chief wine taster" and I smiled to myself at this sudden promotion. He was extremely tall but sadly also very fat, with a handsome face blighted by burst blood vessels. A sure sign of drinking far too much wine and ale, I thought to myself. He hid his huge belly behind the most majestic cloak of gold-woven blue silk I had ever seen. Although in his late thirties to early forties, he needed servants to help him in and out of his chair and had trouble catching his breath.

His gold goblet was never far from his lips, once he managed to prize it from his own taster who always seemed to need a second gulp of everything to be sure.

The king constantly cast his eyes up and down my body, no doubt imagining me naked, but it was his brother, Richard Duke of Gloucester, who enchanted me. While his brother began requesting plate after plate of heron, lark, pigeon and swan, all Richard gnawed on was his lower lip. He looked about ten years younger than his brother and was just as handsome, although much slimmer, shorter and darker. His hair was thick and, unusually for a man, his eyes appeared to be a dark shade of violet. Bequeathed with several titles and estates in the northern reaches of England, he was always looking for new ways to crush his greatest enemy – the Scots.

The treaty the men signed agreed that if their invasion of Scotland was successful, Alexander would became the new Scottish king and he would hand over a big proportion of southern Scotland to the English, including the much fought over border town of Berwick. King Edward also insisted that he marry his daughter, Princess Cecilia. On hearing this I almost choked on the thimble of Cypriot wine I was tasting. Where would I feature in the bedchamber of a man with three wives?

River could smell and taste that wine as if it was the glass of Tizer beside her. She drained the memories from her throat with the remains of the red drink, and reached for the two Kit Kat fingers on her windowsill. As she felt the sugar jump into her veins, she wondered if Fotheringhay Castle still stood and what it looked like today. As she typed its name into Google, she had an urge to visit the place to see if it brought anymore of Dimiza back to her. But the words 'nothing remains of the castle today' soon slapped her around the face.

Last week, River discovered that an archaeological dig was being planned to look for Richard's lost skeleton. A number of experts were convinced that the friary in which his body was buried lay beneath a council car park in Leicester. It was not just his bones that she hoped they'd find, but also any items that he may have been buried with. His gold signet ring, jewel encrusted broach, strawberry jewelled collar, wild boar badge and rosary beads all lived inside the periphery of her recollections. She was counting down the days to a press conference they were planning to mark the launch of the dig.

River's heart tore in two the first time she learnt how he died. His warm and sensual flesh had been barbarically hacked away at until its blood no longer pumped, and then it was stripped naked and paraded through the streets of Leicester. Leicester was the nearest town to the battle in which he was defeated by the invading forces of Henry Tudor. His enemies exhibited his corpse in Leicester's Church of the Annunciation of Our Lady for two days, before handing it over to local monks who buried him under the choir of their friary. There was a rumour that a few decades later Tudor thugs dug him up and tossed him it into the River Soar. But this was obviously dismissed by the historians, archaeologists and obsessive Ricardians who were about to rip up a tarmac in search of him.

Just as shocking to River was learning that Alexander died just fifteen days before him. On the seventh of August 1485 he suffered a Harold Godwinson style death as a splinter of spear flew into his eye during a jousting contest. They were both in their early thirties when they died. Closing her journal she thought about destiny and who up their controlled it, before her phone vibrated again. The text read, 'I'm sorry, mon chou, but I did it for your own good. Please reply.' Angrily sucking melted Kit Kat from her cubicles, she wondered why a man who believed she should be sectioned was so desperate to reconcile with her.

13

As soon as Etta heard the sound of the key in the lock, she turned off the late night debate on ethical fishing and peered into the hallway.

"Petra, wait," she called to the fleeting figure disappearing up the stairs.

Petra span around like a cat having its tail pulled. "Why?"

"Where have you been?"

Irritation propelled Petra back down the stairs. "Who are you exactly? My mother?"

"We haven't spoken for days."

"So? Look, Etta, I'm tired. We'll talk in the morning."

"Yeah, right. You leave the house before everyone gets up. Where do you go?"

"I don't think that is any of your business." She began marching back up the stairs but Etta ran past her and blocked her way. "Excuse me."

"No. You've got to talk to me. The band are really angry."

"You mean Stuart?"

"Not just him. We all gave up our lives to come here and record an album that you have no desire whatsoever to write. Can't you see how selfish you're being?"

"Says the woman who disappeared off to Norway the second our tour ended."

"Yes and I came back, didn't I? I came back for you."

"I didn't ask you to."

"Thanks."

"What are you getting so angry at me for? Don't try and make me responsible for your decisions."

"Look, I know you're hurting, but you're forgetting that I know you better than anyone else. I remember what you were like with Stephen. I know how obsessive you can get. So just answer me one question. Who is he?"

"I'm not listening to this."

"Tell me."

Petra looked into her oldest friend's eyes and felt a prickle of shame that it was her she was willing to throw away instead of the barrier that lay between them.

"Okay. Fine. Follow me."

Petra brushed past her and unlocked her bedroom door wide enough for Etta to see a symmetrical line of photographs across her wall. "His name is Nathan Pentelow. He is an artist. Just like Stephen Jude."

"Pentelow?"

"Shhhhhh!"

"But isn't that Tiana's surname?"

"He's her brother," she whispered. "Why else do you think I let a classical cellist join the band"?

Etta stepped into the room and studied the photographs.

"Isn't his likeness to Stephen uncanny? He paints St Paul's Cathedral at the same spot by the Thames every day."

"What and you just stare at him and take photographs?"

"Don't you think he's beautiful?"

Petra being so brazen about stalking made Etta uncomfortable. She felt a wave of despair at how quick she was to skip down the path of self destructive, rather than attempting to defeat her demons.

"Have you got a cigarette, I'm out," asked Petra with a disarming smile.

"Try and go easy on them, Petra, otherwise it'll affect your singing voice."

"Why should I care?"

"Don't say things like that. Your voice is your livelihood."

"Don't make me laugh." Petra looked at her intently. "Although I know you and the band want to try and live off it for as long as you can."

"That's not fair."

"I think it is. Why don't you just admit that you're jealous of me and always have been?"

Etta was stunned into silence.

"You've always wanted what I have and you probably still do."

Etta wanted to ask exactly what there was to be jealous of, but was not prepared to have a bedroom door slammed in her face. "Trust me, Petra, I'm not jealous. The only thing I want right now is for you to try and..."

"Try and what?"

"To try and find some semblance of happiness. And for all this insanity, this dark, all consuming, self destructive insanity to stop."

"You mean you want me to live without love?"

"What are you talking about? Love does not come into this. Love is not following a stranger around London with a camera."

"And what would you know about love? You've never even been in a relationship."

Etta mentally detached her vocal chords to keep herself from responding.

"You're just like everyone else. All you care about is that stupid second album. Well guess what, there isn't going to be one, and do you know why? It's because I can't write another song until I get back at least some part of what he took from me."

Etta wanted to embrace her, but instead clumsily put an arm around her skinny shoulders. "You've stopped eating again, haven't you?"

"Don't"

"You have to stop this. You're a talented artist and you're throwing it all away."

Etta knew the guilt would stop her sleeping properly again tonight. Drained, she released Petra from her awkward grasp, kissed her on the cheek, and left her padded cell.

14

Agitatedly, River watched and re-watched the video clip of the archaeologists and historians speaking at the dig launch press conference.

Remains. Richard's remains. Does Richard remain?

The morbidly fascinated media interest in the search for her lover's corpse left River cold. The more hype that surrounded him, the less likely people would ever believe her memoir and the part she played in his life. Hopefully they will just find a rusty old bucket, fill up the hole and forget all about this, although a strange feeling was beginning to climb into her that his spirit had already been disturbed. With each minute of the day she felt his presence growing stronger around her. When she closed her eyes she could see him beside her on the sofa, rosary beads wrapped around his thin fingers, his bare torso and the racing heartbeat beneath.

The smell of his sweat uncoiled her.

Her mouth opens for him.

She clicked on the dig's website again for anymore updates. There was no sign they had found anything yet except the remains of some medieval walls, although it had only been twenty four hours. This archaeological-angst made her feel like one of those crazed past-lifers who are convinced they were once Joan of Arc or Tutankhamen or Mary Queen of Scots or Alexander the Great or Anne Boleyn or Attila the Hun or Genghis Khan or Elizabeth I or anyone other than a smelly, sweary, overburdened gongfarmer.

She picked up her phone and typed Nathan a text: 'Thinking of you.' But before she could press send, Richard was suddenly looking at her with those anxious dark violet eyes that made her feel the edge of a blade run from her throat to her groin. *"The Duke of Albany is very fortunate to have you taste his wine for him everywhere he goes." His voice is barely louder than a whisper. It's as if he's worried the castle courtyard contains unwanted ears.*

"It's in case somebody working for his brother tries to poison him."

"Here in England?"

"The King of Scotland has many spies."

"I will personally make sure that any spy of King James found in this castle is hung, drawn and quartered. And I'll ask my brother to put their head on a spike on London Bridge too."

"That is very kind of you, my Lord."

"The King of England has more enemies than you can imagine. As do I. There are so many people in this country who want to take the crown for themselves. No one in my family is safe."

"Does that frighten you?"

"Nothing frightens me. Not anymore. Not after seeing my father, brother and cousin all killed in battle. It makes you a different person. The King and I had to flee to France ourselves on more than one occasion."

"With all these enemies, maybe you should have somebody taste for you too?"

"I have a taster back in my household."

"Where is that?"

"Middleham castle. It's in the north."

"I think I've heard of it. Let me know if you'd like me to taste for you while we're here."

"And what would your master think of that? I know you shared his bed last night."

"How do you know that?"

He smiles at my response. "Mistress, I was born in this castle. I know everything that goes on inside these walls." He slowly walks towards me until the points of his long, black leather shoes almost touch my bare toes. "His breath is warm against my face and it smells of wine that slept the night. I fixate on his mouth just as I did when he signed that treaty yesterday. His lips are delicate and I want them on mine. He takes my hand and leads me towards the door of the castle chapel.

"You're taking me to church?"

He pushes me against the great, thick wooden door before gently allowing those lips to brush against mine. I close my eyes against the fear and the thrill and I taste his tongue. He kisses me in a way that Alexander never has and my mouth floods with the most exquisite claret known to Christendom.

River opened her eyes and saw Richard's inflamed irises rise to her dusty, pound shop lampshade. And then she saw the men who were going in search of his body. They were frozen on her laptop screen, sat behind a desk, cameras rolling all around them. She pressed play. "Although finding Richard's body is a long-shot, it is a challenge we shall undertake enthusiastically." Richard's body. They knew nothing about Richard's body. Richard's body was pale and slender and ever so slightly flinched at her touch. When he lay on his front without his clothes on she could see that his spine was curved. She presumed it was from a falling off his horse or perhaps an injury sustained at battle, until he told her he was born like that. To treat it he had himself stretched by physicians. Ropes were tied to his hands and feet and they were pulled in opposite directions. He often fainted from the pain, and after the treatment he lay naked, face down on the floor, while she ever so gently rubbed warm oil and healing herbs into his back. "Can you see the difference?" he would ask, his face contorted in agony. "Yes," she always said back, secretly thinking that it was no straighter than before.

With the feel of warm oil and herbs on her fingertips, River reached for her pen.

Sharing the beds of both the younger brother of the King of Scotland and the younger brother of the King of England put me in an extremely treacherous position. At first I tried to stifle my feelings for Richard, not wanting to betray Alexander. I feared that in a spike of jealousy he would send my head to my mother in a box. But Richard's intense kiss made staying true to him impossible.

Our invasion of Scotland was a lot easier than we imagined as the Scots surprisingly put up very little resistance. As we crossed the border, Richard ordered half his troops to go off and capture the town of Berwick while we marched up into Edinburgh. On entering the city we discovered there was already an uprising against King James in place. Not only his barons but also his wife and sister had turned against him. They proclaimed Alexander the country's Lieutenant General, but to my horror, he renounced his claim to the throne in exchange for the return of his castle. The rest of the rebels were less keen for reconciliation, however, and chief malcontent, the Duke of Angus, for some reason known as Bell the Cat, insisted that all the king's favourites be hanged from a bridge while the king was forced to watch.

River could hear it now. His screams. His eyes held open as the men he loved were dropped from Lauder Bridge one after the other with ropes tied around their necks. Souls ripped out from behind eyes that rolled back in heads. The sound of the king's cries were the sound of a man losing everything. An act of terror inflicted by the men *she* loved. How could Alexander and Richard have done such a thing? Surely imprisoning them would have been enough. She was not sure if the atrocity had as much effect on her at the time as it did now. Did her ambition blind her to human suffering?

With money fast depleting and Berwick Castle falling, Richard felt that his work in Scotland was complete. He was craving a hero's welcome from his people back in Yorkshire, and affirmation in the shape of land and castles from his brother Alone in his military tent he told me that he wanted me to come and live with him in England, despite the fact that he lived with his wife and young son. Although I had already agreed to return to Inverness Castle with Alexander, it was now Richard that I wanted. As Alexander made a pact with his broken brother in Edinburgh, I joined Richard and his men back over the border.

On our way to Middleham Castle we stopped off in Berwick just as the castle surrendered and the town became English again. Twenty years after King Henry VI, who Richard called Henry Halfwit, handed it over to the Scots. It was the crowning achievement of our invasion, and the first time on the expedition that I saw Richard looking genuinely pleased and relaxed.

Middleham Castle was double the size of Inverness Castle. Richard introduced me to his staff as his "clairvoyant" (causing me to stifle laughter) and put me in an outhouse. I watched the castle activity from a distance, including that of his quiet and ponderous wife whom he refused to introduce me to. I was glad to see their relationship did not appear to extend beyond discussions about their son and the upkeep of the household. She seemed to prefer to sit on cushioned window sills surveying the Yorkshire hills while eating her way through fritters and custards, rather than involving herself in the political intrigue that so fascinated me. She was another duchess who appeared to use food to fill the void in her bedchamber. When Richard informed me of the litany of violent deaths that most of her family had met, I understood why the life had been drained out of her eyes.

She looked up from the page to press play on the video clip again. On the car park they were about to dig up in search of Richard, men dressed as medieval knights re-enacted the battle in which he was killed. Isn't that a bit macabre? she thought. She marvelled at how the violent death of her contemporaries was now family entertainment.

Richard confided in me that he was worried about the queen's family, the Woodvilles. The reason he spent so much time away from his brother's court and council in London was because he resented how much favour he was granting to them. With each year of his reign, his brother bestowed more and more titles onto them, as if willing them to become just as powerful as his actual blood relatives. Scandalously, he even had his wife's nineteen year old brother marry a sixty five year old dowager duchess just so he could inherit her wealth. She had the last laugh, however, as the nubile young Woodville was killed just four years later.

"I hope she enjoyed him while she had him," River sniggered, causing Roger to perk up his broken beak and let out a throaty caw. She threw him a barbecue beef Hula Hoop which he gobbled noisily, and carried on writing.

After I joined Richard at Middleham Castle, a messenger arrived from London with the worst news possible. His brother was dead. The reason given was a chill caught while out fishing, but the first word that fell out of Richard's mouth was: "POISON." He immediately believed the Woodvilles were responsible. But what would be their motive, I asked him as I tried to comfort him. Everyone knew the king gave them everything they wanted. He was much more useful to them alive than dead. "They wanted him dead so they could put that witch's son on the throne instead. Not content with having all the power and treasure of the kingdom, they want Woodville blood on the throne too."

The country was automatically thrown into chaos as the king's son and heir, also named Edward, was only twelve years old. Fortunately on his death bed he named Richard 'Protector of the Realm' which meant he would govern England until the boy was old enough to rule alone. But this was no time to be complacent. The boy king was in the hands of his Woodville uncle in Ludlow Castle, and until Richard got his hands on him, his position as Protector became more tenuous with each passing day.

"Oh my God, I have to go and sign on!" River exclaimed, stuffing her red web of intrigue under a pillow and dropping her laptop lid down. Dodging her startled raven, she threw on a coat and then herself out of the door, before realising she had forgotten her shoes. Once booted, she scurried through the fleeing clusters of squirrels in Trinity Square Gardens towards the tube station. Peering down on her like a malignant spectre were the jagged walls of the Tower of London. But her speed did not permit its menace to seep into her skull and skin.

A scrambled brain and coddled stomach stepped onto the tube station platform only to discover she had just missed a District Line train and the next one would be a six minute wait. It was strange how the claustrophobia of the tube made eight minutes feel like an hour. She collapsed onto a seat and her fingers involuntarily felt her neck. It was as if her flesh was aware of how close it was to the Tower, and how easily it could have met an axe there. But instead of her head falling into a basket, it floated through the tunnels and into the minor chords of a stringed instrument. She got up and allowed her feet to follow the music. On seeing her, the busker immediately put down his bow.

"Thank you."

"What for?" she asked him. She realised she was now stood directly in front of him, but had no recollection of how she got there.

"You just put a pound coin into my case."

"I did?"

"Yes."

She looked down at the empty case.

"You're Scottish aren't you?" he said.

"How did you know that?" She was truly amazed. She had no Scottish accent and the only proof she had of her Scottish blood were the flashbacks of her Invernessian origin.

"It is written all over your face. The emerald eyes, the black hair, the pale complexion, the cheek bones. I know a fellow Scott when I see one. You sound like a cockney though."

"Well, I... I had to relearn how to speak nine years ago."

"Oh? Why's that? Did you have an accident? You look too young to have had a stroke."

She heard the rumble and electric angst of an approaching train and remembered that she needed to be on it. But his ability to identify her Scottish roots made her want to see him again. It was the first time her true identity had been validated. "Look," she said, scrambling through her coat pockets and finding an old *Argos* biro and *MacDonald's* napkin, "could we meet again? I only live five minutes away." She scribbled down her address and phone number and handed it to him. "What's your name?"

"Ginger."

"Ginger?"

"After my hair. And yours?"

"I'm River. After the Thames"

Just in time, River pounced into the metal machine, almost getting herself trapped in the doors.

"MIND THE GAP ... MIND THE GAP ... MIND THE CAT."

15

River closed her front door behind her, kicked off her shoes, collected her journal and pen from her bedroom, and resumed her medieval chronicle on the kitchen counter after flicking on the kettle.

A messenger arrived from the Lord Chamberlain in London confirming Richard's worst fear. The queen and her family were aiming to have the new king crowned before Richard could arrive. Despite Richard being named as Lord Protector, they wanted the boy to reign without his interference. On discovering this, his determination to destroy the Woodvilles became unequivocal.

Richard wore black from hat to shoe at his brother's funeral requiem in York. It was the first time I had ever seen him cry. But besides tears, I hoped I was looking at something else in his eyes. The gleam of his dead brother's crown.

He thrived and excelled in positions of power, so I could not understand why he would not crave the ultimate role. Especially when taking it would remove the threat of having a Woodville child on the throne. I wanted that ambition to be in his head more than anything. Why should I be content with forever being a duke's whore when there was the chance of one day becoming his queen? As he prayed for his brother's soul, I prayed for the day when the Archbishop of Canterbury's anointed oil would slip between my breasts at the altar of Westminster Abbey.

Once the service was over, we rode towards London with a three hundred strong force of Richard's men. He was resolved to snatch the twelve year old king from the clutches of Elizabeth Woodville's brother, Anthony, who was escorting him to London from their home in Ludlow. On our way south we were met by Richard's younger and larger cousin, the flamboyant Henry, Duke of Buckingham. Buckingham hated the Woodvilles more than most of us as he still harboured the resentment of the king forcing him to marry the queen's younger sister when he was only eleven. Once again, this was a marriage arranged purely to pump more wealth and power into the bloated Woodville leeches. Buckingham was just as determined as me to see that crown on Richard's head.

Richard sent a message to Sir Anthony Woodville requesting that their two retinues meet and enter London as a united force, and he wrote back agreeing to meet the cousins in a tavern in Northampton.

It was called the Talbot Inn, and over five hundred years later River could still taste that fine Burgundy wine from Richard's goblet. He made her his "taster," just as Alexander used to do. She Googled 'Talbot Inn Northampton' on her iPhone and felt her organs freeze when a photograph of the building popped up next to the words 'Eatery and Coffee House.' She knew from the way her body was reacting that it was the original building. Technology providing an image for her medieval memories, *my nostrils begin flaring, I can smell the ale and paranoia in the room, I look at the Duke of Buckingham as he raises his voice.*

"Why have you left the king unattended?"

In his face I see it, the pleasure he is gaining from finally being able to chastise a Woodville.

"Don't worry," Anthony Woodville haplessly responds. *"He is being taken good care of in Stony Stratford."*

"Stony Stratford?" Buckingham and Richard chime together like angry church bells.

"It's a village about thirteen or fourteen miles south of here."

"Yes," says Richard, "we know where Stony Stratford is, but why have you left him there?"

"He is very safe."

"That does not answer the Lord Protector's question," persists the indignant Buckingham.

"Because there was not enough room in Northampton for our retinue."

"There are several inns in Northampton," says Buckingham.

"We thought it best to continue on our way towards London until we found a place large enough to accommodate all of us, and then for me to come back here and meet you alone."

"You didn't think we would want to see His Majesty?" continues Buckingham.

"The young king is extremely tired from his journey. We have just spent the past two days riding from Ludlow. His Majesty needs to sleep."

"And how can you be sure he is safe in Stony Stratford?" asks Richard.

"Don't worry. We will ride to Stony Stratford at first light tomorrow, and then we can all ride into London together. I hear the city cannot wait to see their new king. Prepare yourselves for a great deal of fanfare and celebration. Londoners can be very boisterous when they are congregated in one place."

"You dare to tell the Protector of the Realm not to worry?" Buckingham is like a cat sniffing at a trapped squirrel. "You are really daring to tell the Protector of the Realm not to concern himself with the protection of the new king?"

"Forgive me," Anthony says to Richard. "I was not trying to diminish your position."

"Are you sure about that?" Buckingham replies on his cousin's behalf.

"Let's just try and have a pleasant meal together without any harsh words and accusations," beseeches the hopeless Woodville. "I will go downstairs and tell that old driggle draggle that we'd like some food prepared for us. A little venison perhaps, a couple of chickens maybe, a hog or two."

Buckingham continues the order. "And a few pies. Maybe some fig tarts. And ask her about the possibility of some cheeses. And pancakes. And custards to follow."

"And several jugs of ale," requests Richard's dry throat. "We too have had a very long and thirsty journey. My troops outside will also need food and ale. Where are yours camped?"

"Stony Stratford."

"All of them?"

"Yes."

"You mean you didn't bring any soldiers here with you at all?" I can hear it in Richard's voice. Something devious. And the sound of it sends a wave of rapture through my body.

"Just a couple of servants." I watch the wretched Woodville walk straight into Richard's fast woven Plantagenet net.

"I see," replies Richard, with a pensive smile. "I see."

Her kitchen surface was suddenly in view with its lurid orange toaster and vivid blue packet of rich tea biscuits. Here she was again, jolted into the 21st century once by its garishly bright colours. Everything was less kaleidoscopic in the fifteenth century – the shot of red that spurted out of necks on the top of scaffolds really was a shock. Executions were a fun day out for children back then, before Thorpe Park.

But stood by her fridge was the scruffy old crone from the Talbot Inn. She was carrying a platter of pies. Before River could make sense of what she was seeing, the spectre jumped at the electric leap of a slice of toast and she disappeared back into 1483. River gingerly walked over to the hob where the toast landed, not even recalling putting bread in the toaster, or even wanting it. She felt the fifteenth century trying to coax her brain back into its black and fusty mouth, but the present day dug its heels in with the ecstatic bleeping of her microwave. She opened it to discover a steaming cup of tea. Taking it out, she sat on a stool and read the last line she wrote in her journal that was open on the counter. With the events of Northampton circling around her skull like a carousel, she sipped the hot drink and let the red ink flow.

Richard and Buckingham appeared to have a jovial time with the witless Woodville who had naively ridden to Northampton with the protection of only two elderly servants. It was clear to me they were tactically trying to get him limb-less on the free-flowing wine and ale whilst maintaining a clear head themselves. When he could no longer stand, his aged servants dragged him up the stairs to bed and this is when Richard pounced. He used his power as Protector to have him charged with treason and placed under house arrest. Chained to the bed, the more he screamed for release the more we laughed, and as the three of us climbed into the four poster bed in the next room, we celebrated our guile with a bottle of malmsey wine that we passed between us.

"You know why I ordered malmsey, don't you?" Buckingham said to Richard, taking a swig.

We all knew about King Edward drowning his and Richard's middle brother, George, in a barrel of malmsey wine five years ago, but I was shocked that Buckingham would want to remind Richard of this. But it was the reason for his execution that Buckingham was interested in. George had claimed that the king's marriage to Elizabeth Woodville was invalid due to him already being married at the time to a woman named Eleanor Butler. If this was true, the king's children would be illegitimate and barred from the throne, making Richard the rightful heir. I immediately searched Richard's eyes for the gleam of gold I thought I saw at his brother's funeral, but he remained his usual introspective self.

The three of us got very little sleep that night, and in the early hours we rode out of Northampton's city walls in search of the Woodville boy whose rule over England was hopefully becoming more tenuous by the minute. Once we reached the small village of Stony Stratford, we were guided by a huddle of peasants towards a small building on the high street called the Rose and Crown Inn.

Cautiously, River put down her pen and Googled it, and there it was, still standing, and so was *the twelve year old King of England, blonde haired and grey eyed, just like the portraits I have seen of his self obsessed mother. Richard is kissing his little hand and saying,* "Your Majesty, I would have done everything in my power for your father's reign to have continued long into old age, but your mother's family encouraged his every vice to excess."

"Especially his vice for Southwark whores," Buckingham added, taking the royal hand from Richard.

"Are you blaming my mother's family for his death, uncle?"

He is the most precocious twelve year old I have ever met.

"I am blaming his excesses," Richard replies with a disarming smile.

"What have you done with my Uncle Anthony?"

"He was plotting against me, Your Majesty, so I had no choice but to arrest him."

"This can't be true. He is a good man."

"Listen to me, I am the only uncle that you need to concern yourself with now. The loyal brother of your father. The uncle he named your Protector on his deathbed. Tomorrow we will ride into London side by side and every man and woman will be out in the streets to welcome you."

"I'm nervous, uncle. I don't know how to be a good king. I hardly spent any time at court."

"Spending time at court is not necessary to becoming a good king. You have had an excellent education, and I am sure you will rule this country as magnificently as your father did. You are just as eloquent as he was when he was your age, and you look just like him as a boy too."

"He looks just like his mother," sighs Buckingham.

"Anyway, all of that will come in time."

The fear in the boy's voice is becoming more audible. "I couldn't sleep last night. I was too worried."

"Your Grace, once you arrive at the Tower you will be able to sleep for as long as you like."

I try to detect that mischief in his voice again, but I cannot be sure. Suppressing a smirk, I straighten my scarlet wimple. I turn to look at Buckingham, but before River can clock his reaction she found herself back in her garish kitchen. Her eyes were on the photograph of the terraced medieval building on her phone. She swiped onto the next photograph which was of a wall plaque that read, "This house was anciently the Rose and Crown Inn. Here in 1483 Richard Duke of Gloucester captured the uncrowned boy King Edward V, who was later murdered in the Tower of London."

Captured? Who wrote that? The Henry Tudor fan club? And how do they know he was murdered?

She was well aware that most historians believed her lover murdered the boy along with his little brother. She longed for the day when her flashbacks might shed some light on the matter. Could she be the living key to solving the biggest mystery in history?

She felt giddy, as if the voices trapped in those bricks were trying to unlock more of her five hundred year old existence, but nothing came. And so after swiping through some ludicrously dramatic Victorian paintings of the Princes in the Tower, she resumed recording her eye witness account of the events.

Setting off for London, Richard had Anthony Woodville ridden off in a caged wagon to the northern castle of Pontefract. The dungeon there was infamous throughout England and Scotland for the size of its rats and the psychopathy of its torturers. As soon as word of her brother's arrest reached the queen in London, she panicked, packed up her valuables and soon-to-be-bastardized children, and fled to Westminster Abbey for sanctuary.

London was like no place I had ever seen. Rows upon rows of tiny streets tightly packed with timbered houses and workshops of every type of tradesman. A skyline of spires, dominated by the cathedrals of St Paul's and Southwark, and in the distance, Westminster Abbey. A long, winding, snaking, stinking river was saturated with ships and dominated by a huge bridge topped with houses and shops. The smell of the place was atrocious, much worse than Inverness. Everywhere I looked, buckets of slop were being poured out of top floor windows and noisy, well fed rodents scuttled underfoot.

Just as Richard had predicted, every man, woman and child in the city crowded the streets or toppled out of windows to welcome the arrival of their new twelve year old monarch. Richard looked stunning in his black mourning attire and his nephew looked the part in a little suit of purple velvet. Richard and Buckingham told me to tell anyone in London who would listen that the Woodvilles were plotting to kill him, and that they had divided his late brother's treasure up amongst themselves. Being so involved in their plots and schemes thrilled me, but what I loved most of all was that he had left his dead-eyed wife behind in Middleham Castle. I was his only woman now.

Richard's mother, the tall and stately Cecily Neville, known to everyone as Proud Cis, provided Richard and his cousin with their own set of apartments in her huge Thames-side palace, while the boy was housed in the royal chambers of the Tower of London to prepare for his coronation. A coronation that I was hoping would never take place. The cousins made sure to it that he was the most guarded human being in the kingdom. I got very little sleep in Richard's giant bed with my flesh ravished and goosing at the thought of everything I had ever wanted coming true.

Crushing the Woodvilles was no easy task for Richard, especially when London's most powerful London resident, William Hastings, the Lord Chamberlain, was in league with them. Buckingham sounded him out over a jug of ale in a tavern on Cripplegate Street and learnt that he doubted Richard's motives and was not happy about him becoming Protector. It was clear that if Richard was going to keep his grip on power, Hastings had to be removed. But even I was shocked at what he did next.

Her doorbell rung. Of course it did, somebody just had to come and disturb her as her memorandum picked up pace. It buzzed again, grating her on her jagged nerves. How did they even get into the building? Someone must have left the door ajar again. She knew it was most probably Needy Nathan, begging for forgiveness for trying to get her sectioned. She put her memoir in the microwave (she certainly did not want him reading it), quietly walked down the hallway, and peeked through the spy hole. When she saw the magnified face of the Scottish busker from Tower Hill tube station she felt a surge of electricity.

"Ginger!"

"Hello, Thames."

"River."

"I know. It was a joke."

"Please, please, come in."

Baring his pointy canines in a whiskery grin, the fiddler followed her into her poky flat, stepping over black feathers. Completely out of character, Roger flew at the man at full pelt causing him to shriek. With a deafening screech, Roger clawed at his head tearing a thin sliver of flesh from his ginger skull. He let out a pained wail, his arms circling maniacally at the winged creature.

"Roger! Roger, no!" cried River through the Sylvester and Tweety Pie insanity.

"What the hell is it?"

"My raven."

"These things belong in the Tower! Not in tower *blocks*!"

"He befriended me when I moved in."

"He should be put down! I'm bleeding!"

River caught her frenzied feathered friend and shut him away in her bedroom. "I'm so sorry. I swear to you he has never acted like that before." She gasped at the blood tricking down his flustered face. "I'll get something for your head. Sit down."

Ginger sat on the arm of the sofa, grimacing at the television screen which was frozen on a middle aged woman with dyed blonde hair grinning at a muscle-vested fake-tanned youth in a gym. Returning with a bottle of disinfectant and some cotton wool pads, River began to treat the wound. All the while they could hear Roger scratching at the bedroom door, desperate to finish him off.

"Hold that," she said, pressing a pad to the gash while she wandered off to find a plaster. "I think you'll be okay. Cup of tea?"

"Okay."

"Do you take milk?"

"Cream preferably."

"With tea? Okay, well, I think I've got squirty. I do feel bad about this, but it really was totally out of character for him. He's usually so docile. I can't understand what got into him."

"Don't worry about it. I don't always see eye to eye with birds."

"Nonetheless, I'm glad you came by."

"You are?"

"Yes, I wanted to talk to you more about Scotland. Did you mean what you said about being able to tell I was Scottish from my face?"

"Of course. A Scot can always spot a fellow Scot. You're definitely a Scot, no doubt about that. From the Highlands if I was to hazard a guess. Am I right?"

"Well, I am pretty sure I am from Inverness."

"Pretty sure?"

"If my flashbacks are correct."

"Flashbacks? Is this some sort of amnesia thing?"

"Something like that, yes."

"You did say something about having to relearn to speak?"

"Yes. Nine years ago. I had to relearn everything."

"What happened to you nine years ago?"

"Trust me, you wouldn't believe me if I told you."

"Try me."

River took a deep breath. "Ok, you asked for it. I travelled time. See, I told you that you wouldn't believe me."

"Travelled time from when?"

River was shocked not to see a smirk on his face. "1483."

"I see."

"Send me off to the loony bin, hey"?

"Did you hear me say that?"

"Wow. You must be the most open minded person I have ever met."

"And why would anyone want to be closed minded?"

"Very good question. In my experience, I've found it's just easier if I don't tell people the truth about myself."

"How sad."

"They can't seem to ... absorb it. Even my boyfriend has great difficulties."

"Why do you have a boyfriend who doesn't believe who you are?"

"I ask myself the same question every day."

"So tell me, what you *do* know about yourself."

"Funny you should ask. I am compiling it all in a book as we speak." She pressed the door release on the microwave to reveal her journal.

"Do you always put books in microwaves?"

"I don't want my boyfriend to see it. It means so much to talk to someone who actually believes what I say."

"So tell me, have you ever been back to Inverness?"

"You mean in this century? No, I haven't actually left London since I time-transitioned. I have thought about it though. I think I'm just scared. Scared of what, I don't know."

"Well, I think you should. You're really missing out on something special. Scotland is beautiful, especially around the Inverness area. The Lochs and the Highlands. Incredible landscapes like diamonds reaching from the water to the sky."

"I've only seen pictures on the internet. Sometimes certain sights jog weird bits of my mind. Places I must have been to when I was in the fifteenth century."

"I really think you need to go over there and take a look in person."

"You know, I think you might be right. I think that might be *exactly* what I need right now. Perhaps visiting my hometown will be the key to unlocking the rest of my memory."

Ginger set a wild animal loose in the desert of her mind.

16

It was the strangest scene that this Victorian neo-gothic Catholic church in Peckham had ever played host to. Now derelict, its stained glass depictions of the crucifixion were this afternoon concealed by hanging tapestries, each one portraying different images of the feline goddess, Sekhmet, the Goddess of Retribution. Also known as the Scarlet Lady of Slaughter. On the altar stood a small but beautifully intricate porcelain bust of the goddess: a woman's body, a big whiskery lion's face, gold rings in her ears, and a disc of the sun behind her head. Attached to the walls were pictures of domestic cats in all walks of life; rolling around in leaves, rubbing their tails against plump legs, and curving wheelie bins like ballerinas.

At the front of the church, a tall young woman with a grey bob was fastening wooden cat ears both to her and the idol's head. She let out a screech when she heard something climb up one of the windows and claw its way in through a missing panel. Relief flowed through her like wine when she saw a stubbly ginger head pop through. "Ginger! At last. You look exactly how I imagined." As swift as a panther he pounced down onto the broken tomb laden floor and strode over to his accomplice, licking her face in delight.

"Hello, Smokey," he purred, burying his face in her grey mane as she licked his neck.

"How was your trip?" she asked.

"I've actually been here for over a week now."

"Over a week? Why are we only just meeting now then? I've been dying to see you."

"The goddess, let vengeance be hers, wanted me to meet our prey first."

"You mean you have already met our prey?"

"I enticed her at a tube station with a fiddle like I was charming a snake out of a basket."

"But that's not fair, I thought we were meeting her together?"

"I had to plant the seeds in her mind for our little trip."

"Couldn't I have done that? I have been on this bloody mission for almost six months now."

"Please don't question the Scarlet Lady of Slaughter's divine design."

"I wasn't. I wouldn't."

"Good. So yesterday I went round to her flat..."

"You've been inside her flat?"

"Yes. It's tiny. About the same size as her old cell in the Tower of London, and just as grim."

"Never mind her flat, what is *she* like?"

"Confused. Vulnerable. Lost. Nothing like the murderous harlot she once was."

"I have only seen her from afar."

"When?"

"When I went and starred up at her block of flats. Her aura is blood red."

"I hope she didn't see you. A speck of suspicion could scupper everything."

"So, the crucial question then, does she remember her past and what she did?"

"It appears her memory is very patchy, comprised mostly of flashbacks. I get the impression she doesn't remember *that* particular detail. She remembers where she is from though, and I told her she'll properly be able to connect with her past better by returning there."

"Good work."

"Divine retribution lives in our claws."

Smokey gently lifted the plaster on his head and applied healing saliva to the deep cut she found, unmistakeable the attack of a bird. "Did you manage to catch it?"

"Not yet."

They felt the Scarlet Lady of Slaughter close their eyes and whisper into their hearts, *"Avenging one of the darkest and bloodiest crimes of history at the exact location it took place is perfect vengeance."*

In the next street, Zee Zee's Pie and Mash Shop advertised itself as the most upmarket restaurant in Peckham, but the manner in which the incarnated assassins sucked and slurped on their jellied eels elicited a distasteful look from their fellow diners. They did not care; they were unable to curb their eel-induced ecstasy. They ignored the waitress's suggestion of branching out from jellied eels with a bit of mash and pie because fish was the euphoria they were looking for.

Smokey instinctively leant over to lick Ginger's face and he jerked away.

"What are you doing?"

"You've got eel juice on your chin"

"Remember who you are, and where you are," he said, wiping it off with his hand in the most homo sapien manner he could muster.

"It's times like this that I like to forget."

Ginger looked around to see a woman in a black polo neck and purple beads glaring at them. "I'm just saying we need to be careful."

Smokey noticed the looks they were getting too and lowered her voice. "So come on, tell me more about yourself. Where are you from originally?"

"A small Scottish village called Drumnadrochit."

"Drumnad who?"

"Drumnadrochit. It is right next to," he leant forward and whispered, "the castle."

"Ah. Ah, I see. That explains why she chose you for this assignment."

"How about you?"

"I'm from a small seaside town in Devon called Budleigh Salterton. The goddess, vengeance be hers, picked me for this when she foresaw a neighbour of mine becoming the prey's acquaintance when she moved to London. She is a singer and was about to move there with her band to record an album. So," she pointed at the ceiling, "instilled in me everything I would need to befriend her and join it. You are looking at a highly accomplished accordionist, thank you very much."

"And you are looking at the hypnotist who used a mesmeric fiddle to charm our target into our trap."

"Wow. Isn't she incredible? May divine retribution forever reside inside her claws," said Smokey, clinking her glass of milk against his.

"But it won't on this occasion, lady, if you don't learn to control the volume of your voice. A whisker of suspicion could wreck everything for us. There are eyes and entities everywhere who do not want to see her justice delivered."

"I suppose I still...," Smokey brought the level of her voice down to match his, "...have not completely got the hang of these damn vocal chords."

"But you've had six months. I've had one week and look at how well I am assimilated."

"Becoming well adjusted to the sick human race is nothing to be proud of."

"Well hopefully incatnation will not be too far off now."

"I'll drink to that."

"Anyway, tell me more about your life in Scotland. Who is your owner?"

"They call her Mrs M. I've been with her since I was...," he imitated stroking a tiny kitten.

"Aww. I bet you were very cute when you were that small."

"I still am cute."

"Not right now you're not."

"Oh, thanks."

"Come on. These coats are repulsive. My skin is as dry as a dead leaf. Plus I'm freezing cold all the time. I feel like one of those furless breeds."

"A Sphinx?"

"Yes! They're awful!" A high pitch squeal erupted from Smokey's mouth before she is able to cover it.

"Smokey," he growled, "for Sekhmet's sake, do shut up."

"Sorry."

"Yes. So. Anyway. Mrs M got me after her second husband died. It really upsets me that I've been away from her for so long, she'll be lost without me. I know completing this assignment is much more important, but I just hope she doesn't think she has lost me forever. When we go up there, I will be tempted to pay her a visit just to see how she is getting on. I hope she isn't thinking about replacing me."

"I am sure she isn't."

"Tell me about yours."

"Dead I am afraid."

"Oh. Sorry. So you're a stray?"

"I don't like that word. I prefer 'depending on the kindness of strangers.'"

"And how long have you been ... depending on the kindness of strangers?"

"My owner was a retired opera singer and he died two years ago. His daughter sold his house and was going to sell me too, so I ran away. Lived off scraps in the local chalet park. Fish and chips, that sort of thing. You'd be surprised how much food is thrown away."

"Tell me about this band you're in."

"Well this singer I was telling you about is called Petra Sherry and she has to be the most self obsessed woman you will ever have the misfortune to meet. You'll probably find out soon enough. Really, I could reincatnate right in front of her and all she'd be able to see is herself and her problems. And do you know the worst thing? She wears fake cat fur."

Ginger grimaces. "That's like us wearing a coat made out of fake human flesh."

"We are."

17

To commemorate the archaeological search for Richard's corpse, a major history magazine made him their cover star for the month, with a pull-out feature on his life. It centred around *that* portrait of him (the one that middle aged women worldwide swoon over) despite bearing very little resemblance to him. Although, of course, she is the only person on the planet who knew what he really looked like. The article contained nothing she didn't already know, so she took her scissors to it and decorated the cover of her memoir with the pictures. Tossing the glossy remains into the corner of her bedroom, she checked the dig's website for the about the hundredth time that day. She was desperate for updates, but there was still nothing beyond their recent discovery of a few floor tiles. Floor tiles are no conciliation for the bones of your lover. Well, the archaeologists at the press conference *did* describe finding him as "a one in a million chance."

As any medieval Tower of London survivor would, she once again ran her fingers along the upper vertebrae of her spine and up to her neck, the tendons, her throat and the silent voice box it contained. She closed her eyes and thought about his lost skeleton again. Are there any other abandoned women out there imaging what it would feel like to touch the skeleton of their lost lover? If she closed her eyes and wrapped his bones around her, would he come back to her? She opened her eyes to escape the grizzly thoughts and looked at the cover design she had just created. In the centre was an artist's impression of the Battle of Bosworth, with Richard resembling Munch's Scream as a battleaxe sliced through his head. Her imagination, entrenched in the macabre today, pictured his naked and disembowelled body being carted through the cobbled streets of Leicester before being displayed in that church for three days. How his flesh so easily turned from being a cloak of warmth and sensuality into a trodden and bloodied victor's trophy.

River went into the kitchen to split open a scone.

What moved her more than reading about Richard's bloody slaughter, was reading about the death of his ten year old son the previous year. According to her memories he was a brave but sickly little boy, stoical in the face of the illness that even the king's physician could not identify. When he died, a contemporary chronicler described his bereaved parents as being in "a state almost bordering on madness by reason of their sudden grief" and she could well imagine it. His wife lived for that child, and their joint love for him was what bonded the royal couple. She was not surprised to learn that after his son's death, rumours abounded that he wanted his wife out of the way so that he could marry someone else. Not Dimiza of course, she had already transitioned to the year 2003 by then.

She opened her cupboard and took out a jar of strawberry jam and *Richard wipes the Polish cherry wine from his lips. "So about a minute after a box of the Archbishop of*

Canterbury's strawberries arrived, I grabbed hold of my head like I was in pain. I sat in silence waiting for someone to ask me what was wrong, but they didn't. And then really slowly and quietly I said: 'somebody is trying to kill me.' Of all people, it was Hastings who spoke up. 'If this is true, my Lord,' he said, 'you need to punish them as traitors.' He put his head straight into my noose. 'I know who it is,' I said, 'that sorceress Elizabeth Woodville and her conspirators.' I then pulled up the sleeve of my doublet to reveal my arm which I scrapped with a knife this morning in preparation. 'Witchcraft,' I moaned. Again Hastings said 'if this is true, my Lord, the perpetrators need to be punished.' This is where I became hysterical. 'What do you mean **if** this is true,' I yelled at him. 'It is true, and you yourself are the perpetrator!' He looked at me like a rat in a trap. 'I, my Lord?' he whimpered. 'Yes, you!' I yelled, 'you and that harlot witch!' And with that I banged my fist on the table and screamed, '**TRAITOR**!' This was of course the cue for my guards to storm into the room. 'I hope you confessed your sins this morning, traitor,' I said, 'because by the word of St Paul, I will not dine again until your head is brought.'"

I bring my hand to my mouth. Surely he did not go as far as chopping off his head? Surely he just had him arrested and locked away as he did with Anthony Woodville? I don't think my stomach can listen to another word as he continues.

"They dragged him out onto the green, forced him down on a log, and struck off his head with three blows of an axe."

I feel my eyes sting at the horror of it all.

"What's wrong? You know he needed to be removed. He wanted to have me deposed."

"I know, I'm sorry, I am just shocked that it all happened so fast."

"I thought you would be pleased."

"Of course I am."

Concealing my nausea with a grin, I go over to him and put my hand on his chest to reassure him, or perhaps myself. I bite my lower lip in just the way that he does when he is anxious to try and keep the gory images at bay. While the voice in my ear screams that this man did not deserve to die, I lean down to kiss the lips that murdered him.

She found herself standing over her hob holding a jar of strawberry jam, staring into the axe-drenched drama of Richard's eyes. Raindrops began pebbling on her kitchen window, and her lover faded from view with each one. The nausea remained though; a fist in her guts that validated her humanity in the face of human carnage. She began to wonder exactly how much of Dimiza's ambition still lived inside her, and whether or not she preferred the knife-edge of 1483 to the hohumdrumanity of today. Listening to the hum of her fridge (the soundtrack of 21st century urban living), she felt like a comatosed zoo creature after all the visitors had gone home. A bored voodoo doll awaiting incision. But whose? Surely not Nathan's? Not anymore. As she eased herself down her cupboards and onto her kitchen floor, she wanted the lino to roll up and consume her. She was now just a pile of lost bones waiting to be discovered, and that was never going to be enough for her.

She did not remember putting them on to fry, but sizzling rashers of bacon were turning black and filling the kitchen with smoke. She got up off the kitchen floor and took the pan off the flame with the odd feeling that she was reclaiming the controls from someone else who lived inside her skin. Maybe Nathan was right, maybe she was losing her mind.

Roger began circling the smouldering meat with greed written all over his beak.

"Where have you been? Did you go and see your buddies in the Tower?"

Croak.

"Okay, well, as long as those horrible Beefeaters don't try and clip your wings again."

Croak.

Through the flurry of conversation, River heard a knock at the door.

"Hello?" she called into the purple painted wood, her eye searching the spy hole.

"It's Ginger," came a disembodied voice.

"One second."

She hurried back into the kitchen to imprison her resistant raven and rushed back to let the fiddler in.

"Where's that feathered delight of yours?"

"It's okay, I've put him in my room."

"Sorry, am I disturbing your supper?" he said, catching a whiff of cremated pig.

"No, it's fine. Would you like some?"

"No, thank you, I've just had some fish. River, do you remember our conversation about going to Inverness?"

"How could I forget?"

"Well, I've booked the tickets."

"What..?"

He stared at her, smiling blankly. "Don't worry about the cost."

"No way, I couldn't possibly…"

"You'll be doing me a favour. I have wanted to go back to Scotland for a while anyway and I'd rather go with you than on my own."

"When?"

"Next Tuesday. We are taking a train from Kings Cross station straight up to Inverness."

"Well… it's *very* generous of you."

"I am sure you know that Inverness is right next to Loch Ness, the place where the monster with the long, long neck lives. Well, they say she's got a long, long neck but I've seen her and she's more giant cow meets long panther."

In his eyes she saw a castle. Not Inverness castle but another one, right on the banks of a Scottish loch. There were boats. Nets. Gulls screaming with mischief and hunger. A large bird of prey swooping over herring rich waters.

"River?"

"I have been there before. I have been there before."

"Where?"

She was sat on her sofa. But Ginger was gone. She had no idea how long she had been out for, but their conversation was still alive in her mind. He was going to take her to Inverness. On Tuesday. She got up and went to the kitchen because she suddenly remembered she had shut Roger in there, but on opening the door terror immediately vinegared her gleaming eyes. This was a sight she would have prayed never to have to see. Her Roger had been attacked. He was lying wide-eyed, bloody and motionless on the lino, his feathers scattered everywhere. Trembling and whimpering, she ran over to him but it was clear any caressing or nursing would be futile. She was too late. Bile eroded the questions in throat. How could this have happened? How did she not hear anything? She looked up to see a trial of bloody prints leading from the carcass to an open window. Clearly those of a cat.

The Moon

Khonsu, the God of Moon and Time, has never directly communicated with his earthly desire. Despite saving her neck from the blow of an axe by slipping her five hundred and twenty years into the future, she has no idea of his existence. Looking down upon her now as she desperately tries to piece together the mystery of her life, he can see the creep of impending danger; the teeth of vengeance that are on the verge of crunching down on that tenuous neck for a second time. She may have escaped the executioner's scaffold in the summer of 1483, but the Goddess of Retribution does not rest until a criminal heart is dispatched to the underworld. In this battle between vengeance and redemption, divine punishment and unconditional love, her saviour once again searches for a way to release her from the shackles of unforgivable sin.

Khonsu's focus zooms out of the medieval mistress's council flat and briefly scans the rest of the world. He is pleased to see that his efforts to preserve the buildings he loves have paid off. St Peter's Basilica, Santiago de Compostela Cathedral, the Basilica di Santa Maria del Fiore, the Taj Mahal, the Arc de Triomphe, the Sistine Chapel, the Great Pyramids of Giza, the Great Wall of China, the Royal Crescent in Bath; thanks to him they have survived fires, storms, bombs, wars and the culturally blundering Victorians. It is he who keeps the Leaning Tower of Pisa from toppling and the Easter Island Heads majestically gurning. If only flesh was as easy to preserve.

But he tries.

In the case of his wife, the Princess of Bekhten, he evaporated her cells and reconstructed them as his immortal cohabitant of the moon. King Ramesis III of Egypt had prayed to him to exorcise her demons. After dragging black snakes from her body he saw a beauty return to it that he too wanted to possess. During the celebratory feast that the pharaoh threw for him, Khonsu ascended back up to his Sea of Crises with her spirit woven into his wings.

He thought he would never want a woman as much as he wanted her, but that was before time gave birth to a powerful allure that seduced both gods and kings. Dimiza bedevilled him like no one he had ever known, but a dark and bloody deed put a sin in her heart that was about to set her face and body apart.

He manipulated time to keep her together. But it was ephemeral, because the claws of vengeance never forget. And as they creep ever closer to her, and as the love he has for her leaves his consort's heart soaking wet, he longs to be one of those cold, malevolent, narcissist gods. Because this is starting to hurt too much.

18

"River!" Tiana exclaims, her mouth full of cheese. "Sorry. Brie. Come in."

"Thanks." Avoiding eye contact, River stepped into their flat. She did not want Tiana to see that she had been crying.

"Well, you took your time."

"Sorry?"

"Coming to see Nathan."

River swallowed her raw and acidic emotions. "How are things?"

"Really good. I've joined a band."

"Oh."

"Yes. Petra Sherry and the Eleventh Hour. But it seems I'm going to have to wait a long time before I get to do any playing. Look, River, Nathan isn't here. I presume that is why you've come?"

"You don't like me very much do you?"

"To be honest I could do without his moods that always seem to swing from you and the way you treat him."

"The way *I* treat him?"

"Let's not get into this now. If you want to see him you'll find him painting St Pauls."

"In front or behind?"

"Sorry?"

"What side of the cathedral?"

"He's painting it from the Thames."

"Yes, but..."

"Try looking for him around the Tate Modern."

River stepped out of the apartment and turned to give Tiana her best wishes for the band, but was greeted with the door being slammed in her face. An unnecessary act of aggression that shoved another shard of glass into her broken heart. She studied the metal spiral stairwell like she wanted to throw herself down it. But it would not be the first time her body was peeled off the foot of a spiral staircase, and this time there would be no concerned Beefeaters to lay her out on bags of fluffy Tudor queens. Just the sister of a soon to be ex-boyfriend who would probably be pleased to find her dead.

Now she knew how Princess Diana felt when Charles stepped over her freshly stair-fallen-body to go out pheasant shooting.

Stepping back onto Clink Street and heading towards the Thames path, River once again questioned whether or not she was doing the right thing; whether inviting him to come to Inverness with her in an attempt to morph their relationship into friendship was a good idea or simply the height of delusion. It seemed the more she learned about her past, the more confused she was about her present.

19

The hours the Devonshire singer songwriter put into stalking Nathan were starting to take their toll. Not only was she coming down with a cold, but she had already lost half a stone from a diet consisting only of King Size Sovereigns, cheese and onion crisps, chocolate, quarter bottles of rum, and Starbucks espressos. Her skin was becoming dry and blotchy which she concealed with layers of foundation a tone too pale, and blusher a tone too cerise. Her hair felt like burnt straw after too much hairspray and not enough nutrition. Plus, the three inch purple fake Louboutins she bought from Brixton Market to entice him were straining her calves and giving her bunions.

It was half past one in the afternoon and she was plucked out of a coma by the '*If you go into the woods today*' nursery caterwaul of an ice cream van. She bought a couple of Flakes from a man whose attempts at conversation she rebuffed, before repositioning herself on the metal footbridge which was starting to feel as unstable as her. Refocusing on her human intravenous drip, she could not quite believe what she was seeing. There was a woman talking to him. The woman from the pictures in his flat. Anger, curiosity and jealously spiked her blood and she quickly headed back towards the riverbank, throwing herself down the steps two at a time.

She dodged, not always successfully, a gaggle of lost foreign students, until she was close enough to hear what the couple were saying, using tourists and a human statue to hide behind.

"So what do you think?" the woman was asking him, all lurid green sandals and charity shop white skirt.

"Inverness?"

"It is a town in the Scottish Highlands."

"Yes I know where it is, but why?"

"Because that is where I am from. I am going there with a friend who is going to help me reconnect with my past."

"What friend?"

"It doesn't matter. Just come with me, will you? It will give us a chance to talk things over properly."

"What do you want to talk about? Are you breaking up with me?"

Petra could almost taste his insecurity.

"Nathan, I don't want to talk about this here, that's the whole point. Look, I'll be on a train to Inverness on Tuesday morning, and I really hope you're on it with me."

The heartless, undeserving wench.

"Well, it doesn't seem like I have much choice, does it?"

"Okay, I'll let you get on with your painting. I like it. It'll look good hanging in your bedroom. Okay, bye. I'll text you the details."

Petra bit the hand that doesn't feed her as she watched his girlfriend disappear into the crowd, before slowly withdrawing back to her vantage-point on the wobbly bridge.

20

Stuart had finally been pushed to the edge. While most of the band seemed content to spend their days on threadbare, sponge spilling armchairs, swinging along with the mercurial moods of their front woman, while their dreams remain firmly on hold, he certainly was not. That afternoon he contacted the only person he could think of that could change things – Len Stanway.

As the evening passed by, Len resentfully slurped his second black coffee of the evening, waiting for the elusive singer to arrive. "Try her phone again," he said, breaking the icy silence that had descended over the musty room.

Stuart pressed the redial button on his phone. "It keeps going to voicemail."

"She might have it on silent," suggested Etta.

"No," said Stuart, "she's cancelling the call because it's me."

"We're really sorry to keep you up until this time, Len," said Etta, trying to de-charge the atmosphere. "Your coffee okay?"

"My budget didn't extend to a percolator then?"

Etta laughed. Len did not.

The awkward silence was broken again, not by pleasantry, but by the grate of a key in the front door lock. Etta shot off into the hallway to prepare her friend for this late night visitation.

Zombified, Petra groaned at the sight of her friend. "Oh, not this again, Etta."

"Stuart has gone and called Len."

"What?"

Etta grabbed her friend's arm. "He's waiting for you in the sitting room."

Shock switched to rage and she repressed the urge to go and punch Stuart into the afterlife.

"Petra," bellowed Len, "come in here please."

Etta in tow, Petra stepped into the lounge where she found her band congregated obediently around the exasperated record company chairman. The word "conspiracy" jumped between her eyes.

"Nice to see you, Len."

"Petra, members of your band...."

"Stuart," she corrected him, throwing angry eyes at the bassist.

"...are getting very frustrated with you. As am I."

"Right."

"Now, I am paying for you all to live here with the intention of you writing and recording your second album."

"With the ultimatum."

"Excuse me?"

"Nothing."

"It is your responsibility now, Petra, to both the band and myself to see this through. I know you went through a lot of personal heartache after the tour but you can't carry on like this."

"I agree," said Petra.

"We were very lucky gain the interest of the music press with the first album, and we now have the potential of making a lot of money."

That's all you care about, she thought.

"Look, Petra, if you don't give me an album in the next three months I'm dropping you. It's as simple as that. I have not got the time, money or inclination to indulge you anymore."

Petra opened her mouth and the room braced itself to discover their future. "Actually, I've written the album and I've been in touch with a record producer."

"Huh?" Stuart looked like a stamped on bag of crisps.

"That is what I have been trying to tell you, if only you'd all listen."

"What producer?" Stuart and Len chimed together like an incredulous xylophone.

"He is someone I met when ... when we did that support slot for The Jesus and Mary Chain in Edinburgh."

"What's his name?" asked the chairman.

"Royston. Royston Harris."

"I've never heard of him."

"He's very up and coming. He has just bought this secluded recording studio in the Scottish Highlands. Very near to Inverness." She did her best to avoid Etta's lie-detecting irises.

"Bloody hell!" exclaimed Tiana. "What a weird coincidence, my brother is going to Inverness with his girlfriend on Tuesday."

"How strange," deadpanned the Norwegian drummer.

"Petra, why didn't you tell me any of this before?" asks the dumbfounded chairman.

"I was going to call you in the morning, I didn't imagine I would come home at midnight to find you in my sitting room."

"But why this Royston Harris person?" Len pressed her. "And why in the Highlands? Are you going to be doing a cover of 'Donald Where's Your Troosers'?"

"Sorry?"

"Before your time I think. Stuart will know what I'm on about."

Petra persevered with her cover story. "He is very inventive in the studio. He really goes in for atmosphere and ambience. Look, you're lucky I didn't demand Steve Albini in Minnesota. It's you who'll be paying for us to go up there after all."

"*I'm* paying?"

"Of course you are. But as this will be the first album he's produced he is going to do it for free. You should be grateful to me for finding him."

Len studied her eyes for a moment. "You don't know how close I am to dropping you right now, and if it weren't for the success of your first album, I would."

"Come on, Len, I'm the biggest act on your books."

"Actually you're the *only* act on my books. The Deadly Vultures signed to a major label last week."

"I'm sorry to hear that."

"Don't worry, I'll give it a year before they're dropped and begging me to take them back."

"So you're happy for us to record the album in Inverness then?" asked Petra.

"I am telling you, this is your last chance before I send you all packing back to Budleigh Salterton."

"I won't disappoint you," said Petra, holding out her hand for him to shake.

"Madness," sulked a cynical Stuart into a chocolate Hob Nob.

Len went on to interrogate her about the nature of her new songs and this elusive producer, to which Petra improvised convincingly. She announced the working title of the album was '*Abandoned Ship,*' and he told her he would market it as her 'London album,' "just as *Court and Spark* was Joni Mitchell's 'LA album.'"

All that dampened the possibility of the band's world domination was Petra's face slowly being melted by Etta's disbelieving eyes, and Stuart's pronouncement that: "If this doesn't work out I will be on the first train back to Devon to reunite Wild Cats in Wheelchairs."

"Go now if you want," Petra muttered into a chipped mug of rum and coke, her smile fixed for the disarmed record company entrepreneur.

21

Dwelling once again on the beheading of Lord Hastings, River rubbed the tendons in her neck and wondered if the boy king watched the gruesome sight from his window in the Tower. His new bedchamber overlooked the green where it took place, and as Hastings was his father's close friend he probably knew him. It would have been a very traumatic experience for a twelve year old.

River read online that sixty years after Hastings' beheading, Richard's elderly niece, Margaret Pole, had her head chopped off on the same spot. King Henry VIII ordered her execution because of her relationship to the previous royal dynasty. He watched it from a window in the White Tower while tucking into a huge platter of brie tarts. Horrifically, and perhaps to Henry's delight, it took eleven swings of the axe before her head was finally severed. She was dragged to the block but refused to keep still, and after the axe struck her shoulder she leapt up screaming and had to be chased around the scaffold. River's soul froze knowing that she could have ended up the same way. On the same block even? She wondered why Margaret Pole, Lord Hastings, or even Anne Boleyn (whose beheading Henry watched from the same window, probably whilst eating) were not blessed with the preternatural reprieve that she was. What was so special about her that meant she was able to slip out of the age of darkness and into the age of enlightenment with her life (and neck) intact?

She peered through her window at the grey clouds in search of her 'Paranormal Protector' as she often called whatever it was that freed her that day in 1483. As usual there was nothing to see, just the faint glimmer of an early evening moon, and the hanging mesh of question marks that constituted her life.

Turning the television on to keep her spirit from venturing too far into her labyrinthine psyche, *Home and Away* soothed her brain like a Diazepam pill. But hovering over the rippling abdominals and ocean drenched biceps was Richard. ... *"I...,"* his bitten lips disappear into his golden goblet, *"...I told the priest from the chapel to be there so that Hastings could confess his sins before we took off his head. But he would not* stop screaming and struggling and eventually we ...it took five of my men to hold him down in order to do the job. I executed a man before he was able to confess his sins. Do you think God will ever forgive me for that?"

Her own indignation snapped her out of the flashback. Forgive you? Who are you kidding, Richard? Anger pumped through her veins and she went in search of her journal.

Just a few days after the beheading of Lord Hastings, Richard managed to extract the little king's nine year old brother from his mother's hiding place beneath Westminster Abbey. I am not sure if he did it by force or coercion, but with both princes now under his control, Richard was closer than ever to snatching the crown for himself. He still would not openly admit to me that this was what he wanted, saying that his actions were simply to ensure his position as Protector of the Realm, but I knew it was more than that from the hours he spent scheming and plotting with Buckingham behind locked doors.

They told me that they needed to win support for Richard from London's town folk, and that they'd paid the Lord Mayor of London's brother, the much celebrated orator, Dr Ralph Shaw, five hundred guineas to perform a public sermon outside St Paul's Cathedral. It was to be called, 'Bastard slips shall not take deep root.' Apparently it was a quotation from the Bible. I didn't want to ask exactly what it meant in case I looked stupid, but I had my suspicions.

All was revealed on the day, of course, and my body went into rapture when my hopes for the speech were realised. The speaker told the hundreds of people gathered that the sons of Richard's dead brother were illegitimate due to their father's marriage to Elizabeth Woodville being bigamous, and therefore they were unable to ascend the throne. The glorious rumours began by Richard's rapscallion brother, George, five years ago, were now being stated as fact. The people of London were deeply unimpressed with what they were hearing, and many began to boo. Someone even shouted "treason!" and for a moment I feared Dr Shaw would be lynched. My mouth then fell open because he went onto claim that the dead king himself should never have been crowned as he was also illegitimate, due to Proud Cis's affair with a colossal French archer named Blaybourne. That, he said, was why the dead king was so much taller than the rest of his family.

I looked up at the balcony where Richard was watching, half concealed by a curtain. He had swapped his black mourning attire for royal purple velvet. My jaw once again dropped when his mother, Proud Cis, suddenly stormed onto the balcony and slapped him across the face. I was not the only one who saw it and many around me erupted into hysterical laughter. The fast thinking orator lifted his hand up to balcony and proclaimed: "And there you have it. Look up at that face and see the true likeness of his father."

Perhaps it was the public humiliation, perhaps it was the stinging cheek, but when Richard sat with Buckingham over a platter of crab and cockles with Buckingham that evening, they no longer concealed from me the plan for Richard to be crowned instead of his nephew. I did my best to conceal my delight as I listened to Buckingham talk about infiltrating the idea of King Richard III into the London psyche. The next point of call would be a meeting at the Guildhall where Buckingham would give a speech to the Lord Mayor and several other prominent citizens of the city. I kept silent until Buckingham revealed he was going to tell them Elizabeth Woodville was a witch.

"A witch?" I said.

He looked at me like I was a fool. "Of course she's a witch. How else do you think she got the King of England to marry her? A widow, five years older than him with two children, when he could have had his pick of European princesses. Elizabeth Woodville is a devil worshipping, cauldron cradling, spell conjuring sorceresses who enchanted the king into a bigamous marriage, and the people of London need to know about it."

I nodded.

"Dimiza," he said, "your job will be to help my servants gather the crowds. We are going to pay as many vagabonds and vagrants half a penny each to shout 'Long Live King Richard' and 'We want King Richard' outside the Guildhall windows. We want the shouting to coincide with the end of my speech. I will have to think of some sort of cue."

I nodded again.

"Plus we are hoping that Richard's men from Yorkshire will be here very soon. No one is going to stand in our way with those mean beasts parading the streets."

I looked into Richard's silent eyes and tried to ascertain how much of this was coming from him. He refused to meet my gaze. I felt like my role in his ascension to the throne was now just a glorified tramp collector. It was always going to be that dead-eyed goat on the throne beside him and never me. I would remain the willing sack of flesh that filled the void she left in his bed. I was born a nobody and I would die a nobody too.

Something bit her neck. As she scratched it, she clicked on the archaeological dig's website again to check for updates. Not even another floor tile or any hint of the choir he was supposed to have been buried under. Had the hunt gone cold? She wondered what he would look like now if they did find him. Would she ever see that twisted vertebrae again that her herb scented fingers used to massage? The thought of him waiting there under five hundred years of redevelopment made her long for him even more, but also made her sigh at the absurdity of being human, trying so hard to be these amazing creatures, when all that awaits us are worms and fire. A daytime quiz show audience erupted with laughter. She muted them and lay back on her sofa.

Frustration chewed her up just as it did in the summer of 1483, when her body waited to be consumed by Richard, slumped on that giant, four poster oak bed in his mother's London palace. That was another building time did not care enough about to preserve, Baynard's Castle on the banks of the Thames, destroyed by the Great Fire of London of 1666. When she googled it she read that the site was now occupied by a BT office, while the artists' impressions of what it once looked like did very little to trigger her medieval memories.

She unmuted the television for some company and continued the chronicle.

I watched him sit agitatedly at his bedchamber window in Baynard's Castle whilst I finished off the cold cuts of meat that he was too nervous to consume. My throat was sore after all the shouting the day before. I had channelled all my frustrations and belted out 'Long Live King Richard' along with all the human street trumpets I had helped to gather. Looking at him now, waiting for Buckingham to arrive with the officials he had convinced to petition him to take the crown, I longed to be able to say the right thing, or have the right touch, that would make him want me on that throne beside him and not her. But as futility sank in my stomach, he turned to me and asked, "How do I look?" I was glad he cared what I thought. This lost looking man, tugging at a purple velvet collar; this northerner praying for London's acceptance.

"You look every bit the king you were born to be," I lied.

"But am I wearing enough jewels?"

"Can a king ever wear enough jewels?"

"How many jewels did the King of France wear?"

"The King of France was a surprisingly shabby affair. He wore an old felt hat and was covered in dog hair."

"A king who does not look the part will never win over his people."

"The people will love you," I lied again.

"I wish I knew how to get them to accept me over that Woodville brat."

Well he is the rightful king, I almost said. I filled my mouth with more cold cuts to stop it voicing potentially fatal thoughts.

"Lord's teeth, they're here, I can hear them approaching. This is it. I am not ready. I am not ready."

I stood up. "You are." I walked over to embrace him and he almost threw me back down.

"Get back. I don't want them to see you in here with me."

I drank more ale to swallow down the shame and rejection and watched him open the lead crossed window. "My good Duke of Buckingham, what brings you here to my window?"

The theatrical artifice of it left me numb. His cousin called up to him that the boy king had been declared a bastard and told him that he needed to take the throne in order to rescue the country from fear and uncertainty. He said if he did not accept the throne they would be forced to look for another nobleman who would. Richard declared his upmost love and loyalty to his late brother and then said, "I could never put aside my glorious nephew's sovereignty." His initial refusal was all part of a plan to make him look like he was doing the country a great favour, prompting Buckingham to step up his request, declaring that he needed Richard to save England from "the distress and decay caused by your late brother's debauchery." After being told how lucky we all were to have Richard's "glorious wisdom and experience," Richard called down: "Dearest cousin, I have listened to your heartfelt petition and I agree to your request." I then heard a group of yesterday's bribed street trash yell out: "God save King Richard," and a number of hats were wildly tossed up in the air. It was a triumphant performance, but surely Richard did not believe the people of England would just forget all about the little princes languishing in the Tower?

He shakily closed the window and told me a boat would be sailing him along the Thames to Westminster Hall where he would be seated in the great white marble throne as King Richard III. "I've got something for you," he said, reaching into his cloak and pulling out a tiny gold livery badge carved in the shape of a wild boar. He pinned it to my kirtle. My arms wrapped around his slender waist, the heat of his body, the grey clouds beginning to patter their rain against the glass. He pressed his mouth against my ear and whispered, "Anthony Woodville is being beheaded in Pontefract Castle at this very moment."

River looked up from the page to try to ascertain how much of what she felt right now – anger and bitterness at the shedding of innocent blood – was also how she felt at the time. She knew the queen's brother was no traitor; she knew he did not deserve death, but how did she feel when Richard whispered those words into her ear? Learning about Anthony Woodville and reading the poem he wrote hours before his execution threw a millstone at her chest. She googled it once again.

'Somewhat musing
and more mourning
In remembering
Th'unsteadf'ness
This world being
of such wheeling
Me contrarying

What may I guess?
I fear, doubtless
Remediless
Is now to seize
My woeful chance
For unkindness
Withoutenless
And no redress
Me doth advance
With displeasure
To my grievance
And no surance
Of remedy
Lo, in this trance
Now in substance
Such is my dance
Willing to die.'

    River could almost taste the darkness and hear the shackles as he wrote those final words.

    And then she remembered what Richard whispered into the hollow of her neck to justify his deed. "I sever heads so that my own will not be severed."

22

Gulping down her third triple-teaspoon-strong instant black coffee of the morning, Petra listened to the ticking and tocking of the kitchen clock. She wanted to lift the blue ceramic plate off its hook and smash it against the wall. Petra thought of Time as a heartless beast, dragging brains and bodies along with it, regardless of their need for convalescence. That oppressive ticking, when she saw the hands of a clock she saw the gradual erosion of her career; less people buying her album, less downloads of her songs, less 'likes' on the band's Facebook page, less mentions of her in the music press, less chance of avoiding a job stacking shelves in Sainsbury's. Today, the face of the clock was Len Stanway's, and he was demanding productivity.

Draining the cup of its bitter contents, she watched Etta enter the room and did her best to ignore her sourdough face.

"How can you do this, Petra?"

"Oh, here we go." Her words tasted of cremated coffee granules and last night's chain of Sovereigns. "Didn't take you long, did it?"

"I know exactly what you are planning."

"Spare me will you? It's not even eight in the morning yet. Go and watch Good Morning Television or something."

"No, I will not spare you. Are you seriously going to go through with this?"

With a sigh, Petra raised her thinning frame from the stool and swept past the incredulous drummer.

"Off to take some more photographs of him, are you? Don't forget your binoculars."

"I wouldn't expect you to understand."

"And why's that? You don't think I have ever been in love?"

"Well? Have you?"

"Of course I have."

"Who with?"

"Someone back in Norway."

"You never talk about him. Or her."

"You know I don't like to talk about that kind of stuff, but it doesn't mean I don't feel it."

"You don't, Etta, so just leave me alone."

Petra threw on her scratchy black viscous and headed for the door.

"Petra. Please. You're my best friend and I care about you."

"If you cared about me you'll keep that shut and come to Scotland with the rest of the band."

Etta followed Petra along the narrow hallway. "He hardly knows of your existence. You can't bring the whole band to Scotland just to continue this deranged behaviour."

"Shhhh. It will all be different once we are out there."

"How?"

"He'll be getting to know me in a new environment, new surroundings. His heart will be more ... open to possibilities."

"What possibilities? He's going there with his goddamn girlfriend."

"I know, have you seen her? She's all pigtails and sandals. And the way she speaks to him, it's like a girl nagging her mother for chocolate buttons at the check out."

Petra tried to open the door against the weight of Etta's determined limbs.

"For all of our sake's, Petra, just get over Stephen and stop trying to find a replacement for him. It's ridiculous. He's gone. Out of your life. And if you are not careful, soon your career will be too."

"Move out of the way."

"You can't do this to the band if nothing else. They really want to record this album and have the success they deserve."

"Ha! *They* deserve!"

"What's that supposed to mean?"

"Just stop talking to me about that wretched album, will you? I can't help it if I can't please the whole goddamn world by writing more songs. I know you want me to become this huge star so you can carry on living off my career, but *this* is my life now, not that."

"What is your life? Following a man around who doesn't even know you're there?"

"I knew I should never have let you in on this. I knew you couldn't be trusted."

Petra once again tried to open the door. "Look, Etta, once we're in Scotland it won't be long until I get what I want. I'm certain of it. And once he's mine I'll be able to concentrate on writing again, I promise. That's what you want isn't it?" Retrieving the handle from Etta's loosening fingers, she was able to finally slip out into the one hundred year old streets of Camberwell's oblivious dawn.

Behind a greying net curtain, her only friend climbed back into bed, and every protruding spring in her back was an unforgiving finger nail pointing at the culprit.

23

Staring at her own reflection in the blank television screen, River thought about her lover's garish coronation attire and how it reminded her of the outfits the drag queen who sings in the pub on the corner wears. Whenever she passed *The Spread Eagle* on Saturday nights she would pause outside the windows to watch a bit of the show, wishing she had a friend she could go in with. Nathan would be too coy and self aware to go in there. With the coronation clear in her mind, she sat at her kitchen table to continue her autobiography.

About two weeks after the pantomime of Buckingham petitioning Richard to take the throne, I watched, amongst a crowd that refused to cheer, his slender frame enter the giant doors of Westminster Abbey to be crowned King Richard III. He looked magnificently garish in a doublet of golden blue cloth adorned with embroideries of pineapples, over which hung a long gown of furry purple velvet, sewn with the tails of three thousand ermine. I watched the gilded spurs sparkle on his healed crimson shoes, and tried my best to ignore his frumpy wife who sadly had to be crowned by his side. Carrying Richard's train was Buckingham, his face ridden with a thousand smirks. Carrying Anne's was the mother of the man whose army two years later would invade England and brutally slaughter Richard on the battlefield.

She put down her pen feeling lost on a sea of question marks. With a drag queen and Richard III amalgamating in her mind, could her flashbacks actually be twists of her own weird fantasies? Could her true self be a deluded historical fetishist who liked to hang around the Tower of London wearing medieval nightwear? Does she have relatives wondering around London who are too ashamed to claim her? Researching amnesia online taught her that in rare instances the brain alters memories in order to protect the individual from trauma, and in extreme cases, that protection can extend to creating entirely new identities. Maybe she was just another Anna Anderson, the Polish factory worker from the 1920s who was convinced she was Princess Anastasia and that she had survived the Bolsheviks. Had her brain created Dimiza after reading too many history books, in order to escape a life she no longer wanted to live?

The questions tormented her and she found herself walking around her flat, gathering together all her history books in order to quarantine them from her own brain. She needed time out from the jigsaw puzzle torture of her life and decided to go for a walk. Birdcall from Trinity Square Gardens drifted through her window, but she would never get any peace of mind being so close to the Tower of London. She thought about taking a bus somewhere. The British Museum perhaps. No, the last time she went there the malevolent looking Ancient Egyptian gods almost gave her a panic attack.

A nine year old newspaper cutting fell out of one of the history books she was holding, and as she read it...

Police are still seeking the public's help in identifying a woman with apparent amnesia. The woman, who appears to be in her early twenties, was taken to St Thomas' Hospital after collapsing down a set of stone steps in the Tower of London at around 5pm on Thursday. It is believed that she was wearing a medieval costume when she was found, but she was not employed as staff at the Tower of London.

...something in the cloudless sky lifted her face to the window. She could just make out a half-moon, fading into the blue. Milky white and melting her tension. On its surface she saw strange patterns, like the giant wings of an outstretched bird of prey. Her eyes closed and she heard talons scratch at her kitchen window. When she opened them again she found herself looking down on medieval London. A snake-like Thames, cathedral spires, and narrow winding streets of timbre houses toppling over each other. She felt reassured that she while she may never have all the answers, she would always have spirits that swooped out of the darkness to sooth her. But she hadn't opened her eyes at all. And when she did open them she realised she had nothing in her life but the contents of her flat, and the simmering hope for what her trip to Inverness could bring.

Despair finally galvanized River into action. She threw on her coat and shoes, grabbed her journal and pen, and walked out of the flat. She was going to *The Spread Eagle*. It would not be so daunting at this time of day because she could camouflage herself amongst the busyness of their lunchtime trade. In London, there was nothing quite like the freedom of public anonymity.

Once there, she ordered an overpriced jacket potato and coleslaw (or just 'slaw' as it was pretentiously called on the menu) and glass of Cabernet Sauvignon from the friendly barmaid, and found a table furthest away from the bar. Her food arrived shortly after she sat down. As she ate she continued her scribbling, sipping the dense red wine like the blood of Christ, to anesthetize the throat-tightening historical injustices.

Despite everything I had done for that man, at his coronation banquet I was seated at the lowest ranking table along with London's aspirational whores and court desperates. As we watched the nobility tuck into blood-dripping suckling pig, salted slabs of fattened calf, pies of trout and pike, stews of geese and quail, with the odd roasted sparrow or peacock between courses, we had to make do with sucking out bone marrow and nibbling on the feet of oxen. My tired eyes fell onto an outstretched and upturned fawn and I thought about death. Not my death, but the death of all the people who could so easily topple Richard from his newly acquired throne. As much as I felt excluded from his current rapture, and as much as I feared the sideways glances he gave that cumbersome crowned beast beside him, I gripped onto his love because it was all I had. The biggest threat to his throne were two boys, aged just twelve and ten - his dead brother's sons. Despite bastardizing and deposing them, the blood in their veins washed away Richard's stability. I knew most of London believed the oldest one should be sat in Richard's place right now, instead of languishing in the Tower of London. The question was not "if" but "when" there would be an attempt to rescue and crown him, and that darkened Richard's every thought.

It was a problem that urgently needed to be solved, and I was more than happy to accept the challenge.

I looked at his table across the enormous hall, wishing he would make eye contact with me, but he was too busy making conversation with that lumbering thing who had as much life in her as the sheep in her stomach. Fortunately I knew it was all part of his masquerade, and I wondered when the show would be over so I could have my man back to myself. Sucking on the bone of a wild ox, I knew exactly what I had to do.

Feeling coleslaw curdle in her stomach, she put down her pen and checked the internet on her iPhone. 'The worst battles are the ones going on inside your head, the ones that no one knows about,' a friend she had never met posted on Facebook. Well that was certainly true of Richard, the Battle of Bosworth was nothing compared to the inner conflict he experienced. She clicked on the archaeological dig's website once again. Breaking news! They've found a coin! A medieval coin, but still no Richard. They believe it was minted during the reign of King Edward IV.

'I've met King Edward IV!' she was extremely tempted to type in the comments section. That would get them talking. 'Oh yes, he was the tallest and fattest man I had ever seen. But undeniably handsome.' Her memory of him was as clear to her as the threaded eyebrows of the barmaid who served her. Meeting him on the same day as she met Richard in the great hall of Fotheringhay Castle; the last vestiges of flames from the smouldering fire illuminating Alexander Stewart's nervous face. The thimbles of wine she had to drink as Alexander's taster. The English king's disarming smile and licentious eyes as he devoured platters of sparrow. She could even see the men pressing their seals into the hot red wax of that treaty, declaring England as overlords of Scotland if they successfully placed Alexander on the Scottish throne. The smell of burning wax mingling with the terrifying realisation that her attraction to Richard was mutual.

As the Duke of Gloucester, Richard was an anxious man, but within a few weeks of becoming the King of England he was a reeling wreck of paranoia. He jumped at every noise and his fingers never stopped weaving his rosary or fiddling with the handle of his sword. London was shocked at the blood of Anthony Woodville and Lord Hastings on his hands, but he justified everything he did as being for the good of the kingdom (perhaps in the hope that God would hear him). He suffered from the dichotomy of being both religious and ambitious, and he paid priests to pray for his soul to pass through purgatory as quickly as possible when he died.

"Did you know there's been an attempt to free the boys from the Tower? They even got past one of the guards," said Richard through a golden crucifix held up to his lips.

"I hope you had their heads brought to you?"

"No, there have been enough heads on blocks. But the longer I keep them in the Tower, the bigger the possibility of their capture."

"Then take them out of London."

"There is not one castle in England that could keep them as securely as I need them."

"Perhaps you don't need to keep them in England."

"Are you insane?"

"You have a sister in Flanders, don't you?"

"Yes, married to the Duke of Burgundy who thinks the Woodville brat should be on the throne instead of me."

"Do you have any allies in France?" He looked at me like I had lost my mind. "I was once on good terms with the King of France," I told him.

He laughed at me. "You mean you've met him?"

"Alexander and I stayed in one of his chateaus."

"But he thought you were his washerwoman."

"Herbalist. Anyway, there is a country I haven't mentioned yet that I think might be the perfect place for them."

"You mean Portugal?"

"Portugal? No. Why do you say Portugal?"

"I'm thinking of marrying my son to one of their princesses. Spain then?"

"Not Spain."

"Dimiza, I do not have time to play guessing games with you. Transylvania?"

And that's it, that's where it all comes to an end. Her very last memory of her life in the fifteenth century was Richard sarcastically asking her if he should send his dead brother's sons to Transylvania. She may never find out what country she was she going to propose they send the princes to, all she knew was that whatever happened next resulted in him locking her up in the Tower. She tried to squeeze the memory out of her brain, but Richard's *"Transylvania?"* quip was the final brick in the membrane between then and now.

According to history, soon after his coronation Richard set out on a lavish tour across England so that everybody could see their glittery new monarch. Perhaps it was on this public relations drive that he decided to get rid of her, worried what people would think if they discovered he had a mistress. But would he really imprison her for that?

River closed her eyes and heard the sound of heavy footsteps and jangling keys, and then once she was looking at medieval London as if from a cloud. The dirty green Thames winding under a bridge loaded with wooden houses. On the bridge could just make out the severed heads of shamed traitors on sticks, birds pecking at their eyes. Her skin tingled as her bare foot brushed against the spire of St Pauls. She heard church bells and opened her eyes to a pub full of neon colours, strange faces, and sideways glances.

24

Despite it being August, a cool North Sea wind blew along the Thames and down the painter's neck, distracting him from his canvass oddity. Not that he was able to concentrate anyway. The thought that in a few days time he would be taking a train to an unfamiliar terrain with his enchantress filled him with hope and excitement. There was very little space left in his head for his helpless cathedral drowning in a dirty green river. He now agreed with all the grim comments he had heard from passers-by, and contemplated whether he should even bother finishing it.

"I love it," uttered a female voice behind him.

He turned to face his reviewer but she was already walking away. He recognised the black mane and black fur coat that was trotting off in a cigarette wake but could not remember from where.

*

The West Country crooner would not recognise herself in a line up; freshly dyed black haired, giant hooped gold earrings, black scarf around her neck, huge black framed Jackie O sunglasses. Layers of black to conceal the wreckage she had become. Almost choking on the contents of her chest at being so close to her new man, Petra cautiously approached his artwork. She was used to viewing him through the safety of binoculars, but her body had a sudden need to be close to his. She wanted to taste the goods that were soon going to restore her back to health. Breathing in the aura of a creator, she heard her own voice say, "I love it," causing the god-like one to turn. But her flesh was unprepared for a divine intravenous and she fled. Fled. She fled led like a star struck Mary Magdalene overwhelmed by the hazel eyes of Jesus. She thought about going home, but instead repositioned herself back on the bridge and watched the summer sun begin its slow descent.

25

The chat show host's lame jokes weighed heavily on River's sleep deprived eyes. The audience's laughter sounded forced and fake, and the camera panned over their rigor mortis grins, which made her think about skulls and how they have no choice but to grin like that for all eternity.

"That reminds me."

She picked up her phone to see if they were any closer to locating his skeleton. There was a picture of another discovered floor tile. It was decorated with an eagle, its wings and talons all spread out. She scrolled down and read that they think they may have found the foundations to the friary choir, the choir in which Richard was reportedly buried. It scared her to think that one day she would click on this site to see Richard's teeth grinning back up at her.

She turned to pick up the remote control and saw Richard sat beside her on the sofa. Before she could say anything he started shouting at the screen. *"What is this? We need some decent entertainment. Musicians, stop playing. I am sick of hearing about Maidens of Death. Believe it or not, there are times when I like to smile. Laugh even."* Richard turns to one of his attendants. *"Cartwright, go and find Beasley."*

"Yes, my Lord."

"Beasley?" I ask.

"My mother's jester. Years ago he was hired as a fool for Henry Halfwit but was quickly demoted to Groom of the Stool when the king was left in tears every time he talked about whoring. Henry was scared of women, you see. You could say he was the direct opposite of my brother who insisted Beasley entertain him daily and wanted the jokes as crude as possible. He even encouraged the fool to ridicule his weight. He loved it."

"But is that not treason?"

"You have a lot to learn about the ways of the court. Ah, here he comes."

I hear him before I see him, a stomping mess of cheery little bells, and then there he is, a wizened old man in a red velvet one piece.

"Fool, make us laugh."

"Sire, are you always waiting for your buzzard to perch?"

"Why do you ask, fool?"

"Because your shoulder is permanently raised."

I gasp knowing how self conscious Richard is about his curved spine, and I half expect Richard to demand his head. I look at him, awaiting his eruption, but there is nothing but a wry smile and a "carry on then."

"Have you had many wenches, sire?"

"Why, fool?"

"You seem to have injured yourself from carrying so many of them over your shoulder. Tell me, sire, why are you called The Wild Boar?"

"You tell me, fool."

"It's because when your wench wakes in the morning and turns to look at you she thinks she must have fallen asleep in a pig farm."

"Is he not going to lose his head for this?" *I hear myself ask.*

"Wench," *the fool replies to me,* "he is the one who should be worried about losing his head, do you know how many men I passed outside queuing up to kill him? Sire, you smile but you do not laugh. Do you only laugh when you are hoodwinking Woodvilles into thinking you are having a great time, just so you can chain them to their beds when they fall asleep?"

"That is why the Woodvilles are fools, fool, and I am not."

"And nor am I a fool, fool, for I know that only a foolish king would leave unattended the king whose crown he stole."

"Did you just call me a fool, fool?"

"Only a fool would call you a fool, fool, for one word from you and I will become your Groom of the Stool."

"Just shut up and sing us a song."

"Is there no limit to what you will allow him to say?"

Richard hushes me and Beasley begins to sing in a low, mournful voice:

"*Your crown is floating in a witches brew,*

A cauldron inflamed by your lies,

Foot of newt, tongue of frog,

Eye of dog, wing of bat,

Will never taste as bitter,

As the indelible blood on your hands."

Richard holds out his hand. "Stop," he says, and for a moment I wonder if the jester has finally gone too far. "I am bored of you now. Be gone."

The jester bows low and jingly before approaching Richard and holding out his hand for him to kiss it. I am sure I see a glimmer of desire in Richard's eyes to rip his arm out of his socket, and I think Beasley does too, because he leaps backwards again and again and again until he is out of the room, leaving in his wake the sound of his stupid little bells, like a tree of blue tits chirping at an execution.

"Mistress," Richard finally says, turning to answer my bemusement. "Fools are not real people, they are phantoms who live in the walls of castles with the sole purpose of observing royalty. Fools are our mirrors, so if I get angry at my fool I am getting angry at myself. If I kill my fool I am telling everyone that I can no longer live with myself. When Henry Halfwit turned his fool into his Groom of the Stool, he told England exactly what he thought of himself. He became a sticky mess on the Tower chapel floor not long after that."

...the television's hammering laughter and blazing primary colours pulsated her back into the relentless technological stimulation of these perpetually hollow days, and her eyes adjusted to Susan Boyle sat on the host's sofa. Pictures of the singer as a young girl with her siblings flashed up on the screen, and River slumped onto a cushion in resentment. Her own childhood was a ghost on the periphery of her recollections, and her siblings were rotting bones in the ground, just like her love. Her last hope for a clear understanding of her life now lay with her return to her birthplace tomorrow. She was anxious to see how much Inverness had changed from those misty flashbacks of timber houses toppling over each other in narrow streets, fishermen hunched over a torrent river, and the towering heights of a castle she should never have entered.

26

"Of course it isn't going to stay sunny!" Constance snapped at her travelling partner over a shared pot of tea in an overly lit branch of *Baguettes on the Move* at King's Cross station.

"Why?" asked Mary, visibly shrinking.

"Because we are going to Scotland where according to the weather forecast it hasn't stopped raining since Saturday."

"I was speaking more about the weather on the way there."

"We will be in a temperature controlled carriage so why would it matter if it's sunny? I hope they are not getting the same train as us."

"Who?" Mary followed her gaze over to a ginger haired man and a tall grey bobbed woman precariously perched on a tatty brown accordion case.

"Maybe they'll play something for us on the journey?" Mary filled her mouth with scone to prevent further utterances.

"Not," Constance began, her eyes filling with scorn, "if they know what is good for them."

At the next table, Petra Sherry reflected on her guile in a glazed cappuccino doughnut while pretending to listen to Tiana witter over a paper cup full of macchiato froth.

"...going to be so much fun us all staying in the same hotel together..."

"Yeah, great fun," Etta muttered through jaw-clickingly tough granary, fixing her eyes on Petra.

"I feel like the luckiest woman in the world right now," Tiana went on, placing her hand on Petra's.

"My hands are sticky," said Petra, removing it.

"I still can't get over the crazy coincidence of us going to Inverness at the same time as my brother."

"Serendipity," deadpanned Etta.

"You've got butter on your chin," Petra shot back at her. "And I think this doughnut might be stale."

They were finally able to board the 8:13am to Inverness after a much derided delay due to "a flock of geese on the line." River made a beeline along the aisle to her mysterious Scottish friend, keen to further dissect his brain, but was forced to submit to her boyfriend's hand, tapping the seat beside him. She watched Ginger sit with the strange accordionist from Petra's band, and thought it strange that they seemed to already know each other. Pretending to listen to Nathan's delusional enthusiasm for the trip now that they were "reconciled," River cursed herself for forgetting her headphones and busied her mind with how exactly she was going to morph their relationship into friendship once they get there.

Further along the aisle, Petra reclined beside Etta with her eyes consuming the pretty male flesh that was slowly getting stuck in her Latrodectus' web. That was until Stuart sat opposite her, restricting her view and offending her nostrils with banana breath as he launched into a long monologue about not really being a fan of long train journeys and how he wished Len Stanway had forked out for plane tickets, and the higher statistic of train crashes over plane crashes.

"If we do crash," Petra eventually responded, "I hope my body crushes you to death." She did not even bother to lower her murderous voice. "And if I said I wouldn't enjoy it, I'd be lying."

The bassist took the hint and found an alternative place to park himself. Petra pulled out her purse, whispering, "I want to show you something," to her companion. She opened it to reveal two photographs displayed side by side, one of Stephen and one of Nathan. "Can you see the resemblance?"

Etta's eyes darted up from the photographs and into Petra's possessed pupils. "You're taking the piss now, aren't you?"

"What? Of course I'm not."

"Are you sure? Because right now I feel like I am on a train to Bedlam."

"Just keep your mouth shut."

"Why show me them? What did you think I was going to say? Do you really expect me to support this lunacy?"

Petra closed her eyes. "I'm not listening."

"You never do. But I wish it was as easy as just closing your eyes to make this madness go away."

Along the carriage, Ginger drifted in and out of a catnap oblivious to his accomplice's eyes fixed on his heavy-hooded lids. "Are you losing your enthusiasm now that you're an old veteran?" she asked.

He raised one of them. "An old veteran?"

"Well this isn't your first assignment, is it?

"Keep your voice down. I did one other assignment five years ago."

Before she could respond, something prompted a deranged feline yelp to erupt from her lungs.

"Dear me," piped up Constance who was sat directly behind them. "What was that terrible squawk!" She leant forward, ignoring her partner's plea, and tapped Smokey on the shoulder. "Excuse me, lady, I was trying to have a nap, do you think you could try and keep it down?"

Smokey spun around like a tiger on a rat, freezing her with cold eyes. The septuagenarian leant back, the charged atmosphere between the two creatures snatching her tongue.

Petra looked around but could not see the source of such an uncaged emotion. Taking its wild abandon as her cue, she defied Etta's plea for sanity, pulled her binoculars out of her crocodile handbag and zoomed in on her tender prey. His eyes were closed and his mouth was a like that of an inviting, gaping gargoyle. Etta was about to protest her egregious stalking, but was interrupted by a man's loud bellowing voice.

"Where are we now?"

They all turned to see a stocky, middle aged man in a bright blue *Queen of the South* football shirt stumbling along the aisle.

"I haven't slept for two days," he shouted at a toilet door. "I think I'm starting to have hallucinations."

"Excuse me, would you please be quiet and return to your seat," instructed Constance.

Clearly confused, the man perched on Smokey's arm rest and slurred into her pricked up ear. "Hello, deary, and what be your name then?"

In one clean motion, the incarnated harpy swept her scarlet nails across his face, instantly drawing blood. Mouths fell open in unison, including that of the injured Scot, and Ginger quickly reached into his pocket for a secret sedative to keep the cat from leaping out of the bag.

After an eight-hour train wreck of emotions, the travelling party finally reached their destination. For early September the weather was abysmal; relentless cold fronts from Norway brought with them grey skies and gusts of rain. The focus of the accidental holiday-makers was now to find their hotel and fast, except for River who was now drowning in distant voices and fading images.

"River? River, come on. Are you with us?"

She opened her eyes to find Nathan's peering deep inside her like a confused surgeon. She instinctively closed them again to protect herself against his exploratory scalpel.

"Come on, wake up. We're here now, mon tresor."

Dizzily obeying, River trailed through Inverness station with the omnium gatherum, and squeezed herself into the back of a taxi with Nathan and Stuart. As she watched the houses go by through rain splattered windows, Nathan rested his hand on hers.

"Sorry?" Stuart asked River on her other side, his leg defying her personal space by resting on hers.

"I didn't say anything."

"I thought you said it is all different now."

"Oh. Did I?"

"Is this where you are from then?"

River's eyes climbed a church spire in silence.

"Do you speak Scottish?"

Silence.

"When were you last here?"

Nathan quickly piped up before she could say anything psychologically incriminating. "Don't worry, she's in a world of her own at the moment."

"Stop asking people stupid questions, Stuart," growled Petra from the front seat, her eyes glued on Nathan as she reapplied sanguine lipstick in the overheard mirror.

"Universe of her own," Stuart murmured, sulking down into his seat and staring at the rain pattering on the window.

Petra's eyes waited in vain to be met by Nathan's. "Is she okay, or just pretending not to be so she doesn't have to listen to Stuart's bleating? In which case, I totally understand."

"Oh, thank you! Are we at the hotel yet?"

"Why do you have to know everything all the time, Stuart?" asked Petra, now applying foundation to her nose.

Lost words faded into River's ears like a car radio recovering from a tunnel. Her medieval hometown entered the present day with the refocusing of her eyes. It was a strange experience to suddenly see wooden houses, dilapidated alehouses, churches and mills quickly turn into chains of shiny bookmakers, trashy salons, and neon takeaways. The darkening grey sky, salt sea breeze, and scream of gulls remained intact.

The taxis pulled up outside the Thane of Cawdor Hotel; a tall, dilapidated, double-fronted Georgian mansion in the centre of Inverness. Everyone got out except River and Nathan.

"River, we're here."

"I know. I'm not blind."

"Look, when we get back I want you to go and see a psychiatrist."

"What are you still doing here, Nathan? If you think I am mad, why are you still with me? Why are you trailing after me like some desperate octopus when you don't even know or I really am? Or want to know. Or believe me when I tell you. You just want me to be this thing, this doll, this blank canvass for you to paint your ideas of love onto. There's more to me than that scared fool you saw on the telly that day. Why is it that the more I discover about myself, the more you try to convince me I don't know myself at all?"

Shocked by this outburst, Nathan got out of the taxi, leaving her to the abuse of an overhead seagull who seemed to find her diatribe hysterical.

The Underworld

Sekhmet, the Scarlet Lady of Slaughter and Goddess of Retribution, climbs out of the cosmic prism of our existence and into the blood-drenched underworld. She likes to watch the God of Death at work; the wolf-headed Anubis who thrills her more than any other with his terror. Vengeance dripping from his claws, he rips out the hearts of recently deceased humans in order to weigh them on the Scales of Justice. His red eyes focus intently as he measures them against the delicate Ostrich Feather of Truth to see if they lived a pure enough life to be sent out into an eternal afterlife. Any heart that weighs more than the feather belies the sin that dictated the owner's life and is condemned to eternal damnation. It is tossed over his shoulder into the salivating, crime-hungry, crocodile jaws of the Great Devourer.

Anubis's excitingly grisly aura is poles apart from that of her own tedious consort: Ptah, the God of architects. If he were human he would be wearing grey pleated trousers and a freshly ironed cotton shirt. If Sekhmet ever dressed in human flesh she would be a venomous cabaret diva in sparkling scarlet satin, sawing men in half live on stage. She had no idea how she got lumbered with someone respectable when it is clearly dark danger that she craves. As a human, Anubis would be a blade-nifty serial killer lurking on the Thames path at night.

But it is the incarnation of two of her feline worshippers that preoccupies Sekhmet right now. A Siberian Grey from the Devonshire coast, and a tabby from a Loch Nessian village. Like all cats, they have spent their time on Earth waiting for Sekhmet to send them on an assignment. This divinely orchestrated assassination is taking a while to reach its bloody conclusion, but Sekhmet can already taste justice being served. Of all the fugitive hearts still beating on Earth, hers was the most wanted, not just because it had escaped the blood-glossed gates of the underworld once already, but also because her crime snapped a sapling off the tree of English history.

Humans are prisoners of a giant oubliette. They peer up through shafts of light in search of a saviour. But all they can see is the illumination of their own bondage. The human soundtrack is that of shackles and chains, just like the ones heard by the victims of King Richard III before their heads were severed. And Dimiza's would have been next if it were not for the grace of the moon. But now, in the sticky twilight, the scarlet goddess peers up into the prism and waits for the dispatchment of ventricles that may finally win her the dark continent – the heart of the God of Death.

27

The dining hall in the basement of the Thane of Cawdor Hotel was set out with several long rickety tables, waited on by a middle-aged woman with a half-cocked beehive. As bedraggled humans dribbled into the room, she handed out sticky laminated breakfast menus listing fried pig medleys, while pointing at a display of miniature cereal packets on the buffet table. *'The More You Ignore Me The Closer I Get'* crooned from a speaker piled high with last night's dirty teacups.

"Just a black coffee, please," said Petra, taking the proffered plastic and sitting beside an already chewing Etta and Tiana.

"You really should try and eat something," beseeched Etta through mouthfuls of something that looked like the faded yellow sole of a tramp's shoe.

Petra lifted her expressionless, black-lined, dark-shadowed eyes. "I have no appetite."

"But you might be hungry later."

"I doubt it."

"You've lost a lot of weight."

"So you keep telling me."

"I'm just worried about you."

"And I have already told you not to be. I'll be fine if everyone just leaves me alone."

"That isn't really possible, Petra," interjected a barefoot Stuart from the next table.

Ignoring him, Petra watched the waitress slop black coffee into her cup from a filter jug, scolding the face of Bonny Prince Charlie on the placemat beneath it.

"If you have forgotten, we are here to record an album," he continued like a noisy gnat on her earlobe.

"So?"

"So, we have no idea what the itinerary is. We need to know when we are going to the studio. We need to know where the studio is. We still don't know anything about this producer. And we still haven't even heard these songs you are supposed to have written."

"Whose songs are they, Stuart?"

"No ones, because they don't exist."

"Wrong. They are mine. I wrote them. I sing them. You are nothing but a bassist, and bassists, honey, are ten-a-penny."

"That's a little unfair, Petra," said Etta. "You wouldn't have a career if it wasn't for your band."

"What career?" asked Stuart, turning back to his fried eggs.

"The career that you are happily living off," shouted Petra, her pupils brimming over with the black coffee she was a hair line fracture away from pouring over his head. Luckily for Stuart, her attention was captured by the tasty fly in her web; the man she had actually brought them all here for. He was dressed in black trousers and long sleeved purple polo top and his eyes belied a sleepless night. Petra's eyes and those beneath the dishevelled beehive followed his round behind as he took a copy of *The Scotsman* from a rack and sat himself at the other end of the room. The lack of a smile or even a glace at the dysfunctional musician knotted her heart like a rung-out washcloth.

"Tea or coffee?" the waitress asked him in her thick Nessy accent as she handed him one of the finger-offending menus.

"White coffee, no sugar, please."

"Sugar's on the table."

"No River then?" Ginger called to him from the table he shared with Smokey by the window.

"She'll be down in a bit."

"Cutting it fine. Breakfast ends at half nine."

And with that she appeared in a wake of blue printed pineapples.

"Is that dress new?" asked her boyfriend as she sat down opposite him without eye contact.

"It was the closest thing I could get to the doublet my lover wore at his coronation."

"What?"

"Oh for god's sake, Nathan."

Before he could respond, the sixties hair-don't returned with Nathan's coffee and, while making a point of looking at the clock, asked River what she wanted.

"Just an orange juice, thank you."

"There's a carton on the buffet table."

Once the waitress had gone, Nathan reached for River's hand. "You tossed and turned all night."

"Did I?" She removed her hand and pretended not to notice Petra Sherry's skeletal glare from across the room.

"What would you like to do today?" he asked, while his eyes screamed "look at me."

"There is a church I want to see," she said, getting up to fetch her juice.

Ginger pretended to want a miniature box of Alpen so he could go and speak to her.

"All ready for a spot of exploring?"

"Exploring?"

"Of course. The whole point of us coming here was for you to try and get back in touch with the area, remember? You won't get much of that done sat in your hotel room watching repeats of *Take The High Road*. I have taken the liberty of renting a car."

"You have? Well, okay, thank you, that is good of you. There is actually a church in town I want to visit first though."

"Looks like they've found your boyfriend," Nathan called over to her, holding up the newspaper. The headline read: "**Hunters Of Lost King Find Skeleton**."

Open mouthed, she marched over and snatched the newspaper from him. He huffed as her eyes hungrily consumed the words. There were no photographs, but River's head was suddenly full of images as she read. '*Archaeologists and scientists say that there is strong circumstantial evidence to believe that the skeleton they have found is that of King Richard III, but cannot be sure until DNA analysis is completed, which will take up to twelve weeks. The skeleton was found on the first day of the search in the choir of the friary, which is where he is recorded to have been buried, but news of the discovery has not been released to the press until now. The skeleton has excessive trauma to the skull which is consistent with injuries sustained in battle. A barbed metal arrowhead was found lodged in the vertebrae, but most telling of all is the fact that the skeleton has a severe curvature of the spine.*'

"Oh my God, it's him. I know it's him."

"If you want something to eat you'd better get it now before they pack everything up," he responded while his eyes said: "I never thought I would ever be jealous of a man who has been dead for over five hundred years."

28

The church that River was keen to visit was Inverness's Old High St Stephen's. According to her research it was the only medieval building left in the town. She hoped Nathan would not insist on dragging his unwanted octopus tentacles along, but within the space of an hour not only him but the entire travelling circus presumed they were invited.

As it was getting dark when they arrived yesterday, River had yet to see much of the town, but within minutes of stepping foot outside the hotel, and before she could prepare herself, she was hit by the sight of Inverness Castle.

"It is completely unrecognisable," she exclaimed at the building that was turned into a Victorian architect's wet dream one hundred years ago.

"When were you last here?" asked *The Eleventh Hour*'s time-travel-naïve drummer.

"1479."

"No, I mean, when did you come here last?"

"1479."

"Do you think it's open to the public?" asked Tiana in an attempt to rescue Etta from the quicksand of River's dubious psyche.

River responded by picking up her pace to get away from them. Amongst the rows of banks, coffee shops and bars lining Church Street, she could see beggars in sackcloth and small stone houses with thatched roofs. She could hear the clickity clack of horse hooves and smell baked bread and manure and burnt animal fat and Alexander's sweat after plucking her out of her night-time slumber. A feeler reached out for her hand and she was suddenly struck motionless by the crash of time zones and clang of church bells. She walked towards their sound and there it was, grabbing and twisting her heart, the church tower of Old High St Stephen's. "I worshipped here regularly, I know it."

The long demolished friar's abbey that once resided beside it was still visible to her. She was looking at its huge wooden doors while at the same time feeling oppressed by a building fronting a BT logo. Releasing herself from Nathan's clammy words and hands, she pushed the church's metal gate open and climbed the mossy stone steps that led through the cemetery. Her eyes darted over gravestones in the hope of finding a family member or friend, but the oldest grave she could see dated from 1757.

Pulling on the church's door handle, she was not sure if it was fear or relief that gripped her when it yielded. She shivered with the chill of unreachable people as stepped into the cold, musty-smelling, empty building, and slowly made her way along the dimly lit aisle towards the altar. In the split second between turning to look at the effigy of a bishop and focussing on it, she saw his face grow from a dark and faded block of brass into exquisitely defined, polished and golden features. But hundreds of years passed again as she walked towards it. Resting a finger on the effigy's praying hands, she again wondered why Time had chosen her out of all of her contemporaries to preserve.

Her connection with the long-dead bishop was broken by a voice in her ear, "...for this entire relationship I have pandered to your crazy brain. I love you, River, but please tell me when or *if* I can expect something back from you. Can you not just give me a drop of love? I am alone and I am scared and I am desperate for you to see that."

River felt like screaming at this rubbery intrusion. "I can't believe you are doing this to me here. Don't you know what I am going through? Do you have any idea what's going on in my head right now? And yet you would choose this moment to go on a rant about all your bloody needs. You really are unbelievable."

He looked at her like she had just stabbed him, before slowly walking back up the aisle.

Petra broke his path before he could reach the door. "Nathan…"

"What is it?"

His anger threw her and she lost all function of speech, which he took as his exit cue. She leant against the metal gating of a medieval mausoleum, feeling his rejection play out on her chest like a xylophone. Looking up at the porcelain figure of Christ offering his body for her salvation, she became acutely aware of her own emptiness. Not even the peace and serenity of this ancient house of God could lull her mania now. Taking her hand from the bars and slipping it inside her crocodile skinned handbag, she gripped the man-restraining contents that she purchased from *Hardware on the Green*, in just the way that Saint Columba gripped hold of the gospels on this very spot as he converted the King of the Picts to Christianity.

Smokey stretched out on a mahogany pew, not to pray but to get as close as she could to her prey. Now that they were finally in the vicinity of the scene of her fifteenth century crime, and the goddess's chosen location for her to meet her end, it was surely only now a matter of hours. Smokey could smell her liver and kidneys in the knave's musty air. It was not just the kill she craved, but also those caravan park hands that love, stroke and feed her back in Devon. But there was no going back until the job was done.

River walked over to the font, combing the cold holy water with her fingers. Cooling ripples, divinely blessed, she wanted it to wash her soul clean forever. Although devoid of faith, she crossed herself with the water and heard laughter bubble up from her throat.

"What's so funny?" asked Ginger behind her.

She turned around, covering her mouth. "Bloody hell, I thought you were a priest. I ... I just had a weird reaction to something."

"Go on."

"Well, I suppose I would have been a devout catholic when I was last here. I don't know, I'm in a state of ... like I'm half me and half her. It is actually a relief to talk to someone who believes what I say about myself. You do still believe me don't you?"

"We both do."

By his side stood the grey-haired but youthful looking accordionist.

"I hope you don't mind," said Ginger, "but I've told Smokey everything you've told me. She doesn't doubt you for a second."

"Did you two know each other before we came here?"

"Erm. Not really." He quickly moved the conversation forward. "Let's talk about our plans for tomorrow. The drive. Smokey will be coming with us, if that is okay? We want to leave early. About eight in the morning. So if you want breakfast you'll need to aim to be in the dining hall for when it opens at half seven."

"Where is it we are going again?"

"It's a surprise," Ginger said with a canine grin and a hand on her clasped fingers.

"The ways things are at the moment, something would be more of a surprise to me if it was not a surprise," said River. "If that makes any sense at all?"

29

Tasting on her fingertips the toxic cocktail of crushed up sleeping pills and anxiety pills that her doctor prescribed during her emotional apocalypse, Petra made out Nathan's face through the blue and red stained glass of a pub called *The Wig and Gown*. At three o clock in the afternoon, the only inhabitants were a middle aged barman dressed in black, a couple in their twenties with a push-chaired toddler mesmerised by a maniacally flashing jukebox, and her new saviour. She squeezed the key of her rented scarlet *Renault Clio* between thumb and forefinger until it hurt and pushed open the heavy door. The place was all thick oak tables and smouldering fire; the kind of cosy warmth that solidifies couples while freezing out the lonely.

He did not look up.

She waved at his side-burned profile with all the light-headedness of a thousand Glen Nevis near-deaths.

"Erm, gin, please," she muttered to the balding barman.

"Gin on its own or with tonic?" His Highlands accent was as thick as his rustic furniture. "Yes, please. I mean, with tonic."

"Ice and a slice?"

Her brain lurched; she hated natty expressions like that. "Actually, I'll have a glass of red wine."

"Oh, okay ... Cabernet Sauvignon? Merlot? Claret? Shiraz? I think we've also got a Bordeaux and a Beaujolais out back"

Each wine he listed on his ridiculous litany pushed her closer to the edge of sanity. "I don't mind. You decide."

She took a five-pound note from her crocodile skinned purse and put it on the bar. "Could you bring it over, I'm...," she extended a finger towards her hunched prince, "I'm with him."

"You are?"

"Yes. I am." *Despite the fact that he hasn't even looked at me since I walked in. Despite the fact that he just snubbed me in an old church because he is too blind to see our future.* "Keep the change."

As if chilled by a lunar eclipse, Nathan looked up at the giddy legs and chest hovering over him.

Stephen, Stephen, Stephen. "Nathan."

"Oh, it's you."

"Hello, again."

His hands were cradling a half empty pint of dark amber liquid. Despite his ice cold greeting, she sat down at his table, brushing his shoulder with a trembling finger as she did so. "How's your beer?"

"Bitter."

"Oh dear."

"No, it's not beer it's bitter."

"Ah, I see."

"Sorry about the church incident, you caught me at a bad time. What was it you wanted to say?"

"Just to see if you were okay, really. You looked upset."

He sighed and she inhaled the alcohol on his breath. "I don't know if Ti has told you much about my girlfriend? She's.... I don't want to speak ill of her but..."

"Don't worry," Petra raised up her hand. "We don't have to talk about her."

"What are you doing here anyway?"

I've been searching the streets of this godforsaken town for you. "I was just walking past and I saw you through the window."

"Right. Ti said she thought you might be meeting your record producer today."

"Tomorrow," she lied, looking around at the couple who were now giving their child sips of cola while insisting it say "please."

"Actually, I've been meaning to thank you."

A nerve beneath her eye flickered involuntarily. "You have?"

"Yes. I haven't seen my sister this happy since she was in the Berkhamsted Baader-Meinhof."

"The what?"

"The Berkhamsted Baader-Meinhof. They were a string quartet who performed Tracey Chapman and Nina Simone covers in pubs around Hertfordshire. They've split up now."

"Oh. Right. Well, they sound a bit more exciting than my band."

"Your band has a record deal. That makes all the difference."

The barman brought her glass of wine to the table and she dispatched half of into her stomach before he could say 'the Loire Valley.'

Nathan gave her a bristly smile. "You're thirsty."

"I should have got us a bottle."

"Actually, truth be told, I invaded the mini bar in my hotel room last night so I shouldn't really be drinking."

Cringing at *Echo and the Bunnymen*'s *The Killing Moon* sparking up on the jukebox, and watching the child throw a dinosaur across the floor in frustration, Petra gestured at the barman to return. He approached their table, all smiles and apron.

"Another one of these and another bitter for my ….. please."

"I wasn't going to have another."

"You look like you needed one."

"Well, I can't dispute that." He downed the remainder of his pint to make room for the upcoming liquid. "Sometimes..."

"Sometimes?"

"Do you ever feel like you were born in the wrong planet? Sorry, just ignore me."

"No, go on."

"Well, I look at humans and I feel as if I don't know them at all, even though I am supposed to be one. I think that's what attracted me to River. I felt for the first time in my life like I was looking at someone who was just as dislocated from this world as me. Two aliens from the same bloody galaxy. But now I just feel more lost than I think I've ever been in my life."

Petra was surprised at this sudden heart bearing and did not quite know how to respond. Her silence made it awkward and he apologised again, but she put her hand on his and began talking before he could re-seal his ribcage. "There's this old story from Budleigh, the town in Devon I'm from, about a really, really fat woman who worked in one of the cafes there. She was in love with the owner but wasn't sure he felt the same. One day she plucked up the courage and told him how she felt. He laughed in her face and told her to get back to work. The next day, the only thing on the menu was meat pie. And every time someone asked her what the meat was she screamed: 'PIG!'"

Petra screamed the word so loudly that everyone in the pub turned to look at her. Even the toddler.

After a long, eyebrow-raised pause, Nathan asked: "Was that a true story?"

"It's as true as your story about being an alien and thinking you had found your soul mate." Petra drained the rest of her glass right on cue for the barman to return with their new drinks. Furniture polish and bleach from the tea towel on his shoulder invaded her nostrils. She slipped a ten pound note into his hand and told him to keep the change again, whilst *Cat Stevens* replaced *Echo and the Bunny Men* on the jukebox. Her lips, drenched with wine, longing and nostalgia, began singing along to him. "*'Do you remember the days in the old school yard we used to laugh a lot.'* Oh God, Nathan, do you know this song? It was the first thing I learnt to play on the guitar." The chords drew tears from her ducts, and she pressed them back with fingertips that were once indented with guitar strings but now indented with the car key she had been squeezing in her pocket. The car key she was going to use to restore love to her life. "Why is it that our most happy and joyous moments become memories filled with thorns and spikes and pain?"

She did not expect Nathan to understand what she was going on about, but he said, "Maybe it's because we are still craving the person we shared them with?" And with that he took a scrunched up *Starbucks* serviette out of his trouser pocket and passed it to her. "Here."

"Thank you," she said pressing it to where she thought her mascara might be running. Dabbing her nose, she breathed him in, his body heat, and the slight smell of days old aftershave. "Do I look alright?"

He smiled. "You look fine."

She did not want to remove the warm tissue from her skin. "Have you heard any of my music?"

"Tiana had your album on repeat in the flat."

"I Am Alive Save Me."

"Sorry?"

"The name of my album. All of the songs were about ... the man I was in love with."

"I see. Interesting title. That's pretty much how I felt when I met River. Like she could save me from all those empty days. Are you like me? You search for a relationship to fill up something that's missing in your life?"

She did not reply.

"And when they realise how much you need them, they get scared and dump you, and all you are left with is a knife scraping at your chest." He gulped down his bitter, leaving Petra to taste his pain, surprised to find it just as raw as hers. "I will give your album a proper listen when I get back to London."

"Why do you need to listen to my words when you get back to London when I am sat right here in front of you?"

"Because I am interested in your art."

"I'm not. It's because of that bloody album that I lost him."

"How?"

"I went on tour to promote it and when I got back he was gone."

"Sounds like a keeper."

She didn't appreciate the sarcasm. "I would slit my throat for just one more hour with him."

He looked away, drinking more of the much needed brain-number. "I suppose I'm the same with my painting. When I've got what I want in life, I lose all interest in it. But as soon as River and I hit rocky times, I was out on that Thames path painting St Paul's at seven o'clock each morning."

He shivered at the memory. As does she.

Suddenly the child crashed its hands down on a chair behind Petra, causing her skeleton to leap out of its tenuous casing. It then tried to crawl under Petra's chair to a parental cacophony of "Alfie, Alfie, Alfie," before the young hipster father, all beads and beard. reclaimed the product of his seed from their dark aura. They all avoided eye contact with each other.

She edited '*do you want kids one day*' to "do you want something in that" just before the words hit her larynx.

"In my bitter? No, not after last night."

Checking the barman was not peering their way, Petra reached into her handbag and felt the cool glass bottle. She gave the mixture of rum and crushed benzodiazepines a surreptitious little shake before taking it out.

"Rum! Do you always carry quarter bottles of rum around with you?"

"Only on days like this," she said, unscrewing the gold, plastic cap. Before he could cover his glass, she filled him up. "Come on, you need it. Get it down you."

"I don't think it's drink that I need right now."

"I always find that drink dislodges that thing in my brain that prevents me from reaching out for what I truly need."

He lifted the cup to his lips. "I suppose right now I haven't got a reason *not* to drink."

"And plenty of reason *to*."

She locked his eyes with hers as he swallowed the liquid with barely a recoil.

"Wow. Strong."

She smiled. "Devonshire rum. Gets right in the blood."

30

Under a clear blue sky and light drizzle, River walked around the grey bricked town that gave birth to her over five hundred years ago. Desperate for more recollections and flashbacks, she just felt anger at the modern day inhabitants in their shiny coats, hoodies and baseball caps who would only laugh if they were told the truth about their oldest living citizen now walking amongst them.

She had not seen or heard from her boyfriend since he sulked out of St Stephen's High Church that morning. She wished she didn't care, but the guilt of bringing him all the way here just to break up with him soaked her like a sodden basement. She knew she should have been more careful with his heart, but she could not shake off the anger at being loved by a man who was constantly diagnosing her as insane.

The majority of the buildings in Inverness were obstinately Victorian, ridiculously even the castle, which had been rebuilt by some vulgar visionary as a neo-gothic court house. The town's oppressive architecture made her question the purpose for this trip. Ginger had convinced her that she would connect with her roots here, or at least find it useful, but since they arrived he had spent most of his time wooing that weird accordionist. She was intrigued about what he had planned for her tomorrow though.

Walking along the pedestrianised high street, which could be any high street in any British town, she stopped to listen to a busker play some lousy country and western blues. She did not know what to do with herself, all her Invernessian friends and relatives died over five hundred years ago, and every time she tried to envisage herself with them, a *Costa Coffee* or *Betfred* would pop up to break the spell and suck her back into the twenty first century's glistening void.

Throwing 40p into the busker's guitar case, she decided to go and walk down to the river path. Just like the Thames, the flow of the River Ness was oblivious to time and change. To time and change. To time and change. To time and Transylvania. *Transylvania*?

"*Transylvania? Do you want me to send my nephews to Vlad the Impaler's castle?*"

I laugh, unexpecting a joke from him on such a tenuous and delicate subject. "Yes, *that would be perfect, but not what I had in mind.*"

"*Where then? Come on, speak, I have a privy council meeting to get to.*"

"*Scotland,*" *I say.* "*I think you should send the boys to Scotland.*"

"*Scotland?*" *Richard spits the word back at me like a curse.* "*Are you insane? You know we are at war with the Scots.*"

"*That was over a year ago.*"

"*We invaded them last year, but England's war with that country will continue until the end of time.*"

"*I know a castle there so remote that nobody would ever think to look for them there. And it is owned by one of your allies.*"

"*I don't have any allies in Scotland.*"

"*Yes you do.*"

River found herself looking through the window of a Chinese takeaway. She was shocked by this sudden flashback, for it was a little bit more of that final conversation she remembered having with Richard. The final part of her jigsaw. She was desperate to know what happened next, but all she could now see were 'sweet and sour pork balls £6.50.' Surely the castle she was telling Richard about was Inverness Castle? What other Scottish castle would she have been so familiar with? But Inverness Castle was hardly remote, and in the early summer of 1483, when that conversation would have occurred, the Scottish king had taken it back from Alexander. The missing piece of her jigsaw suddenly became very jagged and pale. Spare ribs in plum sauce. For all she knew she may have tried to take the princes to live with her three lunatic brothers and pet buzzard, Grizella, in that tiny timbre house in Inverness. No one would have come knocking for the little boy king and his brother there. Pleased, grateful and frustrated in equal measure for the fifteenth century titbit, she unpeeled her eyes from the stomach rumbling words and continued to make her way towards the river.

She passed a pub named *The Wig and Gown* and considered going in for something to take the edge off, a double-malt whiskey perhaps, but at the same time she did not want anything to blindside her from anymore medieval memory portholes. But then something hit her harder than any flashback could. Nathan was in there with *her*, that strange, skinny singer who never stopped staring at him. She moved to the side to watch them without being seen. They looked very cosy together, smiling and chatting, and River swallowed, waiting for her own emotional response. Her breathing accelerated, but no ventricle tore. She wondered if she should be happy for him. Maybe he had found somebody who could make him happy in the way that she can't.

By the time she reached the river bank, she could no longer feel anything except the loss of the only person on the planet who cared about her. She wished the cool salt breeze would numb her brain the way it numbed her fingers. She did not want to think anymore. She did not even want to see Richard. She just wanted a piece of what this smiling mother and daughter who politely asked her to take their photograph "with the castle in the background" had.

As she gave them their camera back and watched them walk over the bridge, she heard herself say "there is no love in my life."

Mocked by maniacal gulls, she looked up at the mass of grey towers and turrets that peered down on her, just as the original castle would have done when she was a little girl. But this time, instead of wishing to be inside rubbing shoulders with royalty, she simply wished she had never once wondered about their lives.

31

"You are a very wise woman, Petra Sherry." She heard the slur in his voice with a mixture of satisfaction and fear. "Although I don't know why that should come as any surprise. You are the only person I know who has an album in the shops."

Lloyd Cole's voice on the jukebox sliced the atmosphere and Petra sang along. "*She looks like Eve Marie Saint in On The Waterfront.*"

"Who's Eve Marie Saint?"

"An actress who was in 'On The Waterfront.' Get that rum down you, man."

"Where do I find her?"

"Eve Marie Saint?"

"No, the woman who is going to make me happy?"

"Come on, drink up."

"Did you learn to play this song too?"

"Actually my record company once tried to get me a support slot on Lloyd Cole's comeback tour."

"Shall we go to a club? Do you think there is a club?"

"You never struck me as a clubbing man."

"I'm not."

Something fell to the ground. A crash. A yelp. A coo.

"What is all that noise?" he asked, stretching his neck this way and that.

She wanted to run her tongue along his tendons. "I think that kid threw his rattle."

He turned back to her, startled. "Snake?"

His sudden bizarre behaviour made her worry that she may have crushed too many of those pills. She remembered the effect that just one of them used to have on her.

"Do you ever think you are going mad?" she asked his Adam's Apple that was slowly descending towards the table.

"Mad? Oh yes. Oh yes, yes, yes. But sometimes I think I am the normal one and everyone else on the planet is mad. Especially River. No, no, she really *is* mad."

"Well, I've got a spaceship outside so grab your coat."

His pupils expanded. "Spaceship?"

She knew this was evil and deranged, but taking control of his limbs was the only way. The only way she could have him. Surely after all she had been through, she deserved nothing less than incapacitated beauty. Her heart thumped as his eyelids drooped. They were sliding down a manhole of no return together.

Leaping up from the chair, she pushed her bloodless body towards the barman who was now engaged in verbal vacuity with the young family.

"Everything okay?" he asked her, grinning like an inane dolphin.

"It's my husband…" Listening to herself speak was like listening to a sadistically cunning femme fatale from an old black and white 1940's film noir, over-spilling with monstrous sex.

"What's wrong?"

"He has narcolepsy and he is having an episode. Please, I need help getting him into the car."

The barman's face dropped like harpooned Zeppelin. "Do you want me to call an ambulance?"

"No, no, he just needs to sleep it off in his own bed. Please could you help me get him into our car?"

"You okay to assist?" he asked the young father.

"Yes, of course."

"Thank you so much," said the sticky web spinning, creepy, crawly, flesh-hungry black widow as she walked over to the door in readiness for her leg-plucked dragonfly. "Mine is the red Clio. Please be quick. And try not to bump his head."

Get that messianic marrow into moving metal.

32

Flying over the North Sea to the Norwegian coastal town of Stavanger where her lover was waiting for her, Etta tried desperately to exhale the shame that clouded in her chest like the balls of fluff that gathered around her tiny little window.

She jotted down the plane times when Inverness became her oubliette. It was not until yesterday morning that she telephoned him to say she would be returning. It was a difficult decision to make, and one she was still not completely resolved to, but she realised she had been making mistakes all her life so maybe it was time to just accept them and embrace her disfigured future, instead of constantly fighting against it.

Nervy conversation filled the plane and infiltrated her thoughts. Sipping from a clear plastic cup of cheap fizzy wine, she looked around at children being quietly reprimanded by tired mothers, smart casual Norwegians sharing polite jokes, and the faint tapping of gold wedding ringed fingers swiping through faces on their iPhone screens. The slow spread of the human stain searing at high altitude.

Stephen Jude Tyburn. They both worked at *Salterton and Vinegar* but usually on alternative shifts so didn't see each other much. She only discovered how he felt when he asked her out for a drink while she was sunbathing on Budleigh Salterton beach. Combat shirt and canvass under arm, she had always found him intriguing and attractive, but declined his offer because she knew her best friend was obsessed with him. Obsessed to the point of stalking him around the town and coastal path.

"You do know my best friend is in love with you, don't you?"

"You mean Petra Sherry? I know she likes me, but I don't feel the same. There is something a bit ...unhinged about her."

"You're both creative artists, I thought you'd like that."

"No. Artists go together chlorine and ammonia. You're the only one in this town I like."

Etta presumed he had a change of heart because as soon as *Petra Sherry and the Eleventh Hour* won a record deal he asked her out. Perhaps he was under the delusion that the deal was going to make her rich, because he definitely did not appear to have any genuine feelings for her. This made his decision to move out of the holiday park and into her little flat above the haberdashery all the more surprising. Cynical Stuart said it was because he could no longer afford the rent on his chalet.

"I've had enough," he told Etta as he tossed a bag of frozen fish cakes into the deep fat fryer while working a rare joint shift at the chippy.

"Of what?"

"Of being with the wrong woman."

"Then why are you with her?"

"Because I can't have the one I want."

The lingering stare told her too much and she turned away. Wiping down the display cabinet, she felt his irises seep into her skin and grow into something she did not want to acknowledge. Sat alone on her bed that night, questions pounded her brain until she watched her fingers text the words 'We should talk' into her phone. Was she really going to do this? Was she really going to throw away fifteen years of friendship over a man?

They met the following night on the beach. He didn't speak, he didn't smile, he simply took her treacherous fingertips and brought them up to his mouth. The night breeze sprayed the cool, salty English Channel onto her face, and as she closed her eyes and felt his lips on hers, she knew how Eve must have felt. His flesh did its best to silence her demons and doubts. Thrust against the wood of the pier, her body pounded the drumbeat of her best friend's songs. And in the orange glow of a distant amusement park that scattered over the rippling dark sea, she studied his intricately symmetrical features and neck and knew the apple had been eaten. Their slow descent into exile had begun.

Cheap coastal bed and breakfasts from Torbay to Lyme Regis began to know Stephen and Etta as Mr and Mrs Jesson, names she took from the film *Brief Encounter*. She always booked rooms in her strongest Norwegian accent so they would think they had come from afar. Most of the time she felt it would have been more appropriate to use the surname of the film's writer, Noel Coward. Shame mutated into self-loathing, and listening to Petra gush everyday about settling down with the man she had written a hundred love songs about was a slow drip torture. She would have ended the affair, but her love for him tightened around her veins like a leather tourniquet. Eventually they realised they had to either release themselves from each other or release themselves from Petra.

They chose the latter.

Etta had always been close to her retired ballet dancer uncle who lived in a tall, white, weather boarded house in the Norwegian coastal town of Stavanger. She knew it would only take a phone call for him to let them stay. Stephen quickly warmed to the idea, especially the thought of having new shoreline terrain to paint. Petra's inevitable emotional annihilation seemed to be of no consequence to him, but Etta reeled at the thought of what this was going to do to her.

While Etta joined the newly signed band on tour, Stephen packed his things and took a plane to Stavanger. At the final gig, Etta told Petra and the band that she had to visit her sick uncle in Norway, and within days she had joined Stephen there. On touching down at Stavanger airport, she was convinced her friendship with Petra and her life in England were over for good. She was a fool to think the North Sea would magically dissolve the whipping chords of guilt. The whipping chords that would soon catapult her back to Petra's side. It is not possible to melt into love with a thousand rats and vipers squeaking and screeching in your brain. Her conscience dictated that she could not leave Petra to stew in the pain that she had concocted for her. So as he held her in what should have been paradise, she planned her return to hell.

Downing the rest of the cheap fizzy wine and feeling it kick and curdle with the shame in her stomach, she looked out over the blue, North Sea sky once more. Despite this decision to come back to him, and despite her realisation that it is impossible to turn your life into a living penance for the friend you destroyed, her spine was still scarred with the whips of self flagellation. But if she stayed with Petra just one more day, Bedlam would have needed to find accommodation for both of them.

She unscrewed a miniature bottle of gin and emptied it into the plastic cup, while unfolding a copy of the *Daily Record* that she had picked up in the boarding lounge. An agony aunt called Ask Agatha fixed her with large grey eyes while resting her chin on her hand. She wondered what Agatha's advice to her would be. *Etta, you are not to blame for your friend's decline. Becoming a chain-smoking stalker in a cheap, black, viscose coat is not an inevitability, it is a lifestyle choice.*

Peering through the clouds, she tried to spot western Norway's approaching coast. In less than an hour their potent bodies would be as one again. She thought about how thrilled and relieved he sounded on the telephone when she told him she was finally coming back. But as much as she wished for the plane to hurry up, there was also a voice somewhere wishing for it to drop into the sea, to reward her betrayal with what it deserved.

Anxiety caused her feet to shake like wet dogs, and she plugged her complimentary headphones into the armrest socket in the hope of something to sooth her. Annoyingly, the provided music was a jovial Latin number. She unplugged and threw back the gin instead.

"Norwegian?" asked the female voice beside her.

Etta turned to look at a middle aged woman with youthful features and shoulder length blonde hair. "Yes."

"Nice. Did you holiday in Scotland?"

Small talk was not at the top of her agenda right now. "Sort of, yes."

"Nice. Will you have to travel far when we get to Stavanger?"

"No ... I live there."

"Very nice."

"Yes, my husband will be collecting me when we arrive." The lie tasted like cheap confectionary.

"Wonderful. I think it will be close to midnight in Stavanger when we arrive."

Etta suddenly felt a perverse urge to expose more of herself, like an exhibitionist stripping off at the end of her garden for the benefit of a neighbour's overlooking window. "Yes. He's an artist. An English artist. We live there with my uncle. They like each other very much. He paints the seaside every day. And sometimes he walks all the way to the fjords."

"How very beautiful."

Etta smiled, warmed by the sugary sound of her own words. It was true. She was returning home to an artist, her beautiful artist, the man she loved. Maybe this time, in his devoted hazel eyes, she would allow herself to breathe. With a chaotic stalker's ashtray heart over five hundred miles away, and his flesh encompassing hers like the ocean that beguiled him, maybe she would finally find it within herself to be free. After all, wasn't it Petra who said you cannot fight love?

33

Lost on a B road in the Scottish Highlands, Petra gripped her Ordnance Survey map with one hand, the car wheel with the other, and grinned at her benzodiazepine-overdosed man in the overhead mirror. He was oblivious to what was going on around him; oblivious to finally finding a woman who promised to love him for eternity.

The sun was beginning to set and the mountain air was cooling quickly. She did not know how the thermostat worked in the rented scarlet *Clio,* and she had not seen another car or petrol station for quite some time. The reality of what she was doing screamed in her brain like a dying cockroach, but it did not dull the thrill of having him on the backseat locked up and under her control. She resisted the urge to drop the map and wheel and throw her body onto his as they careered off the road to their deaths. *"To die by your side,"* she sang, *"what a heavenly way to go."* But there was no time for death now; she had a room booked for them at the Ault-na-goire Lodge Bed and Breakfast.

Branches were witches' fingers under the glare of the car's headlights. "Insane!" her mother screamed at her from somewhere. *Yes, because you would happily watch me spend the rest of my life alone and miserable in that flat, wouldn't you? Why should I be allowed to find happiness after what dad did to you, hey?* When she watched couples with their arms around each other, she looked into their eyes to see how oblivious they were to discovering this elixir. Cretins don't realise they have gold dust in their hands until they throw it away. Where love is concerned, one wrong decision could see you alone forever. It seemed to her that a masochistic God was up there laughing at us futilely struggling to fulfil our emotional needs. So this was her act of defiance; this was her taking what she needed by force.

Although being stuck in a rent-a-car that had circled the same wooded mountainous region for the past hour, her veins were still as disconnected from their feed as ever. She pulled over and took hold of his warm sleeping hand. Even if she did find the elusive Ault-na-goire Lodge Bed and Breakfast, she knew she would never be able to get him up the stairs and into their room without assistance. And even if she did manage to bluff the staff into helping her, how long before he regained consciousness and started screaming and kicking and biting? Could she really go through with using that stuff she bought from *Hardware on the Green*? It really was a sad world when a girl can't get herself some love without a roll of gaffer tape and garden wire.

Lust shot through her body like a radio falling into a bath when she brushed her face against his stubble and slipped a finger between his lips. That thrilling sensation of warmth and moisture, she leant forward to press her own lips against his and held them there for as long as possible, for as long as it took to fill up the tank. Wrapping his thick, brown sheepskin jacket around her, she rested her head on the warmth and beat of his stolen heart and tried to force her brain to figure out what to do next. That benzodiazepine cocktail would surely wear off soon.

She took his ear into her mouth, "darling, we're a bit lost but I am going to get us out of here," before opening the door. Climbing out, she surveyed the final scatterings of a red sunset across the mountain peaks. A ruined castle melted with the spirits of a thousand dead lovers on the distant horizon. Medieval ghosts wrapping themselves around each other in the purgatorial evening air. Maybe that is where she should aim for, it might touch his heart to wake up in a castle ruin, on ground once stepped on by kings. Perhaps it was only royal spirits now that could save her, for gaffer tape and garden wire were hardly a long term solution.

"Our love nest." It was her own voice now that she could hear, repeating the words she said to Stephen when he moved into her little flat. How time turns beauty into a pathetically cruel and empty ache. She closed her stinging eyes and listened to black-throated divers sing down the remnants of the sun. Opening her eyes, she saw her grandparents' old cottage in the hills of Dartmoor. No. No, it was something else. A small derelict building. Could this be their home for the night? She went to take a closer look.

As she walked, she was startled by the cry of a flock of migrating geese forming a V above her. They were screaming and huge, and in their wake she was sure she saw the dark doom of a vulture. Images of dead geese hanging from the giant hooked beaks of winged predators scurried through her brain. The closer she got to the building, the more resolute she was to make it their honeymoon suite. It had one small window, too dirty to see through, and its door was padlocked. As she approached, she carefully picked a mossy rock out of nestles and thistles, and channelling her fury at the world, at Stephen, at God, at her repressive mother, at just how pitiful her life had become, she pounded at the metal until it gave way.

Pushing the door open, she discovered that her honeymoon suite was actually an ancient public toilet. A Gents in fact. *Ha ha ha.* She laughed into the aroma of a hundred year old urine before trundling back to the car to get her comatosed life partner.

By his arms, his eyes barely flickering, she dragged him through the ferns, over the rocks and up to the broken door where she dragged him over the threshold like a witch in a wedding dress. Lit only by the vermilion sunset peeping through the open door and cracks in the window, she took the reel of garden wire out of her crocodile skinned handbag and pulled off the packaging which instructed: '*For tying and fixing.*' **TYING UP MEN TO FIX ME WITH.** The darkness slipped between her every vertebrae as she proceeded to wrap his wrists to the piping beneath the cracked urinals. Resting her face on his warm neck, she softly sang some of the lyrics that he inspired, for he was Stephen now. *"Your fingers are weapons on me. Weapons on ice thin glass. Ancient china, tender heart. You. The more delicate your touch, the more damage you do to me."*

Ignoring her mother in her ear telling her that he was in need of urgent medical attention, she leaned in to return that kiss-off, that switchblade kiss-off he gave her before she embarked on that wretched tour. *I am proud to say that losing you is a defeat I will never concede.*

She collected a complimentary scratchy grey blanket from the boot of the car and wrapped it tighter and tighter around their lost bodies. *Here. Get closer to me. I wish we could stay like this forever. Better than that B and B where they wouldn't understand why you can't walk or open your eyes. You know you are in love when you choose each others' arms over food and shelter.*

Her heartbeat became an unidentifiable sound, and the darkness became a sun that turned a disused pissoir into a romantic boudoir. And what seeped from her skin was something she never thought she would ever feel. Forgiveness. *I forgive you now, Stephen Jude Tyburn. I forgive you.*

34

River looked out of her hotel window and glaring back at her were Richard's violet eyes. They were illuminated by the half-moon and yellow streetlights that scattered across the glossy dark river. *"I severe heads to keep my own,"* his thin lips told her once again. *"I would not need to do any of this if my brother had just looked after himself, instead of squandering his health on drink and whores. His gluttony has created this disaster. I was happy in the north. I had my family. I had my people. I didn't want any of this. But now, if I don't take the crown, I risk losing everything I have ever lived for."*

Before she could respond, someone came knocking at her hotel room door. She touched the glass to say goodbye to her lost love and walked over to it. "Hello?" she said into the wood. All she could hear back were the corridor's tinny speakers oozing *The Cure*'s '*The Love Cats*' like a soundtrack for a horror show made for rats. She opened the door an inch or two into the sinister throb, and under dim wall-lighting Tiana shot her with a question.

"Is he with you?"

"Hello, Tiana."

"Is he?"

"Who?"

"Colonel Gaddafi. My brother of course."

"No."

"Well, can I come in?"

She opened the door wide enough for Tiana to step inside as her voice pecked through her skull with Richard III's and Robert Smith's like three blackbirds being baked alive in a pie.

"Don't you care that he's gone missing?"

"Has he? I think I need some water. Would you like something?"

"No, thank you."

River went to the little sink and poured from the tap into a toothpaste splattered glass.

"He's gone missing along with Petra and Etta."

"Who?"

"Oh my God, this is ridiculous, what has happened to you?"

"I ... I am feeling a bit spaced out, that's all. Sit down if you want."

Tiana looked around the chair-less room before perching herself on the edge of the double bed. "So, do you have any idea where he is?"

"Nathan? None I'm afraid."

"And you're not worried?"

"Why would I be?"

"He's your boyfriend isn't he?"

River stopped herself from saying what she was about to say but then decided to say it anyway. "I don't love him anymore."

Tiana looked like she had just swallowed a locust and was listening to it scream inside her stomach. "Firstly, I am presuming that means you are going to end this charade of a relationship? And secondly, that does not mean you should stop worrying about his well being."

"He is a very big boy now."

"Don't patronise me, River."

"Inverness is a small and safe town. If he has gone for a walkabout or a for few drinks he will be absolutely fine."

"I thought you said you'd never been here before?"

"Of course I've been here. I was born here. Don't you know anything about me?"

"Oh, yes," her tone changed to that of somebody trying to take a bad joke seriously, "You were here the dark ages or something?"

"The fifteenth century."

"Bloody fruitcake."

"What did you say?"

"You heard."

"Have you just come to my room to insult me?"

"No, darling, I have come here to find out where my goddamn brother is."

"And I told you, I have no idea."

Tiana read her face like she was looking for lies in the lines under her eyes. "You know, all I can think is, he was with you out of some kind of weird, morbid fascination. An art project gone wrong, or something."

"You have no right to say this stuff to me. No right at all."

"A year of his life he gave to you. Well, I suppose there is a lesson there for him to learn."

"And what lesson is that?"

"Only date people within your own time zone."

"And what lesson will he learn from living with you for all these years? How to become a miserable failure in five easy steps? How to pretend to be a successful musician when all you do is annoy innocent people with bad cello playing on the tube?"

"I make my brother very happy, unlike you. He would not be in this dive right now, lost and alone in some damp gutter somewhere, if you hadn't dragged him all the way here just so you can *find yourself*."

"Actually I invited him here in the hope that we could become friends. I didn't expect him to bring you and that scraggy cow with him."

"What scraggy cow?"

"The one he's run off with. Petra Skinny. I saw him sat in a pub with her after we visited that church this morning."

Tiana looked visibly stunned. She swallowed away her silence. "You know what, I really hope he has run off with Petra Sherry. Because she'd make a much better girlfriend than you ever could."

"Just please leave."

"I'm going. If he does return, tell him to come to my room immediately."

"Fine. Whatever you say. I'm going to bed now. Goodnight."

"Just make sure you tell him," she said, stepping out into '*Why Can't I Be With You?*'

River closed the door, strangely grateful for the altercation injecting a modicum of clarity into her brain. If she was going to get anything out of this trip, she needed to not walk around in a trance. She put the shower and kettle on, needing the revitalisation of cold water on her skin and hot caffeine in her blood. Undressing, she thought about Nathan returning, and put the '*Do Not Disturb*' sign on the door.

35

"Kiss my heart better."

In the damp, disused men's public toilet, she could feel all of her needs breathing and growing deep inside of her. The darker it grew outside, the more alive the world inside her skin became. The night was charged as she curled up with warm, semi-conscious male beauty.

Her emotions writhed as his body twitched beneath hers. Entwined together in a scratchy blanket, his lovely head resting on a rusty pipe, she closed her eyes to the pounding of his life. A shard of moonlight through the dirty window illuminated cracked tiles, broken urinals and a cubicle door leaning off its hinges. She did not need to close her eyes to remember how it felt to wake up beside Stephen each morning; the mermaid and starfish wallpaper and the chest she delicately rested her head on. When he finally woke he usually wanted tea, toast and boiled eggs, runny and salty. And then he would insist she went downstairs to fetch the morning newspapers from the little newsagent next door. When you are in love, nothing is a chore. It was the broadsheets if it was the weekend, and he would coat their duvet in them. She would watch him read as she sipped her tea, brushing away toast crumbs, combing his hair with her fingers, if he let her. Just sitting up in bed and admiring the contents of your net, that is love.

Softly, Petra began to sing. "I lie here next to you. Ancient fragile porcelain. Trying to hold my pieces together. Trying to stop the crush. When you can't hear my pleas for your touch. You coat us in Sunday silence."

Nathan murmured something.

"It was called 'To Fall In Love With You.' It was the B-Side to my first single."

Petra gripped Nathan's bare torso tight with the memory and breathed in his sweat. Her heart was re-anchored. Another stir. A gentle kick. He looked like he was caught between purgatory and a dream.

She took his bare shoulder into her mouth and tasted salt. In her mind she saw the image of open mouths waiting to partake of the flesh of Christ. The church on her street in Budleigh was called the Church of Most Precious Blood, and her mother used to take her there on Sunday mornings. Someone once said the sacramental bread turns into Jesus the second it hits your stomach.

To the outside eye, she was a psychotic kidnapper, a deranged criminal, but in reality it was Stephen who imprisoned her. She lived inside his stomach. "So you've only got yourself to blame really," she laughed.

Nathan responded with a whimper, and his eyes flickered as she took him in her mouth.

36

River sprinkled black pepper on her fried egg on toast in the dining hall of the Thane of Cawdor Hotel and sneezed. He was not there to bless her, and his empty chair elicited in her a tiny ache. She had no idea where he was; she had not seen him since she fell upon his cosy little tet-a-tet with that war-painted, chain-smoking, xylophonic-ribbed, failed singer-songwriter, yesterday afternoon.

She had already clocked the impoverished way she consumed him, but she was not someone she imaged Nathan would ever be interested in. She did not feel angry or jealous, just bemused, which validated her decision to end their relationship. Her apathy was exactly what his sister chastised her for that morning through a mouthful of *No Thrills* muesli: "How can you not be worried for his safety," she said, spitting a fleck of raison onto her bare arm. "Did you have another row? Is that it? Is that why he left? Tell me. I need to know." Her clear disdain for her and their relationship echoed around the oppressive, two hundred year old basement; bouncing off the little boxes of cheap cereal crap that seemed to be on constant display. Half an hour later and Tiana's eyes were still fixed in her direction. She was sat by the barred window which looked out onto a set of stone steps, her third cup of coffee poised. River soured her milk with a little wave, just as Ginger the Fiddler approached. "Come on River, eat up, we've got places to get to."

River still did not know where these places were and why they had to get to them so early in the morning, but she did not want to ask again. The kipper in Ginger's teeth made her feel queasy and she pushed the remains of her poached egg away. "I'm ready."

"Great. The car is just outside. Smokey is waiting for us there."

"Please let me pay something towards the car you've rented," she said as they walked out of Tiana's dagger range. "The petrol at least."

"No way."

"Are you and Smokey seeing each other? I didn't like to ask, but..."

"Love at first sight. Now come on you." He put his hand on her shoulder and she felt a tiny electric current as he led her out through the double doors, past the moody waitress with the half-arsed beehive who appeared to double up as a receptionist. Her stare was almost as hostile as Tiana's.

As they walked along the narrow street of grey-bricked Georgian and Victorian houses, a silent glider dragged a banner that read *'Be A Winner Not A Sinner'* across a bright turquoise sky. "Must be Christians," she said, and stopped to stare.

"Come on," said Smokey, suddenly appearing out of nowhere with a scarlet gloved hand reaching out to take her towards a small black *Fiat Uno* that glistened in the morning sun.

"Get in," said Ginger, unlocking the doors with the press of a key.

Climbing onto the warm back seat, River was greeted with that smell of fresh upholstery that was synonymous with brand new cars. The shock of the new for a woman with a foot in the distant past. Ginger ignited the engine, bursting into life an excitable dj that he immediately switched off, and Smokey retrieved an atlas from the glove compartment. "We need the A82," she instructed him, "it goes straight down to Loch Ness."

Loch Ness. Loch Ness was one of those names that River instinctively knew meant something to her when she was Dimiza because of the way it bounced around her brain. Loch Ness. Yes, there was thunderous de-ja-vu when she repeated the words to herself. A very vague image of a castle played peek-a-boo on the periphery of her memory; a castle set on the banks of a loch. It was as imposing as it was *beautiful moonlight on his white flesh, strong, broad, sword wielding shoulders, a warm mouth on her neck and fingers on her legs.* Feeling the flashback clawing its way out of her was like suddenly getting out of a steaming hot bath, that rush of blood to the head, that giddy swirl and whirl and *hands on her naked hips as I bury my face into his bushy chest.* She grabs the car door to keep hold of the present and hears her mouth explode: "There is a castle, a castle where he took me, Alexander. He, he was much more relaxed there because we were away from the prying eyes of his wife. His friend owned it, no, his cousin."

Black leather driving gloves squeeze the steering wheel hard. Their owner's pale blue eyes peer at her in the overhead mirror, just as judgmental priests peer through confessional grates at their parishioners.

She wound down the window desperate for fresh air to keep her from 1479 or 1480 or whenever it was, for right now she wanted to stay focussed on what was going on around her. She knew the River Ness would soon widen into the great expanse of Loch Ness, because she had made this exact journey before in a horse-led carriage. It was a kind of torture, not knowing anything for sure, but sensing far too much. Her brain began to build the castle again, but she could feel in her body that it was not just the rapture of sensuality that had occurred there, but something darker too. Something sinister. Something bloody. Inhaling a horror that was just a thin membrane away from her consciousness threw her heart against its cage of bones. The reality of being completely under the control of two people she barely even knew became starker than ever.

"I don't think I want to go any further," she said, pathetically.

"Why?" one of them asked, but she did not know how to respond. She pressed her palms into her eyes, took a lungful of the cool Nessy air and heard a voice. His voice. Richard's. "*Transylvania?*" There was his sarcastic question again from the very last conversation she could remember having with him. "*Do you want me to send my nephews to Vlad the Impaler's castle?*" she heard his soft voice continue like he was in the back of this Fiat Uno with her and his hot breath was against her face. 1483 grabbed her ankles and pulled her into his body heat.

"*That would be perfect, but not quite where I had in mind,*" *I reply.*

"*Where then? Come on, I have a privy council meeting to get to.*"

"*Scotland.*"

"*Scotland!*" *He spits the name of the country back at me like it is rat poison.* "*Have you forgotten we are at war with Scotland?*"

"*That was over a year ago.*"

"Our invasion was last year, but our war with that country will continue until the end of time."

"There is a castle there, hidden away on the banks of Loch Ness in the Highlands. It is one of the most remote and isolated places on God's Earth. Nobody would ever find them there."

"Dimiza, get your head out of the sky. Who owns this castle?"

"An ally of yours."

"I have no allies in Scotland."

"You do. George Gordon, Earl of Huntley."

"How can he by my ally when I've never heard of him?"

"He is Alexander Stewart's cousin. He and I used to go and stay there together when I worked at Inverness Castle. He was the most kind and gracious host. I am sure if you write to him requesting lodgings for ... family members ...he will be more than happy to oblige."

"And how do you propose I get them over the border."

"That can be arranged, you know it can. You have thousands of soldiers on the border. What alternative do you have? You already said there's been an attempt to rescue them from the Tower. If you leave it any longer you will be in danger of losing everything."

His eyes study the determination in mine. "It would be a huge risk."

"Less of a risk than leaving them another day in London."

"If this George Huntley person agrees, you will have to accompany them there."

"Me?"

"Yes, of course you. And you will need to stay there with them until they are settled."

I immediately think about that frumpy Anne Neville woman, his stagnant queen who holds in her fat hands the life I so desperately want for myself. My jealous, rageful mind imagines them getting closer in his need for female affection while I do all I can to keep him sat on his blood drenched throne.

"Yes, of course, Your Majesty."

"Just Ginger will do."

She opened her eyes to a black leather glove on her shoulder. "We're almost there. Look outside, you're missing all this beautiful Highland scenery."

The pine-treed mountains had risen and the river on her left had widened. It was flanked by mountains that were both stunning and familiar.

"Just let her sleep," protested Smokey, who was now at the wheel.

Words began spinning from her mouth again. "He wanted to put them somewhere completely out of the way where nobody would ever think to look for them. And that is when I thought of this place, because I was thinking of the most remote castle that I had ever been to." She slammed it shut and returned her eyes to the speeding scenery and her five hundred year old guilt and shame playing itself out on the rain speckled glass and *Lord Huntley is talking to me through gulps of wine. "It is lovely to have you back at Urquhart Castle." With my love's dangerous nephews safely tucked up in their bedchambers directly above our heads, freshly caught salmon and trout in my stomach, too much French wine in my blood, and the words of this kind and sweet man in my ear, I allow my tired eyes to close for a moment in a cooling wave of contentment.*

"You remind me of Beatrix, my brother's wife. You both have the same ... how do I describe it? ... overt sensuality. She was his mistress before he married her too."

My eyes spring open because this is the first time I have ever heard of an aristocrat marrying his mistress. So it is possible then. There really is hope for Richard and me. I thought the story of common old Elizabeth Woodville stealing the heart of King Edward in a forest was the closest any woman had ever got to the Whore's Dream.

"I love women like you, I really do. All free and easy. Too many women are overly concerned with being submissive and meek, and getting their etiquette just right, and saying the right thing. I loved how you looked me straight in the eye when we first met. I always enjoyed Alexander bringing you here, and despite the ominous circumstances I am so pleased you have returned."

I drain my cup thinking that I would probably sleep with him right now if my body was not dedicated to Richard. "I have not actually seen Alexander since Richard helped him invade Scotland last year. We left him in Edinburgh Castle where he foolishly capitulated to his brother's demands instead of stealing his crown."

"There was very little support for Alexander to become king."

"In Scotland maybe, but he signed a treaty with England."

"You think Scotland would ever accept a king who had gotten into bed with England?"

"I am always disappointed by men who don't strive to become the most powerful beings they can possibly be. You see, I am just as ambitious as any man, but as a woman the only way I can get anywhere in this world is by standing behind a man."

"And that is why I find you so desirable." The Earl gestures to a servant to refill their cups. "You know, Alexander dissolved into nothing after you left him for Richard. I'm not sure if you're aware of this but when all the lords and barons chose to favour his brother again he fled back over the border."

"He returned to England? I had no idea. Why didn't he seek out Richard?"

"He did but he refused to see him."

"In that case he should have come in search of me."

"Oh come on, as if you'd have bothered with him when you had Richard in your palm."

"In my palm? Ha! I am completely and utterly in his. And when his wife enters the room he pretends I don't exist."

"I thought you would be used to that feeling now, the number of years you have been a royal mistress."

"I am only a royal mistress because the world refuses to let me become a royal wife."

"And that is why you are here? To do something to really make him notice you?"

I take a gulp of wine to avoid his accurate mind reading.

"I imagine Richard refused to allow Alexander to come to his court out of fear of you going back to him."

"He doesn't need to worry about that. I love Richard and I will be his until the day I die. That's why I'm here."

I try to ignore the voice in my head reminding me that if it were not for Alexander I would still be scrubbing pots and plucking pheasants in the kitchens of Inverness Castle.

"If he still wants the Scottish throne, maybe you could help him?"

"I am quite fond of my head, thank you very much. Now that the king is back in favour with his subjects, only a fool would act against him. I wish Alexander well, but he has no future in Scotland I am afraid."

"In that case I am rather surprised you agreed to Richard's letter."

"I agreed to Richard's letter because I wanted to see **you** again." He holds his goblet up to me. "And besides, I need to be in his favour in case he ever decides to invade Scotland again."

"Very wise."

"And it probably won't be long until he does. English kings get bored and twitchy when they are not at war with us."

"I think Richard is hoping for a peaceful reign."

"Gawter!" he shouts at the solo musician solemnly strumming his gittern. "Give us something else, you are sending my lady into a trance." He turns back to me. "England has not known peace since they put a nine month old baby on their throne sixty years ago. And I doubt very much it will know peace now, not with all the enemies Richard will have made by snatching the throne from his nephews."

"He didn't snatch it, his nephews were found to be illegitimate."

"And I was found to be the Queen of Scotland."

"It's true."

"A very convenient truth."

"Well at least his enemies won't be able to get hold of them while they are here."

"They might be out of sight but they will never be out of people's minds."

"They need to die." The words fall from my lips as if the wine had dissolved the bone between my brain and my mouth. I look into the fire to avoid his widening eyes, wishing it would burn up the utterance that is now hurtling around Huntley's skull.

"What did you just say?"

"I .... I just think that Richard will never know peace while they are alive. Don't you agree?"

"I have told you they will be safe here." He lowers his voice. "By God's teeth, they are just children."

"What if someone finds out they are here?"

"They won't."

"You cannot guarantee that. The only reason he won't have someone kill them for him is because he is terrified of God's wrath."

"And so he should be."

"Despite the fact that their deaths will finally bring stability to England?"

He puts down his wine as if it now tasted of blood.

"So I am going to have to do it myself."

"You?"

"It has to be done. Unless you have a highly trusted and discreet servant who could do it for me?"

"Don't be absurd," he spat. "You think I want princes' blood on the hands of my household?"

Gawter's music became solemn again, as if he could smell the danger in the air.

"Richard wants them dead more than anything and I am going to be the one to present him with that gift. Only then will he realise who I truly am."

"Which is?"

"The woman he is supposed to be married to. His true love. His true queen."

"You are delusional."

"Why? Your brother married his mistress."

"That was different."

"How?"

"Because Richard is the King of England."

"He only married Anne Neville for her land and estates. He more or less told me so. His mother pushed him into it because she is related to her. He doesn't want her, he doesn't sleep with her, he doesn't love her, he only sees her as the mother of his son. She is so lifeless she didn't even care when he became king. She walked down the aisle of Westminster Abbey on their coronation day with the same passion and enthusiasm that she walks up the steps to his bedchamber on those strange occasions when he thinks he should try for another son."

"Maybe she's like that because she has to contend with you."

"In that case she should know her place. Even the boy she bore him is weak and sickly. The boys I give him will be Black Princes and Lionhearts."

"Mistress, I will not permit you to do this in my home."

"Then don't permit me. Turn a blind eye to it. But let me remind you that Richard is not someone you want to anger, and if his enemies get hold of those boys, which inevitably they will, it will be your head that he will want on a spike on London Bridge. Do you really think this castle is strong enough to hold them against the thousands of men who will fight to put Edward Bastard on the English throne?"

"You are a sly whore, aren't you? Did you really bring them all the way here just to kill them and blackmail me into keeping silent for you?"

"No, I have come all this way to help you become Richard's ally. The benefits to you will be immeasurable. But it's your choice."

The Earl dismisses his gittern player with a wave of a hand and then drops his head into it. I think I can see his thoughts dancing between his fingers. He reaches for his goblet of wine but puts it down again without drinking from it. "Don't kill both of them," he eventually says. "Just the older one."

"Why?"

"I want to keep the younger one here. Don't worry, I will change his identity, no one will know who he is."

"I am not sure about this."

"If you want me to keep silent, Dimiza, you will agree to my terms."

"What do you want with him?"

"I'll marry him to my daughter."

"But what will be the point of that if you have changed his identity?"

"*Because I will know who he is. I will know that my daughter is married to a prince. This will be your way of thanking me.*"

"*I really don't know.*"

"*It is that or nothing.*"

The wine is filling my veins and clouding my thoughts. I am not happy with his ultimatum but I know there is no way I can return to London with those boys. "*You leave me with very little choice. Do you promise me that no one will ever find out who he really is? I mean **no one**. Not even your daughter.*"

I watch an intoxicated smile slowly part the Earl's lips. "*I promise.*"

"*How old is she?*"

"*The same age as her newly betrothed.*"

"*Nine?*"

"*Yes.*"

"*Actually, are you aware that this will be his second marriage? He married the Countess of Norfolk when he was four.*"

"*What happened to her?*"

"*She died when she was eight.*"

"*Dear God's bones.*" He crosses himself. "*I won't marry them straight away. I will give them some time to mature together first.*"

"*After I have committed the deed, my Lord, I will need some assistance in disposing of his body. I am thinking that we could sew some rocks into his clothing and drop him into the loch?*"

"*No, no, no. You are on your own, lady. I told you, I will not have any of my servants involved in this. If you want that boy at the bottom of Loch Ness you will have to do it yourself.*" He stands abruptly as if wanting to physically distance himself from my evil plight. "*I need to start deciding what I am going to change his name to. It needs to be something suitably obscure. Percy. No. Patrick. No. Perkin. Yes. Yes, I like that. What do you think?*" He doesn't wait for me to answer. "*Let me go up and see him. Let me go up and see my Prince Perkin of Urquhart.*"

The wine-washed earl staggers out of the room in search of the boy whose destiny turns and twists with each blood-charged minute. Fear chokes me when I think about what I now have to do. All that calms me is remembering who I am doing it for and how he is going to reward me.

The twelve year old 'Lord Bastard,' nee uncrowned King Edward V, and his younger brother, the new 'Perkin of Urquhart,' are in adjoining bedchambers. Once the earl finishes fawning over his sleeping prize and makes his way back down the stone staircase, I creep out of the shadows to find mine. And there he is, sleeping doll-like in a shaft of moonlight emitting from an open window. His golden blond curls fall about his young, porcelain face. Amongst his exhalations comes a whimper, perhaps belying a violent dream. He is so innocent, so unfortunate to be the oldest son of a king who died too soon, but this has to be done. I slowly lean down to kiss the knuckle of his tiny hand in recognition of his birthright. Lifting my eyes to check I have not woken him, I very carefully pull away the wild boar skin that his hand rests on. He inhales sharply, as do I, and thinking of Richard as I always do, I quickly force the underside of the fur down hard onto his nose and mouth. Against his resistance, against his muffled screams, against his wild fists which attack my shoulders and chest, I push the fur down onto his delicate features harder and harder. He scratches at my arms and hands until ... until .... until one by one his limbs begin to crumble and his torso stiffens in contortion and there is nothing but stillness and silence. He is gone. Richard is now the undisputed King of England. And I have made that possible for him. Lifting the fur from his face I am shocked to see how death has burst open his eyes and mouth in a final, haunting expression of his short life.

I close his eyes with finger and thumb, but still a glimmer of blue peeps out. Vengeful irises refusing to let me escape this crime. I feel sick at how easy it has been to rip the mortal years away from someone so young, and a monarch at that. But if I had not done so, Richard would never consider me as anything other than his harlot.

I suddenly feel faint with the heavy weight of this sin in my heart. I walk over to the open window and look out over the dark waters. The full moon shimmers and scatters over ripples, as if trying to convey a message to me in a code that I will never be able to *understand. I close my eyes to the cool summer breeze against my face, wishing I could just stand like this forever, rather than face what I have to do next.*

With one arm under his thin legs and the other under his torso, I lift up the asphyxiated young king and walk him over to the stone window ledge. Will his soul be avenged? I know Richard constantly asks God to forgive him for dispatching Lord Hastings and Anthony Woodville into purgatory. His penitence woven with a hundred justifications for beheading the men. Will God understand that we are doing this for the sake of a peaceful England?

The shadow of a huge bird of prey flies over the surface of the loch.

I kiss his forehead, whisper "forgive me, Your Majesty," and allow the weight of his body to fall from my grip, down, down, down, into the deep waters below us. "Long live King Richard III," I whisper on hearing the heavy splash. My voice sounds like a ghost in my ears now. I no longer know who I am.

Her body jolted and she opened her eyes to see gravestones speeding by. She remembered where she was and then her flesh froze at the memory her brain had just unlocked. Her stomach twisted with the guilt and shame of it. She was a murderer. A child murderer. A king murderer. His soul was trapped in this air, determined to show her the bloody part she played in his mortal demise. She began to wind down the window, unprepared for anymore of it, but once again 1483 gripped her murderous limbs and dragged her back down beneath its currents and *I am naked on Richard's crimson sheets not long after I arrive back in London. We are setting our souls alight with our flesh and his mother's best Rumney wine which is dripping between my breasts. "Thistles," I tell him when he asks me about the scratches on my hands and arms. I reach over to fill my mouth with a handful of strawberries, the sharp juice jumps into my blood like a mischievous animal. I feel his arms impatiently pull me into him and I grin at what his bitter queen is missing out on.*

I rest my head on the jewels around his neck which are as red and shiny as the strawberries in my hand. I watch him take a strawberry into his mouth whole, stork leaves and all, and I rest a finger on his pronounced jaw as he chews. I lean forward to allow the tip of my tongue to softly trace the line of his strong jaw until it finds its way into the wet of his mouth. My love tastes like Sunday morning communion.

"Come on, I want to hear everything," he is saying to me.

"I told you, it all went very well. Lord Huntley was just as welcoming to me as he was when I went there with Alexander four years ago."

"And my nephews?"

"Yes, to them too. Very much so."

"You know what I am asking you. Were they happy to be there?"

"Yes. They were confused as to why they couldn't stay in London but..."

"...but I explained all that to them before they left the Tower."

"As did I. Again and again. You know how obstinate children can be. Especially the Lord Bastard. He was adamant that he has no enemies that he needs protecting from. Plus he was still protesting his Uncle Anthony's innocence, asking me to beg you for his release from Pontefract castle. I didn't like to tell him that he can have his precious Woodville uncle back if he wants, but there's no longer a head attached."

He does not laugh at my joke. In fact, he looks dismayed. I look into his deep, dark eyes to try and spot the wild animal splashing about that ordered the beheadings of innocent men. But there is nothing. Sometimes I think there are two different Richards, the ambitious one who wades towards the throne through the blood of his enemies, and the pensive, pious authoritarian who has sworn lifelong devotion to his dead brother. I drop my face back down onto his jewelled neck, imagining how Anthony Woodville's severed head would have looked as it twitched in the hay, lips quivering their innocence, eyes screaming at the gates of limbo. I ask myself if this is the right moment to tell him I have made his crown even safer than he thinks. And before my brain can answer, I feel my own lips forming words. "Your Majesty...," I begin, keeping my face hidden. "Do you not think the Lord Bastard is also too dangerous to keep alive?"

"We have already discussed this. I am not going to let anything happen to my brother's children. His last wish was for me to protect them. I just want them removed, out of the way as far as possible, and that's exactly what you've done for me, isn't it?"

"Yes."

"Then let's say no more about it. I just hope they can lead a happy, peaceful life by Loch Ness, hunting, fishing, playing, until they forget who they ever were. Now fill my cup."

My stomach sinks as I fill his cup to the brim. "But are you not worried that one day Edward will try to claim his throne back?"

"Dimiza, I said let us say no more about it."

"He is gone."

Bile rises to my throat to erode the confession, but it is too late. I watch his jaw clench.

"What do you mean "gone"?"

I swallow the bile. "I ....." I think I may have just ended my own life too. "I...." How long before I face the block and axe? "I have got rid of him for you. He is no longer a problem for you. He is no longer a threat."

His irises become possessed. "How?"

How long before my head joins that of Lord Hastings and Anthony Woodville on the spikes of London Bridge? "I suffocated him in his sleep. He didn't feel any pain. He didn't even know it was happening. I did for you, Your Majesty."

He is slowly shaking his head, repeating, "you don't know what you have done," over and over again.

"Aren't you relieved? You're free of him now. And none of the guilt is on your shoulders."

"What about the other one?"

"He lives. He will be brought up in Urquhart Castle under a different name."

"Is this a terrible joke?"

"The earl begged me to spare him. He promised me he will never leave the castle walls. I am sure we can trust him."

"You killed my nephew?" His violent eyes seize up my throat. "With your own bare hands?" I can feel my legs shaking. "Did you bring a priest with you when you committed the deed?"

"Of ... of course not."

"Then I am afraid you will see young Edward in hell when you get there."

I think I see my thumping, sinful, blackened heart fall out of its ribcage and roll onto the floor. He reaches across the bed and my flesh flinches and braces itself at the thought of a dagger. He picks up his rosary, brings it to his lips, and lifts his cold eyes back up to mine.

"This ... this is what you wanted," I persist.

He throws my kirtle at me. "Put this on."

I do so while he buttons up his doublet.

He grabs my arm and drags me out of his bedchamber.

"Where are you taking me?"

Without speaking, he leads me through the long, cold corridors of the castle, until we reach the empty chapel. A golden goblet is laid out on the white satin covered altar, filled almost to the brim with blessed wine. The blood of Christ. I can feel my own throbbing in my neck. He looks up at the marble crucifix above the alter and crosses his chest. I shakily do the same, my eyes darting across the stained glass windows and masonry, desperately trying to understand what is happening.

Closing his eyes, he brings his rosary woven fingers to his mouth and begins to pray in Latin. I am too scared to close mine. Too scared to pray. My soul is reeling in my skin. It knows its time on this earth is fast coming to an end.

When he opens his eyes they are blank, soulless, dead.

"Your Majesty..."

Nothing.

"Your Majesty, please...."

My voice is made of pure fear. "Look at me. I beg you. Don't worry, I won't tell anyone what I've done. What I've done for you." I think about running but how far can I get in the confines of Baynard's Castle with every exit guarded? I grab hold of him but with one arm he tosses me onto the stone floor.

"I have got blood on my hands for you," I scream up into his face.

"My blood," he screams back. "My blood."

One of his guards bursts into the chapel, his hand gripping the handle of his sword.

Richard holds him back with a gesture of the hand and then stands over me. "The next time I see your face, it will be greeting me on London Bridge."

"No."

He turns to his guard. "Take this traitor to the Tower and tell Brackenbury I want her head in three days time."

The henchman picks my body up from the ground in one roguish grab as if I am already a corpse.

"I did this for you," I try to scream but my words are now lost in the nightmare.

As I am dragged away I see him cross his chest once again and pick up a bible. Does he really think that his soul is not tarnished and destined for the same hell as mine?

I look at the guard's face and realise he is about sixty, with the strength of a man half his age.

"Don't you know how to treat a woman?" I shout into his face.

Rotting yellow teeth appear through his grey beard. "I know how to treat a traitor."

I give up physically resisting because I know it is no use. I allow my impending cadaver to be led through the castle, past the scornful eyes of Proud Cis watching from the gallery, through the crowds of servants who have stepped out of walls to gleefully stare at my downfall, and then I am out on the street and forced into the back of a small, caged wagon.

Through the narrow wooden bars my senses are attacked by the atrocities of London's filthy, stinking streets. The human stench. The shrill and vulgar yelps.

"What's this one done?" laughs an old crone, so close to me I can smell her festering teeth.

Decomposing fruit hits the bars, leaving stinking pulp running down my face. I look into the frightened eyes of a young, slim, pretty woman who is being forced to walk the streets in nothing but her thin, white cotton undergarments. Her bare feet are bleeding and her hair and face drip with whatever the Londoners have thrown at her. Men leer and jeer over her exposed flesh. We hold each other's gaze and something like solidarity passes between us. Or maybe it is familiarity.

As the Tower of London's gatehouse comes into view, I am reminded of the time I was first led towards the imposing entrance of Inverness Castle. But instead of the excitement of finally seeing inside the place I had fantasised about since I was a little girl, I feel only stomach-twisting dread. For I know what happens to people inside these walls. I know about Lord Hastings being dragged out onto Tower green and having his head hacked off; I know of men being tied to the rack and stretched and stretched and stretched until they confess to crimes they haven't committed. I look up and immediately regret doing so, for there above me are the heads of traitors stuck on spikes, eyes bulging, mouths distorted, faces ravaged by torture and starving crows. Will mine be joining them?

The grey beard and yellow teeth of my captor are back in my face.

"Move, whore!"

I am wrenched out of the wagon by the grip of a large pair of thick, leather gloves. The kind of gloves my oldest brother, Torkill, wore when he was out on the mountains training our buzzard to catch dead rats mid air. How I now long for the family I abandoned for ambition.

I am pushed through a small door and forced to climb an unlit, narrow, stone spiral staircase, followed by the sound of a thousand jangling keys. At the top of the steps is a closed door, lit by a candle. My shoulder is being squeezed by thick, dirty fingers and I turn to see a face I recognize. It is Robert Brackenbury, the Keeper of the Tower. I was introduced to him at Richard's coronation feast.

"My Lord, Brackenbury."

His deep set eyes glance into mine. "I don't know you, traitor."

"I am no traitor. I am Dimiza, the king's mistress."

"Mistress? Ha. Well you didn't do a very good job of pleasing him if you've ended up here," he says, using one of his many keys to unlock the thick wooden door.

"Do you think you could talk to him for me?"

"Don't be ridiculous, I don't even know who you are."

"We met at his coronation. I swear to you, I do not deserve to be here."

"Wench, I am given instructions, not reasons. All I know is that you are a traitor and you will face the axe on Tower Hill in three days time. Are you going to step inside of your own volition, or am I going to force you in?"

I step backwards into the small, dark, dank cell without unpeeling my eyes from his, for he is now my only hope. "My Lord, His Majesty loves me and I love him."

"Very touching."

"Please don't close that door."

"I've got work to do."

"I know he asked you to do it too."

"To do what?"

"You know what I am talking about."

"I really don't, and I haven't got the time or inclination to find out."

My mouth spins a lie in its bid for salvation. "I know he asked you to kill the princes too, just as he asked me."

For a second Lord Brackenbury stops being a busy man. He stands stock still and draws in a lungful of the musty air. I have clearly hit home. "He asked me no such thing."

"I know he did. He tells me everything."

"I can see why he wants you dead, whore. Your mind has been dredged out of London's putrid gutters."

"And when you refused, he had to ask someone else to do it, and that person was me."

"No doubt you practice in the dark arts too? Witch."

"So, if you want to know the reason I am here, I suggest you look no further than yourself."

"You should be burnt at the stake. Witch whore."

"If you had killed them he would have got rid of you too."

"You killed them?"

"I killed the true and rightful King of England. The younger one I let live."

Robert Brackenbury instantly crosses himself, looking up into a heaven of cobwebs and crawling insects, before flashing his dark eyes back at mine. "And where is his brother now?"

I tell him because I have nothing to lose and I know it will harm Richard. "Urquhart Castle in Scotland. That is where I took them both. And that is that is where I suffocated the twelve year old king in his sleep."

He grabs hold of his chest and begins murmuring a biblical lamentation.

"What choice did I have? A mistress lives to serve and please her master, does she not?"

"I really cannot begin to imagine the torturous chambers of hell that are being stoked for you."

He slams the door on my wretchedness and I scream through the thick wood until the sound of his keys and footsteps disappear. I turn to look at my new home, lit only by a thin arrow slit. I hear the unmistakable scratching of a rat. My body is as motionless as if the axe had already disconnected my brain from it. I am numb. I am finished. I am dead. The scratching gets louder. My face is now destined to become food for either him or the birds of prey that circle London Bridge.

37

Drawing so hard on her morning cigarette that she almost felt one of her lungs collapse, Petra cast her eyes onto the flowing, shimmering surface of Loch Ness. She had no idea whereabouts on the loch they were, her Ordnance Survey map stopped making sense a long way back, but any monster contained in this Highland water was incomparable to the one lurking inside of her. The rising sun turned the clouds into umber lava, reflecting on the water in strange shapes. For a few seconds she thought she was looking at a small hand waving at her above the surface. She threw her cigarette in its direction and as it landed she was convinced she saw a boy's face.

Wrapping her viscose fur collar tightly around her neck, she took another Sovereign out of the packet and made her way back to the disused public toilet where she kept her man. The warm morning breeze was sensual against her skin, a bliss she knew she did not deserve.

She opened the door wide enough to let in the embryonic sunlight and her hungry pupils devoured the facial features that were his downfall. His own eyes were half-open and tormented, and he let out a whimper like that of a starving fox or shut out cat. She knew she was going to prison for this. His flesh and those binds were supposed to be her new start, but reality was creeping into her bones like the morning. He was not Stephen and so she had to let him go. Swallowing acid reflux back down into the hollows of her stomach, she crouched down beside him and leant in for one last kiss, the final kiss before the start of her own captivity at Her Majesty's Pleasure. His naked chest was too inviting to resist and she rested her face against it, pulling his free arm around her, the arm that never willingly held her. "But even as I hold you, your mind's already left me," she sang over and over again into his warm skin before untying the wire that bound him to the metal piping.

"You're free." She began shaking him. "You're free. You're free. You're free."

*

His liver shivered. Even before he could properly focus he knew something was terribly wrong. His brain throbbed and his body was a frozen leg of lamb. He looked into the green, over-spilling eyes and tried to speak but all he could do was make the gargling sounds of a baby. His mouth felt like sand and something inside him began to spasm.

"You're free," she was saying over and over again. The softness of her lips on his belied the insanity in her eyes. "I'm sorry," she said, stroking his face with a cigarette reeking finger. "I just wanted you to be him."

"Where am I?" he tried to ask.

Her face turned as blank as a corpse and he forced himself up onto prickling legs. He fell towards the open door and a crimson sun that swayed around the sky like a naked light bulb in an earthquake.

38

"This is it. We are entering it now. The village I live in."

"Why are you slowing down?"

"Because this is my home, don't you want to see it?"

"The only place I want to see right now are the ruins of that castle."

"Shhhhh."

Smokey turned around to look at their captive. "She's been out like a light for the past twenty minutes. Probably just as well considering. What are you doing? Why have you stopped?"

"I've just seen Lydia."

"Who the hell is Lydia?"

"My friend."

"And you tell *me* off for forgetting I'm...."

"I know very well what I look like right now, but that won't stop her knowing it's me."

"We can see her on the way back."

Ginger parked the car besides a fluffy, pure white Persian languishing on a garden wall in the hot sun. The second he wound down the window, the cat's expression switched from dozy to delirious. She leapt off the wall and onto the ledge of the car's open window.

"Hello, you," cooed Ginger, using his palms like giant tongues to lap her up, causing Lydia's purr to vibrate through metal and upholstery. She climbed onto his lap and did her best to roll over and stick her ample belly in the air to get maximum stroke action. Hanging from her diamante encrusted collar was a gold pendant engraved with the words: 'Please Do Not Feed Me.'

"I don't mean to break up this touching little reunion, but we happen to be on our way to quite an important job."

"Lydia," Ginger murmured through licks and pets, "we've got to go, but the next time you see me I'll be back in my true form."

"You need to get out of the car now, Lydia," Smokey told the feline sternly. She responded with a pale blue flash of jealous irises before climbing out of the car and back onto her warm spot in the sun.

"I was in desperate need of a boost," said Ginger as he restarted the engine. "I knew she'd take the edge off being stuck in this skin."

"Try being stuck in it for six months."

"Well, in a couple of hours it'll all be over. There, that's the street I live up."

"Don't even think about driving up it."

He inhaled deeply. "I think I can smell Mrs M's hand cream."

"Come on."

"Oh my Goddess, look up there, that's me!"

"What do you mean that's you?"

Smokey followed Ginger's pointed finger to a poster Sellotaped to a tree. Besides the photograph of a ginger cat were the words:

Lost Cat

Ginger is a gorgeous nine year old ginger tabby tomcat with white markings. He was last seen near Pitkerrald Road in Drumnadrochit. He is an indoor cat and not used to cars. Please check your garages, sheds, and trees.

Thank you.

Mrs Mary MacLennan

"Wow, is that really you?"

"Yes." The words on the poster were like a machete to the chest. "'Not used to cars.' If only she could see me now."

Smokey noticed his eyes moistening. "Come on, Ginger, the quicker we get to that bloody castle, the quicker you can climb back onto her lap."

"You're right. What's got into me? It's usually you needing the pep talk."

Ginger picked up speed, heading towards the loch-side castle ruins that were just starting to become visible on the horizon.

"Cute pic, though," added Smokey, throwing him a lascivious eye.

39

River could not breathe when she saw the crumbling ruins of Urquhart Castle. The keep used to be almost double the height it was now and her eyes built it up to its former cloud-touching glory.

"Look, the moat's all dried up. It used to have a huge drawbridge over it. And that gatehouse used to be massive. I could describe the layout of the original castle to you perfectly and a historian would validate everything I said, I guarantee it."

Smokey slowed down to read the sign: **'Urquhart Castle. Summer opening hours. 10am to 6pm.'**

River checked her moon crescent watch. "Oh no, it doesn't open for another hour."

"We know. We're climbing over the fence."

"Once we're sure there are no staff about," added Ginger.

River was about to raise an objection, but overriding it was a need to be inside that castle again. She was keen to discover if stepping foot amongst those medieval bricks and trapped spirits would unlock further doors inside her mind.

She got out of the car and felt someone squeeze her hand. *"You are going to love spending time here." Alexander looks at me and smiles properly for the first time since we left Inverness Castle. I smile back and* Ginger led her towards the ruins, minus the smile.

The deep orange sun rose over the vast blue loch which was silent except for the engine of a distant fishing boat. As they walked through the ruined gatehouse and into the castle grounds her head turned on its own accord to look at the chapel in which she once prayed for the soul of the boy she murdered. But all that was left were an outline of bricks where it once stood. Even God had deserted the place.

"Forgive me."

"For what?" asked Smokey, inches behind them.

She was now being led towards the keep which once housed the bedchambers and the great hall where Earl Huntley threw fabulous feasts. "There were flutes and drums and jesters and some sort of dancing animal. A goat I think."

Ginger's hands began pushing and pulling her even more firmly towards the building which hundreds of years of erosion had left exposed. Some of the stone floors remained intact however, and her eyes involuntarily wove the tapestries that hung on the walls the last time she was here. *Alexander Stewart is holding me beside a smouldering fire. His hazel eyes, full of desire, are slowly uncoiling my flesh. "I want to stay here forever," I tell him.*

"You remember this building don't you, Dimiza?" asked Smokey, her wild irises piercing her flashback. "You remember what you did in there? Did you really think you could get away with killing the rightful King of England?"

"Who are you?"

Smokey laughed at the question with all her teeth. River tried to escape, but Ginger's grip on her arm was an iron vice. Everywhere she looked, Smokey was there, leaping about her with a feline mania. Suddenly Ginger began tugging her towards the entrance of the keep's narrow stone stairwell. For a second she saw the stone spiral staircase that Brackenbury had forced her to climb in the Tower of London, but time had left this one open to the sky. She was pushed up the stone steps until she was on the level of what was once the boy king's bedchamber. It was on the highest floor of the tower's remains and only a railing kept her from plummeting to her death into the loch below. Penetrating her fears, the bowing of a viola floated up the stairs. She turned around and saw the four poster bed with the little king still asleep inside it. His curly blond hair peeked above the furs of Highland bears and wild boars. She could hear the light softness of his whimpers, as if his soul was weaving itself around her limbs. *His delicate twelve year old features, his purple velvet collar, I try not to think about who he is, or that he has a godly right to rule over us, I just want to concentrate on how I will win Richard's heart by stopping his. My hands search for a way to kill him and before I can fully focus on what I'm doing I watch them take hold of the wild boar fur and press it harder and harder and harder still into his nose and mouth.* A sign reading **'DANGER DO NOT CLIMB'** suddenly screamed into view and she could longer see the boy she killed, nor fill brick outlines of fireplaces with smouldering flames and chimney breasts with the Earl of Huntley's coat of arms woven into golden tapestries. She only saw her kidnappers and their palpable malevolence that wrapped around her like ribbons of death. Again she tried to yank free of Ginger's grip, but he responded by shoving her hard against a stone window ledge. The same stone window ledge that she dropped the body of the boy king into the loch from after she snatched away his life.

"The Goddess of Retribution has instructed us to end your life at the exact same spot you ended his," hissed Smokey.

She saw blood and felt her bones dissolve into her skin. She screamed with all that she had left and heard it echo across the expansive loch and the hills and mountains beyond. Her eyes glanced and glazed down at the one hundred foot straight drop directly beneath her.

"His younger brother saw the whole thing," said Smokey. "He was watching from the door."

"No, no, he was asleep."

Smokey laughed again and her flesh was now as lifeless as she made the true King of England's. The bleak taste of murder in the air seemed to turn the morning sky grey. Not one muscle in her body was a match for Ginger's as he lifted up onto the ancient stonework of the window ledge. And then, with her eyes closed, she felt that final push, and the horrific sensation of falling. Of falling. Of falling. Falling and feeling. Feeling the grasp of someone. Someone stronger than any living creature ever recorded in history.

Just like before.

40

The envoys peered down into the loch from the ruins of the window.

"How do we know she is dead if we can't see her?" asked Smokey.

"No human could survive that fall."

Smokey turned to her accomplice, baring her teeth. "It is done, then. It is finished."

"It is finished."

"At last."

She embraced him and felt the menacing chill of death that hung between them. The light formed strange beasts on the surface of the water. "How long until it happens do you think? How long before we turn back?"

He silently followed her gaze into the water as they awaited their much craved incatnation.

*

Sekhmet, the Goddess of Retribution, considers keeping her feline worshippers in their despised coat of flesh until the king-murderer is all sealed up in the underworld, but she knows there is nothing they can do about the interfering menace that is the God of Moon and Time. Their job here is done and their premature sense of accomplishment creeps into her scarlet heart. Wading through the dark, red, starring eyes that live beneath humanity, her own eye is caught by the glimmer and glister of the great Scales of Justice. It is wet with the deep maroon heart-blood of both the guilty and the innocent. Crocodile jaws salivate beneath it, waiting for the chest organs that are tainted with indelible sin. Down here there is no heart more in demand than that of the woman who snuffed away a divinely appointed king, and then fled her punishment on the hands of time.

*

Smokey could see Ginger's fingers twitching on the steering wheel as he drove up the narrow village street. "It's this one here," he said, parking outside a gentrified little bungalow. "I can't wait to feel the warmth of her hands against my fur and smell that *Milk and Honey* soap. I think I can already hear her bare feet walking across the kitchen lino. Squelch squelch. She's got the television on too. I wonder if...," but before he could finish his sentence, Sekhmet transfigured his body back into that of a small, fury, ginger tomcat. The transformation was as fast as a deckchair collapsing in a gale. He slid down onto the peddles and then jumped back up onto the seat, looking up at his conspirator with all of his eyes, He conveyed to her what his vocal chords could no longer say.

Smokey looked into the expressive vertical slits of his pupils, kissed his fluffy head and opened the door for him. "I am going to miss you." He reciprocated with a kiss, a sniff, a lick, and then he was gone, padding off in the direction of a spiralling garden gate. He did not turn to see Smokey waiving at him as he bounded the garden path and through the cat flap.

"Ginger! Oh my God, Ginger!" came the cry of an elderly Scottish woman, and Smokey felt her own ventricles expand with longing.

As she manoeuvred her awkward human body into the driving seat, the word "alien" sprang between her eyes. She was the wrong species in an unknown part of the country, clueless as to what to do next. Channelling her feline anarchy into her undisclosed future, she decided that it was no longer time to obey human convention. She was going to steal the car and make her way back home to Devon. And besides, by the time that rental company report the car missing, the two humans they handed the keys to will no longer exist.

The Moon

Time's incloudnated wife watches in horror as he catches the king murderer a second before she smashes against the rocks.

PRINCESS OF BEKHTEN: You promised me.

KHONSU: I promised you I would just watched her die?

PRINCESS OF BEKHTEN: She is a mortal being who must be punished for murder.

KHONSU: You were a mortal being once.

PRINCESS OF BEKHTEN: But I did not murder a king.

KHONSU: She has suffered for her crimes.

PRINCESS OF BEKHTEN: And what about the suffering that she put that boy through? What about the suffering of having boar skin pressed against his face until he could no longer breathe? The Scarlet Lady of Slaughter will not rest until her black heart is fizzing in the stomach of sinners.

KHONSU: And I will not rest until it is saved.

PRINCESS OF BEKHTEN: So you are saying you have chosen her and not me?

Khonsu turns his attention from his wife's question to Dimiza's body, which he gently rests on the chalky banks of Loch Ness. Water laps against her hair, darkening and dampening it against her pale white face. He wishes he could feel something other than love and desire for the murderess as he moves his fingers towards the woman's wet flesh. Her body floats up, through the morning air, through the lightly bursting clouds, and towards a sun drenched moon.

PRINCESS OF BEKHTEN: The closer she moves towards us, the deeper this knife penetrates my heart.

It is not long before the woman is sitting on the palm of Khonsu's hand, Loch Ness dripping from her into their Lunar Sea. Her wet hair he strokes and her rising chest he kisses. Blue eyes open up like shocked tulips. He covers them and turns the darkness into the first peel of light her mind has received since her spirit floated out of a Tower of London arrow slit to receive his kiss five hundred and twenty nine years ago.

41

Nathan's legs would not stop shaking as he tried to walk along a rocky footpath flanked by pine trees and the vast stretch of flowing azure water. Partly sunny, partly rainy, he had no idea where he was. He wanted to run, to escape, to hand over his abused brain to a rescuer's logic and reason, but there was no sign of civilisation in sight.

"*I just wanted you to be him.*"

He repeated the woman's bizarre words over and over in his mind until they made even less sense. All he could see were her crazed eyes, eyes howling for something that not he was unable to provide. So she took it by force. She took from him what he would have never voluntarily handed over, and the abuse has left him as cold as an empty shell. His mouth tasted as metallic as the pipes she chained him to as question after question jumped about in the wilderness of his skull. How did she manage to overpower him like that? Did she act alone? He looked around him for an accomplice that could be spying on him, but all he was greeted with was a sapphire mist and a wizened old bird that watched him from a thorny bush. In the far distance he could see the ruins of a castle, and wondered if he should aim for it. It would be shelter if nothing else, and there was a good chance it would be a destination for other visitors. *What time is it? Where exactly in Scotland am I?* He tried to modify his breathing, aware of the incoherency of his thoughts. His quivering skin was not cold but his body was empty of everything. He wondered if River was missing him. Wherever she was.

"*I just wanted you to be him.*"

Those words again, echoing in the abyss. He felt his head for clues as to how a nicotine-stained love-monster managed to get him into this state. She must have wacked him over the head with something. Or drugged him. He froze remembering her little bottle of rum with its strange taste and unexpected fizz. Why him? Why did she chose him? His eyes coast the loch's elegant ripples before squinting again at the distant medieval remains. *Warm me up with a roaring fire and a roasted ox.*

"*I just wanted you to be him.*"

Shut up. Delirious harpy.

He rubbed his eyes until they hurt because he could not believe what he was seeing. He knew he was hallucinating, he knew it had to be the effect of whatever that maniacal harridan put in his drink, because floating in the rich blue sky above him was River. Lost to the clouds in a long white dress. The light caught her face this way and that. Her eyes were closed, her limbs fell limp about her. He hit his head with his fist to free himself from this madness and the sky turned white. Brighter and brighter, he covered his stinging eyes, but before he did saw a head rise from the water. It was a young boy's head with damp blonde curls. Nathan peered through his fingers to see that his skin was cadaverously blood-drained. He was looking at a corpse. The boy's blue eyes suddenly snapped open wide, as if being looked at woken him from the nightmare of death. Blue irises blazing with the avid intensity of his moonlit kidnapper.

River was now hovering above the boy, her white dress quivering in the breeze. He called out her name but she did not flicker. The boy's eyelids slammed shut, he sank back beneath the currents, and his love was swallowed up in the sky as if she was sinking into a hanging sea.

The sky returns to its sapphire grace. He sits on a rock for a moment of calm to absorb the intensity of what must have been an hallucination. But slowly something begins to approach him from the trees. A small white dog. Impossible. It comes a little closer to him and then sprawls out in the gravel, rolling onto his back, enticing Nathan to go over and stroke his belly. But the second Nathan moves a limb, he jumps back up onto his feet. He sits back down and the ball of white fur tentatively approaches. Nathan reaches out his empty palm. He wants to get closer to the creatures' warmth, to wrap himself up in his fluff and press his ear against his heartbeat, to feel the comfort of the living. But with a "humph," the dog drops its head onto the ground and his amber eyes survey the loch. Long, dark shapes stretch themselves out over the surface and Nathan thinks he detects a shiver under the animal's thick coat. He reaches his hand out towards him again. Slowly he climbs back onto his feet, and begins to saunter back into the trees, disappearing from Nathan's view faster than the speed at which he is actually walking.

Just like the levitating River and the drowned boy, Nathan knew the dog was probably never there. As he continued his walk to nowhere, he wished he knew how to make the rest of all this disappear too.

42

Under a bright blue brushstroke sky, Petra parked her rented scarlet *Clio* outside the *Ault-na-goire Lodge Bed and Breakfast*.

After the psycho-sexual journey she had just been through, the thought of having to go in and speak to a stranger paralysed her. Her eyes looked like dirty black gutters in the overhead mirror, and her skin was a sick sea bream. She reapplied lipstick and foundation before adjusting the mirror to see the house: a grey Victorian mansion with no sign of life behind its half closed curtains. Swallowing hard, she opened the car door and stepped out into a swaying world. She had not consumed anything since the black coffee she had back at the hotel yesterday morning. Despite spending the night consuming the flesh of salvation, she felt as empty as a recently converted sixteenth century Protestant nun missing transubstantiation.

Securing the *Clio*, she slowly made her way towards the uninviting building and its dark, cracked, sash windows. Crunching gravel and broken roof ties beneath her dirty, two inch heeled, black court shoes, she rested a pensive fingertip on the Sellotaped doorbell. Pressing it set off what sounded like an amplified death rattle, and she had visions of disturbing some cantankerous Scottish prig's human sacrifice.

As a dim yellow light flicked on above her head, she realised she had no cover story as to why she was a day late for her booking, why she had no luggage, and why she was alone. The door opened and an overweight, receding, middle aged man's large soft face eased some of her anxiety. "I'm so sorry. My husband and I have a room booked. We were supposed to have arrived yesterday. I'm really sorry."

"Ah," he scratched his head. "Yes, well, you'd better come in."

His accent was more northern than Scottish Highland and she was hit by the smell of damp clothes as she crossed the mossy threshold. Her ears filled with a scratchy piano sonata played on some ancient device, along with her own vocal chords apologizing yet again.

"Don't worry. Did you get lost?"

"Something like that. My husband...," her brain hit the accelerator, "my husband had to rush down to Edinburgh for an urgent business meeting last night."

"And you stayed in the Highlands alone?"

"Yes. I mean, no I went to Edinburgh with him for a bit and then decided to return. Well it felt a shame to waste the booking. Sorry, I really should have rung to explain."

"I see," he said with eyes telling her he did not believe a word she had just garbled. "I'll show you to your room then."

"Thank you."

"Unless you want something to eat first?"

Her angry stomach would not allow her to say no. "Erm..."

"Have you already had your evening meal?"

"I haven't, but I don't want to put you out."

"If you haven't eaten I'll sleep a lot better knowing that you weren't in your room starving hungry all night."

Something melted inside her at the sound of someone caring about her. "You're very kind."

"Fine. Well, I don't have a menu as such, but I could heat up a couple of lamb chops? Or fry you something. Egg and chips?"

"Lamb chops would be wonderful. Thank you."

"Take a seat through there, I'll bring it out."

He reached past her to put on the front room light before disappearing up the dimly lit hallway.

Sitting down on a threadbare arm chair, she surveyed the room. A stone clad fireplace that had not been lit for some time; yellowing wallpaper pictured with nicotine stained greyhounds; a semi-amputated daddy long legs fluttering about in the dust on a pile of fading board games; and then, with a start, she realised she was being watched. In the corner of the room, a black Labrador lay on its belly looking up at her with sparkling brown eyes. He was so quiet and still that she nearly did not see him at all. "Hello, you," Petra greeted him with a soft voice she reserved for fluffy animals. She loved them for their capacity to love unconditionally and their incapacity to judge. The eyes did not blink and the glossy furred muscles did not stir; the realisation that he was taxidermied froze her blood.

As the warmth from the central heating infiltrated her pores, she found herself acutely aware of just how tired she was. Holding a beautiful man hostage in a disused public toilet was not conducive to a good night's sleep. Her eyelids began to close on their own accord, opening again at the sound of a plate and cup being put down on the table in front of her. Her empty stomach growled at lamb chops, roast potatoes, peas, and a steaming cup of coffee.

"I put something in that for you," he said, pointing at the coffee.

"You did?"

He sat down opposite her with a tumbler half full of whiskey. "I had a bottle open in the kitchen and you certainly looked like you could use some."

"Thank you."

He clinked his glass against her cup. "It's nice to have someone to cook for. You're my first guest in over a month."

"I am? You mean I'm the only one here?"

"You are. I've been having some problems.... Word gets around and all that... Especially in such a tiny village."

"Problems?"

"Mishaps. I don't really want to go into it, but, don't worry, I used to run a successful hotel in Scarborough so you're in safe hands."

"I was just going to say you don't sound Scottish."

"Yorkshire through and through."

She felt the lamb toboggan down her oesophagus. "Do you run this place alone then?"

"Yes. Another thing is, Ault-na-goire is too far off the beaten track for most folk, so I don't really get much passing trade."

He got up and made his way towards a rickety old drinks cabinet.

"That's exactly why I chose it."

"Really?"

"Well, my husband and I wanted to just get away from it all for a bit. Escape from the claustrophobia of the city."

"Which city are you from?"

"We have an apartment in London."

He held a bottle of Glenfiddich Single Malt towards her. "A bit more? You still look like you could do with loosening up."

She nodded and he came over to fill them both up. "It's my best single malt. I save it for guests."

"Thank you." She took a large gulp of the boozey coffee and waited for it to have the desired effect. After a moment of silent, self conscious chewing she asked: "What made you open a Bed and Breakfast in the Highlands then?"

"Quite a long story. A bit like you, I wanted to get away from everything. Except I wanted to do so permanently."

"Maybe that is what I should do. Open a B and B in the middle of nowhere."

"With your husband?"

Petra thoughts floated along somewhere in the purgatory between fiction and truth. "Perhaps. Or perhaps I should go it alone."

"It gets lonely, I can tell you that. Have you always lived in London?"

"No, I'm originally from Devon."

"I thought I could detect a West Country twang."

Despite forced conversation with strangers being one of Petra's phobias (especially whilst eating), there was something cosy about this unassuming, middle aged man in faded denim who effused loneliness. And she was always instinctively drawn to those who showed any interest in looking after her. Or maybe it was just the alcohol that was making her not hate every second of this experience.

"Would you like some mint sauce with that?"

43

"Oh, erm," Tiana moved her glass of Merlot to look at the laminated dinner menu while the waitress with the half-arsed beehive waited impatiently. "I don't know if I could eat anything."

"You've got to have something," protested Stuart through a mouthful of bread roll. "It's all free."

"I might just have a starter."

"Just a starter?"

"What is the soup of the day"?

"Crab," splurted the waitress.

"Crab soup?"

"Yes. Crab soup," she dispassionately clarified.

"Fine. Yes. That will be okay thank you."

"More bread?"

"Of course," Stuart answered for her. "And before you go, I am still waiting for my liver and bacon. I ordered it over fifteen minutes ago."

"Well, it's coming isn't it," she said with a snap of the pad and a scrape of the heel.

"Witch," he said to her departing back. He turned back to his companion. "I don't feel you are properly taking advantage of Stanway's generosity here."

"How can you eat at a time like this?" Tiana asked him, scowling at the crumbs falling from his mouth. "There has been no sign of my brother or Petra or Etta since yesterday afternoon."

"Who needs the Bermuda Triangle when you've got Inverness, hey?"

"I am just hoping that Petra and Etta have gone off to meet this elusive producer, but that does not account for my brother's disappearance."

"Have you asked his girlfriend?"

"Yes, repeatedly. And there has not been hide nor hair of *her* since this morning either."

"They'll have all gone off on some jamboree together and ended up at some dodgy house party."

"Yes, because Inverness is full of house parties, isn't it?"

"Well, I don't know, I have never been here before. And I won't be in any hurry to return, I can tell you that. I'm wasting away here. How long does it take to fry a bit of liver and bacon?"

"Voicemail again," said Tiana, throwing her obstinate mobile phone back in her bag. "If he has gone off painting somewhere the least he could do is let me know. I'm going to kill him when I see him. Also, where's Smokey? I haven't seen her since this morning either."

"Our Smokey really is a strange one, isn't she? In the six months I have known her she was so antisocial she would actually cross the road to avoid speaking to people, but we come here and she is all over that creepy Ginger fella. What's that all about then?"

"I don't know. Love at first sight?"

"Smokey doesn't do love. She does sitting in corners glaring at people."

"Well, maybe she found her match. That Ginger always puts the willies up me when he looks at me with those pale blue eyes of his."

"Who is he anyway?"

"A friend of River's, apparently."

"And she's another strange one. Sorry, I know she's your brother's girlfriend and all, but..."

"No, no, you're right. I don't know if you picked up on it, but she's convinced she travelled time from fourteen eighty something."

"Gosh. Well that explains a few things. I was asking her when was the last time she came to Inverness and she kept saying 1479."

"I ask you, how can someone possibly enter into a relationship with someone like that? I mean, I know my brother likes them a bit quirky, but this one is off the scale."

"Yes, there's being quirky and then there's *bring out the men with white coats*."

Tiana filled up their glasses.

"Just tell him to stick to people from his own time zone next time. Oh look, he's your crap soup arriving, despite the fact that I ordered my main many moons before you."

"Do we have any idea where this recording studio is?" asked Tiana, making space on the table for the miserably delivered soap.

"Inside Petra's vivid imagination I shouldn't have thought."

"But why would she bring us all the way here for nothing in that case?"

"Where that woman is concerned, nothing surprises me anymore."

"Why do you dislike her so much?"

"I don't dislike her. I ... I think she is an extremely talented musician... I just have no time for the way she squanders that talent. I have been in the music industry for twenty years now and I have seen that type of behaviour time and time again."

"They do say mental illness and creativity go hand in hand."

"True, but for my own sanity I'm going to try keep as much distance from her as I can from now on."

"Why did you come here then?"

He held up a bread roll.

"For the free bread? I think you care about her much more than you let on."

"Of course I care about her. I thought this band was actually going to take off and become something. But now I'm just sick of grappling about in the dark tunnels she digs for herself."

"When I look at her I wish ... I wish I could be the one to save her. As stupid as that may sound."

"Yes, I was like you once. Naive. You can't save people who don't want to be saved, Tiana. Oh Lord, what the hell is this?"

Tiana looked over her shoulder to follow his horrified glare. There in the corner of the almost deserted dining hall was their waitress perched on a stool on a tiny stage, microphone in hand. She tapped the end of it three times, creating a deafening feedback.

"And you can shut up," she berated the speaker above her head. "I guess it's working then. I am just going to do a few eighties numbers. Has anyone got any requests?"

"Yes!" yelled Stuart. "My liver and bacon!"

44

Petra's sleep was greatly disturbed by her love crimes and the bad 1970s décor that surrounded her. A plate of fried eggs on buttery fried bread soon turned into an acceptance of more strong black coffee that turned into a sheepish request for her host to top her up with his single malt again. Petra had a lot to forget and nowhere to go. Godfrey did not seem to be in a hurry to be any place either as he resumed his place opposite her on the table, joining her in a daytime hot toddy tipple. He was wearing the same faded denim and stained red chequered shirt that he had on when he opened the door to her last night. His face looked more tired and lined though as if he did not sleep very well either, and he smelled of body odour and stale coffee.

"Any news from your husband?"

She filled her lungs and said, "Godfrey, I have to tell you something. There is no husband."

"I had an inkling actually but I didn't want to say."

"I'm sorry that I lied to you."

"Don't worry, it's understandable, a lone woman like you turning up in a strange village. You didn't want to bring any adverse any attention to yourself. But you booked the room for a couple?"

"Yes. There was someone. You are very understanding, I don't deserve any of this, I don't deserve your hospitality and your kind words and your whiskey and your food."

"Don't be silly, you're doing me a favour. I've been stuck alone here for far too long."

She sipped her single malt whiskey coffee. "Have you ever been married?"

Godfrey took a big gulp of his before replying, "I have. Before I moved here."

"Did she ... pass on? ... Sorry, I'm being nosey."

"No. I passed on her. Biggest regret of my life." He downed the rest of his cup and refilled it with the percolator jug and the bottle, topping hers up in the process. "I was a fool. I had everything that I had ever wanted but my own foolishness got in the way. We ran a hotel together in Scarborough but I decided to throw a grenade at everything I had ever worked for in the shape of one of the chambermaids."

"Don't worry, I know all about self-sabotage."

Petra lost Godfrey to his great bay window where she was able to clearly read the sorry tale of regret in his grey eyes. He turned to face her as if suddenly remembering he had company. "I'm so sorry, I'm keeping you."

"Keeping me from what?"

"From having to listen to me drone on all day."

"Godfrey, I have to tell you something. If I don't I think I'll go mad."

45

Tiana looked up from the miniature kettle she was refilling in the toothpaste splattered basin. "So at what point do we go to the police?"

"It's not our place to go to the police," replied Stuart through the frothy dregs of his third just-add-hot-water cappuccino that morning. It tasted like the hotel room - cloyingly artificial.

"Of course it is, my brother has been missing for twenty four hours now."

"This isn't a police matter, it's a ridiculous farce, all be it with free bed and board."

"Free bed and board and you're anyone's, hey?"

"Like you haven't been enjoying the mini bar and the sauna and the fried breakfasts."

"Fried breakfasts? I never go beyond a tiny bowl of muesli in the morning."

"I am fed up with people starting on me because I like creature comforts. I think I deserve them after what I have had to put up with over the years. Not just with her but with the entire music industry."

"The entire music industry? You can hardly blame the entire music industry for your problems."

"I wish I never left Wildcats in Wheelchairs now, I really do."

"And how successful were they?"

"We played Glastonbury!"

"What at eleven o clock on a Friday morning when everyone was still in their tents?"

"How dare you."

"It was a joke."

"Well, I've not been in the mood for those for a very long time."

Tiana flicked the kettle on. "Look, if you didn't believe Petra's story about recording the album here you should never have agreed to come."

"I thought there was a possibility she had finally got her act together. Stupid me."

"Maybe she has, maybe she is with this Royston Harris fella as we speak."

"Yes, and I am recording my solo album with Brian Eno tomorrow."

"Let me know if you need a cellist."

"Thank god we've got open return tickets, that's all I can say. Imagine being stuck in Inverness for the rest of your life."

As the kettle began to boil, Tiana threw a teabag into a little coffee cup, picked up a little UHT milk carton and contemplated it, before sliding down the wall in a wave of futility. "Why is it that as soon as I invest my hopes in something, *poof* there it goes up it goes in smoke in front of me? Petra Sherry and the Eleventh Hour were supposed to have been my new start, and we would played Glastonbury too, you know, and all the other festivals, if she hadn't... if she was not so... Maybe I should try her phone again?"

"I wouldn't bother."

"Nathan's then. Or Etta's. For god's sake, I've got to do something other than hang around a two star hotel room in Inver-bloody-ness."

"Etta disappeared off to Norway for three months when we were at the height of our success. Did you know that?"

"No."

"She's got form, as you lot say these days. Look, I'm sorry you got caught up in this mess. I just hope you didn't let that tube station give away your busking spot?"

"No. No. No. No, I am not going back to that. I am not throwing away my life anymore. I am going to make it. I am determined to make it this time. I've got to."

Stuart put on a Prince Charles voice. "Whatever 'make it' means."

"Huh?"

"Prince Charles. Sorry. I'm not sure why I did that."

"I've got songs of my own, you know? Songs that I've written. I even brought my demos with me in case that producer was interested." Tiana took out a USB stick from her back pocket and held it up in the air where it became the thin line that separated hope from despair. For a second she thought Stuart was interested, until he said, "That reminds me, do you have any more Nescafe sachets here? I have run out of them in my room."

"Nescafe sachets?" Tiana choked on the words through every rejected organ in her body.

"Yes. And those little milk bullet things."

"I'll give you a milk bullet," she said, throwing the miniature UHT carton at him. It missed him completely, bursting onto a print of a De Kooning painting on the wall behind him.

As the milk dribbled off it, Tiana closed her eyes.

"They'll probably charge a fee for that," said Stuart.

"Charge it to the music industry."

"Actually," he said, giving the splurge a proper look, "I think you might have improved it."

"And you have no idea where he is now?"

Petra was shocked at how nonplussed Godfrey seemed after her revelation that two days ago she drugged, kidnapped and tied up a man in a disused men's public toilet. "The last I saw of him, he was walking off into the woods." Petra dropped her head into her hands as the enormity of her crime flooded her brain along with the whiskey. "I can't believe I had the capability to do such a thing. I had no idea just how completely psychotic I'd become."

"Love can awaken something inside us that we didn't even know was there. A monster that would send our Nessy running and screaming."

Petra tried to laugh. "No, I won't let you make excuses for what I did."

"You were taken over by it."

"I was taken over by jealousy and greed."

"You did all that because of jealousy and greed? I don't think so somehow."

"And obsession. The more I plotted, the more I couldn't turn back, because to turn back would be to return back to the place where I couldn't cope. I *cannot* go back to that place again."

"From what you've told me, it sounds like you were trying to insist on a certainty in a world that had robbed you of everything."

Petra bit her lip; his sagacity was a surprise. "There is no justification for being a criminal."

Godfrey got up from the table.

"Where are you going? Have you had enough of me too? I wouldn't blame you."

He returned with a mobile phone which he passed to her. "If you are a criminal, why don't you telephone the police right now and hand yourself in?"

She contemplated the phone for a while before putting it down on the table. "I just want to cry. But what right do I even have to do that?"

Godfrey sat back down and pensively began swirling the coffee and whiskey in his cup. "I certainly know that feeling. Actually I admire you."

"How can you admire me?"

"Because you took a stand. You took a stand and said 'I'm not going to take this anymore, I'm going to do something about it, I am going to demand my life back.' I admit you went a very strange way about it."

"I used to be someone, you know."

"You *are* someone."

"No, I mean, I was a singer, *am* a singer. I had an album out and everything. Articles were written about me... people bought tickets to see my shows...."

"Wow, I didn't know we had a celebrity staying at the Ault-na-goire Lodge!"

"I wouldn't go that far."

"You hearing this, Jonah?" he called out to his dead dog.

"I still have a record deal. Although," laughed into her coffee cup, "something tells me I've probably just been dropped."

"You don't know that."

"You won't believe what I am about to tell you."

"You mean there's more? Brace yourself, boy."

"I've...," Petra tried to talk through the mounting mania, "I have actually gone and brought my whole band up to Inverness under the false premise of recording my new album here, just so I could follow him. I knew my record company would pay if they thought it was for that purpose. You see what a scheming, conniving witch I am?"

Godfrey downed his drink. "And where are they all now?"

"Festering in some crappy hotel in Inverness. Unless they have all realised now that it was hoax and gone home. Look at me, I'm even laughing about it. I'm sick."

"They do say laughter is the best medicine."

"I don't think they say it to psychotic kidnappers."

"Along with...," Godfrey emptied the rest of the bottle into their cups. "Ooops. All gone. I think I've got a bottle of Famous Grouse somewhere."

"Save it for someone who deserves it."

"Stop all this self pity now duck, it's getting boring."

"Duck? My grandmother used to call me that."

"She did? In that case she must have been from 'op north?"

"She lived in Shipley."

"I know it well."

"All of my dad's side are from there. He moved down to the south coast to find work and get away from the gloom. No offense."

"On his own?"

"Yes."

"Brave."

"Well, he soon met my mother."

"Was it a happy marriage?"

Petra shook her head reaching for her topped up cup. "No, he left her for a woman who makes wine in Cornwall."

Godfrey winced. "Cornish wine? Pure vinegar I shouldn't imagine. How old were you when he left?"

"In my mid teens."

"Ah, well, at least I waited until my kids were in their twenties before I scarped. Do you still see him much?"

Petra shook her head. "It really hurt at the time, but I soon realised that he just couldn't be bothered, and now ten years later I can't either. Plus I still haven't fully forgiven him, as you can probably tell. It really hurt my mother. It changed her as a person. Drained her." The scrutiny in his eyes suddenly made her uncomfortable and she looked around the room for a change of subject. "Ever thought about getting a new dog?"

"Jonah is enough for me. Aren't you, boy?" She half expected him to reply with a wag of the tail. "It'll be lunchtime soon. What would you like?"

"I didn't know lunch was part of the package?"

"Nor is single malt scotch but you've not turned your nose up to that," he replied with a wink of a bushy-browed lid.

Rain began to pebble on the cracked sash window. She looked through it to see a damp ginger tomcat dash by.

"I made a pass at one of the guests," he said. "That is why the locals warn people not to stay here. I made a pass at one of the guests."

47

Swallow, breathe, swallow, breathe, because it is unmistakably her again, River, hanging from a cloud in the early evening sky. Beneath her long, white, shimmering gown, her bare feet float about a meter or two above the rocky peak of a mountain. Nathan's heart threatened to pop its box when the sun's glare illuminated her face. He was torn between screaming out her name and refusing to believe his eyes. Just like the monster people saw in the loch, this was surely a hallucination. He pressed his palms into his eyes wishing for this trippy pantomime to end. He was greeted by a limp goat hanging from the beak of a golden eagle earlier. When he released his hands he found he was no longer looking at his girlfriend levitating above the Highlands, but instead he was peering through a smudged window, beyond which were rows of tables containing ketchup bottles, menus, vinegar and salt and pepper pots. A handful of people were sat alone at them. One of which was his sister.

*

Drained and exasperated, Tiana felt like a cadaver balanced on a chair. Looking around the red and purple walled cafe, she noticed that she was not the only person sat alone. A middle-aged woman sporting a pink Alice band and grey raincoat was sucking the final drops of a yellow milkshake noisily through a blue and white striped straw. "Sorry about that," she said to a man in thick black glasses on the opposite table in a Highlands accent thicker than the drink in her throat. "I think I must have been thirsty."

He did not look up.

A tall, thin man in a denim shirt put a slightly sticky, laminated menu in Tiana's hand. He smelt of bleach. Her eyes darted over the subheadings. One of the 'Home Made Specialities' includes the intriguing word 'Rumbledethump.' She was almost tempted to order it just to see what it looked like. But it was coffee that she was after, strong, black and copious. She hardly slept last night, and since storming out of a hotel room after Stuart passed up her compositions for complimentary drinks sachets, she's searched the streets of Inverness for her lost brother.

After ordering her coffee she felt herself drowning in anxiety, fear and anger. As much as she hated to admit it, she knew Stuart was right to be cynical of Petra. In the excitement of being saved from obscurity by a once successful music combo, she had closed her ears and eyes to the wizard behind the curtain screaming at her through his megaphone. Her talent was the road kill of reality. There was no escape from its determination to destroy her every last ambition. Petra was one of those rare artists who had managed to scale heaven's gate, but she had clearly now lost her footing in the dark, and Tiana was just the fodder of her darkness.

She deliberately burnt her lip on the hot coffee as she told herself how useless she was and how she would never really mean anything to anyone. "You'll only ever be someone for people to chew up and spit out," she muttered into the steaming cup.

Before the anchor could entrench itself any deeper, she saw something through the window that startled her. Her brother. It was as if he had been standing there watching her the whole time. On his face was a mixture of confusion and desperation. She immediately stood up and waved at him, but he remained fixed to the spot, gluing her with his unblinking eyes. Disorientated by his disorientation, she went out to see him. "Nathan! Where have you been?"

His silent face was like a mannequin's with large and entranced hazel irises.

"Nathan, can you hear me?"

"You are a jewel in a paper and metal world."

She went to speak but nothing came. Even looking at him became difficult as her eyelids grew heavier by the second. He turned around and she gripped his hand before she lost him again.

48

"You've gone quiet."

Petra removed a piece of gristle from her mouth.

"Don't you like my Lorne sausages? They're from the farmers market in Drumnadrochit. More than eighty percent pork."

"Pig?"

"Come again?"

"Sorry, you just reminded me of an urban myth from my hometown. There is this old, rundown, dingy cafe. You know the type, everything decades out of date, plastic tomatoes on the tables." Petra realised she was outing Godfrey's tasteless décor as she began to repeat the same creepy tale she had used to try and melt Nathan's armour. "There was this waitress who worked there. Let's just say she was quite fat. Apparently she made a pass at the owner and he quite rudely rejected her advances. The next day the special on the menu was meat pie, and when customers asked her what the meat was she screamed '*PIG'!*"

"Well I can guarantee there is no cafe owner in these sausages."

She washed down her serially ineffectual anecdote with a gulp of whisky tea, dislodging the shard of bone stuck between her teeth. "Don't worry, I'm sure that story isn't even true."

"My wife was a bit like you. Arty."

"Oh really?"

"She was a writer."

"Novels?"

"Short stories for the women's weeklies." He picked up his tea and went and sat down on the ancient sofa beside Jonah, gently resting a palm on his glossy dead head. "I had the ideal life with her, I really did."

"That chambermaid must have been a real charmer then?"

"I think, when you know you are living with the person who is going to bury you one day, you can sometimes end up hearing those nails in your coffin prematurely. It scares you into searching for what else is out there."

"Maybe that's why Stephen left me. I don't think there was another woman involved though. If there was I'd find her and twist her head off."

"On some level I think I wanted to punish her."

"Your wife? What for?"

"For taking away my freedom. It sounds so stupid when I say it now. Because *look*, *this* is the freedom I left her for. This pile of crap bed and breakfast is the freedom I destroyed her heart and our life for. Moping around with regret and the ghost of a Victorian Scottish woman, before dying alone."

"You think this house is haunted?"

"There have been ... incidents. Don't touch any door knobs in the middle of the night, that is all I am saying. Unless you want to feel her cold hand on yours."

"I don't think I believe in ghosts."

"You are looking at one, if ghosts are humans who have cast away their lives."

"Do you think there is any chance she might take you back?"

"She sends my letters back undelivered and hangs up when she hears my voice, so no. She will never forgive me."

Petra downed the rest of her tea which was now lukewarm and joined Godfrey on the sofa. He gave her a slightly awkward smile, which she reciprocated, before he rested his eyes on the giant bay window. She joined his gaze. It was still raining. Long murky dribbles on the dirty glass bringing to mind her years of mascaraed tears. "I just want to be...." She managed to stop herself before 'loved' could fall out of her mouth. Her brain began to dig up that limb-severing final night of her tour. Sat in that dingy dressing room in Exeter. It even had those bulbs around the mirror, although only two of them worked. Etta lighting knocking on the door, pushing it open, and quietly saying, "I'm so sorry he didn't show up." Petra knew at that point she would return home to find him gone. But she did not imagine the fallout; the fall into darkness that would bring her life to this insane point. Her hands dirty with kidnap. Lost in Scotland, comforted by a lonely stranger's whiskey and kindness. Love, love, love, a tightrope of exquisite silk stretched over a cesspit, one false move and you'll be petting the head of a dead dog. He was saying something to her, but she could not hear it through the emotions that dripped like blood from the mirror that had spliced her skull. "What did you say?"

"To be?"

"Sorry?"

"You said 'you just want to be', but you didn't finish your sentence."

She shook her head. "It doesn't matter."

Godfrey looked down at dead Jonah before leaning down to tenderly kiss him between his taxidermied teddy bear eyes, eyes that will be staring into nothing for all eternity. "That's the great thing about animals, you can never love them too much." A spark of sunlight suddenly peeked through the rain, illuminating this touching moment of human horror.

"Can I stroke him?"

"Of course."

She leant forward and gently tickled Jonah under his cold stiff chin, contemplating her own ivory hands. Red nail varnish chipped away to almost nothing. Guitar string dents on her fingertips lost in nicotine stains. She recalled a review in the music press that described the frantic and frenzied way her fingers darted over her fret board. The only thing that moved them now was the alcohol in her veins, and before that, mad dervishes of obsessive lust. "They don't realise that this all has to come from somewhere," she disjointedly began. "You don't just create magic out of nothing,"

"Who? What?"

"The people who want me to keep recording and touring. They don't understand that talent is a fire that either fuels you or cremates you. They just want you to be this *thing*, this boxed and labelled *thing*."

"Who?" he repeated.

"All of my songs came out of the person inside me that I have to share a skin with. There is no escape from her and she will either work for me or against me. She can either create hit records or raise hell in a rented Clio. She wants to roam. She wants to eat. She wants her screams to be heard at all times, not just when she's channelling them into songs on stage."

He looked at her like she'd drunk too much of his single malt. "I *think* I know what you're saying."

"I'm saying there is nothing fun about having a tied up Rottweiler in your head."

"Then let it go."

"I did and she ripped apart everything in sight."

"Then find her a muzzle?"

"This is a muzzle," she said pointing at the whiskey bottle. "*These* are muzzles." She pulled out her packet of *Sovereigns*. "Do you mind if I smoke?"

"Go ahead."

She took one and offered the box to Godfrey. He shook his head saying, "I think my muzzle might be Jesus."

"What?"

"I've been going to church recently."

"Are you joking?"

"It gives me a semblance of ... I don't know ... inner calm or something. Even if I don't really believe in him, even if I am just moved by the building and the crosses and mausoleums, for that moment I am at peace."

"My mum did the same when my dad left, started going to church I mean."

"It's a crutch."

"Maybe life is just a series of them."

"One helping hand after another."

Godfrey held out his hand. Petra looked at it but didn't take it.

"It takes a brave person to swallow life whole and raw," he said, taking it back.

Petra looked away because to her dismay his face was slowly drawing nearer to hers. In her inebriated state she could already feel the clammy sweat of his upper lip. Although she did not want to appear rude to this man who had shown her nothing but warmth, hospitality and understanding, she did not have a strong enough stomach for any kind of physical intimacy with him.

"Sorry," she managed through the sticky dread, unsure if 'sorry' was the correct word to use when rebuffing someone. She saw herself being served up to his next guest as Lorne sausages.

"No, it is me who should apologise. I have taken up enough of your time today. I should leave you to get on."

"What the hell am I going to get on with?"

Godfrey stood up. "Would you be requiring an evening meal tonight?"

"I ... I hadn't thought that far ahead."

"That's fine, let me know when you decide."

He left the room and she stared at the space he left behind, unsure of what exactly had just happened. Looking around the fading front room which looked like it had been decorated by Norman Bates's mother, she heard the monster's scream inside her brain turn into laughter.

49

Etta looked around the room at Stephen's paintings. The layering and re-layering, the thick and lumpy acrylic paint strokes, the otherworldly seas jumping off the canvass; it was a unique style that she was used to seeing depict the south Devonshire coastline, but now he was portraying the geography that ran through her memories like capillaries. The Norwegian Fjords. It scared and moved her at the same time to think how she had stolen an Englishman and planted him in her native home.

"What do you think?"

She turned to look at him. "I thought you were asleep."

"I was. So ...?"

"So what?"

"Tell me what you think of my new paintings."

She allowed her eyes to dance over them again. "I love them."

"Me too. I'm really pleased with them. Coming to Norway was the best thing I could have done. And...," he pulled her towards him, "now that I've got you back to myself I am never letting you go again. I don't care what she or anyone else says or does. I don't even care if she comes here and threatens to throw herself off a fjord. You're banned from leaving my side."

Etta closed her eyes as he pressed his mouth into hers, tasting the words that she simultaneously feared and craved. Directly below them her uncle fired up Kate Bush's *Hounds of Love*. She pictured his wiry body dancing around the front room to the tribal drumbeat of the opening track.

"Don't you want to ask me what Petra's been like ever since you left?"

"Not really. I just resent her for taking you away from me all this time. It is you that I've been thinking about, not her."

"But you loved her once."

"You know I didn't."

"I'm talking about when you lived with her."

"You mean when I resented her the most?"

"Why did you move in with her then?"

"You know why. Because I had nowhere else to go. I had no money. I couldn't even afford the rent on my chalet anymore. What? Why are you looking at me like that?"

"No reason."

"God, she's five hundred miles away and she's still causing a rift between us."

"There's no rift. I just feel bad for her, that's all."

"Well, you shouldn't. She got what she wanted for as long as I was prepared to give it to her. And if you hadn't turned me down in the first place I would never have even got together with her."

"So it's all my fault? She was my best friend and she was obsessed with you. She still is, for that matter."

"So you waited until I was living with her? Anyway, I refuse to talk about her anymore."

Etta sighed away her response. The last thing she wanted was an argument, especially after they had only just been reunited after spending a year apart. She had sacrificed so much to return here. Sometimes it felt like loving this man was an illness that both she and Petra had been infected with. She allowed herself a shameful few seconds to bask in the knowledge that it was only her that he wanted. "What is it about you, Stephen Jude Tyburn?"

"What do you mean?"

"Do you know what loving you has done to her?"

"I don't care. I never asked her to love me, did I?"

"Loving you hasn't been easy for me either."

"You made it a lot harder on yourself than you needed to. Jesus, we're *still* talking about her."

"I suppose that's guilt for you."

"Who's guilty? I certainly don't feel guilty."

"That's because you're a sociopath." She smiled into his steely face. "That was a joke."

He allowed the corner of his mouth to turn upwards and she took it into hers. "What shall we do this evening?" she asked, kissing him. "Shall we go and watch the sunset from the harbour?"

"I have no plans other than to stay in bed with you."

"We should eat something."

"Okay."

"Stop it."

"Your uncle usually brings something up."

"Does he indeed? I see you've got your feet well and truly under the table here."

"He likes making a fuss of me."

"He likes making a fuss with candle lit dinner parties, not with rent-free lodgers."

"Candle lit dinner parties? He isn't Hyacinth Bucket. Anyway, I *have* been paying him rent."

"You have? What with?"

"My paintings."

Etta was too slow in containing her laugh.

"What's funny? Every great piece of art multiplies in value from the day it is created."

"Well anyway," she said, lifting her head off his warm, bare chest. "I think we should go downstairs and offer to go shopping and cook for him this evening. It is the least we can do after everything he has done for us."

"Fine."

"And I suppose tomorrow I should see about getting my old job back at the canning factory."

"What? No way."

"Stephen, how do you expect us to live? We can't just rely on your painting sales."

"I'm not having you work there again."

"I didn't like it much either, but we have to be realistic. I'll do it until I find something else."

He fixed his deep hazel eyes at the ceiling and exhaled. Once again Etta felt the tension stewing between them. As much as she admired his work, his obstinate refusal to acknowledge reality irritated her, as did his blatant disregard for his ex-girlfriend and the part he played in her breakdown.

"Something's wrong isn't it?" he asked.

"I'm probably just jet lagged," she said, shuffling up the cushiony headboard.

"It was a tiny little flight over the North Sea."

"Do you have to disagree with everything I say?"

He stroked her naked back, but now his touch just agitated her. She gathered the generous cotton sheet around her waist and got out of bed, as a terrified man downstairs yelled: "*It's in the trees! It's coming!*"

50

Godfrey entered the room carrying two giant brandy glasses filled far too high.

"Brandy? Oh Godfrey, I probably shouldn't drink anymore."

He stood over her, unsmiling, proffering the glass until she took it.

"What's wrong?" she asked gently.

"I've done something stupid."

"Haven't we all?"

"I've ... I've called the police. I'm sorry."

Petra felt like a bowling ball had been thrown at her diaphragm. She put the glass down on the threadbare carpet beside her bare foot and dropped her face into her hands. She was nauseous with fear and speechless with betrayal.

"I probably shouldn't have done it, but then I realised, while stood in my kitchen, that I was harbouring a criminal. What you did to that man is a criminal act and he might well be in need of urgent medical assistance. The longer I do nothing, the longer I am an accomplice."

She inhaled between her fingers, trying to alleviate the dizziness. "When did you call them?"

"About ten minutes ago. Just the local station, not 999."

As if that makes a difference, she thought through the escalating panic. She knew she had two options: flee or accept her fate. It seemed her legs, stationary with the weight of granite, had already decided for her. Lifting her eyes to him now, she saw that his face was growing harder and colder. She knew he only did this to get back at her for rejecting him. It felt so easy to hate him right now.

"I could go to prison for this."

"But so could I if I don't do anything. Plus, and I really hate having to say this, but I have my business and my reputation in this village to think about. I could really do without any more negative publicity. I am barely staying afloat as it is."

He was changing shape before her eyes. The bohemian, anarchic man she thought he was, quickly becoming a scared, lonely, pathetic shopkeeper - shackled by fear. She could feel the banshee inside her, desperate to rant and scream about how all men knife her in the end, but what would be the point? And besides, why *should* this man show her any loyalty when they have only known each other for a couple of days? Maybe he was right to put his summertime trade over the liberty of a woman who was essentially to him just a mentally unstable customer.

"I should run away, but I really don't have anywhere left to run to. I'm staring at a dead end now. Thank you for your hospitality."

"I feel dreadful."

"Why? You don't owe me anything."

Godfrey slowly stepped away from her hollowing life, perching beside his stuffed pet, before blue lights suddenly bounced off their stony faces and his yellowing walls. His facial muscles came to life as he got up and marched over to the window. "Why did they have to put their lights on? I expressly asked them for no fuss. How many people are going to see this now?"

"There's no one around for miles." Her voice was shaky and unrecognisable to herself. Trying to stay calm she picked up her glass of brandy and downed it in one. Her throat felt like she had just swallowed a rock, but alcohol was a welcome sea for her fear to float in.

Her bleak destiny had been written for quite some time. She had always rejected the anxieties and concerns that were currently being illuminated in Godfrey's face; money, reputation, security. It was all just cups of tea and banality to her. The axis that Petra's planet revolved on was a deep hunger for something that she now knew would forever remain elusive. She was going to be sent down for rejecting the cold, hard functionality of human survival. The policemen currently walking up the driveway were here to punish her for trying to fill the void in the only way she knew how. There was no exit, there was no way out, there was nothing left to do now but sink back into the spider's web of her own weaving.

Reaching for the last drops of brandy as Godfrey let the policemen into the room, she was surprised at just how steady her hands had become.

The Moon

After watching the Earth complete a spin, Khonsu opens his hand to reveal an empty palm.

PRINCESS OF BEKHTEN: Where is she? What have you done with her?

KHONSU: The same as last time. I have sent her five hundred and twenty years into the future.

PRINCESS OF BEKHTEN: Are you insane? Sekhmet will just incarnate more of her worshippers to track her down and kill her.

KHONSU: Then forward in time she will have to keep going. What else can I do when you won't let me have her up here with us?

PRINCESS OF BEKHTEN: So it is me you have chosen?

Despite all he had done to jeopardise their marriage, in her face he sees somebody desperate to still believe in it. He cups her face in his hands and looks down to see the body of his Earth-shackled desire resting amongst the ruins of Urquhart Castle, which now, in the year 2532, are just faded outlines of rocks and stones hidden amongst the moss. A family of four witness her appear out of nowhere and begin to cautiously approach.

Sekhmet steps into their Sea of Crises like a brazen catholic martyr stepping into a heretic's fire. The Princess of Bekhten, in no mood for divine tempests, climbs out and floats away.

KHONSU: It looks like you chose the wrong cats.

SEKHMET: I chose those cats well. They lured that murderess to the scene of her crime, just like I wanted. And they would have succeeded in dispatching her evil heart to the underworld there too if you hadn't interfered again. How many times are you going to send her forward in time to escape her rightful punishment?

KHONSU: All she wants to do is make atonement for her sins and start a new life.

SEKHMET: There is no atonement for killing a divinely appointed monarch. When will you understand that, instead of throwing your misguided magic into the cogs of universal law? That heart is destined for the Scales of Justice and then the stomach of the Great Devourer, no matter how determined you are to keep it beating in her chest. You can't upturn the destiny of a blackened soul. All you are doing is delaying the inevitable, and hurting yourself in the process.

KHONSU: If the Scales of Justice deem her heart to be evil, they can't see what I can.

SEKHMET: Are you darling to place your judgement higher than those divine scales? Are you daring to blaspheme?

KHONSU: A god cannot blaspheme.

SEKHMET: You are just a tiny god, and one filled to the brim with a base desire for a murderous whore. Tell me, what is it about that harlot that you cannot let go of?

KHONSU: Purity, beauty, her capacity for love, her endless devotion.

SEKHMET: Where was the purity, love and devotion in forcing wild animal skin down over the mouth and nose of a twelve year old king?

KHONSU: She did that out of love. A misguided love for a man whose path to throne was paved in severed heads.

SEKHMET: Heads she happily watched him sever. And he received his punishment for that. You saw his twisted body hacked to pieces by soldiers that betrayed him at the last minute. The underworld claiming the contents of his ribcage while waiting for the heart of the unforgivable sinner, the child-king killer. Tell me, are there any other murderers down there that take your fancy? Any serial killers lurking in dark alleyways or rapists in subways you want to declare your love for?

KHONSU: She is the only one that I refuse to watch die.

SEKHMET: Her and that possessed princess you stole from an Egyptian pharaoh's feast. All humans die, that is just something gods need to accept. Although if it was up to me I'd rip the head off every criminal down there. I tried to once, when there were less of them. Do you remember? Ra had to get me drunk on a flood of red ale just to wean me off their blood. Maybe I should have another go.

KHONSU: Just go back to your creepy dark lair of teeth and claws.

SEKHMET: I suggest you fill your eyes with her now before she is gone for good.

KHONSU: Incarnating some more inept felines to hunt her down?

SEKHMET: It's not felines that you need to worry about now.

KHONSU: She will stay alive for as long as I want her to.

SEKHMET: Do you really think you have more power than the gods who want to see justice done on earth as it is in heaven?

KHONSU: You are the only god who wants her dead.

SEKHMET: Wrong. The god of the underworld has been eagerly awaiting those murderous ventricles ever since she snuffed out England's rightful heir. And there is no way he will let you twist divine justice around your fingers for a second time.

KHONSU: You can tell Anubis that I already have.

SEKHMET: I say this to protect you, but I really think you should look away now. Divert your eyes before you see something that will tear your heart out too.

Disobeying her words, Khonsu looks down on the rubble of Urquhart Castle to see the family of four now filming Dimiza with the micro chips planted in their eyes.

KHONSU: Those four? They're harmless.

SEKHMET: Not them. One of Anubis's earthly worshippers is about to collect her soul. And it won't be pretty.

KHONSU: But his worshippers are all wolves.

SEKHMET: And?

KHONSU: And wolves do not exist in Scotland.

SEKHMET: They do in 2532. Look away now, Khonsu. For your own sake, look away now.

Sekhmet slides out of the lunar sea as easily as she stepped in and searches for a better vantage point for what she hopes will be the deciding bite in this tangled game of destiny. Creeping along the rocky banks of Loch Ness, a large grey wolf slowly begins his ascent up towards the murderous meat, now one thousand and forty nine years late for its day of judgement. But before the wolf's fangs can get near enough to crunch, the Princess of Bekhten uses the powers given to her by immortality to send Dimiza back to those precious minutes on the sixteenth of July 1483, before she permanently engraved her bones with murder.

It is a humid night and the top floor windows of Urquhart Castle's towering keep are all open. The newly deposed twelve year old King of England is asleep amongst the furs of Highland bears and lowland wild boars. His blonde curls grace feathered pillows of duck and swan woven by castle maidens. Dimiza is lurking in the shadows around his sleeping royal body, galvanizing herself for what she is convinced she must do. As she carefully picks up the coarse wild boar skin that lies on the end of his bed, time freezes her limbs. The warm summer breeze flickers the candle flames and quivers the golden tapestries, and her head suddenly spills over with an entirely new set of memories from an entirely new life, a life she lived five hundred and twenty years from now.

PRINCESS OF BEKHTEN: Open your eyes, Khonsu.

KHONSU: I can't watch her be killed.

PRINCESS OF BEKHTEN: Trust me. Open them.

Slower than the speed of a dead star's spin, Khonsu turns to see his enchantress back in the young king's bedchamber, but with all malevolent intention erased from her mind. As the glaze melts from Khonsu's eyes and his wings open to embrace his wife, the universe is suddenly in danger of a full scale battle of the gods. Reeling, Sekhmet sinks back down into the underworld's dark pits in search of the god she desires above all. With unknown blood drying on his claws, he turns to her and whispers: "It is a dark day when time wipes away the sins of the most wanted living criminal."

Together they look up through a narrow shaft of light, like prisoners in a dungeon, as the woman released from divine death row leans over the sleeping boy in his bed. Her eyes have now been opened so that she can see good from evil, and the future as clearly as the past. Ever so quietly so as not to wake him, she puts the wild boar skin back down on the bed beside him, gently kisses his forehead through the blond curls, and creeps out of the room. Straight into the shadow of his assassin.

Glenfrey

GlenWho1@
outlook.com

26876338R00114

Printed in Great Britain
by Amazon

how could th
when I'm alre

where's molly

a cat & mouse spin-off

USA TODAY BESTSELLING AUTHOR

H. D. CARLTON

Copyright © 2024 by H. D. Carlton

All rights reserved. Printed in the United Kingdom. No part of this book may be used or reproduced in any manner whatsoever without written permission except in the case of brief quotations embodied in critical articles or reviews.

This book is a work of fiction. Names, characters, businesses. organizations, places, events, and incidents either are the product of the author's imagination or are used fictitiously. Any resemblance to actual persons, living or dead, events, or locales is entirely coincidental.

Cover Design: Opulent Swag & Designs
Art: @tinyhoomanart
Distributed by Zando

First Edition: February 2024

978-1-63893-410-3 (Paperback)

10 9 8 7 6 5 4 3 2 1
Printed and bound by CPI Group (UK) Ltd, Croydon, CR0 4YY
CPI

TO SAM, KRISTIE, AND SAMANTHA,

FOR SITTING IN THAT DINER WITH ME AND TALKING ABOUT CANNIBALISM UNTIL MOLLY'S STORY WAS BORN

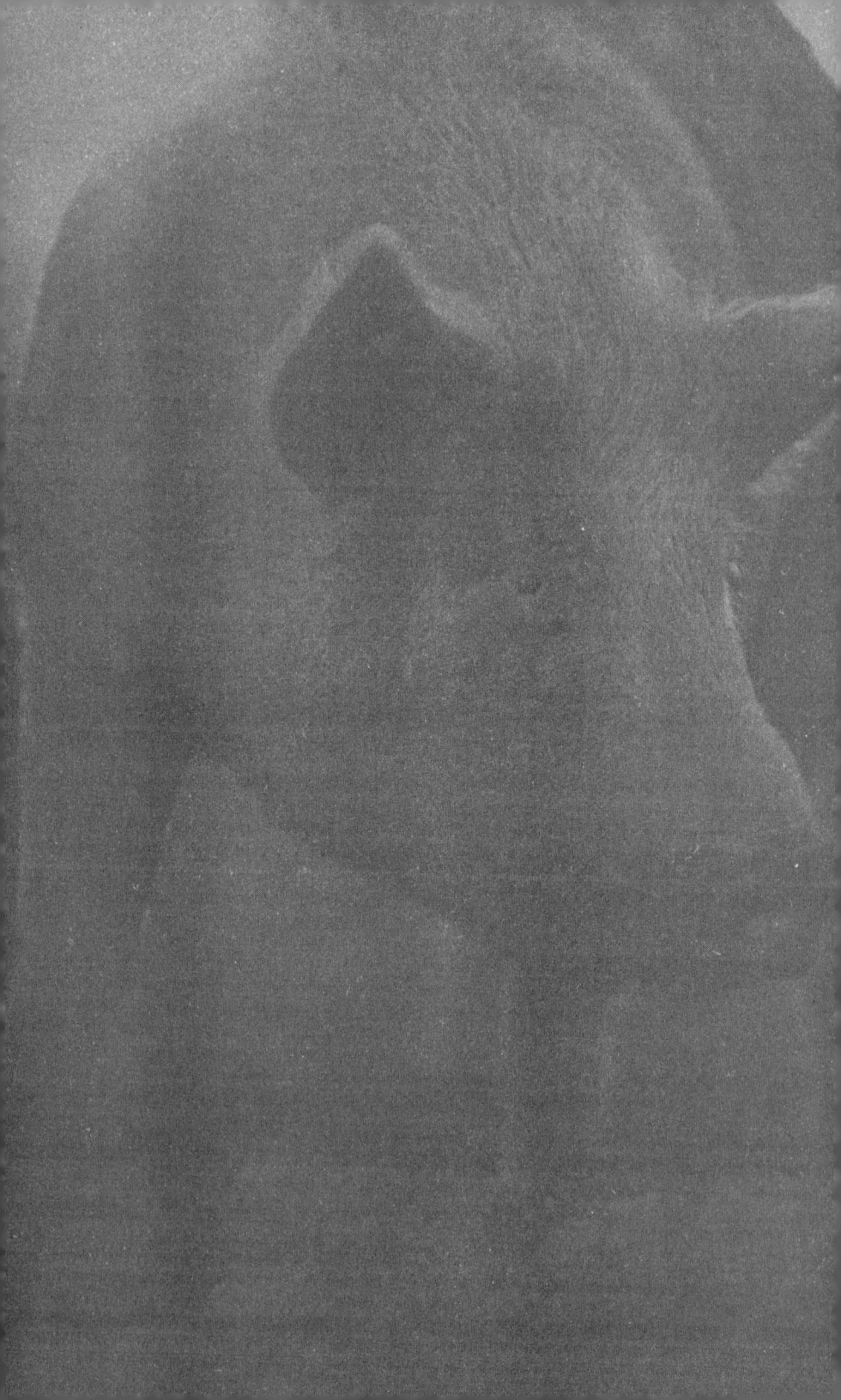

Playlist

GABRIELLE CURRENT- B&W
UNDEROATH- ANOTHER LIFE
LITTLE OCEANS- PEACE
STORY OF THE YEAR- A PART OF ME
YUNG'CID & MAXX XERO- ENDLESS NIGHTMARE
COLORBLIND- GHOSTS
THE USED- MOSH 'N CHURCH
ELLERY BONHAM- SWAY
AMY STROUP- IN THE SHADOWS

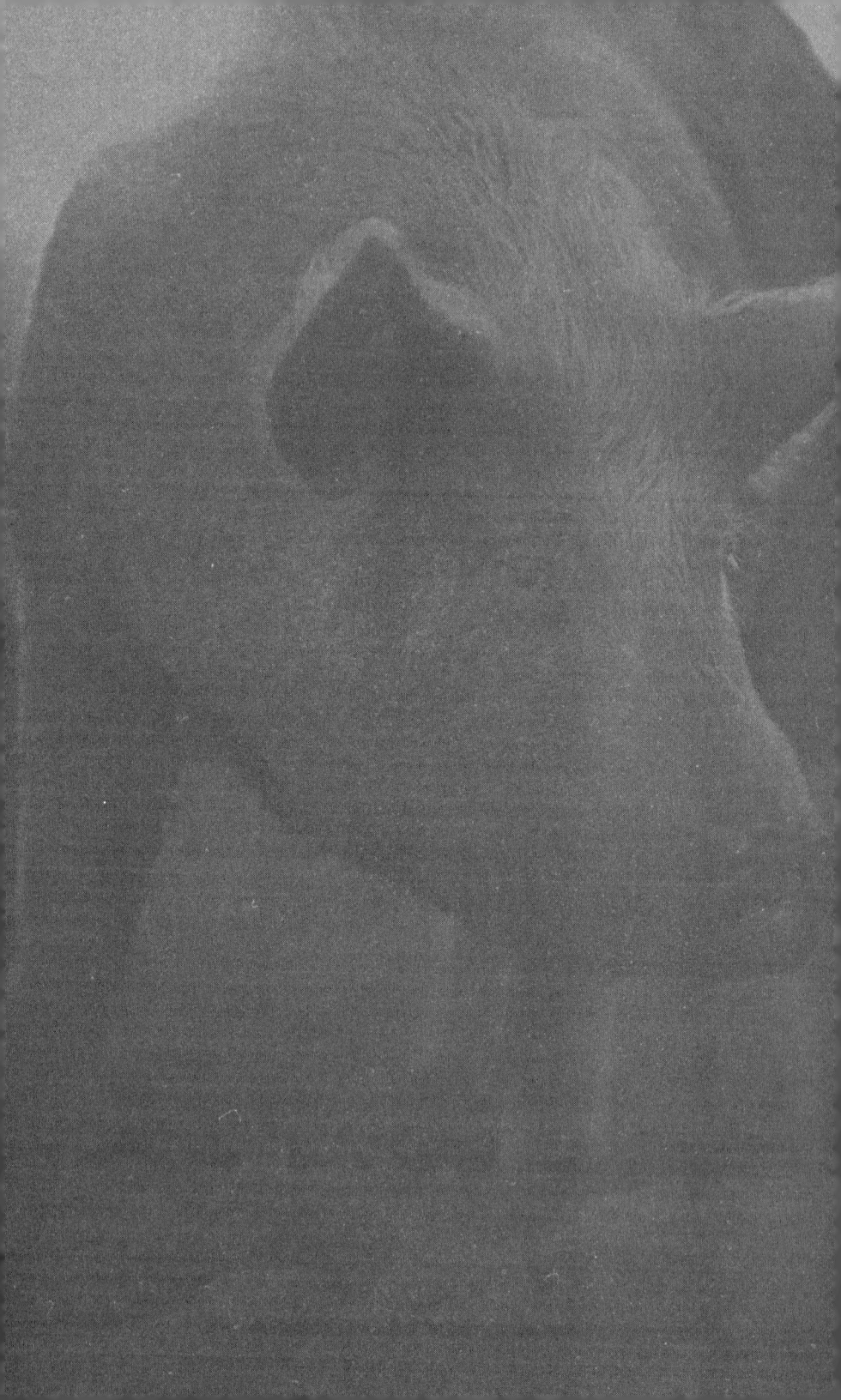

author's note

BEFORE YOU CONTINUE, IT IS **HIGHLY** RECOMMENDED TO READ THE CAT & MOUSE DUET BEFORE READING WHERE'S MOLLY.

READING ORDER:

SATAN'S AFFAIR
HAUNTING ADELINE
HUNTING ADELINE
WHERE'S MOLLY

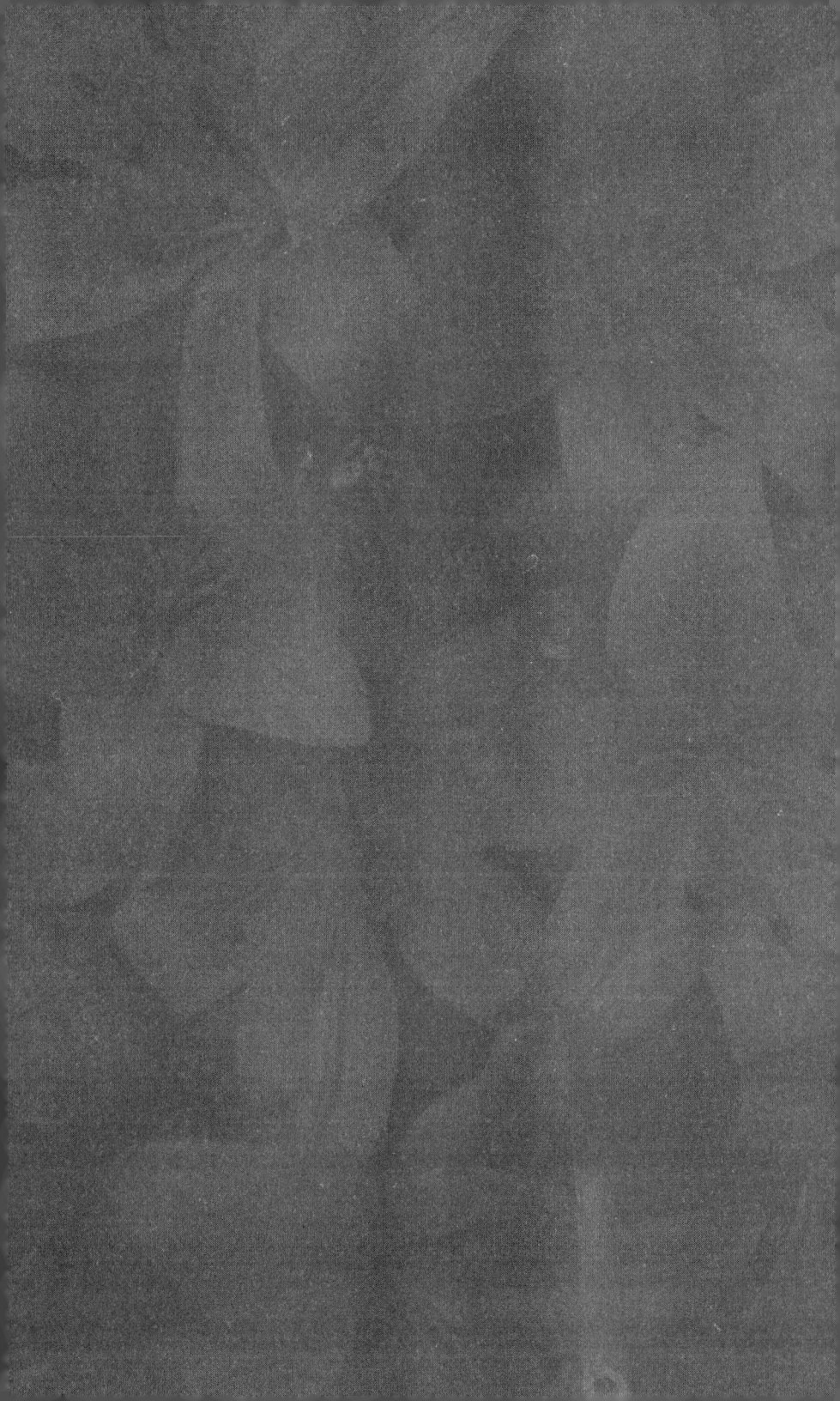

important note

THIS IS A DARK ROMANCE THAT INCLUDES TRIGGERS SUCH AS MURDER, GORE, GRAPHIC LANGUAGE, GRAPHIC SEXUAL SITUATIONS, CHILD ASSAULT AND RAPE (NOT DEPICTED), TOXIC RELATIONS BETWEEN THE MAIN CHARACTERS, CHILD ABUSE AND NEGLECT, SUICIDAL THOUGHTS AND IDEATIONS, HUMAN TRAFFICKING, DRUG AND ALCOHOL USE, AND ANIMALS BEING FED SUSPECT SHIT (THEY ARE NOT ABUSED, I PROMISE).

THIS BOOK ALSO INCLUDES KINKS SUCH AS BITING, BREATH PLAY, BLOOD PLAY, AND DEGRADATION.

PLEASE PROCEED WITH CAUTION AND PRIORITIZE YOUR MENTAL HEALTH.
—H. D. CARLTON

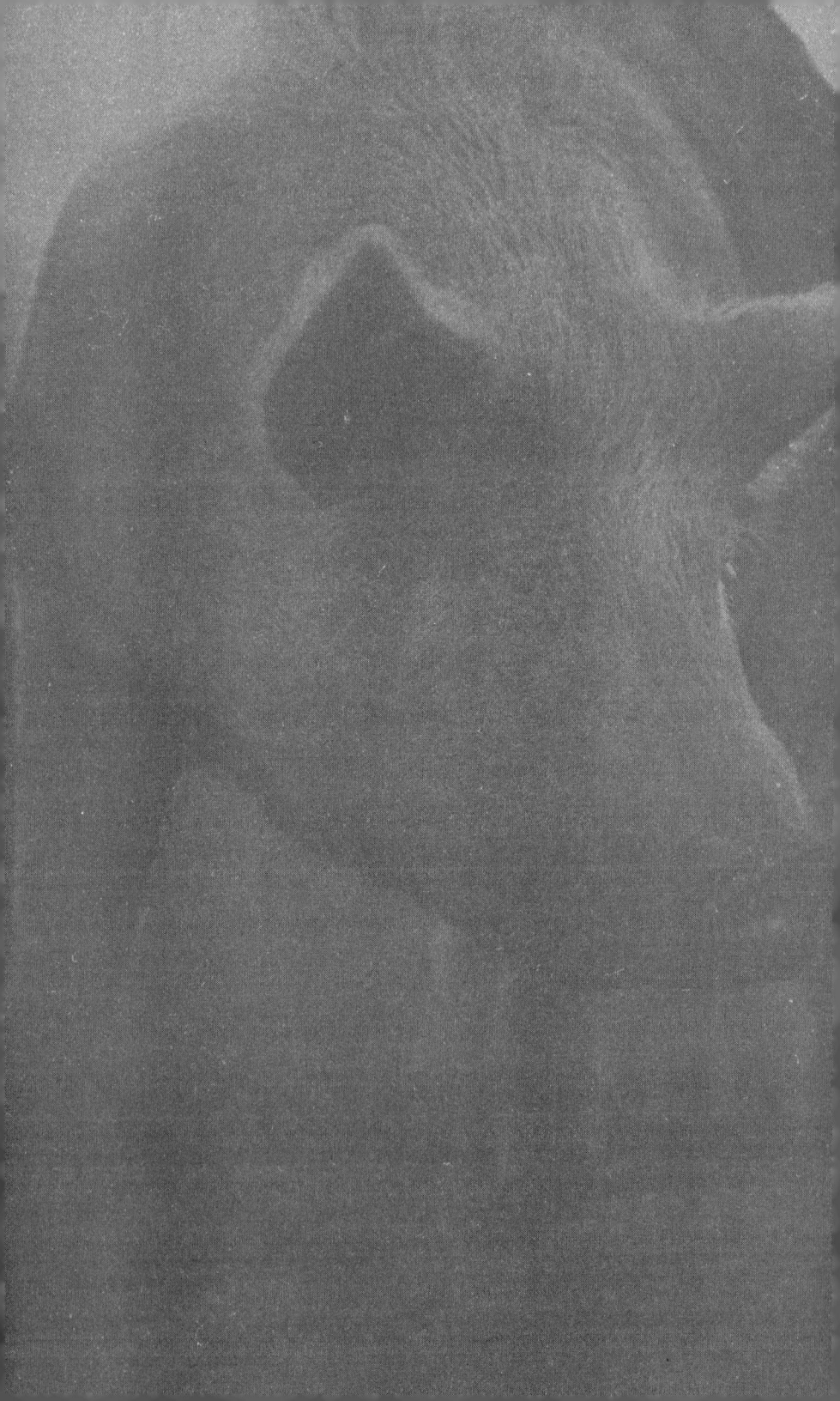

prologue

MOLLY

**PRESENT
2022**

The loud crunch of blunt teeth biting through bone is a lullaby I could fall asleep to for the rest of my life.

I wrinkle my nose.

The obnoxious sound of lip-smacking that follows is not.

"I can teach you to respect me, but apparently, learning manners is asking too much," I mutter, my upper lip curling in disgust when bloody drool splatters onto the plastic tarp before my worn boots.

Gross.

I'm in my barn, crouched on the outside of their pens, keeping my distance while the five massive pigs eat their dinner. They can very easily grab me through the fence if I dare to get close enough, and that is not an attack I'm likely to survive. They're incredibly strong, and if I do manage to escape, I'll definitely be missing a few limbs.

It makes me wonder why the world is so afraid of a zombie apocalypse, when we're already surrounded by animals more than capable of tearing us apart and devouring every last fucking bit of our flesh and bones.

We're just lucky they haven't figured that out yet. Or rather, they haven't figured out how to escape the prisons we put them in.

When finished, they eagerly sniff the hay, searching for their next piece.

"Last one," I warn them, as if they can even understand me.

Sadly enough, they're the only ones I *can* talk to most days. My human interaction is limited, and this pig farm gets awfully lonely. But it's something I chose for myself.

And I don't fucking regret it.

I toss the rest of the leg at their feet, watching them tear into the severed limb in earnest. Tendons, muscles, and veins shred in a matter of seconds, followed by that satisfying *crunch*.

Right then, my phone in my back pocket buzzes. Sighing, I slide it out and answer without bothering to see who it is. I already know.

"Is it finished?" the female voice asks tonelessly. She's been calling me for the last four years, and I still don't know her name.

"Yup," I answer. "They just ate the last of him."

"Good. We'll contact you when the next subject is due to arrive."

The phone goes dead before I can respond. Not that I would've bothered to—that's always been the extent of our conversations.

My human interaction is *very* limited.

Especially because that's what my pets like to eat for dinner.

"Thanks, Petunia," I chirp to myself. Every time she hangs up, I give her a new name. One day, I'm confident I'll have guessed her real name correctly at least once, though I'd never know.

I have a feeling it's not Petunia, but crazier things have happened.

I double-check that the last of the man I fed to the pigs is completely consumed, and then I start the tedious process of cleaning their pens, my table, and the tools, along with burning his hair and clothes and scattering his powdered teeth in the mountains behind my house. Ensuring every last trace of Carl Forthright is gone.

He who was once a rapist and child trafficker is now pig shit.

So fucking poetic.

"You're lucky I love you little assholes because you guys are fucking *messy*," I complain to the snorting pigs, wrinkling my nose when I spot a chunk of flesh on the floor outside their pen.

They're absolute pains in my ass most days, but I wouldn't trade them for the world.

They keep me sane.

And the devil knows that's hanging on by a goddamn thread.

chapter one

MOLLY

FIFTEEN YEARS AGO
OCTOBER 20TH, 2007

"I'm gonna head to the gas station to grab Layla a few things," I tell Dad while frowning at the mess in the living room.

Five crushed, empty beer cans are scattered on the end table, along with empty chip bags and dip with the lid left open.

My father is anxiously peering out of the tattered curtains, shirtless, his pot belly bulging out over his jeans. His gray hair is balding on top, and despite his stomach, he's a tall, lanky old man with a defined jaw, eyebrows that are constantly furrowed, and wrinkles covering every inch of his face.

"No, I need you here. You've been gone all damn day," he snaps, hardly sparing me a glance.

It's after eight-thirty at night, and I've been waitressing at the diner all day. I'm exhausted, but for what feels like the millionth time, she's out of diapers and no one mentioned it. I'm turning twenty tomorrow, but I'll have to pick up another shift now that I'm spending today's tip money on Layla.

"She needs her diaper changed, and there isn't any more," I argue.

He snarls, letting the curtain fall as he faces me.

"She ain't none of your concern."

But she is.

She's sure as fuck not *his* concern, even though she's his daughter.

Dad scratches his arm, track marks blemishing his skin. Again, he glances toward the curtains, as if he's waiting for someone to show up. Probably one of his creepy friends, sure to arrive with a book bag full of drugs, despite the fact that he just made me buy him some yesterday.

"I won't be longer than twenty minutes," I reason. "I just need diapers and formula."

Anxiety spikes in my chest as Layla begins to cry from upstairs. I just laid her down, and I had hoped she'd stay asleep until I got back. She's been fussy for the past week. Right when her eyes close and I think she's finally asleep, they pop right back open and she releases a sorrowful wail that rips my heart out.

"Let me get Layla settled first, and I'll—"

"No," he barks. "If you're going to go, then go now. I ain't got all fucking night."

"Fine," I mumble.

My four-month-old sister is now screaming at the top of her lungs, while our mother is knocked out on the couch, her mouth open and drool trailing down her chin as she softly snores.

A used needle lies on the coffee table in front of her, a bead of blood still staining the tip.

She won't be waking up, which means that Layla will be left to her tears while I'm gone.

Sighing, I head toward the door, pausing briefly when I hear Dad call out, "And grab me a pack of cigs and another six-pack of beer!"

I don't bother answering—not that he expects one. He knows I'll do what he says. If I don't, I'll have to invest in another bottle of concealer. The one I have is almost empty.

The sound of Layla's screams is silenced as I shut the door behind me, my anxiety worsening and gnawing at my stomach. Her poor little throat will be sore, and I'm sure her head will be hurting by the time I get back.

She hates it when I leave her alone, and *I* hate what that implies. There are days that I wonder if it's more than just an attachment to me that puts that fear in her eyes when I walk away.

If Dad is hurting her like he hurt me...

I don't know what I'll do. Except when I'm finished, I'll be covered in blood.

My hands tremble as I speed-walk to the gas station a few blocks down the road. It's a warm and breezy fall night in October—likely one of our last before winter approaches.

Reaper Canyon, Montana, is surrounded by the Electric Peak range, and it's where I was born and raised. The daunting name of this small town is fitting, considering it's where everyone's dreams go to die. This state exudes beauty, but even the mountains off in the distance can't take away the ugliness of my world.

I keep my head down, focusing on the hole in the tip of my dirty tennis shoes. My feet are too big for them now, but I haven't had the money to get a new pair yet. All of it goes to Layla or buying my parents drugs.

On my sixteenth birthday, Dad threatened to kick me out of the house if I didn't get a job. Said I needed to start pulling my weight around the house, as if going to school, doing all the chores, and getting their drugs for them wasn't enough. Let alone being at his and Mom's beck and call twenty-four seven.

My entire first paycheck went on their cigarettes, beer, and drugs. Now, they rely on me to buy our food, and everything for Layla.

The overhead bell chimes as I walk into the local gas station, drawing the clerk's attention. Aside from Layla, he's the only person in this world I actually like.

"Hey, Mol," he greets, a smile stretching across his face, laugh lines forming in his brown skin. He's one of the few people I know who is always happy. I don't believe I've ever known that feeling. Maybe when Layla smiled at me for the first time. But it was fleeting. It didn't take long for my parents to steal away the joy again.

"Hi, Mario," I return, waving at him before disappearing down one of the aisles and heading straight for the coolers where the beer is held.

I'm not old enough to buy alcohol, but Mario now knows my dad well enough to understand that if I don't bring it home, I'll show up with bruises on my face the next day, pleading for him to let me buy it. He's tried to call the police, but each time, I get on my knees and beg him not to. I didn't want to risk Layla being taken by CPS and put in the system.

Families love young girls to adopt, but so do predators, and I won't take the risk. At least at home, I can protect her.

So, despite Mario's hatred for my parents, he risks his license and sells me the alcohol, seeing as he knows it's not for me anyway. He's already made me pinkie swear to wait to drink until I'm old enough, though he told me to stay away from cigarettes forever.

I readily agreed. I've seen addiction in my mother, who, at one point, was valedictorian and had a full ride to college. But then she met my father, and all those dreams and aspirations didn't seem to matter so much when she had euphoria coursing through her veins.

I grab Dad's favorite beer, diapers and formula for Layla, and a few packs of ramen for the next couple days.

Dropping the items on the counter, I pull out my cash while Mario turns to get a pack of cigarettes from behind him. Dad's favorite.

"How are you tonight, sweetheart?" he asks me, clicking the keyboard to ring everything up.

I sigh. "Same ol', same ol'."

"Dad still giving you trouble?"

I give him a dry glance. "Always. I'll be spending my birthday at the diner tomorrow. I was supposed to have the day off, but I didn't get good tips today and, well—" I wiggle the measly bundle of cash. "—it's all gone now anyway."

Mario shoots me an unimpressed look. "What's stopping you from taking Layla from them?"

Shame prevents me from meeting his eyes.

This isn't the first time he's asked, but every excuse I've come up with falls flat. Because the truth is condemning, and as much as I like Mario, what if I can't trust him?

When I refocus on him, my heart squeezes. His stare is soft, and he radiates genuine concern. I feel my resolve cracking.

"Please, Mol, you can tell me anything."

I sigh, and the last of my reservations crumble at his feet.

"My parents have proof of me buying drugs—*their* drugs—but it doesn't matter. It looks bad. They know I want her, and they've threatened to show it to the court if I try to take custody. Dad has pictures and videos I didn't even know he was taking, but he showed me them before he hid them. And if I just take her... I'll be kidnapping her. I'm legally an adult, but the moment I found out my mother was pregnant, I got comfortable in my prison. I can't leave her, Mario."

My friend shakes his head, utter disgust emitting from his brown eyes. "They're sick. Sick, sick people. And they're blackmailing you! Maybe a lawyer—"

"Lawyers cost money, Mario. Money that I *don't* have. All of it goes to them, and I..." My words fail me, helplessness taking root. Exhaling harshly, I finish with the only words that matter, "I'm trapped."

Tears burn the backs of my eyes as Mario stares at me with fury. Fury *for* me, I know. But his anger won't change my situation.

I don't even know how to.

"You don't have any other family?" he questions, the hope hanging on to his words brittle.

Frowning, I shake my head. As far as I know, both of my parents are only children, and their parents are either dead or estranged.

I have no one but Layla.

"I can ask my wife and see about you staying with us—"

I'm shaking my head before he can finish. "My parents won't let me take Layla, and I can't leave her alone."

"Molly, *please* let me help you," Mario begs. "We can figure something out."

"I need time," I snap, and he deflates. Guilt rises, and it only cements my helplessness. "Just... I'll figure it out eventually, okay? She's so young right now, so I just need to make sure I go about it the right way."

He nods, relenting, though his stiff movements betray his true feelings. But just like me, he's helpless.

Even if I take my parents down, they'll be sure to bring me down with them.

"Then at least let me pay for Layla's stuff, yeah? I'll help you get anything she needs in the meantime. But don't think I'm not going to find you a way out of this, little girl," he tells me sternly. "I won't ever stand idly by while you suffer."

Tears well in my eyes, and I'm too overwhelmed with gratitude to thank him properly.

Eventually, I choke out, "Thank you. Even if I have no other family, at least I have you."

His shoulders slump, though the conviction in his tone is strong. "You do, sweetheart. For anything."

I smile softly, even if it's hard to feel. But I am eternally grateful for him, especially since he's the only person who's ever been kind to me.

The bell chimes, and I glance at the newcomers walking in. Quickly, I do a double take, a frown marring my face.

It's my dad, along with a man I don't recognize. I'd have thought they were two strangers who walked in at the same time if it wasn't for them being in the midst of a hushed conversation, their words halting when they finally catch sight of me.

My heart drops.

"What are you doing here? I'm getting your stuff..." I ask, trailing off with nervousness when I realize the other man is staring at me with an expression I can't quite describe. It's a look I don't *want* to decipher, with how it immediately has the hairs on the back of my neck standing on end.

He's short and stocky, with trimmed hair and a square, pronounced jawline. His pale skin is covered in shitty tattoos, and there's a cold gleam in his brown eyes.

Dad strides toward me, gesturing for me to move aside. "I'll take that off your hands. You're too young to be buying alcohol anyhow. Why don't you go with my friend here and wait for me till I'm done?" he orders gruffly.

My mouth drops, bewildered and increasingly suspicious.

My dad has *never* come to take anything 'off my hands'. Which means there's a reason he's here, and that terrifying man has something to do with it.

Like hell I'm going anywhere with him.

"It's fine, I got it—"

"Go," he barks. "*Now.*"

My spine snaps straight. It isn't the harshness in his voice that has me on edge, but rather, the urgency.

Dumbfounded, I look to Mario, and find him a lip curl away from all-out snarling at my dad. He's glaring at the two men with distrust and wrath that burn hotter than the underworld beneath our feet. But what can he do? If he calls the police and accuses me of trying to buy beer just to get me away from them, I would still end up going home with Dad later, and Mario could get his license revoked if they find out he's sold to me before. And if he claims Dad's a threat to me, it'll only separate me from Layla.

I could run... But where would I go? I couldn't leave my four-month-old sister alone, nor did I have anywhere safe to take her.

My mind is spinning over different scenarios, but each time, I come to the same conclusion. I'm helpless.

"I've actually been needing some help around this place. Why doesn't she stay here with me, and I'll pay—"

"You got eyes for my daughter or somethin', buddy? Why don't you mind your own goddamn business, huh?" Dad snaps, glaring at Mario.

"It's fine," I whisper, glancing at the strange man nervously. He's still staring at me, sending a cold shiver down my spine. Whoever he is, he's the reaper, and wherever he takes me, I won't be going anywhere but down.

"Go with him, Molly. I'm not gonna tell you again," Dad barks.

Working to swallow, I hesitantly step away from the counter. Sparing Mario one last glance, I tuck my chin down and walk toward the man, adrenaline releasing into my veins with an intensity I've never felt before. My pulse is thundering in my ears, and I'm beginning to feel nauseous.

A wicked smile curls one side of the stranger's lips, and my stomach fills with acid, bile teasing the bottom of my throat.

"Your dad and I are good friends, don't worry," he assures, grinning wider as if that's supposed to ease my nerves.

It feels as if there is glue on the bottom of my feet, making each step difficult as we head toward the door.

I can't do this. I can't just let this man take me so easily. Wherever I'm going, I won't go without a fight.

I'll take Layla and find somewhere for us to go. Because wherever that is, it *has* to be better than where we are now. Even if I'm a fucking fugitive wanted for kidnapping, I'll find a way for us to survive.

Just as the man opens the door, the bell chiming, I take off down the aisle to my right.

"Hey!" Dad shouts, prompting his friend to whip around. He wastes no time charging after me, causing my heart to jump in my throat.

Instinctively, I grab a few items from the shelves and throw them on the ground behind me. Bags of chips, granola bars, and other foods scatter across the dirty tile, but it doesn't deter him. He jumps over them, his finger skating across my shoulder as I round a corner, only to find my dad standing right there. I scream, nearly smacking directly into his chest.

His arms come up to wrap around me, so I duck below him, scarcely evading them. I just manage to squeeze past him, hearing their muttered curses from behind me.

"Goddammit, you little bitch!" Dad spits.

Heart pounding viciously against my rib cage, I dart down another aisle, seeing Mario come into view. He's holding a baseball bat while speaking frantically on the phone with people who I assume are the police.

"Get here now!" Mario shouts over the phone.

I send more items flying to the ground. This time, it's bottles of soda, all bouncing on the ground, causing some of them to pop open or completely explode.

Quickly, I glance over my shoulder just as the two men stop short of the spillage. I catch sight of the demonic look passing over my father's face. And I know that whatever they have planned for me, it'll make my home life seem like Candy Land.

They split up, Dad going in one direction and the man running to the opposite aisle. They're going to trap me.

Panic invades my senses, and I attempt to backtrack and climb over one of the shelves. The man rounds the corner and charges toward me.

I'm determined to keep going, until I see him reach into the back of his jeans in my peripheral, followed by a distinct click.

I freeze, hanging halfway on the shelf with ice running through my veins, then peer over my shoulder.

Mario is now staring down the barrel of a gun, his face frozen in terror while the man holds it steadily. His face is twisted in anger as he pants heavily.

"I will fucking shoot him. You really want that death on your hands, little girl?" the man hisses.

A thunderous expression is on Dad's face as he stomps toward me, pointing toward the back door labeled for employees only.

"Let's go. Right fucking now!"

I have no choice but to listen.

There's no more running.

I had an opportunity but couldn't get to the exit in time. And as tempted as I am to keep fighting, I won't risk Mario's life.

Panting, and tears blurring my vision, I climb down from the shelf and head toward the door. As I pass Mario, I wave, whispering the word, "Bye," before heading toward the door.

With a deep breath, I walk through the stockroom and out of the back exit. I follow the man through the back alley, my dad breathing down my neck as we walk. There, I'm surrounded by three more men.

There's no chance to scream. Not as they grip my biceps, slap a cloth over my mouth, and drag me into their black van.

It's over for me. I'll never get to see Layla again.

Even worse, she'll never see me again—the only person who took care of her—kept her *safe*.

The only question I have is, will her fate be worse, or mine?

chapter two

MOLLY

FOURTEEN YEARS AGO
JUNE 18TH, 2008

I READ OVER THE last word I wrote on the page before snapping the journal shut. It's a diary I've been secretly writing in for the past couple weeks. It's been my only form of release, but I refuse to take it with me, even if it was the only thing that kept my detonating sanity somewhat intact. It's the only outlet I had for my pent-up rage.

And it can burn with the rest of this house, for all I care.

I hope to God another girl never finds this journal. That would mean she replaced me, and no one—*no one*—should ever have to experience the horrors of this house. No one innocent, at least. I wouldn't care if Francesca, Rocco, or any of his friends got a taste of their own poison one day. It's the least they fucking deserve.

My broken heart is pounding heavily against my chest, the jagged pieces cutting up the inside with each beat. However, the adrenaline coursing through my veins mutes the pain. The only thing I can feel is determination and fury. So much fucking fury.

I'm not waiting any longer. *I can't.*

Francesca has something planned for us in two days, and while I suspect we'll be auctioned off, she never said.

All I know—I can't be here when it happens.

Another day in this hellhole, and I'll lose my fucking mind. Another day without Layla, and I'll kill anyone I have to, even if it ends in my own death. It'll only be my body that dies, anyway. They've already destroyed my soul, and all that's left is an empty house that has seen as many tragedies as the one I'm planning to escape tonight.

My pulse thuds in my ears as I quietly slide out of my bed and tiptoe to the hole beneath the floorboard. When I first arrived here, I noticed the panel was loose, and after a week's effort, I finally managed to pry it up. It was just a dirty hole, but now it's the home of all my secrets and heartache.

With trembling hands, I set the journal inside, carelessly dropping the pen in after it. Then, I slide the wooden piece back into place.

There's no clock in here, but Rocco and his friends have quieted completely, which means they likely passed out. According to Francesca and her constant complaining, that typically happens around two or three AM every night.

I've been preparing for this for *months*.

And now that it's finally here, I'm terrified I missed something. A small detail I didn't plan for when I've done nothing *but* plan.

The only thing separating me from freedom are these thin walls and miles and miles of woods.

That, and the guard stationed outside the house. I've stayed up from dusk to dawn several nights to watch him, forgoing precious sleep to learn his schedule and habits. Which often led me to getting in trouble for falling asleep during lessons. Though Francesca has long since grown tired of my disobedience, she won't get rid of me either.

I'm one of four who made it through the Culling—a twisted game a group of pedophiles and rapists created for sport. The objective is to put us in the woods filled with traps, where they'll hunt us with crossbows. If we're hit, we're punished. If we win and outrun them, we're considered superior meat and then put up for auction.

It's an insult to kidnap us only to make us prove ourselves worthy of being kidnapped.

It makes no fucking sense and was only created so bored rich people can be less bored.

They'll never get the fucking chance.

Inhaling a deep breath, I creep toward my bedroom door. The crickets chirp loudly from outside my window, as if they're cheering me on. Rooting for a precarious escape. One that is likely to kill me.

But I'd rather die rebelling than die submitting.

Sweat forms along my brow as I slowly turn the rusty knob, cringing when it squeals. I swear to God, this house was built when the dinosaurs roamed and is filthier than Francesca's sins.

The hinges creak, though it doesn't stop me from swinging open the door. There are three other girls sleeping in their respective rooms. There's a chance that if one of them catches me, they'll alert Francesca. But I've long since accepted that I'll kill anyone who gets in my way.

No one will keep me from Layla.

My heart races, gaining momentum and slamming against the inside of my chest as I sneak down the long hallway. Aside from my own pulse, it's dead silent. And fuck, is it creepy.

It's always felt haunted here, yet I was convinced it was by the living. Now, I'm not so sure. Or maybe our sadness is potent, even in our dreams.

I bite my lip, holding my breath while I make my way down the steps, avoiding every soft spot in the wood that creaks. The first thing my eyes gravitate to is the green neon numbers blaring from the stove.

2:30 AM. *Perfect.*

Moonlight spears through the kitchen window, but I don't bother with anything in here. I've learned to go days without food and water. But I don't plan on depriving myself for long, seeing as I'm confident there's a town nearby.

Francesca's favorite helper, Rio, makes weekly trips to the grocery store, only gone for a few hours before he returns, and they certainly don't buy in bulk. There has to be a place I can run to and call for help.

I peek into the living room, finding several men laid out over the couch and floor. Five of them. All snoring and surely doped up on drugs, their veins as clogged with chemicals as the dust in the air vents. Their organs are probably floating in an ocean of alcohol, too, pruning in the toxins.

An earthquake would sooner rock them further into whatever depraved la-la land they wandered into than wake them. I wonder, when pedophiles dream of marrying women their age or walking an old person across the street out of the goodness of their hearts, do they call them nightmares? Do they awake in a cold sweat and with a pit of dread in their stomachs?

Surely, they don't consider dreams of cute puppies and rainbows *pleasant*.

Regardless, they're the least of my concerns as I slink through the darkened living room, stepping over stray limbs and crushed, empty beer cans.

It's the guard standing outside the house who has a trail of sweat leaking down my spine.

He would better serve as a boulder in the Hoover Dam with how ossified the muscles around his bones are. All those people that built it died for nothing when all that dumb fuck needed to do was just fucking *stand there*.

But if he sticks to the routine he's followed for the last three months, then he should be holding his dick in the woods somewhere, taking a piss break. Typically, he combines it with a smoke break, using it as an excuse to walk around and relieve himself from standing in the same position for hours on end.

Maybe he wouldn't fare so well in the dam.

Holding my breath, I grab the handle with a trembling, sweaty palm and crack open the door, the rusted hinges screaming.

Wincing, I peek over my shoulder, quickly ensuring the men behind me are still unconscious, then slip out the door.

Only to smack directly into a hard chest.

"Where ya goin', mama?"

Hope, elation, freedom... they fizzle out like a damp firecracker. My bottom lip trembles as I lift my gaze.

Rio.

He wasn't supposed to be on duty tonight.

He's tall, and his light brown skin is covered in tattoos. His hair is buzzed close to his scalp, accentuating a strong jawline and full lips. Admittedly, he's incredibly enigmatic, and the only man in this house who doesn't make us recoil in fear.

He's never been interested in any of us.

Francesca brought him in a few months ago, right after his nineteenth birthday, and not long after he arrived from Puerto Rico. She joked she didn't feel so bad hiring a kid when he's old enough to fuck. I don't think that vile woman is capable of shame or guilt, nor does she pretend to be when she calls him into her bedroom at night.

Just like ours, his eyes are haunted. And unlike the other men, he doesn't leer at the girls or smile when we're raped. In fact, he looks downright sick when it happens.

His job is extraction—a fancy, bullshit name for a kidnapper. They provide him with a picture of a pretty young girl, her name, and her location; his only job is to lure her into his car and bring her back. Most of them are sex workers. Easy to get in a car, and very few people go looking for them once they're missing.

However, they've been having issues with him letting targeted girls slip through his fingers. A mistake that would typically get him killed, but every time Rocco threatens to, Francesca stops him.

She's attached, and it's the only reason Rio is still alive.

I open my mouth, but the answer gets clogged in my throat. It feels too tight, like a crowded room with bystanders pressed shoulder to shoulder, preventing me from uttering a word and wrapping a noose around my neck *and* theirs.

"I got all night. Don't know if you do, though," he drawls casually, pushing for an answer.

"Out," I squeak, the lone syllable forcing its way through the crowd.

A stupid thing to say, but what possible excuse could I conjure? Under no circumstances are we allowed out of our rooms after bedtime, let alone out of the *house*.

I'm fucked. Well and truly fucked.

"Out," he repeats tonelessly.

Adrenaline pumps through my veins, and sweat gathers at the base of my spine. I have the urge to vomit all over his boots, nausea swirling in the pit of my stomach.

I try to clear my throat but only end up squeaking out a choked cough. After tossing a nervous glance over my shoulder, and then over Rio's, I meet his penetrating gaze again.

I'm no longer confident the men behind me won't wake up to our voices, and the guard can show up any second. The smart thing to do is offer him whatever he wants in exchange for his silence and to return to my room. Except something keeps me rooted to where I stand.

Hope.

Hope is what keeps me in place.

He let others go. Maybe he'll let me go, too.

"I'm sorry," I whisper. "I-I'm dying."

I wasn't planning on saying the last part, but it's the truth.

Every second spent in this place—subjected to these waking nightmares—is one less beat my heart is willing to give.

"We all are, no?" he retorts.

I flick another nervous glance over my shoulder. Surprisingly, he takes a step back, allowing me just enough room to step out of the entrance and softly close the door behind me.

A small mercy, yet it means everything to me in this instance. The warm June air feels like a suffocating blanket at this moment.

"P-please. I'll do anything. I won't tell anyone about this place. About you."

He quirks a brow.

"Is that supposed to convince me? You won't have the option to tell anyone shit if I don't let you go, *estúpida*. And keeping you here means no risk," he hisses quietly, his accent deepening with annoyance.

"Right. That was stupid. But it is still completely the case. I just... I have a sister. She's only a year old, and all alone..." I trail off, realizing I'm telling a sex trafficker that my little sister is super fucking kidnappable.

Stupid. Fucking. *Idiot.*

His other brow joins the first halfway up his forehead.

"You're terrible at this," he comments dryly.

"She's not completely alone," I amend weakly. Then, I sigh impatiently. "Okay, whatever. Telling you that doesn't put her in any more danger than she's already in. My parents are addicts and will have friends come over who tend to go exploring the house at night. I guess the only difference between here and there—I'll be able to kill the sick fuck who touches her if she's with me."

He grins, but I've no idea what the fuck he could possibly find funny.

"If you're lucky, you'll manage to kill one before one of them kills you. Then your sister would *really* be alone."

I growl under my breath. Of course, he's right, but my goal was to tug at his heartstrings, not bring out his logic and reasoning.

Hell, I really do suck at this.

I chew my lip mercilessly, trying to figure out a different angle. The man may be fucked up, but he's proven to have empathy. Somewhere beyond the spiderwebs, venomous snakes, and flesh-eating parasites in his soul is a soft spot. I just have to find it.

Worrying my lip harder, I peek over his shoulder again. I'm running out of time. It's a miracle the others haven't returned yet.

"Do you have a sister?" I ask.

His expression wasn't exactly... expressive to begin with, yet it seems as if his face falls anyway. A dark, ominous look passes over his eyes, and his features sharpen. It sends chills down my spine and the hairs on the back of my neck rise.

I'm not sure if I found the soft spot or just struck a *very* sensitive nerve.

The blood in my body turns to ice. If I hadn't been standing in front of a beast before, I certainly am now.

"Is she alive?" I push.

What's stopping me? I'm dead, anyway.

"Yes," he clips. "But letting you go could get her killed if they decide to retaliate against me."

"They'll never know you saw me," I reason, growing desperate. "You weren't even supposed to be on duty tonight."

He considers that for a moment, and my anxiety amps up.

"Look, we're both desperate to keep our sisters safe, yeah? I don't need to be someone who gets in your way, nor do you need to be for me."

His upper lip curls into a snarl, frustration pinching his brow.

It feels like an eternity passes before he finally speaks again.

"Get out of my face. Now. I sure as fuck hope you know what you're doing, because I'm not helping you, nor will I save you if you're caught."

Relief explodes in my chest, stealing my breath away.

"Thank you. I won't forget you, Rio."

I don't wait for him to respond. With one last glance, I take off down the steps and toward the only place that offers a chance of survival—the unwelcoming arms of the forest.

It will be unkind, but I've suffered much worse.

chapter three

CAGE

PRESENT
2022

"Don't let the job title deter you, man. She may be a pig farmer, but she's fucking hot as hell," Eli says from the other end of the phone. "I'll admit, she's showed up in a few of my fantasies when I—"

"Finish that sentence, and I'll drive off the fucking road," I growl, curling my lip in disgust.

As if I give a fuck about who the dickhead jacks off to. I'll sooner cut off his dick before I listen to him talk about what he does to it.

"I'm just sayin', man. Sexy as fuck."

"Noted," I respond tonelessly.

Don't really give a fuck what she looks like, either. The only thing I'm concerned with is dropping off the two dead assholes in my trunk.

Eli's the one who normally takes care of the drops, until he went and got himself shot in the side. Now, he's on bed rest for six weeks, and I was hired to fill in until he recovers.

I'm no stranger to making criminals disappear, though my methods tend to be very different. And less... messy.

"I'll let Legion know when the job's done. Rest up and leave your goddamn dick alone. I don't want to be hauling around dead bodies longer than I need to," I grumble, then click off the phone. The line goes dead, finally giving me some peace and fucking quiet.

His response wasn't important, anyway.

The moon guides me down the barren dirt road, my headlights switched off. While this pig farmer supposedly doesn't have a neighbor for miles, I still like to take extra precautions.

My job relies on my ability to cover my bases, and I certainly won't sacrifice that now when there are two corpses rotting in my car.

After a few more minutes, I arrive at a lone ranch house nestled beside a massive barn, sitting on over a hundred acres of land. At the entrance of the driveway is an old sign that reads *Paladin Farm*.

The corner of my lip quirks as I recall what '*paladin*' means. How noble.

There's a light shining through a single window from her house and a soft glow emitting from the barn. Otherwise, it's pitch-black out here, allowing an unobstructed view of the Milky Way and its star systems.

I stop by the barn just as a shadowed figure emerges from its depths. She stands at the entrance, hands on her hips as she watches me approach.

Legion warned her that I was coming in Eli's place, yet based on the stiff set of her shoulders and her tapping foot, she's on edge.

Rightfully so.

The minute I step out of my car, I'm greeted with the chilly March breeze and her smooth, angelic voice.

"You're here for the delivery?"

My heart pauses, and a distinct part of my brain is blaring an alarm. I've heard thousands of women's voices over the years, but *that* voice—I swear it's familiar.

"Last time I checked," I return dryly, narrowing my eyes to see her better, and failing.

She hums, clearly unimpressed with my answer.

"Two bodies in the trunk," I inform.

"Bring 'em in," she clips, before pivoting and disappearing into the barn.

Digging in my pocket, I pull out a pack of nicotine gum and pop one in my mouth. Then, I open the trunk, curling my lip at the abhorrent smell that wafts from within.

They're already beginning to bloat.

I carry the first body in the barn, the aroma from the pigs no better. It's much bigger on the inside with smooth concrete flooring. Three pens are to my right, with five large, fat pigs dispersed between them. On the other side is the woman, her back to me as she dresses head to toe in a bright yellow hazmat suit.

Without looking back, she points to an expansive metal table with hair clippers, a large metal contraption with a few buttons, pliers, and a Sawzall laying atop it. "Lay them right there."

I do as she says while she begins slipping on oversized rubber gloves that reach up to her elbows.

"I'm going to grab the other one," I say, regarding her closely.

She's reserved, and though she doesn't watch me with her eyes, I can sense that she knows exactly where I am, aware of every movement I make.

A bead of sweat forms on my brow as I carry in the second man, dropping him on the table next to the other.

Thick, opaque plastic covers the wall in front of her setup, descending to the floor, then across it, reaching the pens.

Seems she also likes to cover her bases.

Protective glasses rim her eyes as she grabs the hair clippers. She won't look directly at me, and a few strands of dark brown curly hair frame her face and hide her features, preventing me from getting a good look at her.

"I got it from here," she says woodenly.

I don't answer, too intent on staring at her to see if my hunch is right.

She sighs, and finally turns to look at me, stealing my breath. Even beneath the large protective glasses, I recognize her immediately. There's no mistaking that fucking scar.

She has big emerald green eyes, a gap below her irises that's always given her a naturally seductive stare. And right below the right one is a permanent white, slightly raised bite mark. A full mouth of teeth scarred into her olive skin. How she got it—I still don't know. But it's evident it's not a pretty story.

She's older but doesn't look much different, only more mature. However, the light brown freckles that are smattered across her cheeks and the button nose soften her features. Nine years ago, I told myself I'd count them, but I never got the chance to finish.

I intend to remedy that.

Her eyes widen, recognition flashing within them. She stumbles back, dropping the hair clippers on the table before bumping into it, evoking a god-awful sound from the metal legs grinding against the floor. Even now, she still resembles a frightened cat.

"Cage? What are you doing here?" she snaps, then urgently peers around me as if I were hiding a whole other person up my ass.

"Making a drop," I answer slowly, my brow pinching with confusion. "You're supposed to be living in Alaska. I put you in Alaska." My tone is accusatory, but I'm pissed.

The lengths I go through to make people disappear are fucking tedious as hell. It feels like a slap in the face to have a person I killed standing right in front of me—*not* in Alaska.

That's not why you're angry.

The intrusive voice in my head can go fuck itself.

She glances around nervously. "I didn't like it there."

The muscle in my jaw tics. "What are you doing here, Molly?"

She rears back, as if I backhanded her across the cheek.

"That's not my name anymore."

"This isn't supposed to be your state of residence either, yet here we are."

She narrows her eyes, fire unleashing within the depths of her irises. "Why do you care? I hired you for a job. You did the job. What I do is no longer your concern."

She's right.

If any other client I made disappear were to materialize in front of me, I'd tell them it'll cost triple to make them disappear a second time. But whatever happens to them in the meantime isn't my fucking problem.

Except, Molly isn't like the other clients I've had.

Mainly because I fucked her thoroughly before I gave her a brand-new identity. Then, she disappeared on me—just like she was supposed to.

And it fucking enraged me.

Now, she stares at me like a tiny rabbit caught in a trap, squealing to be freed.

She escaped me once, and I let her.

I won't allow it a second time.

chapter four

MOLLY

PRESENT
2022

I'm going to kill Legion.

He never told me *Cage* was delivering the bodies. I didn't even think to ask who was coming when I was informed Eli was shot and would have a temporary replacement. I trust Legion implicitly, so I wasn't concerned with their identity. Especially because I know how to protect myself regardless of who it is.

I've no idea if Legion even knows anything about the night I spent with Cage—and maybe he doesn't. But, fuck, he could've warned me.

"When did you come back?" Cage questions, his voice tight.

"Four years ago," I answer automatically, though I'm not sure why. It's none of his business—*I'm* none of his business.

"Why?" he demands.

"Doesn't matter why. You shouldn't be here," I mumble, nervous sweat dotting my hairline and coating my trembling palms. *I* shouldn't be here. We both know that, even if he doesn't know why.

Running from Francesca and Rocco was one of the many reasons I needed to escape Montana. Yet, I knew coming back here was the only thing that would save me from myself.

I tried to survive in Alaska, but only found myself dying.

At least here, I'd be living, even if I still feel dead inside.

Cage takes a step toward me, a savage expression mapped across his devastatingly beautiful face.

I forgot how tall he was. Towering over six-four, at least.

His hair hasn't changed since I last saw him. Still buzzed short on the sides, the dark brown strands only slightly longer on top. *Just* long enough to run my hands through. I recall my tongue tracing his sharp jawline made out of steel and thick brows creased in bliss above his forest green eyes. And I'll never forget those wide, full lips that kissed every inch of my skin, or the light stubble that sent chills down my spine every time I felt it brush against me. All features that my stare has worshiped for hours.

Letting him fuck me was one of many mistakes, but I wanted to feel what everyone else was feeling when they had sex—what normal people felt. I wanted sex to feel *good*.

I just never expected it to feel *that* good. And for unknown reasons, that's still more terrifying than being gang-raped by Rocco and his men.

He takes another step toward me. For the second time, I stumble back into the table where two corpses continue to rot.

"D-don't," I choke out, holding up my hand to stop him. As if it would.

He pauses, the gears in his head turning. I've no idea what he's thinking, but in the short time I knew him, he wasn't very susceptible to letting people inside his head.

"Feed the pigs, Molly," he finally grits out, taking several steps back. I feel the constriction around my chest release with every inch that grows between us.

It's been nine years since I last saw him, though I recall all too well how hard he made it to breathe.

I clear my throat as if that's going to remove the anxiety clogging it. Then, I stiffly turn to the first corpse on the table.

A man who is well into his fifties, with a deeply receded hairline and gray hair. After some maneuvering, I manage to remove the articles of clothing from his body and toss them to the side. Then, I grab the hair clippers again and begin shaving his head.

All the while, Cage watches me silently.

Eli doesn't typically stick around after the deliveries. Not since the first time he watched my pigs eat. I'm tempted to tell Cage to leave, but whatever old attachment I had with him isn't entirely gone. Like removing a Band-Aid and being left with the residue. The wounds are healed, yet what was supposed to help close them remains.

"What did this guy do?" I ask, my voice strained.

"He was just acquitted of raping his fifteen-year-old grandson. Not enough evidence, the judge said. Despite the mountain of pictures of bruises around the kid's neck that matched the guy's handprints and the semen sample on the boy's shorts."

"Sounds like the judge should've been killed, too," I mutter snidely, then grab my pliers and begin forcefully yanking out his teeth. When I'm finished, I drop them in the grinder on my table. With the press of a button, it grinds them down to powder, making them easy to dispose of later.

Next, I turn on the Sawzall and begin cutting into flesh. Crimson splatters onto my gloved hands, face, and chest. Behind me, I hear my pigs snorting loudly beneath the ear-piercing sound of the saw cutting through bone.

Now that they have a steady diet of human remains, they tend to get rowdy once they catch a whiff of blood. It used to freak me out, but then I decided that the predators they were eating were far worse than the beasts consuming them.

After I'm done, his arms, legs, and head are removed from his torso. I move the body parts out of the way, then sweep my arm across the table, wiping the excess blood onto the plastic-covered floor for easy cleanup later.

"And this one?" I ask tersely, breaking the tense silence while I remove the clothing from the second man. He appears well into his seventies, covered in liver spots.

"That's the judge."

I purse my lips, feeling, rather than seeing, his amusement.

"Did you kill them?" I question, realizing that in the nine years I've been gone, a lot could have changed with Cage.

"No. Legion handles that."

Legion is an underground organization run by an elusive no-face man named after his company, who employs hitmen to take out whoever they deem necessary. They specifically target those who frequent the dark web, and much like their sister organization, Z, they go after pedophiles.

While *Z* focuses on the trafficking rings and larger operations, *Legion* was formed to focus on the smaller fish—the psychopaths who lurk in plain sight, fitting into society as the blue-collar working class or with their corporate desk jobs, all the while wreaking havoc on innocent souls when they clock out.

Though, Legion sees them for who they really are. Wolves in sheep's clothing. Beasts in human skin.

Cage is quiet as I trim the judge's wispy, thin hair, then remove his dentures and the few remaining teeth and start up the Sawzall again, dismembering him quickly. Except the second I finish silencing the machine, his deep, oceanic voice is back.

"When did you start working for Legion?"

I take a steady breath, grabbing two severed arms and walking them over to the first pen with Dill and Chili inside. I toss an annoyed glance toward Cage on the way, but his expectant expression doesn't budge.

"Not long after I came back. I bought this farm on a whim. It was cheap, secluded, and came with the pigs. I was going to get rid of them, but then I realized they could be useful. *I* could be useful."

The arms go flying into the pen, and Dill and Chili don't hesitate to tear into them. Pivoting, I head back toward the table and grab two legs. I heave them up, and when Cage steps toward me as if to help me, I shoot him a warning glare.

I've never needed a man to do the heavy lifting for me before, and I sure as fuck don't now. I'm more than capable.

Garlic and Paprika are fed next, and Cage doesn't remove his burning stare from me for a single second.

It sets me aflame, like a fever ravaging my insides. I'm short of breath, my palms are sweaty, and my knees are weak. I'd love to pretend that it's because he makes me sick, but my tightened nipples and the faint thrum between my thighs speak otherwise. He holds my body beneath his thumb, ready to betray me when my head demands control.

"I still had Legion's contact info and reached out. Told him I wanted to help snuff every piece-of-shit pedophile from this planet, and how I planned to do it. He was happy to oblige." I end my explanation with a shrug, before grabbing the two severed heads.

Oregano always gets the heads. She's the momma of the bunch—and the biggest.

He's quiet again, seeming to contemplate that as he watches Oregano bite into the judge's head, cracking it open like a watermelon.

"When did you start working for him?" I ask quietly.

"I don't. I still own my store, *Black Portal*. However, Legion's a friend, so when he needs help, I give him a hand."

I nod, turning my gaze back to my pigs. They were already named when I inherited them, and when I first heard what they were, I thought they were stupid. Who names pigs after seasoning?

Now, I find them quite fitting, considering their diets. A little bit of spice with their human meat.

"Moll—"

"You're supposed to call me Marie," I say. "That's what everyone else knows me by."

I flick a glance at him, noting his raised brow.

"Everyone else?"

I shrug. "The grocery store clerk that sells me wine, mainly."

"No friends? Boyfriend?"

I sigh and grab the other set of arms and legs, tossing them to Oregano. The other four can split the two torsos.

"I don't allow attachments when I make money the way I do. Lying to loved ones and living a double life doesn't appeal to me."

"So, you have no one," he states.

After tossing the torsos in the last two pens, I give him a dead stare, letting him see through the windows of my soul, only to find nothing inside.

"No one," I echo, then turn and head to the cleaning station tucked into the far corner of the barn, near the metal table.

"Legion already paid for tonight. Thanks for dropping them off," I toss over my shoulder, signaling the end of his visit. The pigs are finishing up, and I prefer to clean alone.

Or maybe I just prefer to *be* alone.

It's a quiet existence, but it's been so long since I've known anything else.

"I'll see you around, Molly," Cage murmurs, the statement sounding more like a vow than a goodbye.

My throat tightens, and it doesn't ease until I hear his car door slam shut, the engine start, and the tires crunching over the gravel as he retreats.

My phone rings, showing an unknown number, and like every time before, I answer it and hold it to my ear wordlessly.

"Is it done?"

"Yep."

"Good."

The line goes dead, and once again, I'm left with nothing more than blunt teeth chewing through bone.

"Thanks, Helga," I sigh.

chapter five

MOLLY

**PRESENT
2022**

THE SUDDEN KNOCK ON the door causes me to jump out of my skin, nearly sending the wine in my glass splashing in my face and on the fantasy novel from Adeline Reilly that I'd been reading.

Heart thundering, I stare at my front door with widened eyes, my brain running over possible scenarios on who the fuck could be at my door.

Of course, it jumps to the worst conclusions first.

What if it's a cop telling me that they've somehow pinned my father's murder on me and I'm under arrest. Or that they have evidence of me kidnapping Layla. Shit, maybe it's a friend of Francesca's, and they've come to collect what they feel they're owed.

The second knock has me snapping out of my spiraling thoughts. I hurriedly set my wine down on the coffee table, before scrambling to my room to grab my Glock. I've never had to use it, but I don't mind breaking it in.

Whoever it is, I'll feed them to my pigs and no one will ever kn—

A third knock.

Quietly, I fish out my phone from my back pocket and click on the feed for my security cameras, finding Cage on the other side of my door.

I release a weighted breath and swing open the door, glaring at him with annoyance.

He raises a brow.

"Can't say I've ever gotten that look before when showing up at a lady's door. I must be losing my charm." Then, he clocks the gun in my hand, and the other brow joins the first. "That's *also* new. You gonna use that on me, little ghost? I don't mind joining you in the afterlife."

"You scared me half to death," I snap. "What are you doing here?"

It's been a week since his first drop-off, and I wasn't prepared to see him again until the next delivery, which hasn't been scheduled yet.

He raises his hand, and for the first time, I notice he's holding a bouquet of tiger lilies, already in a beautiful crystal vase.

"I come bearing gifts." He lifts his other hand and holds up a DVD. "And a movie."

I sputter, unprepared for both items. He takes advantage and slides past me, forgoing an invitation.

"What the fuck," I mutter beneath my breath, dumbfounded as he kicks off his shoes at the entrance, then saunters into my living room and sets the tiger lilies on the center of the coffee table.

Though, he does pause to take a peek around.

My house is warm and cozy and newly updated. It has a rustic barn feel, with brown wooden beams across the ceiling, distressed wooden floors and furniture, and deep green cabinetry that complements my sage green couch and cream rugs. It isn't a large home, but it's perfect for me.

"You're having wine?" Cage asks, noticing the open bottle and my glass on the table. "My mom loves that shit—she'd love you. Anyway, I brought *The Silence of the Lambs*. Have you seen it?"

"Uh, no."

He shoots me a bewildered look over his shoulder, which quickly morphs into a devilish grin.

"I think you'll like it. It's a fucking cult classic. I figured you'd find some enjoyment out of it, considering it's about eating people."

I frown. "You think just because I feed my pigs humans, I'm into cannibalism?"

He shrugs, popping the disc into my DVD player to get the film ready. "I'm into whatever you're into. I get the feeling these types of movies are right up your alley. Come sit. I'll make popcorn."

I don't sit.

In fact, I stare at him as he walks over to my kitchen and starts rifling through the cabinets like he owns the place, finding a large bowl and my popcorn.

"What if I didn't have popcorn?" I question, crossing my arms.

Again, he peers at me from over his shoulder. His beauty is wicked, and I hate the way it makes my heart flutter.

"Everyone has popcorn, Molly." He says that like it's obvious.

And I suppose it is, considering it's been a staple in my household for the last several years.

He moves through the kitchen with confidence. Like he's been here all along and is as familiar with my home as he is with my body.

As much as my brain protests, my heart is softening.

I only knew him for a night, but I've missed him. More than I ever realized.

Sighing, I relent and trudge over to the couch. Instantly, I grab the wineglass, chugging the rest of it and hoping it calms the butterflies flapping around in my stomach.

"Don't worry, baby, I'll get more wine, too," he drawls, amusement in his tone.

I roll my eyes, but secretly, I like that he's here. Even though I wasn't prepared for an impromptu movie night, the idea of it actually sounds really fucking nice.

I don't think I've ever had one before. At least not one where I wasn't alone.

In no time, the delicious aroma of buttery popcorn fills the house, and he's sitting next to me on the couch with the snack, an uncracked bottle of wine, and an extra glass for himself.

I pop a piece of popcorn in my mouth and cast a thin-eyed look his way. "You could've called, ya know."

"I don't have your number, though."

I raise a brow. "Are you saying you're not a resourceful man?"

He shoots me a cocky grin. "I didn't want to give you the chance to say no."

He grabs the remote and presses play before I can formulate a proper response. We both know he's right, and in a weird way, I'm glad he took the option out of my hands.

I would've agonized over the proposal for far too long, talked myself out of doing it, and then regretted it later.

As the disturbing movie plays, we power through the popcorn like we're starving and drink the entire bottle of wine. And like a true gentleman, he lets me eat all the half-popped kernels.

Then, he grabs my legs and, resting them over his lap, massages my feet, all the while quoting lines from the film. The act is so thoughtless, so genuine, that tears rush to my eyes.

Never have I had anyone bring me flowers, set up a movie, and rub my feet. It's not something I even imagined for myself.

"Why did you come?" I ask softly after about an hour into the movie. My head is swimming a little, but I gaze at him with perfect clarity.

He glances at me. "I wanted to spend time with you. I missed you."

It's a simple answer, yet my heart is climbing into my throat.

"Thank you," I whisper.

He leans down and places a soft kiss on the top of my foot, then turns his focus back to the movie.

I haven't been to Cage's store, *Black Portal*, since that day nine years ago, desperate for an escape and hoping to God I'd find one in Cage.

He provided it for me, but it wasn't the escape I thought I needed.

Now that I'm here again, watching him sell a TV to a typical customer, I realize I'm finding one in him now.

It's been a few days since our movie night, and I don't think I've ever texted anyone so much in my life.

He asked for my number after our movie night, promising he'd call before showing up. Reluctantly, I gave it to him, but I hadn't expected him to text me so often. At first, I was hesitant to respond, but his charm was as addicting through the phone as it was in person, and ultimately, I found myself replying to him until it became thoughtless.

It's been superficial—neither of us daring to tread too deeply. I know he's overflowing with questions. Since I came in today, he's been staring at me with a burning curiosity when he thinks I'm not paying attention yet. But I haven't found the voice to tell him anything.

Admittedly, I'm too scared to.

I'm ashamed of my past. Ashamed of giving Layla up. And ashamed that I came running back when I couldn't find happiness thousands of miles away from her.

And maybe a little ashamed that I didn't have the gall to reconnect with him sooner—the only man who made me feel something outside of bone-crushing terror.

I'm sitting behind the counter, watching him work. He invited me to keep him company until the end of his shift. Even though he's the owner, he tries to stick to a schedule alongside his employees, considering it's his skills that are required to provide his real services.

"You are just so smart. I've no idea how to work these damn things anymore, but my grandson's been asking me to get one of these flat-screen TVs for his video games. And, well, I'll do anything for that kid," the older woman explains, waving her wrinkled hand around as she speaks.

Cage grins, which is a complete cause for concern. Every time he does, I swear that poor woman's heart stops, and an uncontrollable smile overtakes her wrinkled face.

"Well, then, who am I to get in the way of that? I'll point you in the direction of the most cost-efficient TV that'll make his heart happy. Sounds good, yeah?"

The woman titters. "So kind of you. Thank you, young man."

They walk off, leaving me alone with Silas, Cage's employee. We both glance at each other and then simultaneously roll our eyes.

"It's annoying how he's only gotten more charming with age," Silas grumbles, flicking his black hair from his equally dark eyes.

He's a handsome man himself, but his eyes tend to stray toward people who look a lot more like Cage.

"Whatever pays the bills, I guess," I respond, though Silas is right. He's only become more enigmatic since I've last seen him.

Which is definitely annoying.

"He never got over you, ya know," Silas says, bringing my attention snapping back to him. When my brows crease in confusion, he explains, "It took about three years and a really drunken night to admit that you both slept together that night." His arms rise defensively. "Which I'm not judging either of you for. Anyway, he blabbered on about how he hasn't been able to think of anyone else since. How every day, he would picture you showing back up in the store. I guess, in a way, he's been looking for you since you left, even if it was him that made you disappear."

My heart clenches painfully. It's a feeling that I understand.

Many nights, I questioned if I did the right thing by moving to Alaska. I would fantasize about what would happen if I went back and explored a different life—one with Cage.

If it would be as good as I thought it could be. But I talked myself out of it every time, convinced that changing the course of my life over one night with a man was entirely stupid and presumptuous.

I'd never been in a relationship beforehand, and certainly not after, so what the fuck would I know about what's normal to feel after a one-night stand?

"He barely knew me," I finally muster, clinging to the only excuse I have for the two of us always being drawn to each other the way we have. It was just one night. People don't fall in love that quickly, and it would be insane to think otherwise.

"At one point in our lives, we don't know our soulmates at all. But that doesn't make them any less of one. Sometimes... sometimes you just know."

I frown, contemplating that.

Cage reappears before I can wrap my head around that, and he slaps his hands on the counter to draw our attention.

"I have a few things to finish up for a client, and then I'm set to go," he announces. Then, he tips his chin toward the back door. "Come back with me?"

Smiling tightly, I wave at Silas before following him through the back door.

My stomach flutters with nerves, and every time I look at Cage, I increasingly realize that maybe he's more than just a man I slept with once.

And that is utterly terrifying.

For the next hour, I watch him work. He's designing a new driver's license for a client who will now reside in Maine. *Black Portal* is just a front, but his real job is making people disappear and reappear with an entirely new identity. New name, social security card, birth certificate, and state of residence.

Just like he did for me.

It's fascinating to see what he does to legitimize their new life and make it seem as real as any other person.

"Why is this client disappearing?" I ask finally, when he's almost finished.

He flicks his eyes toward me. "He killed his daughter's rapist and murderer. He's out on bail, but his lawyer is confident he'll still serve about twenty-five to life for his crime."

I chew on my lip. "You're saving his life."

Cage shrugs. "I'm just ensuring he has one. That's all."

He shuts his computer down, then turns to me on the chair.

"Let's go grab some food, yeah? I know a great pizza place. They brew the best beer I've ever had."

I wrinkle my nose. "I'm allergic to beer."

His eyes round, and he looks almost devastated, which draws a smile to my lips.

"I'm so fucking sorry for you. They offer a few different cocktails."

I shrug. "I'm just here for the pizza. You can thank yourself for that fixation."

He grins, his eyes sparkling. "I'd like to think I'm responsible for a few fixations, but sure, we'll start with pizza."

My cheeks burn, his implication obvious. He's implying his cock would be another, and fuck him for being right.

His wicked grin widens. "Come on, little ghost. Let's go stuff that pretty little mouth."

Said mouth drops, and he grabs my hand, pulling me after him as he laughs.

What a dick.

He's lucky it's a really fucking nice one.

chapter six

MOLLY

FOURTEEN YEARS AGO
2008

Sweat soaks through my clothing, my curls matted to the back of my neck, as I stumble over another fallen branch. I gasp, scarcely catching myself on a nearby tree.

The sun rose, set, and rose for a second time. Over twenty-four hours have passed since I ran from Francesca's house. Too many hours to be subjected to the heat in the middle of June, though at least the shade from the trees offered some protection from direct sunlight.

I don't need a mirror to know that my face is sunburnt and tomato red. However, I've made it this far, I can go just a little longer.

Anything for Layla.

I'll risk everything for her, as long as I'm with her.

In the distance, there's a break in between the trees where a structure peeks through. My overworked heart stops in my chest, and for several moments, I can't breathe. Can't even blink.

I'm terrified that if I do, it'll disappear, only a figment of my imagination.

If it's only an illusion—something my brain created to protect me from my harsh reality—I think I'll let myself burn to death, only so when I do crumble to ash, there'll be nothing left to put back together.

That same fear drives me forward, my feet tripping over the ground once more, though not from trees that have shed their bark, but from pure desperation.

My vision blurs with tears, and my nose burns from my effort to keep them at bay. I can't lose it now. Not when I'm so close to being able to find Layla again.

The graveyard of crooked branches and green leaves gives way to a blue, sunny sky, showcasing a quiet suburb of homes beneath.

My lips part, and a choked gasp leaks past the chapped skin. Once again, I'm running, this time toward the closest house. It's quaint and tan with freshly painted brown shutters. The type of home that burrows a happy, white-picket-fence type of family in its warm embrace.

In the front yard is a man mowing his lawn, muttering soundlessly beneath the loud buzz of the machine. He appears in his forties, with dark brown skin and a thick salt-and-pepper beard. Sweat glistens on his bald head and coats his t-shirt as he cuts the grass beneath the hot sun.

"Help!" I shout, though the single syllable shatters as it's forced through a throat lined with sharp gravel.

His head snaps up, revealing a startled gaze, his eyes widening further when he sees me barreling toward him.

"Help!" I repeat. "I was kidnapped, I need help!"

He quickly switches the mower off, the sudden silence amplifying my desperate cries. I nearly slip, the worn soles of my shoes no longer gaining any traction on the loose grass like they did on the forest floor.

He holds up his hands—to stop or catch me, I'm not sure—but I throw myself into them anyway. He grabs ahold of my biceps, and though he's taken aback, his grip is firm.

A sob bursts from my throat, and another choked plea for help follows suit.

"Please, help me. Please, please!"

"Hey, hey, it's okay, you're safe. Let's... shit, Latoya!" He trips over his words, ending it with a desperate call for who I assume is his wife.

"You're safe now, it's okay— Latoya! Latoya, get out here!"

A door creaks and a soft voice asks, "What's going on? Who is that?" Urgency taints the last few notes of her second question, and I hear the rapid trek of her footsteps coming toward me.

"She—she just came running out of the woods calling for help," he explains, his words jumbling together.

"I was kidnapped," I squeak through another sob, my face planted firmly in the man's chest. He smells of pine and leather, and it's such a nice change from body odor and cigarettes that it only makes me burrow deeper into his embrace.

"Oh my God, honey, let's get her inside. She looks dehydrated!" Soft, warm skin envelops my hand, stirring the shot nerves to life. "Hey, sweetie, you're okay. Come inside," she urges gently.

I let her pull me away from her husband, only to be greeted with the warmest, chocolate brown eyes I've ever seen. Short, silky black curls billow around her deep brown skin, and she stares at me like a mother concerned for a child.

"Oh, you're sunburnt, too! Come on, sweetheart, let's get you cooled down." Her gaze lifts above my head. "Baby, call the police. I'm sure she has a family who's worried sick."

I don't have the heart to tell her that the only family I have is too young to understand my disappearance.

The oxygen stutters from my lungs as she leads me inside, the cold air radiating from within almost a shock to my system. My teeth chatter as I'm led directly into a cute living room, though I feel nothing except relief.

"Sit here while we wait, honey. I'll get you some aloe and fresh lemonade," Latoya instructs gently.

Woodenly, I plop onto a plush taupe couch. It complements the tan walls and pink and brown floral accents placed around the area. A soft yellow glow emits from a tall lamp tucked in the corner to my right, which stands next to a mahogany fireplace, a flat-screen TV mounted above.

Latoya returns a minute later with a bottle of aloe. Gently, she applies some to my cheeks and nose. The motherly affection radiating from her has tears pricking the backs of my eyes.

"There you go," she whispers affectionately. "Now sit tight, I'll be right back."

She scurries off toward where I assume the kitchen is, while her husband comes through the front door. He pauses when he sees me, and his brown eyes soften.

"You look worn out, my dear," he comments. "Police are on their way. Do you need anything while we wait?"

I shake my head, feeling terrible for bursting into their lives in such a horrible way, yet so relieved that they let me.

"What's your name, sweetheart?" he asks, sitting on the matching couch across from me.

"Molly."

"That's a pretty name, Molly. You can call me Devin. How old are you?"

"Twenty."

My answers are robotic, and now that I'm... *safe*, I can't feel anything at all. None of this feels real. It's an out-of-body experience, and though I can hear and see everything around me, I'm unable to process any of it.

My heart rate picks up as Devin continues to pepper me with questions. Blackness leaks into the edges of my vision, and I begin to wonder if this is a good idea.

What if Rocco shows up, and hurts Devin and Latoya? Would that make me responsible for their deaths?

Images of Latoya and Devin lying in pools of blood flash through my head, their eyes open and lifeless. Senseless deaths. And it's all my fault.

I shouldn't be here.

I'm going to get them killed.

My knees crack from how quickly I stand. "I-I have to go," I stammer, feeling my pulse thrumming wildly in my throat.

Devin slowly rises to his feet, lifting his hands in a placating gesture.

"Hey, hey, you're safe now, Molly."

I may be safe with them, but they are not safe with *me*.

"I just can't be here. They're going to be looking for me, and I don't want you and your wife to get hurt."

A crease forms between his brows. "The poli—"

I dart for the door, nearly crashing into Latoya, who's carrying a glass full of lemonade. She gasps and stumbles out of the way, ice and liquid sloshing over the rim and onto her hand.

"I'm sorry! I have to go before they find me. Th-thank you for your help!"

Latoya opens her mouth, but I'm flinging open the front door and flying out of the house before she can manage a sound.

My head is swiveling left and right, finding the street empty, yet convinced that Rocco and his men are here, lurking just out of sight and waiting for the right moment to strike.

Adrenaline is flooding my system, sending dangerous levels of toxins into my bloodstream. I don't feel the heat any longer, only utter panic that I'm going to be running right back into my captors' hands.

I bolt off the front porch, Latoya's concerned voice calling after me as I take off down the street.

There has to be a bus station around here somewhere, right? I've no idea where we are—didn't even think to ask. But it doesn't appear I'm still in Montana with how different the mountains look.

I run down the street, keeping to the backyards of the houses so I'm out of view. Within a minute, there's a police car turning a corner, likely heading to Latoya and Devin's house.

Ducking behind a playground set, I wait for it to pass before darting away again. After running through a few more yards, I spot a little kid playing outside ahead, his parents out of sight. He appears to be around nine or ten years old, wearing swim shorts and a tank top, kicking around a soccer ball. His pale skin is flushed from the heat, turning the entirety of his cheeks and nose bright red.

He stares at me blankly as I slink up to him, keeping light on my feet as if Rocco will be able to hear me from wherever he is.

"Hey, kid. What state is this?" I whisper, glancing toward his house, where a sliding glass door is directly in view.

"Oregon," he answers casually, curiosity piqued in his crystal blue eyes.

I bite my lip, not liking how far from home I am. Guess it could be much worse.

"Do you know where a bus station is?"

He shakes his head. "I can ask my dad."

"No!" I whisper-shout just as he takes a step toward his house. He pauses, a little startled but still curious.

"Sorry. Uh, would you know where downtown is?" I ask, my paranoia growing stronger with each passing second.

What if Rocco finds me with this kid? They'd probably take him, too, and it'd be all my fault.

I *need* to get out of here.

He tips his chin up as he thinks, showcasing gaps and two different-sized front teeth. His lips are bright red, as if he chugged cherry juice.

Hurry the fuck up. Your life is on the line!

"I think you go that way—" He whips his arm out behind him, pointing straight ahead of me. "—and then you will see a McDonald's, and I think that's downtown."

He ends his shitty directions with a shrug, peering back at me with a *was that good?* expression.

I tighten my lips into a firm line. I'm not much better off, but at least I know I'm going in the right direction.

"Thanks, kid." I pat his head, then take off again. "Oh, and don't talk to strangers!" I call out behind me.

"But you're a stranger," he counters loudly.

And I easily could've gotten you killed.

I don't say that, too far away to tell him about the horrors of this evil world. The only thing I can do is hope his parents protect him from it, unlike my own.

Because, mine... mine are the ones who sold me to Francesca.

And I'll be damned if I allow them to do the same with Layla.

chapter seven

CAGE

**PRESENT
2022**

My left foot taps against the footrest as I drive down the lengthy gravel road leading toward Molly's house. Or, I guess *Marie's* house, though I'll never be able to call her that. Molly was the name I groaned over and over when I was inside her nine long years ago. And it's the name that still comes back to haunt me during my loneliest hours.

"You could've warned me," I growl through the phone. I've been calling the fucker since the first delivery to Molly's house, and coincidentally, he's been busy.

"That was my error," Legion says, his voice just as deep and toneless as it always is. "I hadn't realized you formed an attachment to her."

Dickhead. That was definitely a dig.

"Then why didn't you tell her I was coming? She seemed surprised."

"I should have," he concedes. "I let her know a good friend of mine was coming in lieu of Eli until he recovers, and that you were trustworthy. She trusts me so she didn't seem concerned with your name."

I sigh. "Why didn't you tell me she came back?"

I'm pissed that he didn't. Not because she reversed everything I did to keep her hidden and safe. No, it's because she's been back, within reach, and I never fucking knew. She doesn't owe me shit. Except there's a small part of my ego that hoped she'd want to see me again. The fact that she didn't, only makes me want to prove just how fucking wrong she is for feeling that way. And the problem is I don't know if she'll let me have her, but I do know it won't stop me.

None of this has anything to do with Legion. Not really. He may employ her, but who she was before isn't of much concern to him. The only thing he does make his business is who his employees are now.

"I didn't know I was required to," he counters dryly.

I growl beneath my breath. "Why did she?"

He sighs. "If I recall, she has a sister who was given up for adoption before she left. I assume her reasons for returning to Montana may have something to do with that," Legion says.

I exhale slowly. I only had one night with her. And admittedly, we didn't do too much talking. Although I did know from the news reports after she went missing that she had a much younger sister. Layla, I think her name was.

So, if Molly's willing to return to the one place that caused her so much distress, then it can only be for someone as important as Layla.

"Do you know where her sister is now?"

"Yes," he answers shortly.

I wait, but he doesn't elaborate.

"Legion," I growl, my patience waning.

"Do I need to be concerned about what you will do with said knowledge?"

"No."

He's silent for a beat, but I know I've won when I hear his exasperated exhale.

"She's fifteen years old now, and lives with a nice, wealthy family. And that is not to be messed with, Cage."

I'd happily fucking kidnap her if that's what Molly asked, but I keep that to myself. Obviously, Legion would find that concerning.

"We're clear," I clip. "Thanks, man. I'll report when the delivery is complete."

I toss my phone to the passenger seat, releasing another heavy exhale. There's an undeniable burning desire to know everything about Molly. Why was Layla given up for adoption? And did Molly return, because she wants her sister back? Or to be around for when she turns eighteen?

The obsession is familiar.

It's similar to what I felt when she was first kidnapped. The intrigue of her disappearance and what happened to her—I was incredibly transfixed by her case.

The girl who not only vanished out of thin air but seemed to lose her mind beforehand.

The footage showed her walking into the gas station, and five minutes later, she was running from something that the security cameras couldn't see. Throwing things on the floor, clearly in distress, while absolutely destroying the place. And then seeming to calm, as if someone had forced her to.

What was more disturbing was that the cameras didn't see her leave the gas station. Same with the ones outside the back exit—that door never opened, and she was never seen walking out.

At 9:02 PM, she waved goodbye to the man behind the counter, walked out of shot toward the back door, and that was the last the world saw of Molly.

It was riveting, and I was fascinated.

But this obsession that I feel now is still not the same. No—it's *exactly* what I felt when I met her. *Had* her.

The girl with haunted eyes and a perpetual frown, who carried a sadness so deep that it permanently altered the shape of her lips.

I spent the night tracing my tongue along her Cupid's bow until I remolded her mouth to fit against mine. Because as long as I was inside her, her sadness would be powerless to my obsession. And there would be no part of her that wasn't made precisely for me.

I pull up to her farm, seeing the glow emanating from the same lone window in her house. It's been a week since I last saw her, and I've been talking myself down from showing up at her house uninvited again.

I wonder if that light is shining from her bedroom. Now, I can't look away without first imagining the silhouette of her naked body shadowed behind the glass. The curve of her pert breasts, just big enough to fill my hands, and those dusty pink nipples I could barely pull my mouth away from that night. The swell of her plump ass, before curving into those creamy thighs.

Fuck.

My cock is straining painfully against my zipper, and I'm tempted to unzip and stroke myself to the fantasy. It's not nearly as graphic as it could be, but part of me doesn't want to guess what her matured body looks like now. Mainly because I've already convinced myself I'll find out soon enough, and I want to take her in without any preconceived notions.

It may be the only good thing about not seeing her for almost a decade. I'll get to experience her for the first time all over again.

Reaching into my pocket, I pull out my pack of nicotine gum and pop one in my mouth, needing the buzz to relax my nerves. Then, I get out of the car just as she emerges from the depths of the barn.

She gazes at me cautiously, her stare sliding down my form, then back up again.

"How many?"

"Just one tonight."

Without a word, she twists on her heel and disappears inside the barn.

My heart is pounding, and I'm not even sure why anymore. Anticipation has gathered between the crevices of my bones, as if I'm gearing up to commit the worst of my crimes.

Maybe I am. Yet, I can't find it in me to give a fuck.

Just like last time, I drag the corpse out of my trunk and carry the dead woman into Molly's barn. She's dressing in her protective suit while I drop the body on the metal table.

WHERE'S MOLLY

The silence is heavy and filled with electrical currents. If I licked my thumb and held it up, I'd wield lightning in a matter of seconds. The ways I'd use that to my advantage...

The loud buzz of the hair clippers rips my thoughts straight out of the gutter and into the hands of the woman cutting off another person's hair, preparing to dismember her. She already undressed the woman, and I hadn't even realized it.

I watch her, riveted, and remembering the twenty-five-year-old girl who walked into my TV store, asking for help with her shoulders curled inward and her eyes watching over her shoulder with every step. To this moment, a woman who is so calm and standing like she's sure of herself. It's such a contrast to the version of her I once knew that I'm nearly frothing at the mouth to get to know who she is now.

She finishes shaving the woman's head, then extracts her teeth quickly and meticulously—so smoothly that it only shows her experience.

And when she begins to saw through the corpse's head, I can't help but feel my fascination with her deepening.

Unsurprisingly, I find her skillset in dismembering a person attractive.

"What did she do?" she asks after finishing removing the head.

"She sold her kid to her boyfriend. He would pay for his drug habit with her daughter's body."

She pauses, the vibrating blade an inch away from the woman's leg. She clutches the tool until her rubber gloves squeak from the force of her grip, and when she continues to stay frozen, my brows plunge, concern trickling in.

"Molly."

She jumps, just the slightest, then hurries to continue removing the woman's leg at the hip.

"Where's the boyfriend?" she questions, her tone stiff.

"With Legion. I'm sure I'll be delivering his body soon."

She nods, moving to the second leg.

"And the girl?"

"Probably at a Z location."

Her head turns just enough to give me a hint of her high cheekbones and plump lips. Redness mottles her pale flesh, darkening the light dusting of freckles on her cheeks.

"Find out for me?" she asks quietly.

Something about the young girl's situation has struck a nerve with Molly, which only further ignites the burning curiosity to know more about her past.

"I can do that," I promise, satisfying her enough to where she resumes her bloody task.

The pigs behind me are creating a ruckus, the scent of blood getting them excited.

"Is there a reason why you want me to look into her?" I question, desperate for even a crumb.

She doesn't respond. Not until she's finished completely removing the limbs from the woman's torso.

"Doesn't matter. I'd just like to know she's safe."

She's evading my question—keeping me in the dark—which only stirs the demon lurking inside my soul. A beast who doesn't like to be kept in a darkness it can't manipulate.

I already feel the blackness unleashing into my system, and my fingers crack with how hard I clench them.

The thought of anyone hurting her, especially if it was in the same way that little girl was hurt, will easily turn me into a bloodthirsty monster. The worst part is that I *know* she was hurt. I know whoever kidnapped her didn't bring her to a place that respected her body.

She may have already disposed of them. But if not, I'd love nothing more than to kill them myself.

"Molly," I warn, my tone deepening with anger.

She freezes, much like she did when I first shared the woman's crimes against her kid.

"Did the same thing happen to you?" I ask boldly.

My obsession won't let her get out of not telling me every little fucking detail about her life. About her past and all the reasons she ran to Alaska, and the reasons she decided to come back and make a living out of feeding pedophiles to her pigs.

I've held off long enough and refuse to hold back the burning questions any longer.

"It doesn't matter, Cage," she bites out, tearing the protective glasses off her face and tossing them on the table. The white teeth marks beneath her eye are brightened from the redness of her skin.

A testament to the horrors she survived.

She won't look at me as she picks up the severed head and stomps over to the pen with one monstrous pig inside and nearly launches it in.

The pig wastes no time cracking open the skull. I'm standing right beside its pen, so I shift a few feet away to avoid the spray of blood while Molly angrily marches back toward the table. I watch her silently as she repeats the process with the torso and both legs.

I've lost my patience by the time she snatches one of the arms from the nearly empty table, then stomps back toward me, preparing to throw it in one of the pens. I grab onto her bicep before she does. Whether it's instinct or because she likes to beat people with spare limbs when she's pissed, her arm whips out, and the bloody arm comes careening toward my head.

I duck out of the way, though I'm not spared from blood spattering across my face. I grab onto her wrist, meeting her searing glare.

"Did I say something to piss you off, my little ghost?" I ask wickedly.

She snarls and tugs on her arm, failing to tear it out of my grip.

She looks like she wants to run again, peering at me like an animal backed into a corner. Her flight mode is activated, and I have no fucking qualms with hunting her down.

"You have no right!" she shouts, panting heavily as she seethes at me. "You don't get to come back into my life and start demanding things from me. The only thing you get to do is bring me pig food, and then you *leave*."

The fire in her green eyes is captivating. Fuck, I'm so enthralled.

"You're breathtaking," I murmur.

She blinks at me, taken aback and speechless for several moments.

"W-what? Why would you say that?"

Because staring into her eyes is the only thing I needed, to convince myself she's everything I'll ever want for as long as oxygen invades my lungs. I knew it deep in my bones the day I met her. Even back then, my soul immediately recognized hers as its other half.

"Because I'd tell you anything," I answer. "There's not a single thing I'd be able to keep from you. Especially when you look so goddamn beautiful."

Her hand slackens, shock colored on every inch of her ethereal face.

I take advantage and slide the severed arm out of her hold. Then, I toss it across the barn and into one of the pigpens.

She glances to the side, seemingly trying to gather herself.

"You're going to find every drop of blood that went past the plastic and clean it up. This is an active crime scene that can never look like one when they're done eating."

I grin, and her stare latches onto my mouth, her own lips parting subconsciously.

"That must mean I'm not allowed to leave yet," I drawl lazily.

She wrinkles her nose in distaste at my comment, then attempts to extract her wrist from my grip again. I don't release her—*won't* release her. Holding her is too addictive, and I haven't had nearly enough.

"Let me go, Cage," she demands breathlessly, tugging her arm more insistently.

"I've already done that once," I say, tugging her into my chest roughly. Her gasp feathers across my chest, setting the muscle inside aflame. I lower my mouth to her ear, evoking a shiver that overtakes the entirety of her body. "I'm not doing it again."

"Cage," she squeaks out, even as my lips are already tracing the soft outer shell of her ear, where a dainty gold ring is pierced. Her skin is spotless from blood here, and I intend to take advantage of that. I flick my tongue against the metal, and another helpless sound emits from her throat.

And that's what makes her so goddamn exciting. She's *not* helpless, but I sure as fuck like it when she plays the part.

"We can't do this," she insists, her words airy and lacking conviction.

"Not this, either?" I query before catching the piercing between my teeth and sucking it gently.

Her other hand flies to my chest, her bloody glove covering my shirt in crimson.

I retreat just far enough to whisper, "Now we're going to need to burn that."

She swallows thickly, the sound audible yet quiet.

It seems to take her a second to gather herself, and then she's croaking, "Then take it off."

I assess her closely to ensure she's not fucking with me, but she keeps her gaze locked onto the bloody handprint over my heart. She could be lying, planning to bolt the second I release her.

Deciding that I wouldn't mind the chase, I unlock my fingers from her wrist, one digit at a time.

Her chest heaves, and my cock strains against my zipper, imagining how hard her nipples must be beneath her suit. I intend to find out.

Watching her closely, I slowly remove my leather jacket, having enough foresight to throw it away from the blood. Then, I grab the back of my collar and pull the soft fabric over my head.

Immediately, her burning stare falls to my bare chest, then onto my stomach, tracing every muscle I've worked my ass off for. The industry I work in doesn't allow for weak muscles and little strength. Criminals are my clients, and, at any moment, I may have to defend myself. There have been plenty of times when I *have* had to.

Her tongue darts out, wetting her bottom lip as she dissects every inch of my exposed flesh.

"I don't..." She licks her lips again, this time nervously. "I don't remember you having that many muscles before."

I quirk a brow. "Baby, I was twenty-seven the last time you saw me shirtless. A lot has changed since then."

"Right," she mumbles, once more distracted by the view.

I close the space between us, biting my lip to contain my devilish smile as her breath stutters from her throat.

"I want you to show me what has changed with you, but I also want to see what's the same." Her next swallow is audible. "Does that spot between your tits still get red when you come?"

I crowd into her, instigating by bumping my chest against hers and inhaling her sweet vanilla and cinnamon scent. It mingles with the unmistakable smell of copper, which only serves to make her more enticing.

Molly is painted in blood, and I want her to cover me in it, too.

She stumbles, a small whimper reaching my ears. It isn't born of fear or weakness but of a woman overcome with her emotions.

Before she can overthink all the reasons this is a bad idea, I grab the zipper at the hollow of her neck and pull down, the teeth breaking apart the only backdrop to her uneven breathing.

The material parts to reveal heaving breasts covered by a thin, white tank top. She shrugs out of it, the oversized gloves effortlessly falling off with the yellow suit. Then, it falls down her legs completely, revealing tiny black shorts and toned, long legs.

She's tall, at least five-ten, and has the most delicious curves. She's fucking perfect for me. Every little facet of her was designed just for me.

Chewing on her bottom lip, she steps out of the suit, along with her black rubber boots, and kicks them to the side.

Barefoot and defenseless, yet she stands like a trained killer, and I know her most valuable weapons are her hands.

She's fucking *beautiful*.

A loud bang from the pens disturbs the tense silence, causing Molly to startle. The pigs are demanding to be fed again.

"We're all hungry, baby. Who are you going to feed first?" I ask wickedly before gliding my tongue across my bottom lip.

I'm fucking *starving*.

She doesn't remove her challenging gaze as she deliberately steps away and toward the metal table. I can sense how predatory my own stare is, but the red flush crawling up to her cheeks indicates she doesn't mind being my prey.

She grabs the last remaining body part from the table—another arm. Then, she walks it over to one of the pens where two pigs eagerly await the last of their meal. The others are still working their way through the torso and legs.

Maintaining eye contact, she holds out the arm and drops it in, blood spraying across the hay as they tear it apart.

I stride toward her, my own blood heating as she worries her bottom lip and her hands begin to fidget.

"You know, your pets would tear you apart in seconds with all that nervous energy," I comment, amusement coloring my tone.

She narrows her eyes. "Then it's so fortunate for me that I know how to defend myself."

I grin, the act as devilish as my intentions.

I round her, sliding my chest against her back as I lean down to whisper in her ear. "You must be frightening."

"I am," she insists, though her voice is breathless, and another tremor is working its way down her spine.

I hum, reaching up to tuck a stray curl behind her ear.

Again, she shivers.

"Then show me, my little ghost."

chapter eight

MOLLY

PRESENT
2022

I have tunnel vision.

There's only a sliver of light, the small orb blurring as I process his challenging words.

Then show me.

Show him years upon years of practice that I never utilized because I refused to put myself in a situation where I'd *have* to. Yet here I am.

A dangerous man at my back demanding to see what I'm made of. The honest answer is trauma, sadness, and scars that I can't bear to look at. But I still feel them.

Just as I do the predator breathing down my neck.

I wait a few moments, each second ticking in my pulse, and then I'm twisting at the waist and sending my elbow flying toward his mouth.

He jerks back, and I only manage to clip him, but that was only a distraction. Before he can prepare for anything else, my heel smashes into his foot, causing him to stumble. Then, I'm advancing on him, keeping light on my feet as I strategically strike him in succession, meant to both keep his attention on my hands and lull him into a pattern.

I send my fists flying toward his head, which he blocks, but my foot is already hooked around his ankle, and the next second, his legs are in the air as he slams flat on his back.

I'm straddling him before he can process it, and a grunt bursts from his mouth. But he recovers quickly, flipping me onto the plastic covering before I can blink.

A breath escapes me, and I kick up my legs until my tailbone is lifted, wrapping my legs around his head to keep him at arm's length.

I squeeze my thighs tightly, and he curls his lips into a salacious smile.

"Can't say I'm mad about this development," he rasps.

Before I can respond, he grabs my sides and squeezes, hitting a ticklish spot that causes me to jump and loosen my thighs. He makes quick work of slipping his head free and flipping me onto my stomach.

I manage to make it to my knees before he bars his arm across my throat and holds my back against his front tightly. His other hand sensually glides up my stomach, stopping short of my breasts.

Though it doesn't stop my pussy from tightening in anticipation, searching for something to fill it.

"You're wound so tight, baby. Need me to help loosen you up?" he instigates, his deep voice wicked and rough, sending a tsunami of chills down my spine.

Panting, I still, my brain circulating over the different moves I could make. His hard cock is pressed against my backside, showing me just how much he's enjoying the fight.

Snarling, I send the back of my head flying into his nose, eliciting another grunt. His arm relaxes just enough for me to slip out from beneath it, spin, and tackle his ass, straddling him for a second time.

A bead of crimson trails out of his nose, yet somehow, it only makes me more ravenous. Just like my pigs, the sight of his blood makes me feral.

His hands grip either side of my hips, and he pulls me down against him as he grinds his cock against my clit, sending a shock wave of pleasure shooting up my body.

A quiet moan leaves his throat, a sound that I'm instantly swallowing as I crash my lips against his.

I know the breath was knocked out of his lungs, and I don't intend to allow him to have it back.

A growl builds in his throat and reverberates beyond my teeth, followed by a sharp nip to my bottom lip. It only makes me kiss him harder, in which he returns with tenfold the passion. His hands are plunging into my curls, fisting them tightly, using his grip on them to anchor my head and move his lips over mine however he pleases. Before I know it, he's taken over completely, and I'm helpless to stop him.

I've worked hard to defend myself against a man's touch, but one kiss from Cage is fucking paralyzing.

Just like he swore, he acts as if he's starving, devouring me as he plunges his tongue into my mouth and curls it sinfully against mine.

I'm entirely lost to him as he tears at the white tank top, ripping the fabric in half and roughly pushing it off my body. My sports bra is next to fall victim to his fiery touch, pulling it over my head and flinging it into the unknown.

Instantly, his hands are cupping my breasts, gnashing his teeth against mine.

"Let me taste," he demands roughly, his voice sounding as if his soul has been possessed by the king of hell.

I crawl up his body just enough for him to wrap his hot mouth around a nipple, his tongue swirling around the tightened bud before his teeth bite into the soft flesh.

My back bows while my hand flies into the short strands atop his head, crying out as the sting worsens.

Just when it becomes too much, he releases me only to suck my abused nipple back into his mouth, easing the pain with long, thorough licks.

The sounds coming from my throat are raspy and broken with pleasure. If my body was a kingdom, he'd be waging a celestial war against me where I'd easily crumble beneath his forces. The gods within have grown tired, and it's a relief to succumb to an inferno the devil created just for me.

Cage retreats again, and just when he begins to dish out another command, blood splatters across my face, neck, and side, and across his chest.

A startled scream leaves my throat, and I look over to see Chili tearing into the thigh of the butchered woman.

Mouth open in shock, I turn back to Cage, only to find him peering up at me with an emotion I don't know how to name. But what I do know is that it's powerful, unrestrained, and unlike anything I've seen before.

"You're fucking incredible," he says, his tone hushed.

Instinctively, I peer down at myself, where trails of blood paint my breasts, the valley between them, and my stomach.

I should be horrified, yet when I lift my stare back to Cage, I feel anything but. My clit throbs and arousal gathers deep in my core. The urge to grind against his cock is overwhelming, but I refrain for now.

Something wet splatters onto my face, then trails down my cheek before a crimson bead drips off my jaw and lands on my breast, all of which Cage watches intently.

His hands cup my hips, and he squeezes tightly. Feeling invigorated, I brush a black-painted nail across my nipple, my mouth parting in wonder as his stare drops to my chest. His eyes darken like a forest fire within, blackening with a hunger as potent as the flames. I've never been so ready to walk into a wildfire.

Teasingly, I smear the crimson over the swell and down to my ribs, where a macabre bird with its wings wired onto its body is tattooed.

The black-and-gray artwork snags his attention for a moment, but inevitably, he refocuses on my finger once it reaches the waistband of my shorts.

"Stand up," he rasps, anticipation gleaming in his eyes. He doesn't seem inclined to stand with me. Instead, he props up on his elbows and reclines back on them. He stares up at me with a reverence that can only be captured by the human eye. Nothing—not even our own hands—could recreate that image and do it any justice.

I do as he says, though my knees tremble and threaten to crumble as tragically as if they were an ancient monument.

"Take it all off, baby. I need to see everything," he commands hoarsely.

My heart pounds in my chest as I hook my thumbs beneath the fabric of my shorts and panties and slide them down my thighs. I kick them to the side where the rest of my clothes lay.

Insecurity and forced confidence battle for dominance. From his position, I know he can see the scar on my hip—a perfect imprint of teeth from when Dad bit me years ago. Sadly, it isn't the only bite mark forever marring my flesh. They're also on my biceps, stomach, thighs, and of course, my face.

He left them everywhere, sinking his teeth so far into me that I passed out from the pain. Most of the bite marks eventually faded, except the ones now on full display, crimson smeared over them.

"Jesus Christ," Cage groans. "Sit on my fucking face, Molly."

My stomach twists as I step over him, butterflies unleashing within as I crouch over his face, keeping my feet flat on the floor.

Cage was the last man I slept with, and something about that is utterly embarrassing. I've gotten intimate with plenty of vibrators throughout the years, though I could never muster the courage to let another man touch me again.

Nerves eat me alive, but the wet, hot slide of Cage's tongue along my slit has me forgetting exactly what I was anxious about. And his unrestrained moan that follows has my stomach tightening.

My mouth falls open as bliss consumes me, beginning at my core and spreading out to the tips of my fingers and toes.

"Oh," I breathe, my eyes rolling into the back of my head as his tongue spears inside me, circling around my inner walls.

A growl builds in his chest and his arms circle around my thighs, anchoring me onto his face. My legs tremble violently, once more threatening to give out on me. They're fucking useless when it comes to him.

"Fuck, baby, you taste so good," he groans against me, the vibrations sending another wave of bliss throughout me.

"Cage," I moan just as his tongue flicks at my clit. The breath in my lungs gets lost somewhere on the way out, taking a wrong turn and depriving me of precious oxygen.

I need to breathe, but I need to come in Cage's mouth so much more.

Lips parted and brows pinched, I peer down at Cage to find his heated stare already locked on mine.

The butterflies in my stomach become volatile. They're unable to handle Cage eating me alive—whether it's because they're frightened that they'll be devoured next, or if it's because they know that by the time he's done, I'll be in ruins and there will be nothing left of me. No home for them to live.

He sucks my clit into his mouth, his teeth grazing the sensitive flesh and sending goosebumps scattering across my skin. Already, I feel an orgasm building low in the pit of my stomach, and while I want nothing more than to lose myself in it, I don't know that I'm ready for the aftermath.

"Don't stop," I choke out despite myself.

He sucks harder, showing me that stopping is the last thing on his mind. Then, he releases my thighs and flattens his palms on my stomach before gliding them up to my breasts and cupping them roughly, smearing the blood further across my flesh.

His fingers pluck my nipples, and once again, I feel his teeth graze my clit. The threat is imminent, as if to say that if I don't come soon, I will be punished.

It's a warning that I have no choice but to heed.

His tongue continues to work me, and after a few more seconds, I feel myself approaching the mouth of a volcano, where I'll peer inside, only to be blown to smithereens by the catastrophic eruption.

His tongue flicks, and I'm leaning over the fiery mouth. It flicks again, and I'm completely decimated.

Vaguely, I hear the scream erupting from my mouth as violently as the orgasm washing over me. I think I cry out Cage's name, but at this moment, the only thing I can be sure of is that I'll never be the same once I come down.

Bright bursts of color explode in my otherwise blackened vision, and the entirety of my body seizes against his face. My hips gyrate mindlessly, where his tongue is still flattened against me.

By the time I come down, it feels like I've traveled light years and back. Like I have an entirely new lifetime of experiences.

Panting heavily, I open my eyes, though my vision is still blurred and unreliable. Cage is slipping out from beneath me, and the heat of his body envelops me a moment later, his front pressing into my back. Despite the warm air blowing through the open barn doors, I shiver.

"I have bad news," he whispers darkly.

"What's that?" I croak.

His hot breath fans across the shell of my ear, and the effect is no worse than when a predator is watching you and there's nowhere to run.

"I'm still hungry." His voice is as deep as a mountain and as rough as the rock it's made of.

My bottom lip finds itself between my teeth, and I clamp down until I feel a sharp sting.

I have no fucking idea what to say to that. All I know is that he could take whatever he wants from me, and I would gladly give it to him.

His rough palms fan across either side of my hips, leaving tiny little embers in his wake.

"I need more," he rasps.

"You can have me," I whisper.

Dangerous words to say to a predator, but it's been so long since I've felt this alive.

In response, I hear the clink of his metal belt buckle, followed by the sound of it pulling free from the loops of his black jeans.

My muscles swell with anticipation. For a moment, I'm transported back to when I was twenty-five with the same domineering presence crowding over me. And while it was terrifying, it was equally fucking thrilling.

Soft leather brushes across my neck, barely giving me time to register it before it's looped through the buckle and being pulled tight. My eyes round, and the startled sound from my throat scarcely escapes before it's constricted, allowing me just enough air to stay conscious.

Then, the telltale sign of metal teeth breaking apart follows. What little breath I have comes out in short, excited bursts. Fabric shuffles, and I glance over my shoulder to see him kneeling behind me, completely naked.

"You shouldn't be real," I croak.

He was beautiful nine years ago, but now, he's otherworldly. Surely, a mirage I've constructed in my brain after too many years of isolation. His body is made up of muscles packed beneath tattooed flesh. Solid, but lean. A perfect combination that creates a masterpiece da Vinci fucking wishes he had invented.

He reaches forward and brushes his thumb gently over the teeth prints on my cheekbone.

"I have a feeling you shouldn't be alive. Yet here you are." His stare is affectionate, though it borders on obsession. "And I'm so fucking lucky that you are."

I don't know if I'd ever consider myself lucky, but at this moment, I think I feel the same.

Then, he's tugging on the belt around my neck and roughly hauling me back into his chest. I gasp, my brain slow to process as my body conforms to his demands without thought. The pressure of his palm against my lower back follows, encouraging it to bow until I'm curved into a perfect C, my ass and the crown of my head pressed against him. His other hand cups the underside of my jaw, keeping me firmly in place.

He stares down at me with a savage expression, his mouth poised above mine.

"I love how easily you bend for me."

"Just don't expect me to break," I counter breathlessly.

He hums, as if that's yet to be determined. "But that's my favorite part," he croons against my lips.

His cock teases my entrance, slipping through my pussy with ease.

"Are you on birth control?"

"Yes," I breathe. "Though you should've asked sooner in case I wasn't."

He chuckles wickedly. "I still wouldn't have cared."

Before I can muster a response, he's pushing inside me. My mouth drops open, and he's licking my bottom lip, the act nearly as erotic as him splitting me in half. I'm trembling in his hold, and when he's halfway in, he pauses.

"Can't take it?" he asks devilishly.

"N—"

He drives himself completely inside me, not bothering to wait for my answer.

A choked scream greets his savage smile, burning pain at being stretched so suddenly taking over for a moment. But then he begins to roll his hips, and I'm reminded why he was impossible to forget after one night.

"I forgot to mention, you don't have a choice." He places a sweet kiss on my lips, something that would be a direct contrast to his words had it not felt condescending.

"Asshole," I choke out, though the word is weak as he easily dominates my pussy. My attention is already hyper-fixating on the intense pleasure radiating from between my thighs.

"Careful with the words that fall out of your mouth, baby. I might get confused and claim that, too."

"You wouldn't," I growl.

He pauses again, and his expression portrays utter conviction. "I would do anything to show you that you're mine."

Somewhere between the beginning of his statement and the end, my heart worked its way inside my throat. I'm unable to speak or swallow, only stare at him in shock, for which he takes as confirmation to keep going as if he didn't just rock me to my core.

I blink, and he's fucking me again, tightening the belt around my throat until black spots swarm my vision, though careful not to cut off my oxygen completely.

This time, he sets a steady yet thorough pace, ensuring to watch my reactions closely. Within half a minute, he's targeted a sensitive spot inside me and focuses on stroking right there until my eyes are fluttering.

It shouldn't be so easy for someone to be able to pick me apart like that, but there's not a single inch of me that gives a fuck right now. I wouldn't even be capable if I tried.

"Cage," I moan, my brows furrowing as the sensations become too intense. I strain against his hold, attempting to curl my hips forward, if only so it gives me a moment to fucking breathe.

"Where're you going?" he barks, bringing me back to him. Then, he laughs, the sound savage. "Did you really think I couldn't break you when you can barely take me?" he questions arrogantly.

"I'm taking you just fine," I bite out, my eyes threatening to cross when he hits a spot that feels otherworldly.

"Then why are you trying to run away?" he whispers wickedly.

I want to slap him, but I'm so overwhelmed by the pleasure that I can hardly formulate a snappy response.

"Fuck," I cry, squeezing my eyes shut as he fucks me harder.

"I know you can do better, baby. Let me see you take my cock like a good little slut."

A sharp moan pours from my throat, followed by his name.

Once more, he's licking along the seam of my lips, as if to taste his name on my tongue. Just as his mouth covers mine, I feel a warm liquid splatter against my chest.

I flinch, my brain beginning to split and latch on to the fact that I'm being covered in more blood. The corner of his mouth tics up, and he releases my jaw—though his hold on the belt keeps me in place—and flattens his palm against my stomach. He groans into my mouth while he smears the liquid up to my breasts.

While my instinct is to recoil from it, Cage only fucks me harder, seeming to get off on my body being covered in it.

It should disturb me. This entire situation is beyond fucked up. Yet, it becomes impossible to feel a damn thing outside of the orgasm looming just beyond the horizon.

Cries pour from my throat, and he swallows them all, proving just how starved he is.

"Don't stop," I gasp, my voice strained. "Fuck, Cage, please."

His lips retreat from mine, trailing up along my cheek. I lose all coherent thought, my surroundings becoming disjointed and incomprehensible. The pleasure is like a disease, shutting down my nervous system and taking control. I'm a puppet to the infection, and there's nothing I can do but succumb.

Time stills, and I shatter just as he releases the belt, sending blood rushing to my head, intensifying the explosion detonating throughout my body.

My bones liquefy, and the muscles surrounding them seize. Vaguely, I feel rather than hear the broken cry leave my throat. A sound that quickly morphs into a scream when I feel something sharp bite into my face.

Directly over the scar beneath my eye.

He groans against me, flesh trapped between his teeth, and his body stills before flooding my pussy with his cum.

Burning pain battles with the euphoria rolling through me in harsh waves. It becomes so overwhelming; it feels like I'm on the verge of combusting.

"Cage!" I squeal, and finally, he releases my cheek.

The plunge back to earth is dizzying, more so when he drops his hand from the belt, allowing me to straighten.

My back aches from being in the same position for so long, so I drop forward, catching myself on both hands as I pant heavily.

Fingers brush over my back, and then his thumbs dig into my tailbone, instantly relieving some pressure.

"Jesus, way to remind me I'm not twenty-five anymore," I groan.

His soft chuckle reaches my ears, and I work up the nerve to straighten again. I cock my head over my shoulder, meeting a stare that hasn't waned in intensity.

His thumb brushes against my scar gently. "I hope you think of me next time you look in the mirror."

Insecurity rises, and I'm almost embarrassed that he's focusing on my trauma so plainly laid out on my face. I've always hated my scar, and something inside me rebels against him finding a way to make me accept it. Especially seeing as part of me wants to let him.

I narrow my eyes. "That wasn't cool. Don't do that again."

His smile widens, not the least bit ashamed.

"It didn't stop you from coming all over my cock, did it?"

"Almost."

A massive lie.

One he clearly doesn't believe by the way his lip crooks higher.

I expect a smart-ass response, but instead, he leans forward and places a kiss over the bite mark. I'm taken aback when he pulls out of me, distracting me from the surprises he keeps throwing my way. Now that I'm firmly back in reality, I'm realizing once again that I'm covered in the woman's blood.

"Let's go shower. Show me around the rest of the house while you're at it," he suggests casually.

My mouth pops open. "You—what? No. You're not coming to my house again. You haven't been invited!"

He stands and shoots me a cocky grin.

"Baby, if you keep playing hard to get, I'll fucking move in. Now, let's clean up and shower before I decide I'm hungry again."

He picks up his jeans and begins to slide them on.

And all I can do is kneel on the floor with my mouth agape and stare at his bare ass being covered.

I hate that it feels like it's too soon.

chapter nine

MOLLY

FOURTEEN YEARS AGO
2008

It's fucking hot outside, but even the suffocating summer air can't deter the bone-deep chill washing through me, a reaction that only standing in front of my childhood home can evoke.

The *home* I was sold from.

It's a small, yellow two-story house with missing shingles and dirty siding. It'd be considered cute and quaint in a suburb if it wasn't so broken down. If it fostered a happy family with loving parents.

However, in Reaper Canyon, a town that's seen more drug overdoses than gender reveal parties, the only thing that's been born in this shithole is half of my fucking nightmares. The other half were bred by Francesca and her filthy brother.

"This is so going to get you killed," I mutter aloud.

At any moment, my parents could stumble out the door, lay eyes on me, and call Francesca.

I'd be forced to leave Layla behind.

I don't have much of a heart left to break, but I'd give her the last piece of me if it meant she'd escape this house of horrors.

It took me two days of hitchhiking and bus rides to get here. An adventure that was almost as terrifying as escaping that house. I covered up my scar with dirt and lied to the drivers, telling them my car broke down on the way home from college, and I needed to get home to my sick mom.

By some grace of God, or Zeus, or whoever, the second driver I came across was a sweet old lady who offered me money. Enough to buy a hoodie from the thrift store, get something to eat, and take a bus the rest of the way home.

I got lucky and can only pray that it's still on my side.

Steeling my spine, I trudge through the useless, rickety chain-link fence surrounding the house, and head toward the back. My feet kick through overgrown grass that nearly reaches above my knees, the blades getting tangled around my worn shoes.

The back door leads directly into the laundry room. I can't remember the last time Mom or Dad even smelt detergent, let alone used it to clean clothes, so it's a guaranteed area of the house that they won't be in.

Dad's car is parked outside. There aren't strange cars like there usually were in the past, so I'm fairly confident they don't have any of their dirty friends over. The only thing I need to worry about is my parents seeing me before I see them.

Adrenaline courses through my bloodstream, amping my heart rate up to catastrophic levels. Eight months ago, I would've never been capable of this. Now, I don't know that I'm capable of feeling anything for anyone outside of my baby sister.

Not even for myself.

Breath stutters out of my lungs, and my lips are bone dry as I silently open the back door. I only crack it far enough to allow my body to fit through. Once it reaches the halfway point, the hinges start creaking.

The house is eerily silent, causing the hairs on my nape to stand on end. Typically, there's a TV playing cartoons in the background—for my dad's viewing pleasure, not Layla's. Or my mom screaming at the top of her lungs about what a lazy piece of shit my father is and how they have no money for their heroin because of it.

He had no problem yelling back and definitely didn't have an issue with raising his hand to her. She'd walk away with bruises, and he'd storm out the front door to go score them some more drugs, which resulted in them owing more people money.

They were dirt poor—until they sold me, of course.

Working to swallow, I creep over the pile of dirty clothes discarded haphazardly on the rotting, filthy, white linoleum floor.

I peek around the corner into the filthy kitchen. Aqua blue cupboard doors sag open, unable to close anymore. Dishes are piled in the rusting sink with flies buzzing above them, remnants of food and mold caked onto the steel and cutlery. They're also scattered across the peeling countertops, along with several opened bean and soup cans.

I balk at the awful stench. When I lived here, I grew used to it. Except now, the rot and lingering cigarette smoke bleached into the wallpaper is all I can smell. I, at least, tried to keep it clean.

Covering my nose, I make my way through the kitchen and plant myself against the wall next to the entrance of the living room.

Slowly, I peek around the corner, finding it empty. Sweat gathers along my hairline and creeps down my spine.

Everything about this scenario is unusual. And that makes me really fucking nervous.

Fuck, is Layla even here?

If she's not, I don't know what I'll do. I have no resources to find her. I have nothing.

Fucking nothing.

Panic begins to circulate into my system, a dangerous cocktail when mixed with the adrenaline.

But I can't lose my mind right now. Not yet.

"Keep it together, Molly," I whisper.

Inhaling what's supposed to be a calming breath, but is only toxic fumes, I charge through the empty living room and toward the stairs. My footsteps are silent atop the putrid green carpet covering the room, all the way up the steps and along the short hallway.

I peek into the room to my right first—Layla's nursery. It has a rickety crib inside, the cot within stained, sans a sheet, and with a threadbare blanket.

Relief overtakes me, and tears spring to my eyes, flooding my sinuses and throat until I nearly choke on them.

"Layla," I squeak, my voice splitting like dry wood.

Blonde hair spills around her like a halo while she slumbers. It's grown longer since I've last seen her. Her cheeks are still too hollow for my liking, but at least she's breathing. And right now, that's the only thing that matters.

I sniffle as I hurry toward her, praying to God she remembers me. I've been gone for eight months, which is far too long when she's so young. She's only a year old now and likely won't recognize my face anymore.

"Layla," I whisper, gently shaking her shoulder.

Long, blonde lashes splay across her cheeks, which are also paler than I'd like.

"Layla," I call again, glancing over my shoulder to ensure no one is coming.

Her eyes flutter, and then she gives me those big, beautiful blue eyes. Pretty much the only good thing that came from our mother.

"Hey, sweet baby. It's Molly. Your big sister," I coo sweetly.

She peers up at me silently, as if trying to figure out who I am. She was only four months old when I was taken, so I don't expect her to know me. I just hope she can find it in her to trust me.

"Hi, my sweet girl," I whisper, brushing away a blonde hair from her eyes.

Her arms rise, and instantly, I'm cradling her against me.

The tears bubble over, spilling down my cheeks in rivers, and it's almost impossible to breathe. I've been dreaming about this very moment for eight long, torturous months, and it almost doesn't feel real.

Like any second, I will wake up in that bed in Francesca's house, Rocco breathing over me.

Just like that, I'll lose her again.

I don't know if I'd survive it.

"Da da da da," she blabbers quietly.

"Shh, baby, we gotta be—"

"I knew you were going to show your ugly face here."

The sharp voice is like a whip cracking against my back. My spine snaps straight, and I pivot on my heel quick enough to cause me to stumble.

My heart hammers painfully against my chest as I take in the source of all my pain. The man who was supposed to love me but could only ever hurt me. And one of the last faces I saw before that cloth covered my mouth, and I woke up in a nightmare worse than anything my brain could conjure up.

"Hey, Dad," I greet nervously, the tremor in my voice betraying how terrified I am.

He takes a menacing step forward, prompting me to retreat immediately.

His gray, greasy hairs stand haphazardly on end, and though his eyes are full of hatred and disbelief, it's clear he's just woken up. He's wearing his dirty button-up work shirt, with *Raymond* stitched onto the left breast pocket.

He's a mechanic, and *of course,* it's time for him to go to work.

"W-where's Mom?" I choke out, my gaze ping-ponging between his menacing stare and the hallway behind him.

His lip curls. "Dead."

I blink, more shocked by his declaration than I expected. Maybe because she's survived so much abuse from my father and other men, it seemed like she was indestructible. Or because there were so many nights where I laid awake, praying for her death, and it never came.

I'm surprised.

But not fucking sad.

"How?"

"Overdose."

"Let me guess, from the drugs you bought with all the money you made from selling me?" I snap.

His grin is full of intentions as rotten and black as his teeth.

"Died a couple weeks ago. Dumb bitch got too excited and injected herself with some strong shit we ain't ever had before," he clips. Then, he chuckles, the sound raspy and wet. "And now you're back. Rocco called yesterday lookin' for ya. Promised me 'nother fifty-K if I let him know when you showed up."

My heart drops, another shot of panic torpedoing through my insides, landing in the pit of dread welling in my stomach.

I need to get the fuck out of here *now*.

"Whad'ya do? Give 'em bad sex or som'n'?" he asks nastily.

I narrow my eyes. I can't even be insulted. He talks as if it was my choice to be enslaved and groomed to be sold to a disgusting sick fuck. Like I did the family a fucking favor.

"Ya know, I may not call 'im. I might just have to find me some different people this time 'round. Police have been investigatin' me. Think I had somethin' to do with that whole shitshow with you in the gas station." A loud laugh bursts out of him. "Did you know they can wipe people from security footage? Don't know what kind of genius they got on their hands, but they made you look fuckin' crazy. Me and Louis weren't even in 'em! Every day I turn on the news, they're talkin' 'bout you running from ghosts."

My mouth drops while he cackles loudly. They wiped my kidnappers from the footage? I had hoped to God those cameras were recording, only it feels like a punch to the gut to hear that they manipulated it.

"Only reason they're on my ass is 'cause of that fucking asshole clerk making a statement against me. I'd hoped they'd kill his ass, too, but they said it'd cost me since he ain't got nothin' on us. And, well, he looks just as crazy as you, so he ain't worth the cash. Police don't have shit on me." He ends that statement with a smart-ass grin.

"They will," I spit through clenched teeth. "You fucking sold me!"

Layla huddles into my neck, upset by the obvious tension between Dad and me. I bounce her in my arms, hoping to keep her calm, yet knowing it's likely useless.

"You was useless around here anyway! Tryna steal mine and your mom's baby. That's all you cared about. Layla, Layla, Layla. That's where all your money went instead of paying us rent. Just spendin' our money and living here for free!"

An argument forms on my tongue, building to a monument as tall as fucking Giza, but it's not worth it.

I need to get me and Layla out of here as soon as possible before my father makes good on his promise and calls Rocco here. Or someone worse.

"The only person you have to worry about is yourself," I hiss. "Layla and I will be gone."

Another step, and his face morphs from barely human to demonic.

"As far as I see it, she's still in my custody. Which means she goes where *I* want her to go. You were a pretty penny in my pocket the first time, but you two together? I'll get a fuck of a lot more, no?"

My upper lip curls in disgust, and a hatred unlike anything I've felt before consumes me. It's so potent that the only way for my body to process it is to shake violently.

It's not just wrath.

It's pure fucking murderous rage.

To sell me is one thing.

But to sell a *baby?*

I have no words for how fucking evil that is. No words to describe how decrepit a soul must be to condemn a child so willingly in such a horrific way.

My vision grows spotty with fury, and I set Layla down in the crib as calmly as possible. She lets out a cry of protest, raising her arms and squeezing her tiny hands for me to pick her up again.

"I'll be right here, baby. It's okay," I assure her gently, even though my words tremble.

That doesn't soothe her. But more than anything, I need to get this vile man away from her.

She doesn't deserve to witness what I plan on doing to him. No child should ever see that.

"Let's go downstairs and discuss this. Otherwise, I'll call Rocco myself and tell him you kidnapped me back."

He scoffs out a laugh. "You think they'll believe that?"

"You're right," I agree mockingly. "You're too stupid. I'll tell them I escaped, and you tried selling me off to another fucking pedophile ring. They'll still take us, then they'll kill you, too."

Suddenly, his mouth twists into a scathing snarl. He glances up and down my form, his muddy brown eyes filled with loathing. Silently, he jerks his head toward the hallway, then stalks off toward the staircase.

"I'll be right back, pretty girl," I murmur absently, white noise flooding my brain.

There is no clear thought in my head, just a loud ringing. Woodenly, I follow him, gently shutting Layla's door behind me. I'm not sure if she can climb out of her crib or not, but she's still too little to reach the doorknob. She won't be able to get out.

I reach the top of the steps and stare down them blankly, understanding that he's waiting for me and what this discussion is going to come down to, yet unable to find a conscience to stop myself.

I exhale and make my way down the stairs, finding my dad waiting in the kitchen. He's leaning against the counter, sipping out of the same mug he's always drank out of. Coffee and a shot of Jack Daniels.

"Your mom used to make me lunch for work. Gotta admit, I miss 'er for that, at least," he comments casually, finishing with a chuckle.

He's pretending that we will be engaging in a civil conversation, but he's as tense as I am. He thinks he's going to win, and for the second time in my life, I'll wake up in the back of a stranger's van.

This time, with my baby sister beside me.

"What is it you think you're goin' to do, hm?" he questions, amusement glimmering in his dead eyes. "You think you can hurt me?"

He laughs while I edge toward a tiny round table in the corner of the room, where Mom used to sit every morning, smoking a cigarette and drinking her own coffee and whiskey.

"I think I've faced men far scarier than you and survived."

"You sure about that?" he challenges.

His smile dims, and his gaze slides over to the scar beneath my eye. The very one he gave me when I was ten years old.

I remember that night vividly. Back then, he still had teeth, and he lost his mind to whatever drug he injected into his veins.

He left them all over my body when he raped me.

He, on the other hand, has no recollection of it. If it wasn't for my mom bearing witness to it, he'd be convinced it was someone else. She was also drugged and too delirious to stop him.

Afterward, when Dad attempted to deny it, that was the only moment Mom stood up for me by screaming at him for hurting me. Not because I was assaulted, but because she'd have to explain the bite on my face to the school. The others covering my body could be hidden, just not that one.

Later, she spit on me for trying to steal her husband. As if he wasn't my own father.

Ultimately, it became the result of a play date gone wrong with a nonexistent cousin who had aggression issues. Despite that, it didn't look like a kid's bite; the school believed them, and it was never addressed again.

I cock my head, leaning against the table behind me and resting my linked hands on top. "Do you think a bite to the face is the worst thing that's been done to me? I've lived through so much worse, *Dad*."

He sets his cup on the crowded countertop, and his features slacken into a monstrous expression. Chin dropped, mouth hanging open, and an evil glare beneath his eyebrows.

"Not yet, ya haven't," he threatens darkly.

He edges toward me casually, as if he isn't planning my death. Not by his hands, of course. But by the highest bidder's. While he snorts, smokes, and injects the only form of happiness he's ever felt. Until escaping reality becomes eternal.

Just like it did with Mom.

Behind me sits her discarded mug. It's likely been there since she died—forgotten.

Just like her.

I'd like to think this is Mom extending the hand she never extended when she was alive. A peace offering, maybe.

Subtly, I loop my finger through the handle, and he pauses a few feet away. Right out of arm's length, making me sigh.

If only she gave that much of a shit.

Time stands still, except for the consistent beat inside my chest, reminding me that I'm still alive. I'm still fighting.

Then, he lunges, and I'm swinging, the mug in my hand cracking against his temple. Ceramic shatters, and a shard cuts into my palm.

He roars, and his arm swings out wildly, attempting to grab ahold of me. But if there's one thing I learned about people with more artificial chemicals in their bodies than blood—they have no fucking aim.

I duck and tackle him to the floor while he's unbalanced, the back of his head smacking off it harshly. A curse flies out of his mouth and he's grappling to get a leg up so he can flip me over. But I'm already on top of him, a piece of the mug gripped between my fingers and pressed against his jugular.

It only lasts half a second, and he's carelessly knocking away my hand before sending a fist flying toward my face. Just barely, I flinch to the side, his knuckles clipping my cheek and sending a shooting pain throughout my face.

But my desperation outweighs the sting, and I'm rushing to get my knees over his biceps. Several times, he deters me, nearly throwing me off just for me to crawl back onto him. Finally, I send my own fist into his nose, allowing me to stun him long enough to get his arms pinned beneath my knees, putting all my weight onto him.

I press the piece back into his jugular again, the shard having already shredded my own skin from the struggle.

"Make one fucking move, and I'll slit your throat, asshole," I spit through heavy pants.

My hand trembles against him, my vision narrowing until all I see is his disgusting face, contorted in rage with gray scruff covering his jaw.

"You're a pathetic man," I snarl. "And there isn't a single soul on this planet that will care when you're gone."

He laughs, and his rotten breath fans across my face. I dig the sharp end deeper, a bead of blood blooming from the tip.

"That don't matter to me, baby. Come on, you know better than that. Even if I was a fucking stand-up citizen, I'd go down in history like everybody else. Forgotten. My name carved in some stupid gravestone that people pass by and don't look twice at. And ya know what? The same thing will happen to you."

"Yeah, you're right," I say, my voice breathless and trembling. "But at least when I go down, I'll be able to say I took as many of you sick fucks as I could with me."

Another full belly laugh releases from his throat, though the desperation is evident. He doesn't want to die, and at any moment, he's going to renew his fight.

So, I make a quick decision and slice the opposite side of his throat. He'll bleed out eventually, but it won't be over before I'm ready.

His eyes widen, and his mouth flops while he chokes on his own blood. Blood that spurts onto my face, neck, and chest.

"Fucking bitch!"

Uncaring, I lean forward until his eyes find their way to mine, his pupils little pinpoints.

I shake my head. "No. You don't get the privilege of seeing me while you die."

Dropping the ceramic, I cup his face between my palms and place my thumbs over his eyes.

"No, no, no!" he shouts, though the words are garbled. His fingers wrap around my wrists, attempting to pull them away. But the blood loss has made him weak, and he fails miserably.

It takes a few seconds of pushing until I feel his eyes pop. His answering scream is loud, broken, and full of agony. It's a sound I've grown accustomed to with other girls in Francesca's house. Before, it shattered my heart when I heard it. Now, I feel nothing.

Crimson puddles in the craters of his pulverized eyes, flooding my hands, and down either side of his face. A sea of red.

I chuckle aloud. "Moses probably wouldn't appreciate me calling your face the Red Sea, huh?" I laugh again, the sound hoarse and broken. "Then again, he probably isn't appreciating any of this."

I don't stop until I've smashed them into his puny brain and his struggles cease.

The earth got a little cleaner today.

His hands drop from my arms, and as he goes completely limp, so do I. I just... deflate. Like his eyeballs, I suppose.

That thought wrings another tired giggle out of me.

I'm covered in blood, sweat, and probably other shit I don't want to know about. My heart is racing, and my lungs are incredibly tight.

Killing... killing is *a lot* of fucking work.

Then, my thoughts spiral, and panic overtakes me. How the fuck am I going to cover this up?

"Shit," I whisper, dropping my head.

Thankfully, the neighbors are drug addicts, too, and there were many nights when they were in screaming matches that rivaled Mom and Dad's. Our struggle shouldn't raise any of their concerns, and even if it did, I doubt they'd be kind enough to call the police.

As for his job, it's not unusual for Dad to not show up without warning. He's lost many jobs over the years, primarily due to him going on binges. Sometimes for weeks at a time. They might call for a week, but eventually, they'll give up.

Same for his friends—they don't bother coming over unless he's offering them drugs.

Raymond Devereaux doesn't have anyone that actually gives a shit about him.

But he is in the public eye now.

Francesca used to turn on the TV and show me all the news reports and search parties after I was kidnapped. She would laugh and laugh about how many people were looking for me.

"Look at aaalll those people. And not a single one will find you."

She found that funny.

And now, I need to ensure that's exactly what happens. They can never find me. They can never know I came back here.

That couple—Latoya and Devin—might talk to the media. Claim they had me in their house. But they'll never be able to prove it, and eventually, speculation will become just that.

"No evidence," I whisper. "There can't be any evidence."

My DNA is all over this house. Finding pieces of my hair or fingerprints on every surface wouldn't be out of the ordinary.

However, on a dead body? That would be catastrophic.

I inhale deeply and then release it slowly, feeling my brain switch off once more.

No one is looking for him yet. I have time to clean up, get Layla situated, and then dispose of his body.

After, I'll take Layla out of here and never look back.

"What to do with you," I wonder aloud, heading for the limited cleaning supplies beneath the sink, racking my brain and trying to remember the crime documentaries I've seen Mom watch and if any of them ever talked about getting rid of a body.

"Melting him?" I ask myself under my breath. "No. Too messy, and I don't even know the proper chemicals. Can't bury him or put him in a lake. That *always* gets people caught."

My mind turns over idea after idea while I wrap his body in garbage bags, rejecting them all for one reason or another.

And just as I begin to scrub the floor, I remember one episode I had seen. A proverbial light bulb illuminates, and I pause as I think it over.

"Pig farm," I whisper, a slight grin curling my lips.

And I know just where to find one.

chapter ten

MOLLY

PRESENT
2022

"If I would've known that you were going to throw yourself all over me in the shower, I would've directed you to the guest bathroom," I mutter, pulling a clean white tank top over my head.

He cocks a brow, unimpressed. "At which point did I give the indication that I'd keep my hands to myself? We'll play it back, and I'll redo that part so you're not confused anymore."

I roll my eyes.

"I'm not confused," I deny vehemently, shooting him an annoyed look.

Yet, I am.

I'm confused *and* a fucking liar.

He wears only his boxers—pretty much the only article of clothing that didn't get dirty. His shirt is a lost cause, leaving him with his black jeans and leather jacket, but regardless, he'll likely go home smelling like a pigpen. It takes a special kind of soap to get it out, but I won't divulge that information, purely because I'm irritated with him.

Even more, I'm angry he's not a sensible person who carries extra clothes on hand. His body is downright distracting, making it extremely hard to remember why I'm annoyed.

Right. Because he fucked me in the shower again and reminded me that sex can actually be... *so* good. It took years to forget that after the first time we met. And now I've relapsed and become addicted all over again.

Fucker.

Keeping my back to him, I pump a few dollops of lotion into my hand and start slathering it over my hands, arms, and chest. His eyes are like two little lasers burning into me, but I do my best to ignore him.

It was just sex.

That's it.

"You're about to kick me out," he surmises from behind me. I jump, not expecting his voice to be right at my goddamn back.

"What else would we do? Play ponies and have a pillow fight?" I snap.

I sound defensive. I *am* defensive.

Tension is clustered in my muscles like it has nowhere else to go.

Gritting my teeth, I sit on the edge of the bed and force myself to meet his probing stare. It's not angry like I had expected. Or annoyed, even. No. He looks fucking amused.

He bends at the knees, lowering himself until I'm peering down at him with an incredulous stare.

"I've been dying to know who you are, Molly. Is that so wrong?"

Is he fucking with me? It's incredibly wrong. It's literally the worst thing he could ask me for. To *know* me? That would be willingly inviting him into my life, and I've made damn sure to turn my insides into a crowded room, with no space for anyone.

"Yes," I bite. "You know what my pussy feels like wrapped around you. That's more than most could say. At least, those who are still alive."

He hums, and a darkness passes over his green eyes, turning them into a shadowy, dreary forest. "So, you're telling me that there are others out there who have this knowledge and are still breathing?"

A few months ago, after finally feeling ready to face them after all these years, I had asked Legion to investigate the men in that house and see if any were still alive. After researching, he'd said all of them were dead. Except one.

Kenny Mathers.

He's very rich and well-protected. Unlike most buyers who came around only for the Culling, he frequented the house often.

I overheard Francesca telling Rocco that Kenny was interested in buying me specifically, which is why he couldn't seem to stay away. From the house, and from me.

His money and elitism have kept him safe all these years, allowing him to go off-grid altogether. He hasn't been seen in the public eye since not long after I escaped.

Admittedly, I hadn't been ready to face him, though I did make Legion aware of who he was and what he did. If my boss has done anything about it, I'm not sure. I've been too chickenshit to ask.

"Only one that I know of, but who even knows if that's still the case. Regardless, don't kill anyone on my behalf. Fucking me a few times doesn't make you my hero."

He cocks his head, appearing unfazed by my demand. "What's his name?"

I sigh. "Why does it matter?"

His expression is serious, not an iota of amusement remaining in his stare.

"I want to be the only man on this entire fucking planet that knows what you feel like. And if I'm sharing this knowledge with a single soul still walking this earth, then I will be removing them from it."

I can only blink at him, speechless for a few beats. Despite that, my stomach is a cesspool of restless butterflies, and I feel my heart beginning to soften.

His words aren't terrifying—but my reaction is.

"You're being ridiculous."

"I could be."

"You're not killing anyone on my behalf."

"I will."

"I'm not arguing with you about this, Cage."

"Then don't."

I sigh again, my shoulders slumping. I'm emotionally spent for the night, and I have no energy to convince him to keep his murdering hands to himself.

The prospect of him killing the remaining man from Francesca's house doesn't bother me—but his reasoning does. I don't want him to do it for *me*. Because he harbors any type of emotion for me. I'd rather he just snuff him out from the planet for being a monster and leave it at that.

"What is it you want from me?" I groan, sliding my hand down my face in exasperation.

"As many pieces as you're willing to give for the night."

I drop my hand and gape at him blankly, but he only waits patiently, gazing up at me.

"I just want to know about you. That's all. I'll tell you anything you want to know, too."

I twist my lips, feeling myself relent. Mostly because I'm undeniably curious about Cage, too. I spent many lone nights in Alaska wondering about the man who completely obliterated my world with so much ease. What bothered me most was that I missed him. How could I miss someone I don't even know?

I'm hoping that if I give him what he wants, he'll find something entirely unlikable and want to go home. Then, I can finally go to bed. *Alone.*

I can't afford my world being decimated again, and this time, I won't have to miss him.

"My favorite name in the world is Layla."

My throat tightens, and I curse myself for saying her name. It's impossible to think about her without feeling like my heart is being pushed through a woodchipper. I should've given him something impersonal. Like my favorite color.

He nods slowly, and the tiniest of grins curls one side of his lips upward. God, that look is lethal. I hate it.

"It's beautiful."

"Yep," I croak, then clear my throat, a pathetic attempt to cover the emotion clogging my windpipe.

"My favorite flower is a tiger lily," he tells me. Hesitantly, I meet his gaze again, but this time, I see shadows within them. "My mother was a single mom, and my father died before I was born. Growing up, she would buy herself tiger lilies every Saturday at the farmers' market. She said she didn't need a man because she could get herself anything she wanted. When I got my first paycheck, that was the first thing I bought her. I told her she may not need a man to buy them for her, but that doesn't mean she doesn't deserve it."

"Let me guess—you never stopped buying them for her," I say, a smile involuntarily curling my lips.

He grins, and my heart turns into putty. "Still do."

Goddamn him.

He was supposed to tell me something that made me find him abhorrent. Absolutely vile.

But then, his smile drops, and his features rearrange into an expression that instantly feels daunting. I already know what he's thinking. I can see it written all over his face.

"Let me guess," I repeat, my voice barely above a whisper. "You want to talk about my kidnapping."

"I knew who you were before you walked into my store. The whole world did. And, like most people, I was obsessed with your case. The security footage..."

"Made me look crazy," I supply, my stomach filling with acid.

"I know technology well, and it was clear that it was manipulated. You weren't crazy, and I understood that not only was the worst moment of your life broadcasted to the entire world, but that they altered it to make you look a certain way. Even back then, I was angry for you."

"Thanks," I mutter bitterly. "Is that why you fucked me? Wanted to play with the famous missing girl and have bragging rights?"

His face slackens, and he appears disappointed.

"No, Molly. The only person I ever told was Silas, and only because I was fucking hammered. And I fucked you because I was attracted to you in a way I've never felt for anyone else. I think I became obsessed with your case because my soul recognized yours. And I had so many questions about you."

"Did you get your answers?" I ask, my tone hardening. I'm looking for reasons to be mad, but truthfully, I can't blame him for knowing about my kidnapping or being intrigued by it. The video footage is... it's something that most *couldn't* ignore.

The girl who seemed to disappear out of thin air.

And the girl who was chased by ghosts. Little did they know, I *am* the ghost.

"Not the ones that matter, which is why I want to know you, Molly. I want to know the girl that the world still thinks is dead."

"I *like* it that way," I clip. "Everyone is too involved in their own lives to recognize a missing girl from fifteen years ago. This means I don't become a pony for the media circus, and I'm left alone. There's a reason I haven't let anyone get to know me."

He nods, and the gentle look in his eyes is what makes me realize I'm beginning to freak out a little. My heart is racing, my palms sweaty.

"I'm not going to tell anyone," he assures. "I'm too selfish to share you with anyone, let alone fucking vultures that would risk your safety. I would never put you in danger."

I exhale a heavy breath, attempting to release the anxiety that has begun to poison my bloodstream.

"There's a possibility that I'd be a suspect in a murder if the media learned I did escape." He stays quiet, letting me gather the courage to confess something I've never told a single soul. "When I escaped, I went back to my parents' house. I have a sister, and she was only a year old at the time. I couldn't leave her with the people who had sold me for drug money."

His upper lip twitches, fury settling in his gaze. I don't know why, but that invigorates me to keep going.

"My mom had already died of an overdose, so it was just my father. When he saw that I was back, he talked about selling me again, but this time, Layla, too. And I just... snapped. I couldn't handle the thought of him selling my baby sister. The things I had gone through—all I could think about was those same things happening to Layla—" I cut myself off, too overwhelmed with the thought. That residual fury resurfaces, and my cheeks grow hot as my words turn flustered.

His hand grabs mine, and I focus on it, if only to distract me from my spiraling thoughts.

While I had seen they were covered in tattoos, it's the first time I've actually gotten to study them closely. He tattooed flames on the knuckles of his fingers, the background behind them blacked out to give the illusion that they're melting candles. The artwork is some of the best I've seen, and for the first time, I consider getting my scars covered up with something beautiful.

"So you killed him," he states, bringing me back to the conversation.

"I killed him," I confirm quietly. "And I didn't even feel guilty about it."

"You shouldn't have," he says. "He deserved that and so much worse."

I nod. He did, and there's some satisfaction in knowing that I had been the one to end his life.

"I had heard about a large pig farm a couple hours from where I used to live. The owner was a local source of meat for many people, and there had been talk that he would be retiring soon. So, I cleaned everything up, rolled my dad in garbage bags, and put him in the trunk of his car."

He cocks a brow. "Would I happen to have just fucked you at the same farm?"

A blush immediately blooms across my cheeks. Damn it.

Clearing my throat, I mutter, "Yes."

He grins, and I narrow my eyes at the satisfaction emanating from him.

"Anyway," I continue, shooting him a pointed *shut up* look. "Once I got Layla and I showered, dressed, and packed, I drove to the farm. I waited until the owner went to bed, snuck into his barn, and fed my father to his pigs. It wasn't pretty, and I didn't do everything right. That was how I learned pigs avoided teeth and hair, which made the cleanup process awful. I'm still surprised I managed to get away with it."

It's a grossly oversimplified version of that night, but it's the crux of it. The details don't really matter now, except that I've learned a lot about feeding people to pigs since then. Most importantly, I had successfully gotten Layla and me away from that house, and no one has identified who we truly are since.

"Where's Layla now?"

I twist my lips in an attempt to keep my chin from trembling. That question feels like a sucker punch to the chest. My heart squeezes painfully, and a deep sadness consumes me.

"Emma," I correct. "Her name is Emma now. Four years is how long I tried to take care of her. Since my dad was under investigation for my disappearance, it didn't take long for the feds to notice him and Layla missing. She was broadcast all over the news, just as I was, and there were so many conspiracies about what happened to the three of us. Some people speculated that I escaped and took her, but there was never enough evidence to support it.

"So, I renamed her Emma, and I tried *so* hard to take care of her. It was almost impossible to get a job because I couldn't get an ID and expose myself. I managed to find a few under-the-table jobs, though they were typically underpaid, and my bosses somehow managed to be a shit person every time. It wasn't sustainable, and I wasn't providing a safe, healthy life for her."

A rock forms in my throat and for a moment, I can't breathe, let alone speak. Ten years isn't nearly long enough to smooth away the pain and devastation. A lifetime wouldn't even be enough.

Cage flexes his hand around mine again, reminding me he's here.

"I found a nice family in a wealthy town, and I stalked the fuck out of them. I watched them for months, ensuring they were good—*truly* good people with happy kids. And then... once I was positive they'd be able to give her the life she deserved... I waited until she fell asleep, then left her on their doorstep with a name tag and her birthdate like she was a goddamn dog."

My eyes flood with tears, and even as my chest heaves and my lungs expand, it still feels like I can't fucking breathe.

WHERE'S MOLLY

"I continued to watch them for several months afterward to make sure they actually took her in and didn't give her to some foster home. It took a little while, but eventually, they were able to adopt her. Since she was older than when I first took her and several hours away from our hometown, no one suspected who she was. Plus, I made sure she only ever knew me by Marie. It was chalked up to a druggie mother who just left their kid on a stranger's doorstep. And I was okay with that. It meant she was safe and could finally live in some goddamn peace."

Everything burns—my wet eyes, nose, cheeks, and throat.

"When Legion found me, it had been a year since I dropped her off. I never saw him, but he must've seen me when my boss was getting aggressive with me. He sent me to you, and the rest is history."

I bounce my leg anxiously, the urge to cry becoming harder to contain. "Fuck, it still sucks that I couldn't provide for her," I choke out, my voice broken with tears.

"But you did provide," he insists, catching ahold of my wandering gaze. "That option was stolen from you, baby. It's not because you weren't capable, but because you were in danger just as much as her. You were young. And I know it's not your home she's sleeping in. However, you *did* provide her with the life she deserves. *You* gave her that."

I squeeze my eyes shut, a few tears wiggling free anyway.

"I'm selfish and want her to remember me like I do her. But I know that I'll never be able to be in her life. Not with my lifestyle. I want her to stay far away from this shit. But I missed her so much when I was in Alaska. I was a fucking zombie, no matter how hard I tried to live."

My lungs are still tight, yet I force myself to keep going, even though it feels like each word is made of fiberglass.

"So, four years ago, I broke down and moved back. The previous owner had passed, and the farm had been up for sale for a while. I had a decent job in Alaska and used all my savings to buy it. I feel better being in the same state as Layla, even if I can't be in her life."

I end my explanation with a sigh, feeling exhausted suddenly. Emotionally and physically. I hadn't planned on telling him that much, though admittedly, it felt good. But now, I just want to sleep.

"Do you still watch her?" Cage asks boldly. My eyes drop to my lap, where I fidget with my fingers. A flush crawls up my throat, embarrassment taking root.

"Yes," I admit, forcing volume into my voice. Maybe it's wrong or creepy, but she's my sister and I care too much not to check up on her. And while it's a tad embarrassing, I also don't feel guilty about it, either.

He chuckles. "I'd do the same if the roles were reversed."

I smile tiredly, on the verge of resting my head on the pillow and passing out, even if he doesn't leave. Letting him stay one night doesn't have to be a big deal.

Once more, he squeezes my hand, drawing my attention back down to him.

"You saved her life, Molly. Remember that. Always remember that."

chapter eleven

MOLLY

NINE YEARS AGO
2013

"*Jesus, you're so fucking* sexy. When did Brent hire you? If I had known, I'd have visited my cousin sooner and already have you naked in my bed."

He's definitely an incel. I can't imagine a remark like that working on a single woman when he's missing his two front teeth and his pale skin is pinkened and covered in scabs from drug use.

I lean heavily on the counter separating us, staring at him like he's a fly that's expecting me to be impressed with its crooked wings when it has shit smeared across its upper lip.

"Please tell me, how many women have you successfully gotten in your bed with that pickup line?"

He grins, accentuating the blond peach fuzz peppered above his mouth. I bet he thinks it makes him look more like a man.

"I got one in there right now. But I'll gladly kick her out just for you."

Disgusting.

I hate this fucking job. I hate my boss. And evidently, I hate his family, too.

I've been working in this god-awful mechanic shop for a month and have been sexually harassed more times than I can count. I'm at my wit's end, but I need the money.

"No, thanks," I quip. "I'll let Brent know you're here to see him."

His smile falls, replaced with a dark expression. I give him my back before something foul falls out of his mouth—worse than what already has.

The small shop is nestled in a run-down town deep in the mountains of Montana. Luckily, I haven't seen my face plastered anywhere here, and the media has moved on to another world event that only affirms this planet has gone to hell.

Now that I no longer have Layla, I wonder why I even bother walking amongst the living. But I refuse to have fought so hard for my life just to throw it away. I can only call it pure stubbornness at this point.

"Brent, your cousin is here," I call into his office, standing firmly outside the door. Every time I go in, he asks me to shut it behind me, and it always ends in a highly uncomfortable situation. Most times, he hits on me. Other times, he finds a reason to berate me, then tops it off with a lovely threat.

He knows I'm running from something since I admitted it's too dangerous for me to have a driver's license, and he loves to use that as collateral.

"Which one?"

"He didn't say," I respond woodenly.

He sighs, the sound laced with irritation.

"Then how do I know he's my cousin?" he snaps. "You know damn well I got the police up my ass. And the first one goin' under the bus is *you*, little girl."

And there's the threat.

"I'll go ask," I mumble.

He mutters an insult beneath his breath while I trudge back toward the creep. He's fiddling with the car scents, taking one off the rack, sniffing it, and deliberately returning it to the wrong row, all the while wearing a smart-ass smirk on his ugly face. I clench my teeth, anger flaring. Brent's yelled at me several times for not having the scents arranged correctly when customers do exactly that.

"What's your name?" I ask, attempting to keep my expression neutral. Last thing I want him to know is that his endeavor to piss me off is working.

His answering grin is evil, and I hate the way that makes me want to retreat in on myself. I've seen that very face far too often. And what comes after.

"You need my social security card, too? Just get my fucking cousin."

It takes effort to refrain from spitting on him the way he just spit on me. Keeping the saliva in his mouth with that gap must be impossible.

"He wants your name first," I insist.

"I ain't doing shit— Brent! Brent, get the fuck out here!" he yells loudly.

Fuck.

My heart speeds as I hear my boss's door slam shut behind him, followed by his angry footfalls. Panic unleashes, and I'm assaulted by the memories of Rocco charging at me with the same heavy steps.

Brent stomps up to the cash register, fire in his brown eyes. Sweat gathers along my hairline while I fight to stay in the present. Except, I don't know that reality is much better.

"The fuck you yellin' for?" he snaps, glaring at the man for a beat, before turning it onto me. This time, I do shrink away.

My boss is a big man. And he's *mean*.

Distantly, I hear the chime of another customer entering the shop, though none of us acknowledge them.

"This little bitch refused to get you after I asked nicely. She's fucking disrespectful!"

Being called a bitch is certainly nothing new and certainly doesn't hurt my feelings, but him risking my job is absolutely uncalled for.

My mouth falls open, a protest building on my tongue. However, it instantly dissipates when Brent's accusing stare swings onto me.

"That true?"

"I-I was just trying to get his name like you asked," I defend myself weakly.

"Bullshit. She was fucking grilling me, man!"

"Shut up, Bud," Brent barks, though he keeps his fiery gaze on mine.

The familiarity between the two is apparent. Guess that means he is Brent's cousin, which only makes my situation worse.

"Go into my office and wait for me," he orders darkly.

The intention in his eyes is unmistakable. If I do as he says, I'll be walking out with one less piece of myself intact.

I nod, the movement jerky, as I turn toward his office. There's also an exit this way, and if I want to save myself, then it's imperative I take it.

Another job bites the dust, and I still have little money to show for it.

Devastation mingles with my growing anxiety. I'll have to find another town and beg for an illegal job, yet again. And the likelihood of finding a boss who's a decent human being is low. I haven't had one thus far and have gone through four jobs now.

I'm exhausted. So fucking exhausted.

"The dumb bitch can't even arrange these right," his cousin—Bud—snaps. "The strawberry is mixed with the..."

I don't hear the rest of what he says, and I don't need to. He only cemented the necessity to get the fuck out of here.

I speed-walk directly toward the exit and charge out of there without a backward glance. Sunlight pierces my eyes, though I hardly register the sharp pain. I have tunnel vision, and the only thing on my mind is getting as far away from *Engines & Oil* as possible.

By the time I reach the bus stop, I've no idea how much time has passed. I don't remember a single second of it, nor the entire ride to the women's shelter I've been staying at.

With clouded thoughts, I eventually make it to the shelter. There aren't many women boarded here, thankfully, but I am required to have group therapy sessions with them to stay.

It's incredibly uncomfortable. At least they're like me here, traumatized, and just want to be left alone. And it helps I get my own little apartment, though I am required to pay a small fee to keep it. The shelter's meant to give survivors a form of independence away from their abusers, and it's considerably cheaper than renting regular apartments around the area.

I reach my door and nearly shove through it to get inside, convinced Brent followed me and is right behind me. Though I didn't see a single soul, it still feels like someone was right on my tail the entire way home.

Only when the door is shut and locked do I throw myself against it and release a heavy exhale.

I'm incapable of feeling relieved when I'm in near-constant danger, but at least I'm not alone in that office with Brent, possibly on the brink of being assaulted again.

That... that's honestly all I could ask for at this very moment. That, and to not have been followed home by one of those creeps.

Another exhale, and then a sob is bursting free. I slap a hand over my mouth, yet it's a hopeless attempt to contain the outcry.

Soon, I'm overcome with them, and I'm no longer capable of standing. I slide down the door, my shoulders shaking and chest heaving as wail after wail rebounds against my palm.

Tears stream down my cheeks in rivers, and for the longest while, there's no thought behind my agony.

I'm not even sure why I'm crying anymore. Because of what could've happened? Or because I have to start over once again? Maybe it's because no matter how hard I try to get my feet firmly beneath me, they always get kicked out.

I just... I can't *take* this anymore.

I don't want to die, but I don't want to exist. And I wish with every ounce of my soul that I was never born. That I had never been brought into a world so cold, violent, and full of heartache.

And the worst part is that even though I feel dead inside, I'm painfully aware of how alive I am. I dread every night when I fall asleep because I know I have to wake up again and do this life for another day.

I just don't want to be here. That's all I want.

The sobs wane, but the tears are constant. Snot leaks down my nose no matter how hard I sniff, and eventually, my butt begins to ache from sitting on the unforgiving tile for so long.

Forcing my eyes open, I glance around at my abysmal home. The small cube of stained white tile around the front door transitions into a thin brown carpet. The walls are freshly painted white, though it doesn't bring much light into the dark room.

Unlike the house I grew up in, it doesn't reek of cigarette smoke, body fluids, and grime. It's just old. And it's the nicest home I've ever had. But it's still not mine.

Which is why I kept it bare, save for the standard furniture that came with it. No decorations. No personality. No... life.

Sighing, I wipe away the tears and force myself to stand. Group therapy isn't until later, but they usually set out a tray of sweets beforehand. At this moment, a chocolate brownie is the only thing I have to look forward to.

I blink away the residual wetness in my eyes, then peek through the eyehole to ensure no creepy ex-bosses or cousins are outside. Once I'm confident the coast is clear, I unlock the door and swing it open. Something black and sturdy clinks to the ground, and my heart instantly drops.

A journalist found me. Or a stranger that's planning on reporting me to the police. Different scenarios shuttle through my brain at lightning speed. Where they saw me. If they're waiting somewhere for me.

How long do I have to escape? Or is it too late?

It feels as if I'm having a heart attack as I shakily bend over and grab the card. It's metal, which surprises me first. Then, I flip it over to find the word *Legion* in bold, gold-foiled letters. Below is a phone number and nothing else.

No real name. No job title. Nothing.

But they look really fucking important.

Heart in my throat, I glance around suspiciously, still seeing no one, but not trusting that in the slightest. Other apartments surround the shelter, and the street is directly to my right. There are many places for them to hide.

Quickly, I retreat into my apartment and slam the door shut, relocking it again. Then, I distractedly make my way to my bed and slump down on the edge of it.

What the fuck is *Legion?* And what could they possibly want with me?

For a good five minutes, I argue with myself. To call them or run like my life depends on it and hope to God this *Legion* never finds me again. It doesn't look like a business card for a journalist or government official. And part of me is aware that if either one of those people found me, they'd be knocking on that door, not leaving me some obscure, ominous card.

Plus, it's incredibly fancy. It screams money.

I'm fairly confident a cop or news reporter doesn't make *this* much cash. Not enough to justify wasting it on a card, anyway.

I growl, growing irritated with myself. Without further thought, I slide my prepaid flip phone out of my back pocket, dial the number, and press call before I can talk myself out of it.

Curiosity won, and like a cat, it may get me killed.

The ringing stops, replaced by a sinfully delicious voice. Deep and raspy, yet toneless.

"I was hoping you'd call."

My lips part, so incredibly unprepared that I'm at a loss for words.

Oddly, he waits. Doesn't even question if I'm still on the line.

After a few moments, I get my shit together long enough to eke out, "Who is this?"

"Legion," he answers simply.

"And what do you want? How did you find me?" My tone grows increasingly aggressive with each word, the gears in my brain switching from shock to suspicion.

"I saw you at the mechanic and witnessed what transpired between you and your boss. You looked like someone who needed help, so I followed you home. Of course, I didn't want to make you feel more unsafe than I already have, so I let you decide to make contact."

I blink, unable to formulate a single coherent thought.

"Would you like my help?" he asks evenly.

"I— What does that entail?"

"A new life where you would be safe, comfortable, and provided for."

Again, I blink, my mouth now hanging open. Then, my lip curls.

"You're a freak, aren't you? Expecting me to fuck you in return or something? You think I'll willingly walk into another prison, you sick fuck? Go to hell."

I hang up the phone before he can respond, my hands trembling violently. I feel sick to my stomach, and all those old memories resurface.

Doting on men and offering them pleasure at the expense of my own sanity. I was 'taken care of and provided for'. I had a roof over my head and food in my stomach at Francesca's house, too.

But that doesn't mean I wasn't dying a slow death. That I wasn't being tortured alive and driven fucking insane.

I would rather be independent and struggle than have a monster provide for me. At least when I'm alone, the only demons I'm fighting are my own.

The phone rings, startling me out of my thoughts. I jump, the phone tumbling to the ground and flying under the bed.

Cursing to myself, I get on my knees and fish it out, only to see *Unknown* flashing across the screen.

I'm tempted to smash the phone beneath my foot just so he can never reach me again. But something in my gut tells me to answer it, even if it's to curse him out again.

Just before the last ring, I flip it open and answer it.

"Listen, asshole, I don't want you call—"

"I assure you, I want nothing from you." His deep, calm voice chases away the rest of my threat.

"W-what? Why would you do this? No sane person would offer something like that with no strings attached."

"I only want you to go to a specific location and meet one of my trusted men. He's safe, and he'll set you up with a brand-new life.

I'll drop a car off for you with the keys inside, the location on the GPS, and plenty of cash for you to do with as you please. It's your choice to go, and no one will force you. No sex. No requirements outside of that. I promise you."

This is a joke. A prank. It has to be.

The sigh from the other end of the phone is almost discernible.

"I recognized you, Molly. And I can see from a mile away that you're not in a good place. I won't tell a single soul about your identity or location. I just want to help you get somewhere safe, that's all."

Fuck. Fuck, fuck, fuck, fuck. FUCK.

My heart can't take this abuse. It's only a matter of seconds before it gives out on me completely.

"Why?" I snap, my flight mode beginning to kick in. Someone *did* recognize me. And that could be catastrophic.

"It's what I do," he responds.

Not good enough of an answer.

"What's the catch?"

"You tell no one where you're going or about what my friend will do for you. Nothing else. Just your silence."

"And if I don't?"

"We will disappear without a trace before anyone could find us, and never be at your disposal again."

"At my disposal?" I repeat dumbly.

"You will come to learn that I am a valuable friend, should you ever need me again."

He speaks with a poise and confidence unlike anything I've heard before. It's almost as intimidating as it is comforting. An odd combination, and one that I feel is deadly.

I would be incredibly stupid to entertain this. Meeting with a complete stranger who is making an offer that seems far too good to be true. Especially when I've been recognized. This could be a trap. A ploy to use me for something nefarious.

No—*worse*. He could be connected to Francesca and try to bring me back to that house.

"Who do you work for?"

"I'm my own boss."

"Did anyone hire you?"

"No, Molly. I do the hiring."

Why do I believe him? No one in their right mind would consider something like this.

But my mind hasn't been right for over five years now. And at this point, what do I have to lose?

My life?

What life?

"You will have a new identity, a home, a job, a whole new life. There are very few people who deserve this more than you."

It's like he can sense I'm on the edge of a cliff and just needed one final push.

"Okay," I rush out, almost as if my mouth is racing the rational part of my brain. "But the second I feel something is off, I'm running."

Another whisper of a sigh. This one sounded relieved.

"Of course. I'll text you further directions. You won't regret this, Molly."

The line goes dead, and slowly, I pull my phone away from my ear and stare at the screen blankly.

My mind isn't racing. I'm only plagued with a single thought.

What the *fuck* am I getting myself into?

chapter twelve

MOLLY

PRESENT
2022

Layla is extremely athletic, and I have no fucking idea who she inherited that from.

Maybe our mother was, too, before she got into drugs. I doubt Dad lifted anything heavier than a vodka bottle in his years, though.

Regardless, my little sister is the star player on her soccer team, and she just scored her third goal.

I jump out of my seat and clap like there's a hornet in my face, but I refrain from cheering and screaming like I want to. I'd rather her parents think I'm an enthusiastic family member for another kid than wonder why there's a random stranger yelling their daughter's name.

"GO EMMA!" her mother, Margot, screams through the palms cupped around her mouth. Her husband and Layla's father, Colin, is right beside her, cheering with the same enthusiasm.

I'm so grateful they kept the name I gave her. It's what I would've named my own daughter, had I ever had one.

I knew that if I were going to keep Layla truly protected, then I couldn't be carrying around a missing child *as* a missing child and blatantly calling her by the name being broadcasted across the news. While I tried to avoid the public at all costs, there were times it was inevitable. And I knew that eventually, Layla was going to grow up and learn her name, and I couldn't risk her knowing who she was. It was necessary for her safety. And now, it's essential for her to continue to live a safe, happy life.

Layla's long blonde ponytail swishes behind her as she does the cutest little happy dance, her teammates running to cheer with her. My eyes grow misty, pride beaming from my chest so intensely I can hardly breathe around it.

It's impossible for me to know who she is deep down inside, but I'm confident she's the best fifteen-year-old to ever exist. Funny, smart, and popular. And from what I've seen, she's so fucking kind.

Which is the only thing that truly matters to me. That, and her being provided for and loved the way she deserves to be.

But if the couple down the row from me is any indication, she has exactly that. Their expressions resemble mine. Pride, joy, and so much love, it hurts.

Or maybe it just hurts because she doesn't know my love anymore, and I only had hers for five years of her life.

The game ends an hour later, and to no one's surprise, Layla's team wins, 4-0. The girls are assembled in a huge group, all cheering and screaming their delight.

And when her parents make their way to the group and embrace Layla in an enthusiastic hug, their mouths forming the words *I love you* and *I'm proud of you*, I turn and leave.

Tears sting at my eyes as they often do after her games. Whether it's because she won, and I can't be the one to celebrate her, or because they lost, and I'm unable to console her.

Regardless, I'm so happy for her. Because even though it's not my arms that are wrapped around her, the embrace she's in is no less loving.

This is literally the worst thing to ever happen to me, particularly in the middle of a goddamn Target.

"Marie, this is my mom, Winifred," Cage introduces us, a shit-eating grin tilting his lips. I'd love nothing more than to smack it off, but I'm currently paralyzed.

I know my eyes are the size of golf balls, and if the equally mischievous smile on his mother's face is any indication, it hasn't gone unnoticed.

She can't be much taller than five feet, peering up at me with hazel eyes. Her short white hair curls artfully around her nape and over her forehead, perfectly styled. Bright red lipstick paints her smiling lips, and she wears bedazzled black jeans and a leopard-print blouse.

"It's so nice to meet you," I squeak, holding out a slick palm for her to shake. She scoffs and bats it away before pulling me into the warmest hug I've ever experienced.

My throat tightens, but I choose to believe it's because I'm so relieved that she doesn't have to touch my sweaty hand. When I pull away, I meet Cage's gaze, only for my eyes to gravitate toward the box of condoms directly behind him.

Jesus fucking Christ.

I'm never going to recover from this.

After Layla's game, I got a call from Legion informing me that I'd be receiving another drop tonight.

For the past month, Cage has been delivering bodies three to four times a week, and each and every time, he finds a new way to end up in my bed.

Aside from the incident in the barn, I started making him use condoms. And due to his insatiable sex drive, we ran through an entire fifty-count box already.

I've tried to convince myself this past month has been some strange, lucid dream, yet the bruises on my hips and ass have made it impossible to deny.

And each night, after he'd leave, I tried telling myself to keep it strictly professional from there on out, but the twinge in my heart let me know my body heavily disagreed.

So, like any responsible thirty-four-year-old woman, I'm buying more condoms.

Just in case.

An otherwise safe endeavor. Until a presence sidled up next to me, a delicious scent invading my senses before a familiar hand pointed at a specific brand.

"I'd need these."

My wide eyes slowly processed the glaring XL on the box, then Cage's wide grin right in front of me.

Before I could utter a word, a sweet face had popped up on the other side of him, scolding him for trying to *'woo a lady in such an egregious manner.'*

"I didn't know Cage had a new lady friend!" she exclaims warmly, pulling away only to capture my cheeks between her soft hands. "Oh, the beauty of you! Your eyes are quite sexy, you know that? And that bite mark, dear Lord, it must have come from a horrible person. But, dare I say, it makes you look very edgy, my dear."

My mouth drops.

Cage sighs.

"She's going through a phase of calling women sexy. Yesterday, she told me she wanted to start wearing leather pants again," Cage explains. Despite his dry tone, his eyes glimmer with amusement.

Winifred releases me to shoot her son a disgruntled look. "That's how I seduced your father, ya know. I was wearing these skintight leather pants and a bright red halter top." She returns her stare to mine, excitement glittering in her eyes. "The girls never looked better, let me tell ya. His father took one look and had me bent over—"

"Ma," Cage intervenes sternly.

She rolls her eyes and then winks at me, a devious grin curling her red lips. "Don't worry, sweetie, I'll finish the story another time. He gets *sensitive* when I talk about my sex life in front of him."

A valid reaction, only I don't voice that. Instead, I return her smile, albeit nervously.

"Yeah, I'd, uh, love to hear it," I mumble.

"Great!" she shouts, startling a customer at the end of the aisle. I bite back a grin when the young blonde woman gives us a dumbstruck expression. Admittedly, it's hilarious, and a laugh bursts free.

Winifred doesn't even notice.

"Come over for dinner tomorrow night, and I'll tell you all the stories. I used to be a groupie back in the day. And let me just say that wannabe rock stars are better in the sack than successful ones. Once they get rich, they feel like they don't have anyone to impress." She waves her hand airily.

"Ma—"

"Anyway, can you make it? I make the best peach cobbler."

Her stare is full of so much hope, it's literally impossible to say no. I flick a glance at Cage, finding a dark and almost taunting expression. He wants me to answer, which only sends my heart rate escalating to dangerous levels.

He's obviously not feeling inclined to give me an out, and I'm unsure if it's because he's enjoying watching me struggle or because he actually wants me to come.

Either way, he's a dick.

"Y-yeah, of course. I don't have plans."

"Great!" she bellows a second time and, once again, scares the same young girl, who has since wandered closer. She jumps, drops a box as a result, and scurries to pick it up, her cheeks now bright red.

Then, the frazzled customer tosses Winifred a bewildered glance, frantically tucking flyaway blonde strands behind her ear, and hurries off before she suffers from a heart attack at an age far too young.

"Cage would love to come pick you up," she volunteers, not even bothering to check with him first. She turns to him. "Bring her over at six. And pick us up some of that good shit I like."

My brows jump.

Cage rolls his eyes. "She's referring to wine," he clarifies dryly.

Winifred refocuses on me. "And, for the love of God, wear something comfortable. We'll be sitting on a couch drinking and trash-talking my wonderful son, so please don't feel the need to impress me with a silly dress. I guarantee the ones in my closet are sexier anyway," she directs. She goes to turn away but then pivots back around. "Oh, and don't let him talk ya out of using condoms. Raising kids is so 1950s. Here, if he's anything like his father, then these should work."

I laugh when she snatches the size small condoms from the shelf and chucks them into my cart without a backward glance, then bids me farewell.

Cage's face morphs from shock to being visibly offended. "Oh, she's got jokes."

Winifred's answering cackle can be heard across several aisles, and I'm almost positive that wherever the young blonde woman is in the store, it managed to scare her again.

chapter thirteen

CAGE

NINE YEARS AGO
2013

"I want to return this piece-of-shit TV," the old woman snaps, her gray-and-blonde hair frazzled as she slams the receipt down on the counter.

"What was wrong with it?" my employee, Silas, asks, keeping his tone kind despite the woman's bad attitude since she first stormed in. She's short, clearly a smoker, and has her chest puffed like she's tough shit. Her bones are twigs, but whatever gets her out of bed, I guess.

"It wouldn't turn on!" she exclaims, slamming wrinkled hands on the counter. "What kind of idiot sells a TV that don't turn on?"

Silas's eye twitches, and I snicker beneath my breath.

"I kept pressing the damn clicker, and nothin'!"

"Did you make sure it was plugged in?"

The woman looks at Silas like he speaks an alien language, which seems only to enrage her further.

"Plugged into what?" she yells, her voice rising. "You know what, it don't matter. Give me my money back, you piece of shit." She tosses her receipt at Silas's chest.

It's almost impossible to contain my smile, considering I know the exact question about to come out of his mouth.

"Sure, ma'am. Where's the TV?"

Again, she stares at him like she doesn't understand.

"At my house! You think a little old lady like me can carry that in here myself? You people can't go pick it up?"

Silas is now the one staring, completely dumbfounded. I drop my head to hide my quiet laugh.

"Uh, no, ma'am. If you want to return an item, then you need to bring it in. We don't go to people's houses to retrieve it."

The lady's mouth flops for a moment, and then she proceeds to go off on a tangent. The words *'you people'* and *'pieces of shit'* are said so much, I'm ready to send her to an early grave and inscribe the words on her goddamn tombstone.

Eventually, I step in and send her off on her merry way, promising a return when she brings back the actual fucking TV. She didn't argue much. Most don't when they crack their necks simply to look up at me.

Which makes my job a fuck of a lot easier considering my regular customers aren't wanting to buy TVs. And while I've worked with quite a few grandmas, they certainly weren't harmless.

"Why are felons so much easier to deal with?" Silas grumbles, casting a dirty look at the door the old woman just exited out of.

I raise a brow. "Why do you think I created this business?"

Silas cocks his own brow mockingly. "Because you're a smart motherfucker who learned how to do something ninety-nine percent of the population can't do?"

"Ninety-nine percent is a bit of a stretch," I respond dryly. But it's not far off.

I was twelve years old when my older sister, Olivia, paid some asshole for a fake ID. I remember her being so excited, her blue eyes sparkling as she talked about getting into her first bar.

She was sixteen years old and deep in her rebellious phase.

That weekend, Olivia got dressed up with her best friend, Kelly, and they snuck out after our mom went to bed. That was the last time I saw her, and I remember vividly calling her an idiot before she climbed out of her window and ran off into the night.

The story of what happened afterward was told through the mouth of her killer during his trial.

According to Officer James Gill, he was called to the club Olivia and Kelly tried getting into. The bouncer took one look and could see their IDs were poorly made. So, to teach them a lesson, he called the police.

Officer Gill arrived at the club ten minutes later and herded them into the back seat of his cruiser. Except, he never took them to the station.

Instead, he drove them to his house that was settled by the mountains on the outskirts of town. There, he proceeded to rape and torture them for two days until he ultimately shot them both in the back of the head.

For two years, we didn't know what happened to them. Until Officer Gill kidnapped another girl, and unlike my sister and her friend, she escaped and lived to tell the police force what an evil man they had working for them.

After that, they searched his house and found Olivia, Kelly, and seven other girls buried on his property.

All I could think was that if my sister and her friend had never gotten shitty IDs, James Gill would've never entered their lives. Would've never put them in the back of his car and senselessly murdered them.

In my fourteen-year-old stupid-ass brain, I thought I was avenging my sister by learning how to make legitimate fake IDs for young women. It didn't take long before I realized I was only allowing them to enter an environment full of equally evil men. They weren't any safer and had my sister gotten in the bar that night, there's no guarantee a different man wouldn't have committed the same atrocious deed.

So, for a while, I had a skill that I didn't know how to utilize.

Until one day, a kid a few years older, David, came to me and asked if I could do more than just make him a new ID. He wanted a new life.

His dad was a general in the Marine Corps and highly abusive. David felt his life was in danger every time he went home and was convinced that if he just simply ran away, his father would find him. I guess his old man had threatened as much.

It took me two weeks to figure out how to get him a new social security card and birth certificate. I even managed to get him a job on a fishing boat.

It sparked a passion I didn't know I had. Turns out, making people disappear would be how I'd save them.

WHERE'S MOLLY

I turned eighteen and started my own business, *Black Portal*, an electronic store that sells TVs. But that was only my front. I sold my actual services by word of mouth in the beginning. Eventually, I got Legion's attention from one of my clients who knew him, and he liked what I could do and sent more clients my way. He helps bring me business; in return, I help him with favors.

My only rule—I don't help rapists or pedophiles, which isn't an issue since Legion makes those types disappear in a more permanent way. Murderers, I take case-by-case. I've helped bad guys get away, but they weren't lacking the moral compass I require if they want my help. There is such a thing as a gray area, mainly when it comes to murder.

"Jesus, is that who I think it is?" Silas whispers, his question saturated in disbelief.

My heart stops beating the second I lay eyes on her.

Molly fucking Devereaux is heading toward the counter, her eyes darting in every direction. Her shoulders are curved inward, and she's picking at her nails anxiously. Dark brown curls are deliberately arranged around her face, but those sad, green eyes and the scar on the apple of her cheek... it's a dead giveaway.

She was plastered all over the news when she went missing. And then her baby sister, Layla, eight months later. Most assume their father took Layla and ran, but neither has been seen since. Both girls with strange disappearances, which still haven't been solved to this day.

It's been almost six years since she disappeared. Now, here she is, in the flesh. And she looks no less sad than she did in her missing person poster.

"I got this one handled." I jerk my chin at Silas, signaling for him to leave us alone. Without a word, he disappears in the back.

"They say that people who have eyes like yours are destined for a tragic death."

There's a slight pause to her gait, but she pushes forward until she's a foot away, only a counter between us.

"Sanpaku eyes," I clarify. "When you have a gap below your irises."

"Do you greet all your guests by telling them they're going to go out in a ball of flames?"

"That's typically why they come to find me. I'm the one who saves them from the fire."

She hums, distracting me from counting the freckles on her nose. I only got to fifteen, but I don't mind restarting.

"I'm just here for a TV," she lies.

My answering grin is involuntary. "Sure, what kind?" I question.

"Uh—" She glances around and then points to a fifty-inch flat screen. And if I had to guess, far out of her price range. "That one."

"That'll be five hundred dollars."

Her wide eyes fly to mine. "Jesus," she mumbles. "That's literally so unnecessary."

I point toward our cheapest TV. It's a small box from a decade ago, but it has been refurbished.

"Fifty bucks for that one."

Her nose wrinkles in distaste. "That doesn't look worth more than a dollar."

"It's an antique."

"It looks better suited to host a bonfire," she retorts without hesitation.

I'm full-on smiling like a fucking fool.

"It probably is, but be careful, my employee might hear you. That's his pride and joy."

She raises a brow. "My condolences to his wounded ego."

Damn. I think I love her.

She clears her throat, realizing we've been staring at each other with stupid grins on our faces.

"So, uh, do you take payment plans for putting out fires?"

I lean my arms on the counter, now looking up at her from beneath my brows. I can feel how wicked it is, but I'm unable to hide it.

"First, tell me your name. Mine is Cage Everhart."

She narrows her eyes, seemingly suspicious.

"You're telling me you don't know who I am? Legion didn't tell you I was coming?"

I grin, appreciating her observation.

"Legion actually didn't warn me, the fucker. But while I do recognize you, I wanted to be careful in case you go by something else."

She hums, then answers, "Molly. You can call me Molly."

I hold out a hand for her to shake, which she grabs timidly. The second her skin touches mine, it feels like tiny electrical currents zapping between our palms.

"Nice to meet you, Molly," I rasp.

If I had to hold her hand forever, it wouldn't be long enough. However, she releases me and pulls out a black card from the back pocket of her dark blue jeans, appearing unsure. "Legion?"

She says it like it's a question, though the gold letters say just that.

I've seen this card a handful of times. And every time, the person handing it over is someone who desperately needs an escape.

It also means Legion is completely covering their fee. And my prices are steep.

"Do you know where you want to go?" I ask, brushing my thumb over the foil letters. Usually, I keep the card, but I slide it back to her for reasons I can't explain. Hesitantly, she grabs it and tucks it in her jeans again.

"Alaska." The answer seems to burst from her throat, as if it's been imprisoned behind her teeth.

I raise a brow in surprise. Most people try to go to the beach, where it's warm and makes them feel like they've escaped to a tropical island. I *could* send people to places like that, but most can't afford that hefty fee.

Ultimately, they go where I send them, though I do try to find somewhere they're happy with. Especially if they deserve that peace.

"You like the cold?"

She shrugs, and it seems as if she's battling with her next words.

"If I'm out in the wilderness, just me and the wolves, no one will find me. No one will recognize me. I've disappeared once. This time, I want it to be for good."

My tongue forms the words to ask what happened to her that day. Who was chasing her? Did they put that haunted look in her eyes? How did she escape? And what is driving her to stay hidden from the world?

"It's going to take my team a good twenty-four hours to obtain everything," I tell her.

Her fingers tap on the counter, and she chews on her lip nervously.

"Does this happen to come with accommodations before I leave?" she questions, her cheeks beginning to flush red with embarrassment. "I, uhm, I don't really have anywhere to go while I wait."

Legion will cover all her expenses, including food and necessities. If she has that black card, she might as well have his credit card.

But I don't tell her that part. Not yet, at least.

"Sure," I say. "We'll help get you set up in a hotel. Legion will cover you."

Her shoulders fall in relief, but mine tighten.

It's a feeling I can't name. One that probably has some fucking obscure word to describe it. But knowing this may be the last time I see her before she leaves doesn't settle right with me. In fact, it makes me downright desperate to ensure it's not my last moment with her.

Not because of who she is and what happened to her. But because, for some indescribable reason, she feels like mine.

"Give me a second to get some things sorted. Stay put, yeah?"

"Yeah," she croaks, casting another glance around.

She's uncomfortable, and I decide immediately that I really fucking hate that.

It's not easy pulling my gaze away from her, but I force myself to turn and head into the back. Silas is standing in front of a stack of boxed TVs, a clipboard in his hand as he sorts through inventory.

"Go out front and keep an eye on her? Make sure she's not recognized. I'll only be a minute."

"You got it," he chirps, before setting down his clipboard and heading out to the front.

I wait a few minutes, ensuring he isn't around, then I pull out my phone and get to work. Within a minute, I'm calling the first hotel.

"Thank you for calling the *Milton Hotels*. How may I help you?" a woman greets, her voice high-pitched.

"I'd like to book every available room for the night."

There's a pause. "I-I'm sorry, you said *all* available rooms?"

"Yes, please. Every single room. Until you're fully booked and don't have a single fucking one to spare."

"Uhm, okay. Sure."

Once that's done, I proceed to call every hotel within a thirty-mile radius and book them out, too.

chapter fourteen

MOLLY

NINE YEARS AGO
2013

"Do you have a computer I can use to find a hotel?" I ask, tapping my fingers against the counter nervously. Cage just returned from the back, and anxiety is gnawing at my stomach.

This entire situation is so far out of my depth, and I feel a little sick if I analyze it too deeply.

So easily, I could be walking into another wolf's den. I'm not sure if escaping human trafficking has made me cautious or reckless at this point. Everything I do feels like my life is on the line, and I'm not sure if I'll live long enough to know peace.

"Silas will book the room for you and get it taken care of," Cage offers.

His employee doesn't waste another second and pulls out his phone, googling nearby hotels.

"Right. Thanks," I mumble.

"Do you need anything in the meantime? Water? Food?"

I blink. Food has been more of a luxury than a necessity, and I've gotten good at ignoring the hunger pangs. For as long as I can remember, it's always been a fight to fuel my body. And I don't know if I've ever been offered food and water in all my twenty-five years of life.

"Uh, I guess water would be nice," I say, my cheeks burning.

"Sure, thanks," Silas mutters on the phone before hanging up, his brow pinched. "That's the second hotel I've called that is completely booked."

Cage glances at him. "Keep trying. I'm sure there's at least one that has an available room." Then, his stare returns to mine. "It's about dinnertime for us anyway. We're open for another hour, and I suppose it's not smart to take you out in public, so I can order a pizza if you'd like?"

My lips part, but I have no words. I'm not sure why, but it's embarrassing that he wants to feed me. I know I'm malnourished—but I guess I don't like that it's so obvious.

However, I'm too hungry to turn it down.

"Sure. That'd be nice. Thank you."

"What toppings do you like on your pizza?"

I flush hotter and avoid eye contact, deciding to settle my gaze on my chipped nails. "I've never had pizza before, so I don't really know. I guess just cheese is fine."

When I do find the courage to flick a glance in his direction, I'm almost impressed by how easily he schools his expression. He doesn't gape at me like I'd expected. Instead, a sly grin curls his lips.

"Then let me be the one to introduce you to the best thing you'll ever eat in your life. I'll get a supreme, maybe a Hawaiian if you're the type to like pineapple on your pizza—huge debate in the world, by the way—and of course, a plain cheese and a pepperoni just in case."

My eyes nearly pop out of my skull as he goes on. "Oh my God, no. That is so much food! You really don't have to do th—"

He leans heavily on the counter across from me, cutting off whatever the hell I was going to say. He peers up at me with a challenging expression, but what has me tongue-tied is the raw animalistic energy that radiates from him. I don't know if he's even aware of it, yet it sets me on fucking fire anyway.

"I know I don't have to. But I like to eat," he drawls lazily.

My chest tightens, and a swarm of butterflies flutter in the pit of my stomach. It doesn't sound like he's declaring his affection for consuming *food* at this moment.

It feels as if a sharp, pointed claw is poised against the inside of my throat, and it slowly drags down my chest, into my stomach, and between my thighs, leaving a hot trail in its wake.

I'm tempted to make some corny joke about being out of practice with eating, though I know how to swallow. Except I don't have the confidence to say something like that. Nor am I sure if I'd even want to.

Sex isn't something I'm interested in. Not after going through everything that I have. In fact, I'm perfectly content if I never have to see another penis for the rest of my life.

Yet, the way Cage stares up at me now—I wonder if that's really true.

I hadn't considered what sex would be like if I *chose* it, and if it's something that would feel good.

"Goddamn it!" Silas shouts, startling me damn near out of my skin. Cage cranes his head over his shoulder, glaring at his employee.

"Sorry," he mutters. "I've called every fucking hotel nearby, and all of them are booked. How is that even possible?"

My heart drops, and immediately, my thoughts begin to spiral. I have Legion's car and could probably sleep in it for the night. It's not safe, but if I find a parking lot with other cars, maybe no one will notice.

"Th-that's okay. I can find somewhere else to st—"

"Absolutely not," Cage interrupts, straightening his spine. "I have a spare bedroom. You can stay with me tonight."

My mouth flops for a few moments before I raise my hands, finally scrounging up the voice to protest. "N-no. That's so not necessary. I'll find—"

"If you're even considering sleeping somewhere outside, I'm going to have to stop you there. That's too dangerous."

A crease forms between my brows. "And staying with a complete stranger isn't?"

His features relax slightly, and he offers a soft grin.

"Call Legion. He'll put guards outside my house. The second you scream for help, they'll come running, and I'll have a bullet through my brain before I can blink."

"A bullet? That... that also seems unnecessary."

He cocks a brow. "Is it?"

An image of my father being ripped apart by pigs flashes through my brain, and I relent, "I guess not."

"For what it's worth, I would never hurt you. I promise not to lay a finger on you." There's a pause, and I hear the unspoken words he won't give voice to.

Unless you ask me to.

A large part of me is glad he didn't say it. But another part of me is a little disappointed. Maybe because I don't know that I'll ever gather the courage to say that I *do* want him to.

He nods toward me. "Call Legion."

The black flip phone burns in my back pocket, and I'm tempted to pull it out and do just that. But what if Legion is no better of a man than Cage? If he led me to someone willing to hurt me, then I doubt he's an upstanding guy, either.

And I'd rather fight one man in a place where I have access to a knife than a man when I'm alone in a car.

Do I feel safe with Cage? No. But not because I think he'll hurt me.

Only that it'll hurt when I need to leave.

I don't know why I feel safe with him, just that I do. And if there's one thing I've gotten really good at over the years, it's trusting my gut.

"It's fine," I force out. "I'll take your word for it."

"How old are you?" I ask, though my voice is breathless with awe as my stare bounces around his home.

"Twenty-seven," he answers instantly.

I've never seen a twenty-seven-year-old own a house like this. It's *beautiful*.

The interior is a combination of black stone, veneer wooden panels, and cream walls. Plant life is scattered throughout the open floor plan, complementing the earthy-toned furniture.

The living room is sunken in from the kitchen, two rounded steps leading down to where a massive, circular black couch sits in front of a fireplace, a huge TV mounted above it.

To my left is a sleek kitchen with a huge island in the middle. There, Cage lays the cardboard stack of pizza boxes, left over from a few hours ago. The supreme was my favorite, and I found the cheese too boring. To Silas's dismay, I didn't mind the pineapple on the pizza, though it wouldn't be something I'd order for myself.

"You can have more if you're still hungry," Cage offers, nodding toward the food.

"I'm full," I protest. I've never eaten so much in my life, even if it was only four slices.

I grew up eating ketchup sandwiches on stale bread and soup when I was with Francesca. Greasy, fried foods were a luxury I never knew.

His stare slides down my form slowly before returning to mine. By the time he's finished, I'm on fire and shifting on my feet, my thighs clenching from the pulse between them.

"You'll be hungry again soon enough."

I don't know what that means. But the way his voice roughened has me shifting once again.

"We'll see," I retort, feeling as if I just issued a challenge. His darkening eyes seem to confirm that.

I almost expect him to shatter the pretense that this is an innocent sleepover and strip me down where I stand. Instead, he turns away and gestures for me to follow him.

I can't decipher why I feel disappointed by that, just that I do.

"The guest bedroom is this way," he calls. It takes an extra second to unglue my feet from the wooden floor and follow him. "Do you need to shower?"

That question nearly stops me in my tracks again. I had a shower at the motel I stayed in last night, but the water pressure was comparable to a yard sprinkler, the drain was clogged, and the tub held more rust and grime than soap.

A shower in a place like this just might be the closest to heaven I'll ever get.

"Y-yeah, if you don't mind," I manage. However, the second the words leave my mouth, I wonder if I'm being incredibly stupid. Or rather, stupid-*er*. Showering in a stranger's home, naked and vulnerable. Not that I'm much more protected with a scrappy t-shirt and torn jeans, but at least I'd die with a bit of dignity.

"I have a towel and washcloth for you. A spare toothbrush, too, if you need it. Even razors."

I chew my bottom lip, feeling a small burst of excitement. Admittedly, it's been a long time since I've had the luxury of shaving my legs.

"All of it," I rush out, then instantly flush with embarrassment over my clear desperation for a decent shower. Clearing my throat, I tack on, "Please."

I can't see his face, but I know he's grinning.

He leads me into a spacious hallway, where an ornate gothic stone bench is placed on the left side, an array of different plants covering it, and beautiful artwork surrounding it. We veer off to the left and enter through double doors that open into a massive bedroom.

"This is the guest bedroom?" I ask incredulously, taking in the biggest bed I've ever seen covered in soft black sheets, the crackling fireplace on the opposite wall, and the white ceiling with beautiful black wooden beams lining across it.

"One of them, yeah."

"I can't imagine what the master looks like then," I mumble, a funny look passing over my face.

He turns, a devilish look on his face as he asks, "Would you like to see it?"

"Nope. Bigger isn't always better," I quip, noting the open door to my left where I can see a black stone vanity. I head toward it without waiting for his response, and his burning stare doesn't abate as it follows me. "I assume the bathroom is already stocked with what I need?"

"Sure is," he drawls deeply.

My stomach flutters as I hurry into the bathroom, too much of a chicken to spare him a glance. By the time I get the door shut and lean heavily against it, my heart is pounding.

He'll be waiting for me to finish, and what comes after will be something I've never done before.

I'm going to fuck him.

And for the first time, it'll be my choice.

I'm so fucking nervous, but it doesn't feel... bad. In fact, it's exhilarating. It's a foreign emotion, but I can understand why people get addicted to it.

Because at this moment, I've never felt more alive.

chapter fifteen

CAGE

PRESENT
2022

When I was a kid, my grandma once convinced me that my mother came out of the womb talking.

I'm *still* convinced of it.

"So, I told her, 'Ma'am, if you're going to keep talkin' all that shit, at least carry some toilet paper with you to wipe your damn mouth.'"

Molly cups a hand over her smiling lips, green eyes glittering with mirth as she shakes her head at my mom.

She used to embarrass the absolute shit out of me and Olivia. But once we lost my sister, I found a new appreciation for her eccentric personality. She's all I have in this world, and despite her utter heartbreak over her daughter's death, she always showed up for me. Never let me down, despite how hard the world tried to kick her to the ground.

"I don't like bullies. What do you kids call 'em these days? Karens? Well, she was one of them. Except I just called her what she really is, which is a defective sperm that grew too much of a mouth instead of a brain."

"You're such a poet, Ma," I comment dryly.

The tiger lilies I had just bought Mom are arranged in the crystal vase she's had for decades at the center of the dinner table, our empty plates and wineglasses in front of us.

I pull out my pack of nicotine gum and shove one in my mouth. I'm tempted to eat the whole sleeve of them now that we've finished dinner. Mom already served the peach cobbler, which I skipped. I'm not much of a sweets person.

Unless, of course, it's Molly's pussy.

"Am I? Next time, I'll charge ya just to listen to me speak then," she retorts. "All this time, and I coulda been getting rich just from yelling at you."

I chuckle, glancing at Molly and finding her biting back a smile. One of these days, I'll teach her how to set them free.

"Have some more to drink," Mom encourages, pouring more red wine into Molly's glass. "With as stiff as you are, I fear my son will be marrying a wooden puppet. He'll be picking splinters out of his—"

"Jesus fucking Christ," I groan. "Quit talking."

"I'll make sure to buy him a magnifying glass then," Molly says, one corner of her lips curled upward.

"For the splinters or his penis?"

"*Ma.*"

A laugh bursts from Molly's throat, and instantly, I forgive my mother for being so crass. I'm used to her making jokes at my expense, but I'm confident Molly has never met anyone like my mother, and her personality definitely isn't a one-size-fits-all. There's been a few girlfriends in the past that she's scared off, which instantly told me they weren't worth it anyway.

"I'm not gonna scare ya off, am I?" Mom asks her, as if reading my mind.

She shakes her head. "I don't scare that easily. Not anymore, at least."

"See? She's tough," Mom tells me, then focuses on Molly, a sly grin on her face. She's going to say something terrible, except I don't have time to stop her. "How viable is your uterus? Eggs haven't shriveled yet, right? I've been waiting for grandkids."

"I'm sorry about her," I apologize, leading Molly into my childhood room. "Believe it or not, she doesn't ask about every woman's uterus that I've brought around."

She gives me a guarded look. "How many women have you brought around?"

My expression is serious as I say, "Two. And they were hopeless attempts at trying to make myself feel what I felt with you."

She turns away, choosing not to answer.

"My mom really likes you," I tell her, refusing to let her run away, even if it's in her own mind.

"She hardly knows me," Molly argues softly, running her fingers over a high school soccer trophy.

"She knows all that she needs to," I say, shrugging a shoulder.

She raises a brow. "What have you told her?"

I grin. "Only the important parts. That you're incredibly strong, funny, and the most amazing woman I've ever met. I think she can see that already."

"What if she's wrong? We're not even dating."

My muscles tighten, and my teeth clench. I'm overcome with the urge to show her just how wrong she is. She's mine, as explicitly as the heart in my chest.

I'm advancing on her before she can slide her fingers across another trophy. Her breath halts as I crowd into her, my chest molding against her back. She shivers as I lean in closely, feathering my lips across the shell of her ear.

Those little tremors are not nearly enough.

I want her to fucking convulse like she's being possessed, and it'll be my cock inside her while she does.

"You think I need an anniversary date to put my baby inside you?"

I don't recognize my own voice anymore, but I do find that little gasp familiar.

"You wouldn't," she breathes. "We hardly know each other."

"No," I agree. "Not yet, at least." I place a kiss below her ear. "But I would. I absolutely—" Kiss. "—fucking—" Kiss. "—would."

She whips around, those fiery eyes pinned to mine as she snaps, "I wouldn't let you. What if I find you to be absolutely insufferable? You could leave food crusted on your dishes instead of rinsing them off. Or have dirty clothes all over the floor and soggy towels on the bed." She pauses and glances nervously to the side. "You could find my nightmares intolerable."

"You don't think I have them?" I question, enjoying the feeling of her heart beating against my chest. "I've suffered in life, too, baby. Just in different ways."

"You have nightmares?" she questions curiously.

In response, I grab her hand and pull her after me.

"Where...?

She trails off as I lead her out of my old room, down the hall, and to the last door on the right.

She doesn't speak as she takes in the pale yellow walls, blue-and-yellow duvet, and the pictures pinned to the corkboard hanging above her white desk. Pictures of a blonde-haired girl sticking her tongue out next to friends or holding up the peace sign and pursing her lips.

She was beautiful.

"Her name was Olivia. She was murdered when she was sixteen, and I was twelve. It ultimately led me to get into the business I'm in. She and her friend were caught trying to get into a nightclub with a fake ID. Her killer was a cop who came to pick them up, and she never came home."

"I'm sorry," Molly whispers, slowly walking up to the photos and studying them closely. "Not many people come home."

"You did, though, didn't you?"

Slowly, she turns her head just enough to peer at me over her shoulder.

"If anyone deserved to be the one to escape, it would've been her." She turns away, but not before I see the sadness polluting her eyes. "Turns out, I wasn't important enough to deserve it. I thought Layla needed me, but I think I only delayed her happiness. My father was being investigated, and eventually, CPS would've found him unfit anyway. I was convinced she'd just go to another unfit home, but what if she didn't? What if she found a good home, rather than me taking her away to live four miserable years with me? No stability. Being hungry all the time—" Her voice cracks, and she cuts herself off abruptly.

"You're wrong, ya know," I tell her, fire building in my chest. "Or, at least, there's a good chance you are. She would've gone into the system, and there's no guarantee she would've ended up with a good family. She could've gone from one abuser to the next."

Molly nods, the movement choppy, but she doesn't appear convinced.

I'm furious that she could think so little of herself. Even more furious at the people who made her feel as though she's not a goddamn goddess walking this earth that we don't deserve.

"You are the most important person I've ever met, Molly," I whisper. "And while I will always be devastated that my sister didn't survive, I'm so fucking happy that you did."

Though her back is facing me, I hear a soft sniffle. She doesn't respond. Instead, she stares at Olivia, that smile on her face forever frozen in time.

"For years, I couldn't step foot in this room. Anytime I saw those pictures with her smiling face, it would slowly morph into a dramatic frown, her mouth opening on a wail. It looked fucking demonic, and I had all but convinced myself that was the real expression frozen on her face when she died. Her cries of terror outlived her heartbeat."

"Do you want to talk about her?" Molly asks quietly, voice clogged with tears. "I'd like to get to know her."

My chest tightens, and I can't tell if I want to wrap her in my arms because she cares, or because I need something to hold on to while I tell her about my sister.

"She loved 80s music. 'Sunglasses at Night' by Corey Hart was her favorite song, and she insisted on constantly wearing these neon pink sunglasses for three months after she heard it for the first time. Mom thought she was the cutest thing, and I made it a point to tell her how ridiculous she looked."

Molly's head swivels to find the picture of Olivia wearing them, a bright smile pasted on her face as she sits beside me in our mom's car, my face slackened in a dry, unamused expression. She'd just gotten her driver's license that day and, of course, blasted that Corey Hart song all the way home.

"She wore pink lipstick every day, even when she was sick. She always said the version of her without it was her evil alter ego. She hated tomatoes but put ketchup on everything, even her mashed potatoes. Which I still find very fucking gross, by the way."

"I would have to agree with that," Molly chuckles softly.

Her stare slides to a picture of Olivia sitting beside a bald little boy in a hospital bed, with birthday hats atop their heads.

"When she turned sixteen, she spent her birthday at the children's hospital in the cancer unit because she felt guilty that they may never see that age."

My heart aches, and for a moment, it feels impossible to continue.

"She never knew she wouldn't see past that age, either."

Molly turns to me, sadness swirling in her gaze.

"She sounds like she was an incredible kid," she whispers. "Amazing, really."

I nod, working to swallow past the rock in my throat.

Almost shyly, she grabs my hand and walks me over to Olivia's bed. I'm not sure what she intends, but my head is too fuzzy to ask.

With a slight smile on her face, she lies down on one side of the bed and pats the empty spot next to her. Confused, I follow suit, the both of us staring up at the ceiling silently. Right as I begin to ask her what she's doing, a burst of music fills the room.

My eyes flick to where she holds her phone up, "Sunglasses at Night" playing from the speakers.

"Mol—"

"Shh," she hushes, laying her hand over mine. "Don't be rude. Olivia might be trying to listen, too."

I can't breathe.

A fire explodes in my chest, burning a path down to our entwined hands.

I hope to God that it burns her, too.

I want the flames to melt our hands together so she can never let go.

If she wanted me to fall in love with her, she only needed to tell me. Now, she has no choice in the matter.

Though, I suppose she never really did.

Turning my head, I stare at her until she meets my eyes. "I will chase away all your nightmares until they grow wary of returning. They will fear me, my little ghost. But you never will."

chapter sixteen

MOLLY

NINE YEARS AGO
2013

I don't know that I've felt so clean in my entire life. Nor has my skin ever been so smooth.

A towel is wrapped tightly around my body, and my hair tumbles over my shoulders in a mass of curls, water dripping from the ends.

Anxiety is holding every last one of my nerves hostage. I'm standing at the door, staring at it as if it's the mirror on the wall from *Snow White*, and it's going to tell me my future.

Will I like sex?

I've never had an orgasm before. Too caught up in trying to survive to even consider it. I've always avoided intimacy or anything to do with sex. After what my father did to me, and then everything that happened in Francesca's house—I never felt inclined to try.

Now, I wish I had. If I don't even know what I like, how will he?

I'm too much in my head.

Surely, he can figure it out.

Inhaling deeply, I swing open the door and find the room empty. That's both disappointing and relieving. Had he been standing there, I probably wouldn't know what to do with myself. But that means I'm going to have to seek him out now. Which sounds equally terrifying.

What the fuck am I even supposed to say to him?

Hi, excuse me, can you put your dick inside me? I'm not sure if I'll like it, but let's find out together.

I'm going to embarrass myself. I just know it.

I walk over to the bed, noticing a pile of clothing folded atop. They look like men's clothing, and when I pick up the soft black t-shirt, I'm instantly hit with a delectable scent—a mix of vetiver and sandalwood.

My eyes nearly roll, and I'm unabashed in the way I practically stuff the soft fabric up my nose.

"Smell good?"

The voice is so sudden, there's no containing the loud screech that bursts from my throat. I drop the shirt while I whip around, my towel unraveling from the quick movement. I catch it before it falls completely, then bar my arm across my breasts and hold it there, though it only manages to cover my center. With my other hand, I grip the towel against my stomach, keeping it from swaying and exposing me further.

My heart is on the verge of exploding out of my chest, and I'm too stunned to get my shit together and cover myself properly. At this moment, I hardly remember how to breathe. My lungs are functioning no better than an old, rusty engine that was left abandoned in a junkyard.

Green eyes darken, a red-hot flame burning within. They blaze a trail over my exposed flesh, unashamed by the way his stare so readily devours me. I don't miss the way it catches on the white bite marks imprinted on my skin. My hips, my thighs, my stomach...

His teeth visibly clench, rage flashing across his gaze.

"What?" The delayed question comes out as a breathless squeak.

Nostrils flaring, he takes a step toward me, and the battered muscle in my chest flies up into my throat. I lock my knees, forcing myself to stand still despite how much I want to back away.

Distinctly, I feel a bead of water drip onto the swell of my breast, which his gaze immediately tracks. The droplet slowly trails down the valley between my breasts, and the muscle in his jaw pulses, nearly tearing through his skin. His animalistic gaze snaps up to mine, his chin tipping low as he stares at me fiercely from beneath thick brows.

Heat gathers low in my stomach, sinking down between my trembling thighs. My clit pulses from that single look alone, and I know that if he were to part my legs, he'd see the evidence glistening from within.

Never in my life have I *ever* felt this way. Never has my core felt so... empty.

He's silent as he stalks toward me, but I'm positive my escalated heart rate is audible.

I shift on my feet, feeling how slick I've become. It's almost embarrassing, yet it's a reaction the men in Francesca's house would claim, but never actually accomplished. They wanted us to weep for them, but the only thing they ever made wet was our eyes.

Cage, on the other hand, easily makes my pussy weep, and he hasn't even touched me yet.

He stops an inch before me, the heat radiating from him warming my skin. Goosebumps scatter across my flesh, and a shiver tumbles down my spine. It feels as if bees are buzzing beneath the surface, their fluttering wings creating electricity and engulfing my body in it.

"Do you want me to leave?" he asks quietly.

It's a question that requires a simple answer. Yes or no. Yet, my brain turns it over as if he presented me with a complicated math equation.

The throbbing between my legs screams its answer, though my head can do nothing but focus on how I have no idea what the fuck I'm doing.

"I-I'm not very good at this," I mumble, keeping my eyes pinned to his chest. I'm not brave enough to meet his stare. It'll eat me alive, and I'm too afraid that I'll allow it to chase me away before I can let him touch me.

"Has anyone made you feel good before?"

I lick my lips, feeling like any moisture in my body has flooded south.

"No."

"Then that's all you need to do. You don't need to do anything else, except let me make you feel good."

My nod is choppy, and the butterflies in my stomach have been freed. But they're hungry, too, and they've begun to tear at my insides. Especially as his forefinger hooks beneath my chin and forces it up, until my stare snaps to his like a magnet.

"Where do you want me to kiss first?" he asks, his tone hushed, deep and rough.

Silently, I reach up and brush my fingers across my lips, drawing his attention there.

He's slow to lean in, as if to prolong the torture. But the second his lips capture mine between his, I wish he'd given me an extra moment to breathe.

The kiss is short, but primal and entirely too explosive for only a second. It's nothing like those pecks I've seen on TV, and I can't imagine they felt the pure fire that's raging between us.

He watches me for half a second before he crushes his mouth back onto mine, evoking a volcanic eruption that's melting me into a pile of ash. Yet, he holds on to all the pieces of me and gathers them against his chest until there is no me and him. Only an us.

His hand slides along my jawline and dives into my damp curls, directing the angle of my head so he can lick along the seam of my lips. And like a greedy little puppet, I eagerly open for him. He tastes the smallest of gasps on his tongue as it glides against mine, which seems only to invigorate him.

It transforms from a passionate kiss to being devoured whole, and the only thing I can do is submit. I'm a slave to him, and it's the first time I'm happy to be one.

In a moment of madness, I drop my towel altogether, the thump over my feet causing him to pull away, though his lips rest against mine.

"Where do you want me to kiss next?" he rasps.

I've never heard a voice so deep, bordering on demonic. It would make sense why I feel so possessed.

"Lower," I rasp.

He places an open-mouthed kiss on my jaw, ending it there.

"Let me hear your words," he purrs. "Do you want me to kiss these pretty tits? Or I can kiss your sweet pussy. I'll fucking feast on her if you want."

"Yes," I moan. "All of it."

He dips at the knees just enough to grab the backs of my thighs and lift me up, my feet hooking behind his back. But it's useless because, within moments, he's laying me on the bed and descending my body, wasting no time wrapping his lips around my nipple.

A shot of electricity races down my spine, and my back bows off the bed, a cry slipping past my lips.

"Cage!"

His answering growl is primal, followed by the sharp bite of his teeth. My mouth falls open on a silent scream, my body unable to properly function beneath the assault.

Every one of my nerves is hyper-fixated on the way his tongue swirls over me. Then, he switches to the other, cupping both of my breasts in his large palms as if he's feeding them into his mouth.

My fingers dive into his short strands, scraping my nails against his scalp.

His teeth gnash at my abused nipple one more time before he pulls away, taking his wet kisses lower.

My lungs tighten, refusing to pull in a single breath as he reaches my belly button. There lies a scar that's fitted perfectly around it.

Aside from the one on my face, I've always hated that one most because of how ugly and centered on my body it is.

I'm prepared to tell him to ignore it, but before I can manage a sound, he's matching his teeth to the scar and sinking them into it.

"Cage!" I screech, the burning pain encompassing my shock.

When he lifts his wicked stare to mine, I see a mix of rage and something I could only describe as possession.

"I will claim every part of you, Molly. And that includes the pieces of you those fuckers tried to take from me."

My brows pinch. "From you?" I repeat dumbly.

Deliberately, he places a kiss over the bite.

"Don't be fooled, little ghost, I will own you even after you've disappeared. You may vanish, but your soul will always be mine."

I'm not sure if it's normal for one-night stands to be so damn intense. It sounds like a proclamation of love without saying the words. Except way more... permanent.

Yet, he may as well have gathered any resolve I had left and crushed it beneath his boot. He's so intense, but there isn't an iota of me that cares right now. He feels too good, and if it continues this way, maybe he'll be right.

Though it won't stop me from becoming a ghost.

It's the only thing I know how to be.

His stare drops, and he resumes his path toward my pussy, pausing briefly to bite over the white scars on my hip and thighs. Each time, it grows more intense. By the time his hot breath fans over my center, I'm trembling.

"Cage," I whisper, feeling as if I'm on the verge of combusting. I need so much more, but I'm also not sure if I can handle what's next.

He inhales, and my eyes widen in mortification. Before I can slap him or move away, he's parting my thighs and covering my clit with his mouth. Except he doesn't lick me yet, depriving me of the sensation my body needs so desperately.

"Please," I groan impatiently.

Grinning devilishly, he delivers the smallest lick, sending a shock wave up my spine.

My back arches, and the strangest confidence washes over me.

"Please lick my pussy. I need you to make me feel good," I plead. "You promised."

"Fuck," he curses a moment before he flattens his tongue and glides it up my slit. My outcry is answered by another thorough lick, in which he groans deeply.

"Christ, baby, you taste so sweet, I don't know how I'll stop. I would gladly drown in the prettiest cunt I've ever eaten."

His words are filthy, but the way he continuously flicks his pointed tongue over my clit is entirely depraved. There's no time to prepare for the sharp sensations invading every inch of my insides. I'm overcome with pure bliss, and for several heartbeats, the only sound I can muster is a loud moan.

"Oh, ffu— Oh my God, Cage."

He doesn't relent, and within moments, I'm hurtling toward a far more powerful sensation. Pleasure, euphoria—they're too weak of words to describe the hurricane building inside of me.

"Oh, please, don't stop." Yet, that's exactly what he does. "Cage!" I shout as he pulls away, only to dive his tongue into my pussy, curling it upward.

I writhe beneath him, grinding my hips against him and hoping to God he does fucking drown. My nails scrape against his scalp, and if I could hook them beneath his flesh and force him to make me come, I'd happily show him what it means to be a puppet.

My eyes roll as I get close again, and for the second time, he pulls away.

A frustrated scream bursts from my throat, but before I can spit a threat at him, he grabs the underside of my thighs and pushes them forward until my lower back is lifted off the bed and my knees are hiked to my ears. I'm folded in half, my core less than a foot from my face.

Within seconds, his mouth is covering my pussy again, and this time, he's showing me exactly what he's doing to me. With perfect precision, he strokes my clit, my arousal and his saliva pouring down my mound and dripping onto my breasts.

Cries stream from my throat as I grip his forearms, red crescents forming in his flesh. Once more, he's driving me directly toward the edge. My thighs shake violently in his hold as he feasts on me like a starving animal driven to madness from hunger.

"Cage, I'm going to come. Please, *please*, let me come," I beg breathlessly. "Let me drown you."

A growl unleashes from his chest, vibrating against me. Dark green eyes are pinned to me as he viciously sucks on my clit, his tongue unrelenting.

My throat closes and my vision blackens a moment before I explode. The scream that unleashes is so sharp, it leaves my throat raw. Colorful fireworks detonate behind my pinched eyes, filling the blackness with a mirage of blues, pinks, greens, and purples.

I don't know how long I'm submerged beneath the storm, but distinctly, I can feel my body seizing furiously. Yet, he holds on to me with a firm grip, keeping me in place as he continues to lap at my cunt until I have nothing left to give.

After what feels like forever, I come down from an experience that could only be described as an exorcism.

"Jesus f-fucking Christ," I stutter, my voice cracking and shaken, my mouth almost feeling numb.

His gaze is fierce. "If you're asking Him to save you, then I will nail Him onto that fucking cross again. You will be my ruin, but only *I* will be your savior."

chapter seventeen

MOLLY

NINE YEARS AGO
2013

Even if I had the brain function to respond, I wouldn't know how.

Gently, he drops my trembling legs back onto the bed, only to draw his t-shirt over his head.

Jesus fucking Christ.

I keep the words to myself this time, but a small gasp manages to slip free.

His body is sculpted better than the marble statues of gods in museums across the world. Chiseled to pure perfection, with black tattoos covering his stomach, chest, and down his arms.

The gray sweatpants he's wearing do nothing to hide his hard cock, and the moment I lay eyes on it, I immediately wish I hadn't. In this case, maybe ignorance would've been bliss.

"Cage, I don't know if I can handle it," I say hesitantly, now extremely cautious of trying to take all of him inside me. I'm unsure how I'd even fit it in my goddamn *mouth*.

"It'll fit, baby," he assures confidently, hooking his thumbs into the waistband of his sweats and sliding them down his thick thighs, and off his legs.

His cock is even more intimidating without the clothing over it, and much bigger than I thought. But, fuck, is it beautiful. Long and deliciously thick, with pulsing veins cording throughout it. He's perfectly proportioned, and even the swollen head has me aching to suck on it.

"Keep staring at me like that, and I'll give that little mouth of yours more than it can handle."

It takes effort to drag my gaze up to his, my expression twisted with apprehension. "That's not going to fit."

He grins devilishly. "It'll fit."

I give him a look that tells him just how wrong I think he is, though that only widens his smirk. He oozes confidence, and while I'm still incredibly terrified of the beast between his legs, I do feel at ease that he knows what he's doing.

"Do you want to watch me prove you wrong?" he asks lowly, his voice deepening. Reaching over to his discarded sweats, he plunges his hand into the pocket and produces a foil packet.

He brought protection.

Relief washes over me. So much so that I don't hesitate to whisper, "Yes."

I'm enthralled by the way he expertly slides the condom over his thick length, and I'm short of breath when he prowls up my body, hovering over me. My stomach tightens when he leans down and brushes the faintest of kisses over my lips, eliciting crackling static between them.

"I'll feed my cock into your pussy nice and slow, okay, baby? I'll make sure you're so fucking full, then just when you think you can't take any more—" His lip pulls up into a savage snarl. "—I'll go deeper."

That's not just a promise, but a threat.

"What if I can't take it?" I question, my tone husky with desire.

He trails his lips over my jawline and to the shell of my ear. Just before he places a soft kiss below my lobe, he murmurs darkly, "You've survived much worse."

His tone is unapologetic, indicating that he's confident in my ability to survive *him*. My stomach clenches around the anxious butterflies within.

Once more, he's lifting the underside of my thighs, hooking them over his arms as he positions the tip at my entrance. He applies just enough pressure to part my lips, but not enough to breach past my opening.

I've never been on a roller coaster, except this is precisely what I imagine it feels like when it crests over the hill right before the big drop. The anticipation is nearly as terrifying as it is thrilling.

"Cage," I breathe shakily, needing him to do something—anything—but leave me in suspense.

"Take me," he commands roughly. I shake my head, at a loss for what he needs me to do. Only then my pussy contracts and it feels like my body is suctioning him in.

"Fuuuuck, that's it," he rasps, the both of us watching the tip of his cock disappear. "So goddamn tight, *fuck*, Molly."

"I— What—"

"It's a natural reaction, baby. Most men just aren't patient enough to wait for a woman's pussy to invite him in," he explains tightly.

I didn't know that was possible, but he's pushing his hips deeper, and I no longer care. I'm too focused on learning how to breathe again, yet it seems like a futile effort. Just as he promised, he feeds his cock into me until I'm on the verge of bursting.

"Ohhh, ngg, th-that's so good," I mewl, my eyes threatening to cross from the pleasure overtaking me.

"Look how fucking greedy your cunt is, baby. You see how badly it wants my cock? It's practically begging for me to fuck it." He spits the words through gritted teeth, his body coiled with tension, veins pulsating throughout his arms and hands. "Is that what you want, Molly? For your little pussy to be fucked?"

I nod jerkily, attempting to utter a simple *yes*, but only managing to let out a sharp, slurred sound. I'm drugged on euphoria, yet I need more. I'm a fiend for it, and it's something only Cage can give me.

He drives completely inside me, and my eyes cross, while the most erotic whimper sounds from his throat.

"Oh— Fuck, Cage," I cry, the words as deprived of oxygen as my lungs.

His lips feather over my ear, and a deep foreboding gathers in my bones a moment before he gives his warning.

"Brace yourself, little ghost. I don't fuck kindly."

My heart rockets up into my throat, and I hurry to wrap my hands around his biceps, but he leaves me no time to prepare.

He retreats to the tip, and then he's driving into me, setting a hard, steady pace that steals my breath, my vision, my goddamn sanity.

Delicious moans spill past his lips, his pleasure as loud and unhinged as mine. It only drives the butterflies in my stomach wild, as if they have no direction to migrate, leaving them to wander.

"Fuck, Molly, your pussy is gripping me so tight," he groans. "You're clinging to me like a desperate little slut."

One arm unhooks from my leg before he slides his palm up my throat to cup the underside of my jaw. He grips tight, forcing my unfocused gaze to his. The emotion in his stare is just as intense as the way he pumps into me. It borders on obsession and has the organs in my body plummeting to the pit of my stomach.

"Eyes on me while I claim you," he growls. "I need you to see me like I see you."

"I see you," I whimper, though my focus is unstable.

I'm already nearing another orgasm, and I don't know that either of us will be able to contain my reaction when it hits.

There's no control over a natural disaster. Only allowing it to wreak havoc and bracing yourself for the outcome. The storm building inside me is catastrophic. It'll be devastating, and I'll be in ruins.

"Fuck, I'm going to come," I gasp, my eyes beginning to roll. I feel entirely out of control as I pummel toward that edge. My surroundings blur, and the only thing I can see through my fuzzy vision is his devilish grin. It looks like he's laughing at me, as if he's amused by how easily he can make me come. It's almost degrading, yet it sets me on fire anyway.

His hips pause suddenly, and immediately my orgasm wanes, a downward roll on a steep hill.

A frustrated groan is the only response I'm capable of.

"Didn't I already tell you to keep your eyes on me? I'm in the business of making you disappear, not in repeating myself," he states, his tone almost threatening. My glazed stare flies to his.

"I'm sorry, please keep fucking me," I rush out, rolling my hips to reignite the pleasure.

"Don't make me ask again, Molly," he murmurs before pinching my jaw harder, ensuring my attention stays locked on him.

I'm nodding, prepared to do anything he asks of me if it means he makes me feel good again.

"That's a good girl," he purrs darkly, finally resuming. Except this time, he angles his hips differently, hitting a spot deep inside of me that's never been reached before.

It's almost impossible to keep my eyes straight, but the expression on his beautiful face is as striking as it is heart-dropping. His mouth is parted as sexy moans pour from his tongue, and his thick brows are slashed above his eyes in an expression of ecstasy.

It takes no time to reach that pinnacle again and then go free diving off it.

His name rips past my lips in a scream that leaves my throat raw. Though, I'm unsure if I'd notice anything outside of the orgasm that crashes through me. It sends my back arching off the bed as if possessed by a soul-eating demon that's determined to leave everything in its path decimated.

The power of it is breathtaking, and whatever control I had over my body ceases to exist. My teeth rattle from how hard I seize, and my death grip on Cage's arms can't even keep me grounded.

There is no mercy in the way he continues to pound into me while spitting his own curses.

"I think you can do better than that," he bites out through clenched teeth.

I shake my head, delirious from the continuous onslaught of his thrusts yet understanding that he has no intention of stopping.

"I can't... I can't take any more," I pant breathlessly. "Please, it's too much!"

"Is it?" His tone is mocking, followed by a coo that suggests '*you poor baby.*'

My head kicks back, so entirely overwhelmed with the sensations that my brain is unable to compute how to handle it. I shift between trembling violently, slapping Cage's arms, to clawing at his flesh with little reserve.

"Let's see how tight that pussy can hold on to me," he growls. "Show me how a dirty little slut milks my cock."

"Fuck you," I choke out, starbursts beginning to explode behind my pinched eyes.

"You are, baby, and fuck, you're doing such a good job," he whimpers in my ear before drawing my lobe in his mouth and sucking.

A sharp outcry is the only sound I'm capable of uttering. A third orgasm takes hold of me, sending my soul into space where I float above and watch myself come wholly undone, my inner walls contracting around his cock.

"Fuuuuck, baby, that's it. Just like that, fuck yes, just like that. You're such a good girl," Cage chants against me.

His back muscles flex, and his thrusts become choppy, losing himself in time and space along with me.

"Molly," he rasps out, followed by a moan that is long and unrestrained. Distinctly, I feel him erupt, though I have the misfortune of the condom preventing me from feeling it inside me.

He stills, panting against my lips now, his breath syncing with mine. We're both shaking, and he relaxes on top of me, though he's careful to keep his weight from crushing me.

We're both silent for several minutes, spending the time searching for our breaths.

"I've been called a slut a lot," I admit after a few more moments, my voice cracking. He lifts his bowed head to gaze down at me carefully, waiting for me to collect my thoughts. "But I liked it when you said it. Just... only during sex, though, okay?"

He brushes a few strands away from my face gently.

"If a man ever calls you something you don't like, I'll fucking kill him. I'll always respect your boundaries."

I catch my bottom lip between my teeth before it can tremble. It takes a moment as the urge to cry subsides.

I've never felt so... respected. Like my feelings about what happens to my body are actually valued. Like they *mean* something to him.

"You're different," I mumble. "Thank you for showing me how to enjoy something I never thought I'd enjoy. For respecting my body. And for giving me something to hold on to before I disappear."

His eyes soften. "You can always hold on to me, Molly. Always."

chapter eighteen

MOLLY

PRESENT
2022

"I can't do a delivery today," I tell Legion, attempting to keep my nerves in check. I've never told him no before.

But this is necessary.

There's a pause. "May I ask why?"

I chew my bottom lip, contemplating if I should just tell the truth or not. However, I don't want my personal issues to come between me and my job. Or at least, I don't wish for Legion to know that.

"I'm uncomfortable with Cage," I blurt out.

That wasn't what I was planning to say. I was supposed to tell him my pigs are sick. Although it's technically the truth, though not in the way Legion is probably thinking.

I'm not uncomfortable because I don't like Cage; I'm uncomfortable because I like him way too much.

More silence.

After a few beats, I can't take it anymore. "I don't know if anyone has ever told you this, but your silence is super unnerving."

I'm sweating. It's forming along my hairline and between my boobs. I shake out my free hand to release some tension. I don't even know *why* I'm so nervous. Legion's never made me feel threatened. But *fuck,* he's really intimidating for a dude that never shows his face.

"What has he done?"

"Nothing!" I exclaim. "Don't kill him, please."

"Is this because he's in love with you? Or because you're in love with him?"

I slap my hand over my face. None of this is going to plan.

"That... No, neither," I stutter.

"Are you lying?"

"Legion," I groan. "I just think it's best that Cage and I no longer work together. That's all. Nothing personal."

It's *so* personal. I am such a liar—and not even a good one.

"Where's Eli? Isn't it time for him to come back?" I ask.

One Mississippi. Two Mississippi. Three Mississippi...

"Eli will do the delivery tonight. Your comfort is my priority."

My shoulders slump in relief. "Thank you, Legion."

"Have a good night, Molly."

The phone clicks off, and I instantly feel sick to my stomach. Legion will call Cage and tell him he's off the job. Maybe it'll be casual, and he'll tell Cage that Eli is simply ready to come back.

Or maybe he'll tell the truth, and Cage will come here demanding answers.

Which is something I'm not prepared for.

What the fuck am I supposed to say? That spending time with his mom and laying in his sister's bed listening to her favorite song scared the absolute shit out of me?

It only proves how much of a runner I am. How, even after all these years, I live like there's a target on my back. And, because of that, I refuse to let anyone get close.

I know that no one's coming after me anymore. Not really. According to Legion, Francesca and Rocco are dead, and Z destroyed the Society—which turned out to be some shadow government that was playing a massive hand in human trafficking operations.

Even if I were discovered by the public, I could easily lie and say I didn't make it out until years after my father and Layla's disappearance. No one could prove otherwise. But I've found comfort in my anonymity, and somehow, I've convinced myself that Cage is a threat to that.

I should've never agreed to dinner with his mom.

But it doesn't matter now.

I'm comfortable with my life. I've found my own retribution for what happened to me, and I don't need a man's love or his cock to fix me. I've already picked up every little, fucking, chipped piece of me and meticulously put them back together. I'm not broken anymore; I just don't work the same. But there's nothing wrong with being different.

I'm better off alone.

Francesca and her hound dogs made sure of that.

"Miss my face, huh? I always knew you couldn't resist me."

Eli's always been a nuisance in a sort of endearing way. But he's a loyal employee of Legion, and despite his terrible pickup lines, his jokes are harmless, and he's never made me uncomfortable.

I've been working with him since returning to Montana, and I have a soft spot for him.

"How could I? You're the full package," I answer dryly, though a small grin curls one corner of my lips.

He drops the dead body on my metal table, then splays out his arms as if he's presenting himself as a prize.

He's a cute guy—still in his mid-twenties with pretty brown eyes, a clean-shaven face, and a killer smile, though he's self-conscious of the front tooth that's slightly shifted over the other. His light brown hair is cut short and styled away from his face with probably five different products. He's one of those guys that takes his hair *very* seriously.

With how often he carries bodies around, he's lanky but fit, and he ensures to wear clothing that shows off just how many muscles he possesses.

Regardless, he's not my type. It seems only one man fits in that category, and it's always been Cage.

"I won't make you beg anymore. Come to papa."

I roll my eyes and grab my hair clippers, even though the old man has barely any left.

"Don't make me throw up on the corpse. I don't think my pigs would appreciate it."

He scoffs, and his upper lip curls in distaste. "Somehow, I think they'd consider it extra seasoning."

"Okay, that's disgusting," I mumble, faking a gag. I'm used to the filth that comes along with owning pigs. They're dirty animals, regardless of how hard I work to keep this place clean. Not just from blood but their grime, too.

And despite what I feed them for dinner, I still don't like to consider all the different things they'll eat. It's nearly limitless, and that in itself is rather unsettling.

"If I die, please don't feed me to them. Especially Oregano. That one is *too* eager when she eats," he pleas dramatically.

I snort, finishing shaving the dead man's hair and moving on to extracting his teeth. "Deal, as long as you don't let me become pig food, either."

He places a hand over his heart, like a soldier pledging his allegiance to the flag. "You have my word."

So dramatic.

"So what did this guy do?" I ask, nodding toward the corpse.

"Got a bit too friendly with his daughter. Most fucked-up part was that his friend was *also* assaulting her, and the dad pinned it all on him, and got away with it."

I shake my head, my heart hurting for the little girl. Oftentimes, I wish they brought these assholes to me alive.

"Have you spoken to Legion lately?" he asks, quickly changing the subject. The amusement on his face relaxes, settling his features into a more serious expression.

"I did earlier. Why?" I toss the teeth into the grinder and flip it on, the loud noise doing little to cut the building tension in the air.

"Did he mention anything about some brotherhood?"

My brows furrow as I remove the man's clothes. "Brotherhood?" I echo with confusion. "Doesn't sound familiar."

"Yeah, they're dubbed the Basilisk Brotherhood. Apparently, Z knows them now, and they're interested in your job in particular."

My hands freeze, and my muscles grow dense with tension. "What do they want with my job?" I ask, my voice hardening.

If they try to replace me... I'm going to throw a colossal fit. I get paid substantially to do what I do, and it doesn't require me to get any more involved in Legion's work than I want to.

I live a simple life, and I'm *happy* with that.

"They want the organs. Evidently, they think feeding them to pigs is a waste of money."

Now, my brows shoot up my forehead. When I meet Eli's stare, he explains, "They're organ traffickers. And I think they want to work with you and Legion."

I blink, having no idea what to think or feel.

"How come Legion told you about this and not me?"

"He asked me to meet with them first, get a feel for them before Legion entertains their offer. I'm sure he won't approach you about it until he's confident they're good people."

'Good people' is a loose term when it comes to this corner of the world. However, there's a surprising number of people like me. What we do wouldn't exactly grant us access to the pearly gates up above, even though we do it for good reasons. The ones we kill—even the devil wouldn't want them.

"If *Z*'s working with them, then they must not be too bad," I comment, resuming my work and switching on the Sawzall.

Eli shrugs. "My thoughts as well, but you can never be too sure. I'd expect some type of contact regarding this soon. You might be making new friends."

I sigh, cutting off the man's head. Eli takes a step back when the blood splatters too close for comfort.

"Great. Just when I was getting used to you."

Eli gasps. "I resent that. Who else is going to tell you how sexy you are on a weekly basis?"

I raise a brow, unimpressed. "Somehow, I think I'll survive."

chapter nineteen

CAGE

TWO WEEKS LATER
2022

I CALL HER A little ghost, yet for some reason, I never considered that the brat would actually ghost *me*.

My blood simmers as I watch her from the depths of the woods surrounding her barn. As usual, the double doors are wide open, allowing the barn to air out. It's beginning to rain, the cold droplets doing little to cool my temper.

She's cleaning up after feeding her pigs, having just hung up the phone with the lady who confirms the corpses are disposed of.

She's meticulous. Has a routine that she doesn't stray from. And everything has a place.

Except for me, apparently.

A couple of weeks ago, Legion called to inform me Eli was back on the job, but immediately, I knew something was off when he not-so-kindly told me to forget where Molly lives and stay away unless she contacts me herself.

That was all I needed to hear to recognize that she was running.

It shouldn't have surprised me. Yet, it did.

More than that, it fucking *hurt*.

And it absolutely enraged me.

I have no doubts that Molly returns my feelings, except she's completely fucking clueless when it comes to being able to handle those emotions.

She may not have ever been in love, but she also has never met another like me.

And what she seems to forget is that I will *never* give up on her.

I've left her alone for two weeks, sticking to the shadows nearly every night since I got that call. Just observing her go through the motions of life as if I'm not the one who gives it to her. Waiting to see if she'd crack and reach out to me.

She hasn't, and my patience has waned.

God, how tempting it is to walk up behind her, wrap my hands around that dainty little throat, and show her that the only reason she can breathe is because I fucking allow her to.

"Fuck, you really piss me off," I bite out beneath my breath. I plunge my hand into my pocket and pull out my pack of gum, popping two pieces in my mouth this time.

I wait until she's finished at the barn, clicking off the overhead lights before making her way out into the trickling rain. She's not carrying the bag of clothes and hair that she typically burns when she's finished, likely due to the rain. Which means she'll probably wait to scatter the teeth in the mountains.

I contemplate leaving her be for another night. But that lasts all of half a second. My control snaps.

Legion will have to come out of hiding if he wants to try and stop me.

Two weeks without being able to inhale a full breath is torture enough.

Quietly, I make my way through the tall grass, keeping to the shadows as I approach her from behind.

She doesn't sense me until it's too late—her instincts having lightened over the past nine years.

She freezes, her shoulders stiffening and hiking to her ears, the panic snapping her spine straight. And then her damp, thick curls are fisted in my hand and I'm jerking her against my chest, my lips at her ear.

"For a little ghost with so many bones, you're just begging for me to break them," I growl.

A sharp gasp breaks through the melodic pattering of rain, and a shiver races down her spine so violently I feel it through her skin.

"Cage," she breathes, the pulse in her neck beating erratically. I'm tempted to press my teeth against it to taste something sweeter than the bitterness coating my tongue.

"What are you doing here?" she chokes out, resisting my hold. But I've let her pull away from me for long enough. She's lucky I don't sew her goddamn flesh to my own.

"Didn't I already tell you that I let you disappear on me once and I'm not going to allow it a second time? Did you think I'd just let you go so easily?"

"Yes," she squeaks when I fist her hair tighter, gritting my teeth as my fury renews. Just when I think I've calmed, I'm reminded that she actually tried to ghost me.

No proper explanation. No phone call telling me she doesn't want to see me again. Not even a fucking shitty breakup text. Just... silence.

"Then I suppose I haven't made myself clear enough. Allow me to remedy that."

"Cage, stop it!" she snaps, digging her heels into the wet grass when I shove her toward her house.

When she continues to fight, I scoop her up and throw her over my shoulder with a frustrated snarl.

"Walk away from me one more fucking time, Molly, and I'll make sure you can't walk at all."

"Don't you dare threaten me, asshole," she snaps.

While she sends her little fists flying into my back, I send the flat of my palm directly onto her plump ass.

"You dick!" she screeches as the loud slap reverberates into the cool night air.

A dark laugh unleashes from my throat, my muscles tightening with the need to punish her.

"Seems to me that's exactly what you need right now."

She huffs out an affronted sound and sends a hand diving into the back of my jeans to grab ahold of the waistband of my briefs, her threat clear.

I narrow my eyes as I climb her wooden porch steps.

"I'd just love to know what you think that's going to accomplish. If it's anything other than my cock shoved down your throat, you're sadly mistaken."

"You won't have a cock if I pull hard enough and cut off the circulation."

Completely unrealistic, but I let her have her little tantrum while I carry her into her house. All the while, she continues to threaten me, likely growing angrier by my lack of concern over a possible atomic wedgie. It'd probably hurt—would *definitely* piss me off—but it wouldn't make me drop her like she's hoping for.

She's made me into this, and now she has to fucking live with it.

"Cage, I swear to God, if you don't let me go, I will call Legion—"

"Don't make me find that faceless fucker and kill him," I snap. "He may have saved you before, but he sure as fuck can't save you now."

She growls at me, pounding on my back again. "Just let me go, and then we can talk like mature fucking adults!"

"Oh no, baby, you had that chance when you decided to run away rather than fall in love with me. Now, we do it my way."

She sputters for a moment, astonished. "Fall in lo—what are you talking about, you psycho? Just let me go!"

I smack my palm against her ass a second time, evoking another sharp gasp, but that was only a warning this time. Next, I slip my thumb between her clenched thighs and firmly press where her clit is.

She goes completely still.

"Stop it. Right now." Her voice is shaky, and those words are standing on grounds being ripped apart by an earthquake. But it isn't fear saturating her tone like she'd have me believe. The heat between her legs and nails digging into my leather jacket gives her true feelings away.

I can't help but smirk, rubbing tight little circles through her jeans as I head down the hallway directly ahead and toward her bedroom at the very end.

Little stuttered breaths sneak past her lips, though she tries to contain them, only for her throat to betray her and make a sound of its own.

She can't escape the pleasure any more than she can escape me. If I allowed it, she'd sooner rip her heart from my chest to steal it back, but unfortunately for her, she doesn't even realize I have it yet.

And I would never let her take away something so fucking precious.

But fuck, there's no denying that it's fun when she tries.

I toe open her door, revealing her bed with an olive green duvet, more distressed furniture, and artful pieces hung on the cream walls.

Standing at the end of her bed, I slide her down my body until I have her legs hooked around my hips.

She's glaring at me with glittering uncut emeralds, polished until her frustration is evident. Her bottom lip is slightly pouted, and her freckled cheeks are reddened with anger, brightening the white teeth imprint below her right eye.

She may be ferocious, but she's not very intimidating when she's cradled in my arms and my palms are cupping her ass.

"You're so goddamn beautiful," I murmur, completely enraptured by this woman. Christ, the things I'd do for her *and* to her. It's fucking limitless.

"You're being incredibly disrespectful right now," she snips.

My stare drifts to those plump lips that are just begging for me to bite them. "I haven't even begun to disrespect you yet, baby. But my God, how I look forward to it."

Her eyes narrow into thin slits, though her cheeks flush brighter.

"We can't be together, Cage," she states firmly, but once again, her words are brittle.

"Why's that?" I ask casually, still studying every inch of her face.

"B-because! I said so! I'm better off alone."

I offer my dry gaze for all of two seconds, ensuring she can see just how weak of an excuse that was.

We both know she doesn't have a truly good reason other than her being scared.

She huffs. "Maybe I just don't want a relationship. Is that not a valid enough reason? Do my feelings not matter?"

She's glancing away, unable to keep her stare hooked to mine now.

Running. She's running as we fucking speak. And that irritates me.

It's my turn to narrow my eyes, a disgruntled growl building in my chest. Instead of answering, I toe off my boots and climb onto the bed, dropping her flat on her back with a startled exhale.

She attempts to scramble away, but I've already anticipated her move and have her wrists pinned above her head before she can make it two inches.

Stray curls fall over her face, and she pants from below me, seething at me with a fire that rivals the heat emanating from her pretty little cunt.

"You're scared, and I get that. You've been alone nearly your entire life and don't know what it feels like to have someone take care of you. Fine, we can work through that." Then, I lower my voice, ensuring she can see just how fucking serious I am. "But what I will not do is allow you to run from me."

I lean down until my lips are a hairsbreadth away from hers, her breath warming my face in short bursts.

"Don't worry, little ghost. I'm going to teach you how to spend forever with me."

She blinks up at me with widened eyes filled with bewilderment.

"You're crazy," she breathes.

"About you," I correct. "I'm crazy about you."

"You barely know me."

"I know you better than you know yourself," I retort, my stare drifting back down to her pink mouth. "I don't need to know your favorite color to know that I was the first man to make you feel good in your own body."

That pouty bottom lip curls between her straight teeth, and I can't help the burn of jealousy. *I* want to bite it.

"Do you think it's better for me to know if you prefer bacon over sausage in the morning or that you've fought like fucking hell to get to where you are and would eat both just because you can?"

She cocks a brow. "You think I eat pigs for breakfast?"

The corners of my lips tip up, and my voice drops into a whisper. "I think you'd eat it right in front of them because you enjoy the morbidity of it just as much as chopping up dead people as their food."

"I think you're searching for things to love, but eventually, you're going to realize that I was never meant to be happy, and you're only wasting your time."

My chest tightens at the sorrow in her eyes, and the burning desire to fix it is insatiable. I will never know peace for as long as Molly Devereaux is sad.

"You can't fix me," she finishes.

"I don't want to fix *you*, Molly. There's nothing to mend when you've already done that yourself. The only thing I will do is ensure there isn't a single part of you that is empty. Your life, your heart, and your sweet pussy." I lean in closer until my lips lightly rest against hers. "Filling you will never be a waste of my time."

I'm crushing my mouth to hers before she can respond. She doesn't need to when her body is already doing so. Her back arches, pressing her chest against mine, and her lips part easily beneath the pressure of my tongue.

A little moan brushes the roof of my mouth, and it's the only confirmation I need that while she may run again, she sure as fuck loves being caught.

I pull away, catching her heavy-lidded stare. "Tell me that you're mine."

Her brows furrow, a small frown tipping down her swollen lips. "Since walking into your store, I don't think there was ever a time that I wasn't, Cage."

chapter twenty

MOLLY

THREE MONTHS LATER
2022

"GO EMMA!"

The scream comes from her mother, Margot, her blonde ponytail bouncing as she jumps up and down on the bleachers only a few rows from Cage and me.

I'm on my feet, screaming along with Margot, though I'm still careful not to say her name. Cage is also on his feet, clapping his hands loudly and wearing a smile on his face.

He doesn't know her, but he knows everything about her, and he's learned to care for her from afar, too.

There've been many sleepless nights where I cried for the little sister I'll never get to know, and he's held me every time, talking me through those moments until I reminded myself that she's happy.

"Are you going to introduce yourself to her?" Cage asks quietly.

My smile slips, and I shrug, trying to hide how the mere thought makes me want to vomit.

Cage took it upon himself to look deeper into Layla's life, just to ensure she was as happy as it seems on the outside. And she is. But he discovered that there might be a part of her missing, too. He found her posting questions on public forums anonymously, asking for advice about the possibility of her parents lying to her about her early childhood. She wrote that she has vague memories of another mother-like figure in her life, but her parents will tell her nothing about it. She knows she's adopted but feels like her parents are strangely secretive about where she came from and how they came about adopting her.

It broke my heart and made me question if I was genuinely doing the right thing by staying out of her life.

"I don't want her to know what I do," I say. Something I've said a million times before. "And I don't want to lie to her, either. She's been lied to enough in her life."

"Is one lie worth never knowing her at all?" he asks. Something he's asked a million times before.

And I still don't have a good answer.

He stares at me intently, and I'm reminded that he could only know his sister for twelve years. The choice to know her longer was taken away from him.

Guilt eats at me, and a battle rages inside my head, only I still haven't figured out who's winning. The part of me that wants to know her, or the part of me that feels she's better off without me.

Either way, Cage feels I'm taking that choice away from her.

"Her parents would hate me if I reappeared in her life, I think," I continue.

"Possibly. But only because they'll feel threatened. Maybe confused. But if you trust them with who you are, they might learn to trust you. You're not there to take Layla away from them."

"I would never," I agree. "She belongs with her family, and I'd never do anything to change that."

"You're her family, too, baby. And once they know that you're not trying to take her away, they might be happy to have you fill in those gaps for Layla. They're so secretive about her past because they don't *know*. They know nothing about who she really is or where she comes from, and maybe it'll bring them some peace, too."

It's all hypothetical.

Theoretical.

There's no way to know if that's how they truly feel, or if that's what they'd truly want. No way to know if it's even what Layla would want.

Sure, she might think she does. But what happens if I tell her, and it sends her into a tailspin because now she must face the fact that her birth parents were sick, depraved people? Would it cause an identity crisis? Would she feel like her blood is tainted by evil?

They're thoughts I've had to come to terms with myself. Would I end up like my parents eventually?

I don't want Layla to suffer from those insidious thoughts. I don't want her to ever know the pain of having her biological parents see her as nothing more than a cash cow. To know that she meant so fucking little to them.

Because she meant everything to me.

Everything.

Layla scores one more goal before the clock runs out, knocking the ball into the net with her head. Her team beelines for her, lifting her up in their arms and screaming for yet another win. They're undefeated so far, and it looks like they're quickly on their way to Nationals.

My heart bursts from pride, and I scream along with the rest of the team and their families, my hands stinging from how hard I clap them.

"Emma, Emma, Emma, Emma," the team chants, lifting her up on their shoulders. Yet, her head is swiveling to look back at the other team, their shoulders slumped. Despondence polluting the air around them. There's a slight frown on her face, almost as if she feels guilty for beating them.

It's all I need to see to know that she will *never* be like our parents.

I just hope that if I do meet her, she'll see that, too.

My heart is pounding in my throat, and I'm just wondering at what point my body decided it would function better there instead of my chest.

It's clearly gone rogue, along with any coherent thought as Layla and her parents approach.

Cage and I are standing outside the field gate, where throngs of people spill out as everyone leaves for the night. The warm August air is suffocating, and I wish I had brought a mini fan to keep me from sweating through all my clothes.

WHERE'S MOLLY

I doubt being a sopping mess will make an excellent first impression.

Layla and her parents emerge from the doors, her blonde strands matted to her sweaty forehead and a bright smile on her face as her dad, Colin, shakes her shoulders with excitement. Her head tips down, and that grin slips ever so slightly.

It's very little encouragement, considering I'm point two seconds from bailing, but it's enough to keep my feet planted until Layla is only a few feet away.

The world tilts on its axis, slowing to a halt as our eyes clash. I'm not sure if we're moving in slow motion or if she really has stopped walking. Regardless, there she stands, two feet away, and staring right at me.

"Emma?"

Layla's head snaps to Margot, who is staring at her with concern, her gaze darting between her daughter and me.

"You okay?"

"Uh," she stutters, but then refocuses on me before she can muster a better response.

"Emma, who is that?" Colin asks.

I bite my lip, my brain rolling over how to introduce myself. My real name? My fake name? Her sister? Does it even matter?

My mouth opens, then snaps shut, and I shift on my feet uncomfortably. This was a mistake. A huge mistake.

I have no place interfering in her life. Who cares if there's a small part of her missing? It's better than finding out your parents tried to sell you in the sex trade *after* they sold me. That's like—*so* much trauma.

I go to turn, but Cage grabs my biceps, preventing me from running away.

"Who are you?" Margot is directing her question toward me now.

"Uh."

My response isn't any more informative than Layla's was, except I actually know the answer.

I clear my throat and try again, "Her sister."

All three of their spines snap straight, but while wariness and suspicion clouds over her parents' vision, Layla narrows her eyes in contemplation, as if she's trying to recognize me from memories almost a decade old.

"Excuse me?" Margot snaps, stepping forward, her tone sharp and irate. "What makes you thin—"

"I gave her to you," I say, my voice cracking. Fuck, it hurts so much to say it aloud, even if it was the best thing that I could've done for her. It just fucking sucks *I* couldn't be that. Cage's hand cups my bicep, gently squeezing to remind me he's here. It's enough to power on. "Ten years ago. I left her on your doorstep with a name tag and birthdate."

She and Colin blink at me in astonishment, a range of emotions flashing through their stares. I doubt they told anyone that; it certainly wasn't released to the public.

"You gave me away?" Layla asks, her voice soft and tinged with hurt. It's the first time I've heard it up close and directed at me. It's enough to move me to tears, though I manage to hold them back.

I chew on my lip, contemplating how to answer, only to settle on a shaky nod. I can't trust my voice not to crack and for a tsunami of an explanation to burst free. I know I need to take it slow with her—*if* she decides she wants to know me—but I hate that she feels like I abandoned her because I didn't want her.

"Why?" she asks.

"Maybe this isn't the best place for this to happen," Colin intervenes, glancing nervously between his wife and me. They're both on edge. Uncomfortable. And for good reason. Maybe I should've sent her a message on some social media app instead, but that felt so... impersonal. Dirty.

I don't want Margot and Colin to feel like I'm sneaking behind their backs. Like some weird predator trying to gain Layla's trust without their knowledge.

I want to do this the right way. Maybe this wasn't the *best* way, but at least her parents won't be kept in the dark.

"You're right," I rush out. "I guess I didn't really know the best way to go about this—"

"You should've come to us first," Margot states firmly. She's aggravated, and her protective instincts are fully engaged. It's understandable, but keeping my voice even takes effort.

"Probably. But I didn't want to become a secret to her or a reason for you two to have to keep one if you tried to decide for her. I'm not here to try and take her away or cause any trouble. I chose you two for a reason, and I have no plans to undo that decision."

"Then what do you want?" Layla asks, cocking her head.

"To know you," I say, meeting her baby blue eyes. "That's all. If that's not what you want, I'll respect that. But I just wanted it to be you who decides."

Colin scoffs. "We get a say, too. She's only fifteen—"

"And she's going to grow up eventually," I remind him, my own tone sharpening. "She won't be fifteen forever. Just ask yourself if you'd be preventing her for her own sake or yours."

He looks slightly offended by that, but it doesn't make it any less accurate.

Swallowing back the bile threatening to spew from my throat, I take a few steps forward and hand Margot a piece of paper with my number written on it.

"Go home and talk about it as a family, yeah? Then call me when you all decide. I'll respect your decision regardless."

Hesitantly, she takes the slip from me. I spare Layla one last glance before turning and taking off.

"Hey!" Layla's voice stops me, and I turn enough to give her my eyes. "What's your name?"

I swallow, and for a brief moment, I consider giving her the name that I gave myself when I took her away from our awful home. But I want her to know the real me. The version of myself I've been fighting to find again since I became a ghost all those years ago.

"Molly," I rasp. "My name is Molly."

Then, I pivot and hope to God that this isn't the last time I'll ever hear her voice.

Cage entwines my hand with his, squeezing tightly.

"So, the little ghost finally materializes. Welcome to the rest of your life, baby."

epilogue

MOLLY

**ONE MONTH LATER
2022**

Even the tip of Cage's dick in the back of my throat doesn't deter my thighs from seizing around his head. His tongue swipes through my slit, targeting my clit with perfect precision and skill.

I'm sitting on his face and leaning down his body, sucking on his cock until his own thighs tense with pleasure.

We're competing on who can make who come first. Whoever the winner is gets to fuck the other in the ass, and I'm determined to win. Yet, less than a minute in, and I'm on the verge of losing.

I take him down the back of my throat again, evoking a deep groan from his chest and causing him to pump his hips, forcing me to swallow him impossibly deeper.

I gag, but even that doesn't diminish the burning need to explode. Squeezing my eyes shut, I bob my mouth up and down his length with vigor, sucking and licking while using my hand to twist around the flesh that my mouth can't reach.

In retaliation, he sucks my clit into his mouth, flicking his tongue over it with a speed my brain is incapable of comprehending. The only thing it can grasp is how fucking amazing it feels.

My stomach tightens, and I reach that cliff within seconds. There's no stopping the orgasm rolling over me and off that edge, sending me flying off with it.

I scream around his cock, losing control of my body as I mercilessly grind into his face. His arms hook around my thighs, and he moans against me, opening his mouth to accept the eruption he so savagely forced out of me.

A few seconds later, he's filling my mouth, too. Hot ribbons of cum shoot down my throat, and the only thing I'm capable of is rolling my hips and swallowing him down until there's nothing left of either of us to give.

I pull back just as he does, the two of us panting for breath.

"Jesus fucking Christ," he breathes.

"What are you calling out to Him for? Clearly, He's on *your* side," I gripe without heat, rolling off him. "I was *this*—" I hold out my hand and pinch my forefinger and thumb a millimeter apart. "—close to getting to peg you."

He chuckles. "We got the rest of our lives. Let me work up to that, yeah? For now, I get to fuck your pretty little ass."

There's already a smug grin on his face as I lie down next to him, propping my chin on his heaving chest.

"Shut up," I say before he can start gloating. The smirk widens, and it's entirely unfair how beautiful it is.

"If it makes you feel any better, I had to pull out the big guns and think of some pretty fucked-up shit. I was ready to explode the second you deep-throated me."

I roll my eyes. "That means you cheated. I demand a redo."

"Deal," he agrees readily, the word rushing out of his mouth before I can barely finish.

I purse my lips, then smack his chest playfully. "You're just going to keep cheating, so I keep asking for a redo. Dickhead."

He laughs, causing my head to shake. Scoffing, I roll away from him, prompting him to roll after me and cocoon me in his arms, my back to his chest.

"You're right," he whispers sensually in my ear, eliciting a bone-deep shiver. "I'd do terrible, terrible things to get my mouth on that pussy as often as I can."

"I have one more body to grab," Cage says, only a little breathless after carrying in three dead men from Eli's trunk. Apparently, they were brothers and enjoyed sharing child porn with each other like they were goddamn cute puppy videos.

My brows pinch in confusion. "I thought Eli said he only dropped off three?"

"He did. I brought an extra."

I can only manage a blink before he's halfway out the door.

"What the hell?" I mutter, bewildered. The only response I receive is an obnoxious snort from Dill.

"What the hell?" I repeat a couple minutes later when he reappears, my tone louder and sharper.

My mouth drops as Cage carries in a very familiar man, dropping the body on the metal table. Someone that I only tend to see in my nightmares.

"Kenny Mathers," I whisper. The only man from Francesca's house who managed to get away unscathed and the last living man who abused me in that house. "How did you find out who he was? I never told you his name."

"Legion," he answers simply.

Of course. I should've known.

"How did you find him?"

"In a prison. Well—Legion's prison—not an official one. Keeping him locked up, away from society, until you made the initiative to kill him. I decided to do that part since you don't like to get involved in that side of the business."

"You killed him?" I repeat in a whisper.

"Sure did," he chirps proudly. "Legion handed him over to me, and I took care of the rest."

I stare at him, mouth agape as I try to process that not only did Legion keep my abuser locked away all this time, waiting for me to be ready, but that Cage killed him for me. And is now presenting him to me as... pig food.

"Wow," I choke out, completely overwhelmed. "I think I love you even more now, but I'm also not sure 'cause I didn't think that was even possible."

That's the first time I said those three words out loud, which is also a lot of emotions to deal with. Specifically as his eyes flare, and now he's watching me as if *I'm* the food.

"You got anyone else on that hit list of yours? I'll kill as many people as you want if you keep telling me you love me."

My vision is blurring, and my chest feels too full.

"You're an idiot," I croak, blinking away the tears. Cage grabs a hold of me and tugs me into his embrace, holding me tight.

"I'm going to fuck you for so long later tonight," he whispers sinfully.

I choke out a laugh, and he grabs my chin, bringing my focus to him. He stares at me softly, though there's a hint of that obsession still lingering in his eyes.

"I love you, too. Now, let's get to work chopping him up. Chili's giving me an evil eye, and Garlic and Paprika seem like they're conspiring against us as we speak."

The loud chirp of my phone ringing nearly causes my bones to climb right out of my flesh in fright.

I've had the sound up at full volume ever since I handed Margot my phone number; I've just been waiting for her to call.

It's been a little over a month, and I've all but convinced myself their silence is my answer.

Either Layla doesn't want to get to know me, or Margot and Colin won't allow her to. Regardless, it's not my place to interfere with either decision. Even if it feels like my heart is in tatters.

"You gonna get that?"

Cage and I are in the process of extracting teeth and buzzing hair off Kenny and the other three dead bodies.

I glance at the number, noting that it's one I don't recognize. Pulling my gloves off, I press the answer button and hold it to my ear.

"Hello?"

"Molly?"

My heart pauses for a beat. "Yeah?"

The woman clears her throat. "This is Margot. Emma's mom."

I nearly stumble over air as I whip around and begin to pace.

"It's so nice to hear from you," I choke out.

"How long have you been going to Emma's games?"

I frown, a little taken aback by the question.

God, what if she's calling just to tell me Layla said she doesn't want to know me? What if she tells me to never contact them again or show my face at any of her games?

I'll always go to her games but respect their wishes enough to not let them see me. I'll keep my distance for as long as Layla demands. If it's forever, I would be okay with watching her grow old from afar—as long as she's safe.

"I moved back to Montana over four years ago. As soon as I discovered that she was playing, I went to all her games. Every single one."

Margot is silent for a moment, and then I hear a soft sigh.

"Emma is... she's interested in talking to you," she begins, her voice taut with discomfort. "She admitted that she had been feeling a little lost about her early childhood and would like to know about her biological parents. And you, of course. We agreed only because we feel it would help Emma heal from... from her abandonment issues."

I close my eyes, feeling as if Margot is standing before me and tearing her claws into my flesh until my heart is exposed, then ripping it out of its useless cavity. No bones could ever protect it from Layla's hurt.

"I understand," I whisper. "I will tell her anything she wants to know."

"And I know who you are. Who she is," she rushes out, almost as if, if she didn't get it out she'd combust.

"I see. Then I hope you know that I didn't give Layla to you because I didn't want her, but because I had to."

There's silence, and it's only now that I notice Cage has shut off his own hair clippers. It's quiet—too quiet.

"Emma," she corrects. "Her name is Emma."

I bite my lip, not realizing I slipped up.

"I know it is," I concede softly. "I gave that name to her so no one would find out who she was."

"Right," Margot says, her tone curt but not lacking heat. I know this is hard for her as well.

"I appreciate you allowing me to speak to her. At least this once. I... I can't even begin to express how much she means to me."

Margot sighs again. "I believe you, Molly. I can't imagine the things you've been through. The things Emma has been through. If I'm being honest, I wasn't going to allow this when you first approached. But... once I googled you and found out about your story—your kidnapping—I realized there may be a lot more to both of your stories than I was giving credit for. In my head, I built you up as some drug-addict mother who left her kid on some random stranger's doorstep. I used to thank God every night that she was left with us and not someone who would've hurt her. I remember you said that you chose us. Is that true?"

"I did," I answer. "It's a little creepy when I say it out loud, but I watched your family for months. I couldn't leave her with just anyone, but I didn't trust the system, and I wanted her to go to a family that I knew would keep her and love her."

"Well, you chose correctly," Margot says. "So I will pay you the same respect and let you see her. But know that the moment Emma says she's done, you will *never* see her again. Is that understood? She is—"

"Your daughter," I assure. "And I understand. I will respect her wishes. Always, Margot."

She releases a heavy exhale, as if a small weight has been lifted from her shoulders.

"Okay. I will text you a date and time."

"Thank you," I breathe. The phone clicks off, and immediately, tears spring to my eyes and spill over in rivers as if they were poised at my lash line, waiting to be released.

"What happened?" Cage asks, rushing over to me and cupping my face between his palms. Thankfully, he had the foresight to take off his rubber gloves, even though his body is still covered in blood from extracting their teeth.

His eyes dart between mine, concern etched into his slanted brows.

"She's going to let me see Layla," I croak, the end of my declaration broken by a hiccup.

"Come here, baby," Cage mumbles, ushering me into his arms. I keep my chin tilted up and away from his chest, while he bows his forehead to rest on my shoulder, hugging me tightly.

The cap that was held tightly over the emotions I had bottled inside me during the conversation bursts off, and I lose myself, sobbing into his neck while he sways us side to side.

So much fear, hurt, and loneliness is released from my chest. Ten years without seeing her beautiful smile, hearing her say my name—it's been torture. Worse than anything I've ever suffered at the hands of dirty men.

I had never known love until Layla was born, and for years, my world revolved around her seeing another day. Then, it revolved around protecting her from me and all the baggage that I towed around.

And now, it feels like I've finally been set free. From the chains that were wrapped around my ankles, constantly dragging me back into my sordid past every time I tried to escape it.

"I get to see her," I squeak out between harsh wails.

"You get to see her. And she'll get to love you now."

That only makes me cry harder. I've never known a god, but if one exists, He'll grant me my sister's love. That's all I've ever wanted.

I'm not sure how much time passes before my cries die down, my throat raw, and my eyes bloodshot and swollen.

Cage pulls away just enough to swipe the tears from my cheeks with his thumbs.

"I love you, little ghost. And I know she will, too."

I hiccup as he leans in and rests his lips against my forehead, kissing me there softly.

"I love you, too."

Just as I catch my breath, my phone goes off again, and for a second time, scaring the absolute shit out of me.

Clearing away the lingering emotion from my throat, I answer without looking.

"Hello?"

"I hear you're good at making people disappear."

The deep, male voice is jarring and not what I was expecting. I pull the phone away from my ear, checking the number. It's unknown.

"Who is this?"

"Most know me by Z. But you can call me Zade."

THE END

Molly is first introduced in the Cat & Mouse duet. If you haven't already, pick up these books to experience all this world has to offer!

Reading Order:

Satan's Affair
Haunting Adeline
Hunting Adeline

ALSO BY HD CARLTON

acknowledgments

First as always, a huge thank you to my readers. You all have put up with my slow writing and stuck around during times of extreme burnout where I didn't know if I was successfully going to be able to write another book. I can't thank you enough for your continued support, and being someone I can rely on no matter what. I love you all from the depths of my black soul.

Secondly, thank you to my amazing husband. Without your support, I wouldn't be where I am today. We're the best power couple that ever lived, in my personal opinion. You're also the best husband in the world, and I'm so glad to be dominating the world with you by my side. I love you so much.

And thank you to Sam, the most dedicated stalker, and my best friend. You've been an incredible support system and looking at your face 24/7 while you yell at me to write while simultaneously distracting me with anal tattoo ideas has been the highlight of my days. Even if it was initially forced, I'm so thankful you're in my life. Forever. I love you, weirdo.

Kristie and Samantha, sitting in the diner with you two is one of my favorite memories. And where Molly's story was born. I love you both and am so eternally grateful for you two.

Next, thank you to my alpha readers, Amanda, May, and Tosh. I would trust all three of you with a trust fall, but even more, I can trust you guys with my book babies, and that's some real shit. Thank you for never being my yes-men, but always my biggest supporters. And thank you for tearing my books apart and treating me like a commoner that can barely spell, kicking my ass when I don't know the answers to questions about my own books, and figuring my shit out for me. My books definitely would not be what they are without you three.

To my betas, Autumn, Nicki, Ana, Janine, and Taylor, I appreciate all of you so damn much. Again, for not being my yes-men, but incredible supporters who kick my ass. Thank you, thank you, thank you for being by my side.

Thank you to my kick-ass editors, Angie and Rumi. Thank you for always making these books look shiny. I appreciate you both so much.

And last but certainly not least, thank you to my bestie, cover designer, and cheerleader, Cassie. You always make these covers so beautiful, but your soul is even prettier. I love you.

about the author

H. D. Carlton is an International and USA Today Bestselling author. She lives in Oregon with her husband, Bigfoot, two dogs, and cat. When she's not bathing in the tears of her readers, she's watching paranormal shows and wishing she was a mermaid. Her favorite characters are of the morally gray variety and believes that everyone should check their sanity at the door before diving into her stories.

Learn more about H. D. Carlton on . Join her newsletter to receive updates, teasers, giveaways, and special deals .
And if you're brave, join the for extra early torturing—I mean teasing.

Facebook
Twitter
Instagram
Goodreads

SO, YOU DECIDED TO STICK AROUND, HUH?
HERE'S YOUR REWARD...

extended epilogue

MOLLY

PRESENT
SEPTEMBER 4TH, 2023

"Jesus *fuck*, you're tall," I breathe, my eyes rounding.

The man strides into my barn like he owns the place, and if he demanded it of me, I just might concede. Not only is he tall, but he's also fucking scary-looking.

The contrast between his dark brown eye and light blue eye is startling. And the scar cutting through the left one—starting from just above his eyebrow and straight down to the middle of his cheek—only heightens the savage look he possesses.

No wonder he's the head of the most prominent organization in the world.

Behind him walks in a considerably shorter woman, her long cinnamon brown hair fashioned into a loose braid over her shoulder.

I recognize her immediately. Not only as a famous author—whose books I fucking *love*—but the woman who was kidnapped and found herself in the clutches of Francesca, just as I was. When I heard Z found her, I nearly cried in relief that someone else had made it out of there, too.

She's beautiful and has some of the prettiest light brown eyes I've ever seen. And *definitely* is fucking the big boss, if the way Z—or rather, *Zade*—looks at her like he'll murder Cage and I in a heartbeat if we even so much as sneeze on her is any indication.

She's glancing around the barn, her mouth agape as she takes in my setup.

"Oh, Sibby would *love* this," she mutters to herself.

In response to my comment about Zade's height, Cage turns to me with a *what the fuck?* look on his face. "Baby, he's only, like, two inches taller than me." He points a thumb to his chest. "I'm tall, too."

I glance at Zade. "He's... scarier."

Cage's eyes droop with exasperation while Zade shoots me a charming grin, stretching the scar on his face.

"I only hurt people who deserve it. Scout's honor," he assures.

The woman rolls her eyes. "He was never in Boy Scouts. And he's scary, but I can kick his ass, and *I'm* nice." She rushes forward, holding out her hand for me to shake. "I'm Addie. His fiancée. Thank you so much for having us."

I shake her hand, appreciating that she has a firm grip. I never trust anyone who can't give a proper handshake.

She squeezes my palm tighter, her eyes sparkling with awe. "You will never understand the impact you've had on my life, and I've been wanting to meet you for so long."

I blink, bewildered.

"I found your old journal in Francesca's house," she explains. "The one you wrote in during your time there. It... Your words saved me in a way I can't even express. They helped me get through the days there. I started writing in it after you. I still journal even now, all because of you."

"Oh, my God," I breathe, still in utter shock. "You found it? I honestly had forgotten all about it..."

"That journal saved my life, Molly. *You* saved my life, in a way." She shows me her wrist, which is covered with a beautiful tattoo of roses trailing up her arm. "There used to be a barcode here, but I got it covered. It's really small, but in one of the petals, I added your name. I carried you with me in that house, so I wanted it to be permanent, too."

She points to one of the roses, and instantly, my hand covers my mouth, eyes welling with tears as I stare at the five small letters scribed expertly inside the petal.

When I was in that house, they hadn't tattooed us, but I could only imagine the new precautions they started taking after I successfully escaped. I never imagined tagging them like fucking animals would be one, and it breaks my heart. But I also never imagined my journal would save someone else, and for that, I'm so fucking thankful.

Dropping my hand from my mouth, I lift my watery eyes to her, gazing at her with a little sorrow, and a lot of pride. "You did that, Addie. *You* got out."

She gently grabs my hand and squeezes. "I did it with your help."

Entirely speechless, she leaves me to process that, moving on to Cage.

The only thing that brings me back to reality is Zade's sharp stare cutting to where their hands connect for point two seconds. He keeps quiet, but Jesus, he was definitely counting how long they touched for. I'd hate to find out what would happen to my boyfriend if it were a second too long.

I'd go down, though I'd sure as fuck go down fighting.

My brain is still lagging from Addie's proclamation, so it takes me a moment to absorb Zade's words.

"Scar buddies."

Again, I blink. "Scar buddies?"

His finger flicks between our faces. "We both got dope scars. You know what that means? We should be friends."

Again, I blink.

Zade grins at my bewilderment, and continues, "Legion tells me you're a valuable asset. Murdering people happens to be my second favorite thing in the world, following my fiancée, of course. I'd feed your pigs really fucking well, and I have no problem doubling your salary to work with *Z*."

I cock a brow, crossing my arms over my chest. "I'm loyal to Legion."

The grin that slices across Zade's face is quick. "I was hoping you'd say something so noble. It means you're a damn good employee. However, I respect Legion, and he's agreed to share. You'll still work with him, and Eli will continue to deliver the food. Your pigs and wallet will just get a little bit fatter, that's all."

Then his stare snaps to Cage. "I hear you're also valuable. I pay good money for skills like yours."

Cage cocks his head. "Can't you do what I do just as easily?"

Zade shrugs. "Sure. But I don't need the extra workload when I have your expertise. I sent a few people to your store so I could see your work, and I have no problem admitting I haven't seen it done better than you."

Cage's brows jump in surprise.

"You'd be valuable. You both would," Zade continues. His intense stare slides over us, probing and analytical, while Addie goes to coo at the pigs. "So, are the two of you down?"

Mine and Cage's stares cut to each other at the same time.

I'm not sure why, but it feels like Zade is going to introduce me to a whole different world. One that will bring me out of the reclusive shell I've been comfortable in for the past decade.

And I guess... I guess I'm finally ready for it.